Feeling hopeless my room at the B possibly because holiday-themed boutique had exploded inside.

The walls featured framed Christmas artwork. The antique bureau, nightstands, and bedstead were all decked out in swags of holly, complete with tiny red berries. There were red velvet bows, colonial-style garlands of crimson wooden beads, and plenty of wreathed holiday candles.

I was in Sproutes, Massachusetts. So far, the place felt like Christmastown, USA. I was in love.

I was also hideously awake. I recognized the feeling. It meant there'd be no more sleep for me.

Not wanting to disturb anyone, I got out of bed quietly and tiptoed downstairs.

I'd make chocolate-peppermint truffles, I mused as I reached what I judged must be the kitchen. That was the flavor of my most successful Christmas treat.

Happily envisioning the B&B's guests smiling as they tasted my chocolaty creations, I groped for the kitchen's light switch. No dice. I set down my bag full of chocolate-making gear, and tried again.

The lights flared to life. I blinked against their brightness and crouched to retrieve my bag.

But I wasn't in the kitchen I realized as I straightened. Instead, I was in the dining room. And this wasn't going to be a memorable stay in Sproutes for any of the reasons I'd imagined.

Judging by the inert, awkward pose of the woman sprawled out beside the enormous dining table, splattered by what appeared to be Christmas wassail punch, I'd just stumbled upon another murder.

Books by Colette London

A Chocolate Whisper Mystery series:

Criminal Confections

Dangerously Dark

The Semisweet Hereafter

Dead and Ganache

The Peppermint Mocha Murder

COLETTE LONDON

KENSINGTON PUBLISHING CORP.
http://www.kensingtonbooks.com

KENSINGTON BOOKS are published by

Kensington Publishing Corp.
119 West 40th Street
New York, NY 10018

All Kensington Titles, Imprints, and Distributed Lines are available at special quantity discounts for bulk purchases for sales promotions, premiums, fund-raising, and educational or institutional use. Special book excerpts or customized printings can also be created to fit specific needs. For details, write or phone the office of the Kensington special sales manager: Kensington Publishing Corp., 119 West 40th Street, New York, NY 10018, attn: Special Sales Department, Phone: 1-800-221-2647.

Kensington and the K logo Reg. U.S. Pat & TM Off.

ISBN-13: 978-1-4967-1064-2
ISBN-10: 1-4967-1064-9
First Kensington Mass Market Edition: October 2018

eISBN-13: 978-1-4967-1065-9
eISBN-10: 1-4967-1065-7
First Kensington Electronic Edition: October 2018

10 9 8 7 6 5 4 3 2 1

To John Plumley—you're my everything!

One

Do you know what Christmastime means to a chocolate expert?

It means a little (much-deserved) time off, that's what.

You might not have noticed this before, but there's not all that much *Theobroma cacao* involved in your typical yuletide celebration. Sure, chocolate Santas make an appearance in a stocking or two. Delicious peppermint mocha drinks pop up, and (maybe) homemade fudge. But aside from those chocolaty treats, almost all the sweets involved in the festive season between Thanksgiving and New Year's Eve are of the *non*chocolate variety.

Frankly, it's a missed opportunity for deliciousness, I'd say. But I didn't make up the system. It just so happens that other treats—fruitcake and mince pies, most conspicuously—got there first. They achieved prominence with old-timey treat-loving types before chocolate even got out of the starting gate. After all, chocolate desserts date only to the 1700s or so, when British sailors first brought back drinkable chocolate from South America, launching a worldwide love affair with cacao beans and all their super-scrumptious permutations.

Professionally speaking, I benefit from that chocolate *amore*. That's because I know all about chocolate . . . and everything that's made from it. See, I'm a bona fide chocolate whisperer—the first in the world. Usually, I work on a referral basis, helping my clients make the most of their cupcakes, confections, gelati, candies, and other creations. One day, I'm developing new products for a powerhouse global corporation; the next, I'm perfecting triple-chocolate cookies for a mom-and-pop bakery.

Large or small, I adore my clients. That's why I'm willing to give 100 percent to my work on their behalf. For me, there's no mousse too melty or truffle too tricky; no matter how difficult the job, Hayden Mundy Moore never quits. When the going gets tough (or crumbly or sticky or irredeemably gluey), I have a tendency to dig in my heels and try even harder.

Maybe that's why I keep getting into *non*chocolate-related trouble, though. If I see something that's wrong, I can't help intervening. Even when the thing that's wrong involves—how do I put this delicately?—*murder* . . . I somehow wind up mixed up in it.

At the moment, though, my amateur investigations into the darker side of life had been neatly wrapped up. I was officially at loose ends, facing nothing more perilous than an ordinary day in mid-December. That's probably why I jumped at the first invitation I received to do *something*. Anything. The fact that the invitation in question came from my favorite husky-voiced number cruncher (aka Travis Turner, my friend and advisor) was just a bonus. I was in before I'd even heard all the details.

Usually, Travis vets clients and arranges consulting work for me. This time, he had something more relaxing in mind. This time, I wouldn't be using my extensive knowledge of cocoa to turn run-of-the-mill chocolate treats into gastronomic megastars for my (sometimes secret) clientele. This time, I'd be going to a party, a party in the epicenter of old-fashioned Christmases: in New England. In Sproutes, Massachusetts, to be exact.

Never heard of it? Me either. But since I was currently sweltering in sunny Las Vegas after wrapping up a chocolate job, making a getaway to the chilly Northeast sounded good to me. Snow? Small towns, picturesque covered bridges, and fir trees? Mistletoe? Converted barns? B&Bs wreathed in holiday lights?

"Sign me up, Travis." I turned my back on my hotel's view of the famous flashy Strip. *Those* weren't Christmas lights. I grabbed my trusty duffel, already packing. "I'd love a little New England–style Christmas cheer. It could be any time of year around here. There's barely a nod to the season in the casinos."

A few had leveraged the holiday for the sake of selling specialty cocktails or embellishing their lighted marquees, but for the most part, Christmas didn't incite gambling, carousing, or doing things you'd rather forget. As the city's official motto teases, "What happens in Vegas stays in Vegas." That meant Sin City wanted nothing to do with the Christmas season.

Me? I wanted *everything* to do with it. I *love* Christmas.

I'd been hoping to spend the season at the famous holiday markets in Europe—maybe in Berlin, my favorite. But Travis's invitation did tradition and glühwein one better—especially once he let slip that small-town Sproutes was where he grew up.

My notoriously private "keeper" was essentially offering a guided tour of his largely unknown past, coinciding with one of the most nostalgic times of the year. Given the circumstances, even steady, dependable Travis might be tempted to wax sentimental about the people and places that mattered to him.

Maybe I'd even meet the extended Turner family. I imagined a calculator-wielding clan full of preppy smarty-pants, all gathered for (an organized) Christmas, and smiled to myself.

"There's plenty of Christmas cheer around here," Travis told me on the other end of the line. "Even some snow."

He described the bed-and-breakfast where I might stay, going into detail about its authentic Federal architecture, its expansive grounds, its décor, and its host. Honestly, I tuned out some of the specifics. I couldn't help it. Travis has one of those voices—deep, authoritative, warm, and super sexy—that's an aphrodisiac in itself. I swear, he could record himself reading IRS tax tables, and his listeners would be transfixed.

To be candid, I've always had a bit of a "voice crush" on my financial advisor. Travis doesn't know it, but he has a unique ability to make me giddy. Even long distance. Not that I've ever let on, of course. We work together! Travis monitors my trust fund—the money left me by my beloved, eccentric uncle Ross—and he does an excellent systematized job of it, too.

Thanks to my uncle, I've been bequeathed the all-the-chocolate-you-can-eat lifestyle I've always dreamed of. Not that every day is champagne and gourmet confections. There are strings attached. For one thing, I'm required to travel at least six months out of the year, so my inheritance keeps me on the move.

Not that I mind. With Travis holding the purse strings—and making himself available for check-in phone calls—I feel happy and secure globe-trotting just about anywhere. Sure, sometimes I long for all the standard signposts of a real grown-up life. A home of my own. A regular boyfriend.

A golden retriever. A future that doesn't fit neatly into one wheelie suitcase and a single duffel bag. But for the most part, I'm happy traveling, consulting, and doing my best to make magic with chocolate.

"And your host has agreed to give you full range of the B&B's kitchen," Travis was telling me. "I mentioned that you might want to whip up a few chocolate treats while you're here."

"It's as if you know me." Travis did, of course. We'd finally met—after years of flirtatious phone-exclusive contact—in France, where I'd gone to celebrate the retirement of my chocolate-making mentor, Philippe Vetault. "I could use some time to experiment, actually. It's been a while since I freelanced on any new recipes, just for the fun of it."

Like most professional bakers and confectioners, I kept a book of recipes—formulas, really—which guided me in my work. Making exemplary chocolate isn't all magic. It's science, too.

"I'm looking forward to tasting what you come up with."

When Travis said so in that raspy, memorable voice of his, I couldn't wait to get started. Fondly thinking of him, I cradled my phone. "I'm looking forward to sharing with you."

Unlike Danny Jamieson, my oldest friend and closest confidant, Travis appreciated sweets. Danny preferred to treat himself with fried, salty, or spicy foods. The more intense, the better. But that was Danny in a nutshell. Intense. And loyal.

"It's too bad you won't be here in time for the tree-trimming party tonight," Travis said. I pictured him surrounded by Christmas lights and falling snow, buttoned up in one of his impeccable suits. "It's only an informal get-together, but—"

"But I could have wowed your friends with chocolate?"

My financial advisor laughed. "Yes, but that's not my point. I'm not inviting you here to work, Hayden. You're my plus-one for the premiere party this weekend. That's all."

I nodded. I knew Travis had traveled to New England to be there for one of his childhood friends, writer Albany Sullivan. The fact that he'd taken time off from working in his high-rise office overlooking Seattle's Puget Sound spoke volumes, though.

"Are you sure Albany won't mind my being there with you?"

"We're not romantically involved, if that's what you mean."

It was exactly what I'd meant. "And your family?"

A pause. "My mother lives in Seattle now."

There'd been something meaningful in that pause. I was sure of it. I make it a habit to trust my instincts. "And your dad?"

Another pause. Then, "He never lived in Sproutes."

I waited to hear more. My hopes of meeting the whole algebraically gifted Turner clan were dwindling. "And . . . ?"

"And I'm about to book your plane tickets." This time, Travis's tone was all business. No playfulness. No innuendo. Just efficiency. "Economy both ways. Is that all right?"

"You know it is." Despite my inheritance, I'm a down-to-earth person. I grew up gridskipping with my experimental archaeologist parents, staying in accommodations ranging from hostels to yurts to five-star hotels. I know how to blend in.

"Then I'll tell Zach to expect you later tonight."

Travis meant the B&B's host, Zach Johnson. I wasn't yet finished trying to wrangle more background information from him, though.

Getting people to talk to me—consulting clients, random strangers, people at train stations—is something I'm good at. It's kind of my superpower. It helps me troubleshoot cacao.

"What about your grandparents?" I pressed. "Surely they—"

"They'll be delighted to meet you." Travis's tone said he knew what I was up to. "I've told them all about your exploits."

"Not *all* of them, I hope."

"Only those that didn't involve murder."

"Good." I hoisted my packed duffel and set it atop my wheelie bag. I slung on my trusty crossbody bag, awkwardly using only one hand, then opened my hotel room door. Bye-bye, Las Vegas. "I wouldn't want to shock Grandma and Grandpa Turner."

"It's Grandma and Grandpa Miller, Bessie and Walter. My mother's parents. Don't worry. They're not easily shaken."

I debated climbing another branch of the family tree, then decided not to. Travis didn't want to talk about it. I headed down the football-field-length hotel corridor, pulling behind me almost everything I had in the world. It all came with me.

"Tell me more about Albany," I urged. I knew that Travis's friend had published a sensational "lightly fictionalized" memoir of her life growing up in Sproutes. Now her memoir was being turned into a holiday-themed musical called *Christmas in Crazytown*. Its debut was supposed to be a hot ticket this year.

My advisor gave me a very bare-bones rundown, then quit.

"Once you meet Albany, you can draw your own conclusions," he told me in summary. "Just keep in mind, it's been a stressful time for her. The run-up to the stage show hasn't been easy."

I scoffed. "What's not to love about having your best seller turned into a soon-to-be sold-out show? Sounds pretty easy to me."

"You'll see." Travis's tone had turned . . . ominous? "Bring your couverture spoons and your A game," he added in a lighter voice. "I may have hinted to everyone about your most famous product."

I couldn't believe it. "You didn't."

"I did. Why not? Everyone loves it."

Hmm. The "product" in question *was* a Christmas-themed smash. I had to admit it. So far, it was my only successful foray into persuading a corporate client to embrace chocolate during the holidays. You would definitely recognize it, but . . .

Well, I'm sworn to secrecy. So there's that.

This time, it was my turn to change the subject. "I'll see you tomorrow, then. At seven? Bright and early. Bakers' hours."

They were my hours, too. Up with the roosters, just the way my clients tended to be. I didn't mind. Lately, though, I'd been struggling with some pretty epic jet lag. Crossing several more time zones to arrive in Massachusetts wouldn't help matters.

"See you then," Travis told me, affectionately this time.

Not that we were *involved* or anything. Even after meeting Travis in Saint-Malo, I'd avoided the temptation to become more than friends. For me, one memorable trip down that path was enough. Which only made me wonder, Where *was* Danny these days?

Last time we'd spoken, he'd mentioned a Hollywood client. He'd been cagey about the specifics, but that wasn't a surprise. As an in-demand L.A.-based security expert, my bodyguard buddy often worked for high-profile clients—people who didn't want their names thrown about willy-nilly. Danny Jamieson was nothing if not discreet. Also, tall, dark, handsome, and irredeemably macho. He'd earned two university degrees, but you wouldn't have guessed it to look at him. Danny was, well . . . rough around the edges. We went way back, all the way to our days trawling SoCal dive bars together, acting as each other's wingman. Now those days were behind us. But we'd shared plenty of other adventures.

Do I sound nostalgic? At the ripe old age of thirty, I guessed I was. Or maybe it was simply the season.

I couldn't wait to indulge all my most Christmassy impulses. Eggnog and mistletoe? Multicolored chaser lights? Decked-out fir trees? Wrapped gifts? Santa, stockings by the fireplace, and Bing Crosby on the (virtual) stereo? Sign me up!

All that stood between me and a whole lot of Christmas cheer were one ride to the airport, one five-hour flight, another ride to the B&B in Sproutes, and some time. Easy peasy.

I left a gift box of chocolates with my Las Vegas hotel's concierge, several more with each member of the desk staff, and another with my cabdriver, then headed for snowy New England.

When I awakened that night, I didn't know where I was.

That's not unusual for me, though. Given all the traveling I do, I'm statistically more likely than the average person to forget where I'd fallen asleep and stub my toe on the bed frame while getting up in the middle of the night. Knowing that didn't offer much comfort when grappling for a toe in the dark, though.

Ouch. Frowning, I sat on the bed and clutched my big toe, hoping to massage away the pain. I remembered arriving past midnight, thanks to a delayed plane. I'd fallen onto my room's cheery double bed (made up with red flannel Christmas-print bedding) and promptly passed out. I hadn't changed into sleep clothes. I hadn't unpacked. I'd simply brushed my teeth—my one nonnegotiable—and gone in pursuit of the requisite forty winks.

I was still planning to meet Travis first thing in the morning. My keeper might be famously methodical, but I'm famously determined. I make it a point of pride to keep my word.

We'd agreed to meet at 7:00 a.m. for breakfast. I meant to do that. However, my circadian rhythm had other ideas. My body and brain were still stuck between Nevada, Brittany (where I'd been before meeting my Las Vegas client), and Melbourne (where I'd been working before that). Frankly, I was all over the place.

Feeling hopelessly jet lagged, I studied my room at the B and B. I'd loved it on (bleary) sight—possibly because it looked as though a holiday-themed boutique had exploded inside it.

The walls featured framed Christmas artwork. The antique bureau, nightstands, and bedstead were all decked out in swags of holly, complete with tiny red berries. The rugs and bathroom linens were jolly red and white, bordered with green. There were red velvet bows, colonial-style garlands of crimson wooden beads, and plenty of (currently unlighted) wreathed holiday candles.

I inhaled their pine-and-cinnamon fragrance and couldn't help smiling. I was in Sproutes, Massachusetts, I remembered. So far, the place felt like Christmastown, USA. I was in love.

I was also hideously awake. I recognized the feeling. It

meant there'd be no more sleep for me, not even in that super-cushy bed in that peaceful bed-and-breakfast. I wasn't kidding, either. You could have heard a pin drop. It felt . . . hushed.

Not wanting to disturb anyone, I got out of bed quietly. My host, Zach Johnson, had been asleep when I'd arrived. He'd left arrangements for me to check in and get my room key from a lockbox tucked behind a pillar at the B and B's impressive entryway.

It was a trusting, generous gesture. I liked Sproutes already. If this was the way people behaved in small-town New England, then Travis and I were in for a memorable stay.

Wanting to express my gratitude, I tiptoed downstairs. The treads were in perfect repair; they didn't so much as creak. On the landing, I took in the view, savoring the decorations that Zach had put in place for the holiday. The banisters were adorned with more garlands, these made of fresh evergreens.

Their fragrance led me toward the foyer. From that cheery enclave, another corridor branched toward the parlor on the left and the dining room and kitchen on the right. I veered right.

It was easy to find my way. Even carrying my bulky bag of chocolate-making gear, I could make out my surroundings. I hadn't explored earlier, but now there was enough moonlight to view the B and B's immaculate historical furnishings and Christmas decorations. I glimpsed a towering, ornament-bedecked fir tree in the parlor and almost veered toward it. I stopped myself just in time. I planned to make a handmade batch of truffles to surprise Zach and the other guests. I needed to get started.

I'd make chocolate-peppermint truffles, I mused as I reached what I judged must be the kitchen. That was the flavor of my most successful Christmas treat—the secret one that Travis had mentioned earlier. Why not? My corporate client would never know that I'd done a riff on those popular flavors. I was sworn to secrecy about the goodies I developed for consultees, but that didn't mean I could never enjoy their original formulas.

Happily envisioning Zach and the B and B's guests smiling as they tasted my chocolaty creations, I groped for the kitchen's light switch. No dice. I set down my bag and tried again.

The lights flared to life. Reflexively, I blinked against their brightness. I crouched to retrieve my chocolatiering bag.

But I wasn't in the kitchen, I realized as I straightened. Instead, I was in the dining room. And this wasn't going to be a memorable stay in Sproutes for any of the reasons I'd imagined.

This was going to be a memorable stay for another, more horrible reason. Because judging by the inert, awkward pose of the woman I saw sprawled atop the jolly red loomed rug, beside the enormous dining table, splattered by what appeared to be Christmas wassail punch, I'd just stumbled upon another murder.

Two

My initial hope was that I was wrong.

I didn't want the woman to be dead. I didn't want any of this to be happening. I wished I were dreaming, but I knew I was awake. Gripped by an ominous sense of incongruity all the same, I crept closer. My voice quavered as I called out.

"Hello? Are you all right?"

Obviously, it was a nonsensical question. The woman wasn't all right. She was motionless. Pale. It looked as though she'd fallen atop a punch bowl. I noticed one on the floor near her head. It was made of beautiful sterling silver, embossed and decorated with colonial-style flourishes—and with a few tresses of her long dark hair, gruesomely strewn across it.

Those wet strands were glued to the punch bowl with the same liquid that appeared to have splashed all over her. I smelled red wine. Fruit. A little spice. It was wassail, for sure. Orange slices and cinnamon sticks littered the floor. They were traditional additions to one of the holiday's tastiest drinks.

Wassail was alcoholic, I told myself. Maybe she was

simply drunk? Passed out after too much caroling and tree trimming?

I moved nearer, mentally cataloguing details as I went. She was wearing party clothes—a pair of slouchy gold trousers and a matte black halter top, plus a few expensive-looking pieces of jewelry. I guessed her age to be mid- to late twenties. It was difficult to tell, with her face so ghostly, covered partly by her hair. Her limp position haunted me. My hands trembled.

I'd like to say I felt cool and capable. I did not.

I've seen dead bodies before. Yet the awful reality of it never diminishes. This was someone who cared—someone people cared about. Now she was gone. Unless she was breathing?

I crouched and watched for breath, however shallow. She appeared to be beyond CPR. I felt horribly mindful of the fact that this might now be a crime scene. Should I touch anything?

If I could save her, I had to. Probably only a few seconds had passed since I'd switched on the light, but they felt like hours. My heart pounded; my mouth felt dry with fear. I glanced around the dining room and the darkened kitchen beyond it.

Could someone be lurking there?

No. I was being silly. Murder wasn't following me around the world. That was impossible. I gave myself a mental shake and reached for the woman's wrist. If I could detect a pulse . . .

The moment I grasped her delicate, lifeless wrist, I recognized her. This was Albany Sullivan, celebrated memoirist. Travis's friend. I hadn't met her yet, but I'd seen enough media coverage of Albany to identify her pretty face, flowing hair, and slender body, clad in her signature "antifashion" style.

Albany was—had been—an original. She'd been made for the media blitz accompanying her memoir's release, appearing on every publicity outlet and, by all accountings, acing them all.

I sensed no pulse, only terrifying stillness as she lay amid the disarray of the fallen punch bowl and all the spilled wassail. That sticky liquid had already begun to dry on her neck and shoulder, on her expertly made-up face, on her eyelashes—

Suddenly queasy, I looked away. I reached numbly for my phone, then remembered in a haze that I'd tucked it into my bag of chocolate-making supplies. I inhaled deeply, hoping to dredge up some necessary strength as I retrieved it. I dialed 911.

I'd be lying if I said I spoke calmly to the authorities. I probably didn't. My hands still shook. So did my voice. I did my best to force the necessary words through my tight throat, anyway, taking comfort in the fact that help would arrive soon.

My call was still ongoing, but I needed to phone Travis next. It was important that he heard about this from someone who cared. This tragedy would shake him, maybe more than anything else we'd been through together—and we'd been through a lot lately. I wanted to be there for my advisor. My friend.

On the other end of the line, the emergency worker kept talking. We'd keep the connection open while waiting for the authorities to arrive. Police, I imagined. Maybe EMTs, too. Not that there was any help for Albany Sullivan now.

I steeled myself and peeked at her. Maybe she'd fallen and hit her head? Maybe someone had bashed her in the skull with that heavy, ornate punch bowl? Maybe she'd been shot? Or stabbed?

But I spied no bullet wounds. No wounds of any kind.

I wasn't expert enough to determine what had happened to her.

Frankly, I didn't want to be. I'm a chocolate professional. End of story. It didn't matter, just then, that I'd helped capture a killer a time or two. That didn't make me an expert.

I longed to call Travis. Or Danny. But I settled for the 911 operator, offering all the details I saw. Doing so helped me remember them more vividly, just as though I'd jotted them down in the Moleskine notebook where I keep my formulas and my schedule. Traveling as much as I do— and to the kinds of off-the-grid places I go—you learn to keep certain things nondigital.

When the operator informed me that the authorities were close, I shakily got to my feet and went outside to flag them down. The wintery weather bit into my skin and stole my breath. I was wearing my usual jeans and (in deference to the cold) a sweater, but my sneakers were not up to the job at hand.

I slipped on the icy walkway leading back to the B and B. One of the arriving police officers steadied me. "Careful, ma'am."

"Thanks." I swallowed hard. Jolted by a fresh burst of adrenaline, I kept going. "She's in here. Follow me."

"I'm right behind you," the officer said. "Don't worry."

Her voice, kind but crisp, brought a certain dreadful normality to the situation. This officer was accustomed to handling terrible events with equanimity and professionalism.

I guided the way, even as lights began coming on upstairs. I heard murmurings. Footsteps. The police sirens had awakened the B and B's guests. I hadn't been able to warn Zach Johnson.

In my concern about Travis, I'd entirely forgotten my host.

Uniformed officers strode inside. Two of them passed by me. They seemed familiar with the bed-and-breakfast's layout.

But then, Sproutes was a small town. It occurred to me that some or several of these officers might know Albany Sullivan personally. I had to warn them. I knew Albany had siblings. They were (now notoriously) mentioned in her book. Pseudonymously, of course, with certain identifying details changed. But it didn't take a genius to recognize who the real-life inspirations for those characters were. What if one was a police officer?

I moved quickly. "You should know, it's Albany Sullivan," I blurted in an urgent tone. "She's the one I found in there."

All the emergency workers stopped moving. Either my warning fell far short of comforting, given its hasty delivery, or . . .

I realized that everyone's gazes were trained behind me.

I turned. Travis stood there, wearing a hastily thrown-on B&B robe. He appeared to be clad in pajama pants, too, but nothing more. I stared at his bare feet in shock, full of sorrow.

Gruffly, my advisor cleared his throat. Nothing could have prepared either of us for this. "What's happened to Albany?"

I made myself look up. His frown, behind his professorial horn-rimmed glasses, told me he wasn't ready to hear this.

I reached for his hand. Dumbly, he let me grasp it. But his attention was all for the police officers . . . and the scene that lay beyond them. From his viewpoint, I knew the dining room was largely hidden—or at least, the tragedy waiting inside it was.

"Travis, I'm sorry." I squeezed his hand, my voice

choked with concern. "Albany has had . . . an accident. There's nothing to—"

"Be done," I meant to say, but my advisor shook his head.

He pushed past me, along with a few of the B and B's guests. One of them might have been my host. Despite the lights that now floodlit the multistory house, I couldn't tell. I didn't know what Zach Johnson looked like. I couldn't have picked him out of a police lineup—not that I hoped it would come to that.

One of the police officers belatedly stepped up. He threw his arms wide, then held out his palm. "Stop. Nobody comes in."

But Travis had already reached the dining room's threshold. He was tall, blond, and more muscular than he had a right to be, given his spreadsheets-and-suits life-style. He craned to see.

His mouth tightened. When he turned to me again, gazing over the heads of worried guests and imposing police officers, Travis's expression looked troubled, but not grief-stricken.

A moment later, I learned why.

"That's not Albany," he said. "It's definitely not."

Was he in shock? It seemed likely. Gently, I went to him. "Travis, I'm so sorry. But it looked like Albany to me."

His distant gaze sought out the woman on the floor. Despite every effort, she remained unresponsive. She had to be dead.

"I was awake," I explained. "I came downstairs to make chocolates—you know, as a thank-you to Zach and the B and B's guests for accommodating me at the last minute. But then I—"

"That's not Albany." Travis met my gaze squarely.

I had to admit, he didn't seem like someone in the throes of shock and heartache. Still, I wanted to comfort him.

My relationship with Travis has happened largely over the phone, so I wasn't familiar with how he dealt with tragedy. Maybe with denial? This certainly felt like denial. "I realize this is devastating, given how close you and Albany were—"

"Are. We *are* close. We've been friends since seventh grade."

I regrouped. "Maybe we should get some fresh air."

Before we could, a wail came from the dining room. In sync, Travis and I maneuvered for a better position. I guessed we both wanted to know the source of that raw, inconsolable sound.

Inside, someone had reached the woman. A man had fallen to his knees beside her. Another of the police officers was crouched nearby, probably disturbed in the midst of examining the scene by the keening man's arrival. Was it Albany's father?

It could have been. He was heavyset and graying, with weathered but handsome features and a rumpled, expensive-looking suit. His feet were covered with a pair of stylish sneakers, but no socks. It was clear he'd gotten dressed in a rush, having been awakened by the sounds of the night's events.

By the look of him, he undoubtedly wished he hadn't been.

I peered between the onlookers and watched as he shoved away the police officer. Next, he fell onto the woman's body, giving another hoarse cry. I couldn't help feeling sorry for him.

Heartsick, I shifted my gaze to Travis. I wanted to see how he was holding up. It turned out, he was managing quite well.

There was a woman in his arms. A pretty, dark-haired woman with a slender build and a defiantly "antifashion" ensemble.

I gawked at her. She looked *exactly* like Albany Sullivan.

But then who . . . ? Why . . . ? I shook my head and reflexively glanced back at the dead woman I'd found, utterly perplexed.

Travis wouldn't comfort just anyone so warmly. My keeper was far too reserved for that. Was that Albany in his arms? If so, who was the woman who'd face-planted into the punch bowl?

The two of them were—if you'll excuse the term— dead ringers for one another. They could have been twin sisters. Were they?

Half convinced I'd fallen asleep on the plane and dreamed everything, I blinked. The police officers were still there. So was a *third* lanky brunette—another Albany doppelgänger. She stood on tiptoe at the edge of the crowd, phone in hand, dressed in just flattering enough men's trousers, worn with a silk shirt and eyeglasses. The whole effect was avant-garde geek chic.

That was Albany's style, my memory protested. But although Albany was pretty, this woman was in a league of her own. She was *stunning*. That's probably the reason I shouldn't have been surprised to glimpse my security-expert pal right beside her.

"Danny?" I mouthed in disbelief.

My bodyguard buddy was already headed my way, sporting his usual wariness, tattoos, and bulging muscles. He had grabbed the striking brunette's hand and was guiding her along in his wake.

She appeared more than happy to follow him. Danny Jamieson was like catnip to women, I knew. They were drawn to him, stayed long enough to feel intoxicated, and then moved on. But there was something different about this one. She seemed . . . on edge.

Well, we were at the scene of a potential murder. That seemed like a reasonable reaction to me. I nodded hello to them.

I couldn't help glancing back at the dead woman. Then at the woman in Travis's arms. Then at Danny's companion. *Three* women who appeared identical to Albany Sullivan. How? Why?

Danny handled the introductions with typical brevity.

"Hayden, this is Tansy. Tansy, Hayden."

Struck by a niggling sense of familiarity—one that didn't owe itself to my having just seen three semi-identical brunettes—I stared at Tansy while shaking her hand. Her grasp felt cool and confident; her manner was charismatic. Not quite effusive, but I sensed that, under different circumstances, that would have been her approach. Unlike everyone else, Tansy didn't appear to have been unhappily awakened at 3:00 a.m. In fact, she seemed positively fresh faced. Her hair looked perfect, her clothes the same.

"It's nice to meet you, Hayden." Her voice was husky, tinged with millennial vocal fry. "Danny talks about you a lot."

The man in question scowled. "I wouldn't say 'a lot.'"

Tansy gave him a teasing smile. "I would." She turned to me again, her expression sobering. "Did you really find—"

I nodded before she could finish. I didn't want to relive the moments when I'd discovered the wassail-splattered woman.

Tansy understood. "It's awful. *So* awful," she told me in a low voice. "I mean, I can't say it's surprising, exactly, but—"

A warning look from Danny cut her off midsentence.

I glanced from my bodyguard pal to the woman I surmised was his . . . client? I wondered what was up. "Is it Albany Sullivan?"

They both looked at me as though I were crazy to think so.

I didn't understand. Not even as Danny shook his head to confirm it wasn't Albany. He turned his attention to the hubbub going on nearby, his body language even more guarded than usual.

But then, Danny often has a bad attitude, especially when it comes to authority figures. Growing up tough in a gritty, wrong-side-of-the-tracks neighborhood in L.A.— and then falling into (temporary) criminal behavior—will do that to a person. Danny was reformed now, but getting there had taken a while.

"It's Melissa Balthasar," Tansy volunteered somberly. "One of *Christmas in Crazytown*'s producers. Roger is the other one."

With a nudge of her perfect chin, she indicated the disheveled, silver-haired man who'd crumpled beside the body.

I examined him more closely. "Is he her father?"

Tansy's laughter pealed out, vibrant and inappropriate. Several people turned to glance at us, full of disapproval or curiosity or both. But I was too busy gawping at her to care.

I'd recognized her at last. The "Tansy" to whom Danny had introduced me so casually was, in actual fact, Tansy Park, world-famous sitcom star and bodacious breakout sex symbol.

Without her customary big blond waves, lipsticked smile, and barely there wardrobe (the better to showcase her famous bikini body), Tansy seemed like a different person altogether.

Until she laughed, that is. Her hooting laughter was unique. Everyone in the world has heard her inimitable guffaw.

Tansy's laughter might have been the most endearing thing about her. Or it would have been, under other circumstances. As it was, poor Tansy seemed shamefaced by her lapse in decorum.

Shoulders slumping, she turned away. Danny saw and kindly squeezed her hand, even though comfort wasn't on his list of security services, slated next to surveillance and ass kicking.

"He's her husband," Danny informed me. "Where I come from, the two of them are a legit power couple. Without Melissa, Albany's memoir—and the show in Sproutes—wouldn't be happening."

I frowned. "But Roger has to be fifty, at least. And Melissa—" I broke off, trying to estimate her age. I couldn't.

I felt too haunted by the memory of her pale, waxy face.

"She'd just turned twenty-six," Danny said. "I compiled security dossiers on everyone involved in the production."

Tansy nodded in agreement. I estimated her own age at around the same. But the bombshell sitcom actress was alive and vibrant. Melissa Balthasar wasn't. Never would be again.

She'd been younger than I was, it struck me. Awful.

"You want them?" Danny's voice intruded on my thoughts.

I refocused. "Your dossiers? No, thanks. I'm not going to—"

"Investigate this time," was what came next. But I was brought up short by the appearance of another brunette. I caught sight of her as she wandered inside and down the hallway, like a ghost.

Maybe she *was* a ghost. Because, with an eerie sense

of déjà vu, I thought I recognized her. She looked like Albany. Again.

My staring gave me away. Danny and Tansy followed my gaze to the *fourth* Albany Sullivan mirror image I'd seen that night.

"Albany's sister, Ophelia Sullivan," Danny supplied. His perceptive gaze caught mine. "I know what you're thinking."

He couldn't possibly. Because what I was thinking was preposterous. We didn't even know for sure if a murder had been committed at the B&B that night. Not technically. Not yet.

All the same, I couldn't help wondering, If the worst had happened, *which* Albany look-alike had been the intended victim?

I glanced toward Travis. In his arms, Albany didn't much resemble the self-assured, wisecracking media darling she'd been while making the rounds to publicize her "almost memoir." In the wake of Melissa's death, Albany appeared scared. Sad. Confused.

Her distress seemed genuine. I couldn't help feeling moved.

"You're thinking that Melissa Balthasar might have been murdered," Danny forged on bluntly, clearly startling Tansy. "You're noticing that she wasn't the only tall, skinny brunette around here. You're wondering if someone meant to kill Melissa . . ."

"Or if someone else—a look-alike—was the target," I finished. "Yeah. Pretty much." I couldn't help analyzing the situation. Blame the tumultuous months I'd spent mixed up in murders. I was different now. Danny, my closest friend, knew it.

"No!" Tansy squeaked with alarm. She clutched

Danny's bulging bare biceps, drawing my attention to his brawny bod.

I wondered if the two of them were lovers. Then I dismissed the thought. Danny had his faults. Mixing business with pleasure wasn't one of them. If he'd been hired as Tansy's bodyguard, then he wouldn't be sleeping with her, too. Maybe afterward . . .

"You don't *really* think this was *murder*, do you?" Tansy asked, her beautiful eyes wide. It was difficult not to stare at her. "I mean, Zach's B&B is a really nice place. Surely no one would bust in here and actually *kill* Melissa, just like that."

I remembered her earlier comment that the producer's death hadn't been exactly surprising. Also, the significant look Danny had employed to cut her off. There was something going on here.

But no matter what Danny surmised, I didn't plan on sleuthing this time. I'd had enough of murder and misdeeds—of immersing myself, however reluctantly, in the grim side of life.

I intended to remain on the sunny side of the street from now on. See, when it comes down to it, I'm not cut out for dwelling on disaster. To prove it, sometimes, Danny and Travis give me a hard time for being what they call "a soft touch." For being too trusting. For liking (almost) everyone I meet. But I can't help it. Most people *are* good—or well intentioned, I reminded myself then. A surprising number of people help in a crisis; even more make ordinary days special just by existing.

Who wouldn't want to lean on that? I did. So I did.

Occasionally, I point out to my cynical security-expert pal and his brainy (sometime) adversary, Travis, that while I might consider multiple suspects while sleuthing, only *one* is guilty. That means I'm necessarily suspecting innocent people. I don't want to get too carried away being antagonistic toward them all.

"If someone did commit a murder, the police will find out," I reassured Tansy in what I hoped was a heartening tone.

As I watched the proceedings in the dining room, though, I had my doubts. So far, the police hadn't been especially useful in the murder investigations I'd been involved in. But there was a first time for everything, right? I'd been told to stay put so my statement could be taken. Yet no one had followed up with me. That delay bugged me. Shouldn't I be interviewed before I forgot exactly what I'd witnessed? Wasn't time of the essence?

Memory is a fallible thing, I knew. It shifts with time and circumstance, forming a spectrum of possibilities more than a verifiable truth. But still . . . I wished the Sproutes police were more proactive. Of all the officers there, someone could have taken my statement. For all they knew, I could ID the killer.

If there was one, I reminded myself. That was far from an inevitability. Most likely, this was an unfortunate accident.

The grave expressions on the officers' faces said it wasn't.

Four potential Albanys. Four potential victims. Hmmm . . .

"Harvard said he was inviting you here." Danny scattered my thoughts. His nickname for Travis, his onetime archenemy, almost made me smile. At least it was better than Captain Calculator, another of his favorites. Travis and Danny had cooperated a few times—notably, for my sake—but mostly, they competed with one another. Constantly. "I bet you weren't expecting all this."

"That's for sure," I agreed. Around us, the B and B's guests were starting to return upstairs, looking hollow eyed and full of questions. So far, the police hadn't offered any answers. "All I wanted were a few jingle bells, some candy canes, and maybe a chance to make a snow angel. Have you ever done that?"

Tansy nodded. On her, wistfulness looked totally gorgeous. Next to her, I felt about as glamorous as an unpaired mitten.

It was silly, but despite the seriousness of the situation, Tansy's presence lent a certain surreality to the proceedings. She was such a tremendous star that her sitcom was aired worldwide, dubbed in multiple languages. No matter where I traveled, Tansy's show could inevitably be found on the dial. I couldn't really be standing beside her in the flesh, could I?

Sure, she'd changed her hair color and downplayed her glam persona. All the same, down-market Tansy was still Tansy.

Danny scoffed. "I'm from L.A., remember? If you want snow angels, you'd better ask your genius pal over there." He aimed his chin toward Travis, then gave a cocky grin. "He probably has a formula all worked out, with the right angles and approach."

I didn't doubt it. We shared a smile. "I might do that."

"If you're looking for the best Christmas, though, I can hook you up," Danny went on. "After things settle down, I mean."

He was pretending, for my sake, that Melissa's death had been an accident. I appreciated that. So I played along.

"What I'm looking for is an old-fashioned Friendsmas," I told him. A holiday shared with friends instead of family (hence, the name Friendsmas) sounded pretty good to me. "If I'd known you were here, I could have given you time to plan."

A shrug. "I don't need time to plan. Stay ready. Don't have to get ready." Danny squared his shoulders. "You good? There's nothing we can do here, and Tansy has rehearsals tomorrow. We should get back to our motel. We're staying across town—"

"Danny!" Tansy looked alarmed. Her gaze darted at me.

"You can trust Hayden," he promised.

The actress bit her lip, appearing hesitant. I wondered what she was afraid of. I wondered, too, why she'd hired Danny. So far away from Hollywood, a bodyguard seemed like overkill.

"You go." I gave Danny a good-natured shove. "I'll catch up with you later. I need to stick around to give a statement."

After a few words of encouragement for me (and, let's be real, some advice), Danny left the B&B with Tansy. That left me.

Alone. Watching the police. Waiting for my turn to give a statement. Which was when I noticed the man I now knew as Roger Balthasar crouched forlornly beside his fallen wife's body. I felt for him. I truly did. Until I noticed, from my unique vantage point, that Roger was engaged in what appeared to be a tense conversation—*negotiation*?—with one of the Sproutes police officers.

I squinted, wondering what might be going on. But there was no mistaking Roger's cajoling demeanor—or the effect it had on the listening police officer. A moment later, the officer stood.

"Looks like an accidental death to me," he announced.

As though his speculation had been a signal, the

evidence-gathering team slowed to a crawl. I stared at them in disbelief.

Had Roger Balthasar, influential producer, just made a deal to shut down the investigation into his wife's untimely death?

It sure looked that way. I shook my head—and caught Travis doing the same thing. Our gazes met. His seemed almost pleading.

My keeper wanted me to intervene. Just the way I always did. He was afraid, as I was, that if this was a murder (always a big "if"), then Albany had been the killer's true target.

I was afraid of the same thing. It didn't require rocket science to recognize the potential significance of those four look-alike brunettes. But I was afraid of getting involved, too.

So far, I'd been fortunate enough not to be seriously hurt while engaging in amateur sleuthing. Any day now, however, my luck might run out. I didn't want to become a victim myself.

You should probably know at this point that I'm a fairly tall, reasonably lanky brunette myself. While I don't have a killer fashion sense, I do have shoulder-length dark hair and just enough of a passing resemblance to Albany to feel uneasy.

But there was no help for it. I was in. I had to be. If the police investigation was (maybe) corrupted—if there wasn't going to be a legitimate inquiry—then someone had to help, right?

Someone in Sproutes was hiding a murderous Christmas secret—someone horrible enough to spoil the holiday season. I had to find out who. I had to do it before that person struck again . . . just in case they'd missed their target the first time.

If the killer had made a mistake, he'd realize it soon.

More than likely, he'd attempt to "fix" it. Also soon.

I gave Travis a subtle nod, then went to get started. With only a few weeks till Christmas, there was no time to lose.

Three

"I can't believe the way you took charge last night!" Albany Sullivan said to me over breakfast the next morning.

She'd definitely regained her composure probably thanks to Travis and his comforting company. In the bright light of day, in fact, Albany didn't even seem to be grieving. Maybe she'd already processed her feelings about Melissa? Or maybe, despite working together, they hadn't been close? It was possible that Albany was simply one of those look-on-the-bright-side types.

I hadn't expected to see her when Travis and I met, sticking to our agreed-upon 7:00 a.m. hour despite the awful goings-on last night. But Albany had accompanied my advisor, showing up without explanation, as though *I* were the interloper here, and not her. Given the circumstances, I couldn't complain. Besides, I wanted to know her better. Who *was* Albany Sullivan, really?

At the moment, she was someone who spoke her mind.

"Someone had to do it, though, right? That 'investigation' was a joke." Albany made air quotes with her hands. She rolled her eyes. "I promise you, Hayden, if the chief of police had been there last night, everything would have been different."

"That's what everyone's been telling me," I said.

My B and B's genial host, Zach Johnson, had made almost the same remark, beat for beat, after he'd shown me the way to the buffet this morning. Out of deference to last night's dreadful events, the customary breakfast service had been moved from the dining room to the B and B's cozy parlor. Travis, Albany, and I had chosen a table near the yule fire in the big brick fireplace.

A glance down the hall told me, however, that the dining room didn't appear to be an official crime scene. Contrary to what you'd expect, based on movies and TV detective shows, the room hadn't been cordoned off with police tape. It had instead been considerately closed with a red velvet rope hung across the entryway. The meaning of that was clear enough, I supposed. I was dismayed to have confirmed what I already feared: the police weren't stringently investigating Melissa Balthasar's death.

"Besides, I didn't do anything all that remarkable," I told Albany. I noticed her hand resting on Travis's atop the snowy tablecloth. "It was time to give my statement, that's all."

Albany laughed. She clasped Travis's hand, once, then released it to pick up her orange-cranberry-pecan muffin. As she gave that sweet a dubious look, she shook her head, suggesting she hadn't changed her mind one iota. "You charged over to the head officer and demanded to give a statement. I saw you. That's take-charge behavior. I admire that. You can't wait for life to hand out what you want. You have to take it. Right, Trav?"

Trav. Her familiar shortening of his name brought me up short. I'd thought I was the only one who called him that—usually while employing my customary frisky phone greeting.

Tell me, Trav. What are you wearing right now?

It had become a ritual between us—an imaginary seduction in a make-believe relationship. It was fun, pretending to gear up for some spicy phone-call flirting. Especially with Travis, who was always so straitlaced with me. I thought my keeper enjoyed our repartee, too. But now that game of ours felt slightly less special. I frowned and forced my focus onto my own breakfast.

It was a double chocolate chocolate chip muffin, of course, which wasn't as Christmassy as Albany's choice. But when life hands you two options, I always say, go with chocolate.

"Absolutely," my financial advisor agreed with Albany. He hadn't chosen a muffin, but bacon and eggs instead (of course). His plate lay mostly ignored between his suit-clad forearms.

He looked nice. I wasn't sure Travis owned anything *except* suits. Taking off his tie was about as casual as he ever got.

"That's how Trav got admitted to Harvard. By taking what he wanted and never accepting no for an answer," Albany confided. Her gaze traveled affectionately over his chiseled profile. "It wasn't easy, but he stuck with it." She squeezed his hand again.

I dropped my own gaze to that fond gesture. Seeing it, I felt . . . something. Jealous? Rivalrous? Impatient? Was this the way Danny and Travis felt when they competed with one another?

If so, I didn't like it. I felt uncomfortable. Self-conscious. And I was distracted from finding out what those difficulties were that Travis had overcome, according to cooing Albany.

Full of curiosity and questions, I scrutinized Travis's face to see how he reacted to Albany's touchy-feely approach to breakfast. My advisor's preoccupied expression told me nothing.

When I glanced back at Albany, she was watching me. Her face looked sharp; her features wary. But she smiled instantly.

"We're so glad you're here, Hayden!" she said. "I mean, despite the tragedy with Melissa and everything. We were just saying, Trav and I, the more the merrier, right, Trav?"

Her noticeable use of *we* (and *Trav*) stuck in my throat. I sipped my coffee, then decided to "take charge" again. As a first step in my nascent investigation into Melissa's death, I'd decided it was important to get to know Albany. Her memoir and the resulting show were the reason everyone was in Sproutes for the holiday season. It made sense that, with her work as the backdrop, the murder might have had something to do with it. I couldn't forget those Albany doppelgängers from last night.

"Despite everything, I'm happy to be here," I admitted. I gazed at the parlor's comfortable furnishings and colorful, shiny decorations—and at the dreamy snow falling lightly outside the window, piling up on the mullioned panes. None of the other guests were awake yet; we had the place to ourselves. "I've never experienced a real New England Christmas. This looks like the perfect place to spend the holiday, that's for sure."

Albany laughed again. "You wouldn't say that if you'd grown up here. Right, Trav?" She gave him a companionable nudge. "There's a reason I called my book *Christmas in Crazytown*."

Aha. That was the perfect segue. "Was it really that bad?"

Albany's eyes sparkled. "Define *bad*. In my family, everything is relative. But you have to laugh, right? Especially when your mom burns the turkey, *with* the frozen giblets still inside, by the way, and your sister goes vegan on the spot—"

"Ruining Christmas *every year after*!" Travis chimed in.

In sync, they beamed at each other. I didn't get it. It wasn't like Travis to interrupt. Usually, he was polite to a fault. Yet Albany seemed to have expected him to do just that. Perplexed, I glanced from Albany to my financial advisor. I had the sense this was an oft-repeated ritual between them, but . . .

"Going vegan isn't that bad," I said. "I've had some very tasty vegan meals. In Morocco, for instance, a good tagine is—"

Albany's exasperated, confused exclamation stopped me.

Travis looked at me expectantly, as well. Then, "Hayden, you promised! You had all that time on your flight, too."

Uh-oh. I recognized that edge to his voice. It was the same tone he employed while recommending anti-procrastination apps for my phone and haranguing me into finishing client reports.

I might *possibly* have a *tiny* problem with delaying certain elements of my work. Never the fun, hands-on, chocolate-centric parts, of course. Only the boring, necessary follow-up parts.

"Come on," I protested in my own defense. When cornered, I tend to make jokes. "Does anyone really enjoy doing homework?"

Their impassive united confusion told me everything.

These two *did* enjoy doing homework. Probably always had.

"You didn't read my book!" Albany pouted. She pointedly put down her orange-cranberry-pecan muffin, as though I'd ruined her appetite with my supposed shirking. "'Ruining Christmas *every year after*!' is my catchphrase! It's a through line. After every appalling, hilarious event, the narrator just keeps saying it. It's what people shout at me at book signings. It's what my publisher printed below the starred review pull quotes on the musical tie-in edition. It's how Oprah welcomed me on her show!"

Wow. Humblebragging, much? Still, I felt duly chastened.

It was as though Albany had tested me with that setup, and I'd failed. But Melissa's death was too important for me to quit snooping around now. I still needed to gather background intel.

"*Christmas in Crazytown* is a musical?" I asked Albany. "I didn't know Tansy Park could sing and dance, too. That's cool."

Albany chortled. Her laughter wasn't as enchanting as Tansy's had been. "Tansy's singing and dancing are . . . enthusiastic, to put it kindly. But she's not in the production to excel at performing, you understand. It's like Melissa always told me—"

Albany choked on her next words. Apparently, her newfound breeziness had just worn off. She looked away, sniffling and apologizing. I suddenly felt terrible for pressuring her for details about the show—and even worse for assuming that Albany didn't care about her producer. Despite her earlier bragging, this version of Albany was more likable and less exclusionary.

But I couldn't trust my own judgment when it came to Travis's longtime friend. It turned out, I was having a surprisingly difficult time dealing with their closeness.

I've never been the competitive type—not when it came to people in my life, at least. I was nonplussed by the feeling.

"Tansy is in the production to put 'butts in seats,'" Travis explained, bailing out Albany in her moment of need. "That's how it is with entertainment these days.

Producers want a sure thing. A best-selling memoir is a start, but a bankable star is insurance. Even if Tansy performs poorly, people will come to see her. That was Melissa's philosophy, at any rate."

Interesting. "I guess we'll see if that's true."

Albany's face took on a dour cast. "*If* the show opens. That's not guaranteed anymore, thanks to last night's disaster."

Apparently, Albany wasn't too sensitive *not* to consider her own bottom line. "You think the premiere will be delayed?"

A shrug. "There've been calls to cancel the entire show."

I didn't want to be insensitive myself, but . . . "Can the show go on without Melissa? I'm not sure of a producer's role, but Roger is still here. If he can bring himself to work, that is."

Albany's reply was a snort. "Nothing but his own untimely demise will stop Roger Balthasar from working. He's a machine."

"Really?" Sometimes, the less said, the better. At least when it came to leading (what were essentially) witnesses.

But Albany didn't take the bait. She gave her muffin a halfhearted nibble, then sighed dramatically. "Yes, really."

Humph. That was hardly illuminating. A police detective had once told me that, when it came to murder, it was important to examine the victim's spouse. To consider him or her a suspect.

I was having no trouble believing Roger Balthasar to be untrustworthy, duplicitous, and potentially murderous. I didn't care about the age gap between him and Melissa. I did care about (what appeared to be) his attempts to shut down the police.

Evidently, Albany wouldn't be the one to help clarify that. I chewed another delicious bite of chocolaty muffin (brain food, naturally), then regrouped. I still didn't know all the ins and outs of *Christmas in Crazytown*—the musical show or the book.

"What interested you in writing a memoir?" I asked Albany.

She looked askance at me. I thought the jig was up—I'd been too obvious in trying to extract information—but Travis jumped in.

"Actually, it's a 'lightly fictionalized' memoir," he told me in that very specific, I-alphabetize-my-canned-goods way he had. "That means that, while the people, places, and incidents mentioned in the book are genuine, their portrayals might not be. Especially not in the show, as a matter of expedience."

I frowned at him. I understood *that* much. I'm not a dunce; I simply don't like spending all my airplane time on required reading. The minute Travis had suggested I bone up on Albany's work on my way to Sproutes, my innate contrariness had kicked in. I hate being told what to do. Along with my incurable monkey mind (which always keeps me hopping) and my procrastination tendencies, stubbornness is one of my most defining features.

However, I was familiar with Albany's book. I would have had to have spent the past six months under a rock not to be. Despite being overseas a lot, I'd heard of Albany's media blitz, her sensational memoir, her witticisms on late-night television.

I'm not above playing dumb when it suits me, though. I widened my eyes. "Isn't it difficult to keep things straight in your own mind, then?" I asked Albany. "Memory is malleable, you know. There's research showing that witness testimony, for instance, can be shifted through subtle manipulation. People can be made to believe lots of things."

"Are you suggesting I'm manipulating people with my book?"

"No, no!" *Sure, maybe.* "Only that it's possible your childhood Christmases here in Sproutes weren't so bad. Or so funny. Not as much as you made them out to be, at least."

"Well, of course they weren't." A beat passed while Albany squared off with me. "I *made* them funny through talent, insight, and amazing writing. But the raw material was there. I mean, come on. My parents named us Albany, Cashel, and Ophelia. With names like those, how well adjusted could we have turned out?"

I smiled. I had the sense Albany had employed that quip lots of times. On my mental Moleskine, I noted her siblings' names. I thought I remembered Danny IDing Ophelia last night.

"You're well adjusted," Travis reassured Albany. His deep, sexy tone softened warmly for her. "You overcame a lot."

"Thanks to you!" Tenderly, she stroked his hand. "You're a champion, Trav. What in the world would I have done without you? You were my inspiration, you know. Seeing what you went through—"

"'Went.' Past tense. No need to rehash any of that."

His words were gently said, but Travis's posture had turned distinctly guarded. His shoulders looked stiff, too. That might have been because of his (usual) tailored suit, worn today with an open-collar shirt and spiffy oxford shoes. His jawline looked taut, but everyday handsomeness was probably to blame for that.

"No more trips down memory lane without fuel!" Travis spied Zach Johnson emerging from the kitchen with a napkin-covered basket of what I assumed were baked goods. Jovially, my keeper waved over the B and B's host. "Not that these goodies will be half as tasty as the delicious chocolate treats you create, Hayden."

Okay. Now I *knew* something fishy was going on. My financial advisor was a genius at finance, itineraries, and research of all kinds. He excelled at making connections. But he was the worst at misdirection—especially when it came packaged with a compliment. Empty flattery wasn't Travis's style. Not with me.

It briefly occurred to me that maybe Travis was different—more relaxed—here, where he grew up, with media darling Albany at his side, bolstering him. But I didn't think so. I thought Travis had a secret. I wanted to find out what it was.

"I'll be sure to give you extra helpings next time," I assured him sweetly, promising myself to get to the bottom of this. If my advisor thought he could sidestep me, he was wrong.

I chatted with Zach while he delivered what indeed were more baked goods—muffins and croissants, *pains au chocolat* and flaky fruit Danishes. The innkeeper was friendly, if slightly subdued. I would have expected sadness or a bit of conjecture about Melissa's tragic passing, but Zach hadn't even mentioned it. Along with Albany, Zach seemed not to want to linger on Melissa's death. That seemed odd to me. Wasn't it human nature to talk about such an awful event? But maybe New Englanders were different. Maybe that taciturn Yankee reputation was merited.

The funny thing was that Zach's earlier text messages to me, confirming my arrival and the lockbox routine to retrieve my room key, had been funny enough to make me laugh out loud.

Maybe Zach was one of those people who preferred

digital communication, I reasoned. With certain clients, I'm the same way. But I was pretty sure my persona remained static, no matter what. I didn't think I came across as particularly clever while on Twitter or aloof via SMS. On the other hand, Travis, distinct from most people, doesn't have a single social-media profile. Not even a headshot on his company's "About Us" webpage. He's notoriously private. Now, given the things Albany had said about Travis's difficult past, I wondered if he was hiding from something. Or maybe hiding from some*one*. I wished I knew.

I glanced up from selecting my second muffin (you would have had an encore, too; they were delightful) to see Zach looking at Albany. Specifically, at her hand, which rested on Travis's sleeve. If I appeared half as jealous earlier as Zach did then . . .

Well, let's just say I needed to shake off that feeling. Tout de suite. Because it wasn't pretty to witness or to feel.

Albany didn't look up. "You should really consider offering a gluten-free option," she told Zach. "Lots of people are moving toward cleaner diets these days, even at Christmastime."

Her blithe criticism left poor Zach downcast. It seemed he had hoped for her approval and had been rebuffed. While he and Albany peered judgmentally at his glutenous baked goods, I caught Travis making a face. Unlike Albany, I knew Travis didn't like "fussy eating." He even joked about it. So I almost burst out laughing. Travis saw. He winked, then smiled at me. We were back. Buddies through to the end. My heart swelled with happiness.

You know, just a little bit. As I said, I'm not into Travis. Not passionately. Not unless he's speaking in that dizzying voice of his. But I was pleased to know that he hadn't changed completely. *I* knew a few details about him, too, even if they didn't relate to his past. He apparently still didn't favor a "clean diet." There was hope I'd make Travis fall in love with a varietal dark chocolate, perfectly made to melt in his mouth.

Or maybe something sweeter. Milk chocolate. Or white?

Despite my training and experience, I'm not a snob about white chocolate—also known, when properly made, as a buttery combination of cocoa butter, milk fat, and sugar. What's not to like? Anyone who says it's not "real chocolate" can fight me.

"Anyway, I must dash." Albany tossed down her Christmas-print napkin and rose. She leaned over to kiss Travis's cheek—loudly, with a showy smack of her lips—then laughed and wiped off the lip-gloss smudge she'd left. "I tried to get a hold of the show's cast and crew to let them know about Melissa and cancel today's rehearsal, but I wasn't able to reach everyone. I want to get to the theater in case people show up for work."

"Good idea." Travis's glowing expression suggested it might be the finest idea in the history of mankind. "I'll be right behind you." This time, *he* squeezed Albany's hand caringly.

Whoa. Were the two of them . . . *an item*? I needed Danny's take on the situation, stat. He'd been in Sproutes longer than I had. My bodyguard buddy would know the score. I could count on him for background and solid conjecture. Plus, I wanted Danny's views on Melissa's maybe-murder. We needed to talk sans clients.

While I thought about that, Zach busied himself brushing crumbs from our table. He was still watching Albany, but a lot less moonily now. I guessed I'd misjudged the situation. From the corner of my eye, I spotted a few B&B

guests arriving for breakfast. Life seemed to be moving on, despite last night's catastrophe. Poor Melissa Balthasar. She deserved justice.

Except Albany didn't move. "You're not coming, Trav?" She sounded vaguely petulant, but Travis didn't notice.

"I thought I'd catch up with Hayden for a while," he said.

"Oh." For a moment, Albany seemed annoyed. It was evident that she and Travis had a routine. Then she said, "Okay! Later!"

As she strode lithely away, leaving lemongrass perfume and vaguely hurt feelings in her wake, I couldn't help feeling I'd won. For now, Travis was mine. But that was crazy, right?

Despite Albany's flowing brunette locks, she was the golden girl of the moment. She was stylish, imitated, and widely admired. She'd inspired countless online memes, multiple bidding wars, and bucketloads of salacious speculation—not to mention, a famous skit on late-night TV. Albany was (probably) wealthy and (indisputably) successful. She could have Travis Turner if she wanted to. The question in my mind was, Did she want to?

When I surfaced from my ruminations, Travis was watching me. Patiently, with the same unshakable sense of equability he always possessed. His gaze seemed uncomfortably . . . perceptive.

"I warned you that Albany can be hard to warm up to."

"Don't be absurd!" I protested. "I barely know her."

"Yet you haven't announced that you like her," my keeper pointed out. "For you, that's as good as saying you loathe her."

I laughed, despite noting, worryingly, how hurt he seemed that Albany and I hadn't become insta-buddies. "I don't loathe her! Albany seems . . . intent on reminding me that I *wasn't* in your past. Her cliquishness is a little off putting, that's all."

Travis's expression eased. "She may be overreacting out of anxiety," he allowed. "She's had a difficult time lately. Also, according to Albany, I talk about you *a lot*. She's intimidated."

I hooted. Whatever else was going on with Albany, I doubted she suffered from feelings of inadequacy. "Ooh, you talk about me?" Jokingly, I fluttered my eyelashes at him. "Really? Go on."

But Travis wasn't interested in teasing. "Scoring your account was a big deal, years ago. Albany helped me strategize."

Oh. I hadn't expected business talk. I frowned slightly. "I thought you 'scored' my account because old Mr. What's-his-name retired?" My previous financial advisor had been . . . enervating.

"Either way, it's all in the past now." Travis swept his gaze over my plate of chocolaty muffin, plus fruit and yogurt. "If you're almost finished with that, we can get started."

"But what if I want to talk about the devious machinations you apparently went through to work on my trust fund?"

If there'd been any, of course. It was a good thing Danny wasn't there, I knew. I was sure my security-expert pal still harbored a few distrustful thoughts about the man who helped manage my fortune. As Danny would have said, *I* was the golden goose. I couldn't take for granted that Travis would always have my nonfinancial interests at heart.

But Travis and I were friends now. Close friends. That made all the difference to me. I believed it did to him, too.

His smile seemed to confirm it. "You're welcome to press for details," he said. "I'm afraid you'll be disappointed."

Fine. I knew when to back off. "Okay, then, yes. We can 'get started' with looking into Melissa Balthasar's death."

"I knew you'd be in. Who are your suspects so far?"

"Still TBD." To be determined. "I'm pretty sure Albany might have been the killer's real target, though. Or at least *one* of the four Albanys around here might have been." Travis nodded in agreement. Jokingly, I added, "I can definitely see why real Albany might inspire someone to murder her, though."

Travis remained stone faced. Apparently, my grin hadn't leavened the situation sufficiently. I tried again. "Someone who didn't know her well enough, I mean. Someone who had a grudge?"

"Someone like Tansy Park," Travis suggested with a lift of his eyebrow. "She and Albany definitely didn't get along."

Privately, I had to side with Tansy on that. All the same . . .

"Let's get after it, then. Can we get into rehearsals?"

"Albany is planning to cancel rehearsals today, unless Roger Balthasar says otherwise," Travis reminded me. It was interesting that Albany had provisionally taken charge while Roger dealt with his wife's sudden and unfortunate passing. But then, it was Albany's work the show was based on. "It's still possible the show will be shut down altogether."

Not before I get there to look for clues, it won't be.

If the show's cast and crew scattered, I might miss my chance at identifying the producer's killer forever.

"Then we'd better wrangle ourselves a backstage tour before it's too late," I told Travis as I stood to leave. "*Christmas in Crazytown* is integral to the case. It's what everyone has in common, right? There are bound to be clues at the theater."

I was on the job. Super determined. Powered by chocolate.

Four steps away from the table, I doubled back. I wrapped my chocolate-studded muffin in a napkin and stowed it in my crossbody bag for later. With that accomplished, I headed out again, then bundled myself in multiple layers of coat, scarf, and hat before joining a chuckling Travis at the B and B's doorway.

His gaze shot knowingly to my (now bulging) bag.

"Hey, sleuthing is hungry work," I argued. "Somebody went to a lot of effort to make this scrumptious chocolate muffin. It would be a shame to let it go to waste." I gave my bag a tap, gently enough not to crumble the muffin. "This is just a professional courtesy, and nothing more. Now let's go."

Four

It was a good thing I'd packed a snack, I realized a short while later. Because it was quite a commute between the B&B and the not quite bustling center of town. *Christmas in Crazytown* was being staged at the diminutive Sproutes community playhouse, which bordered the sleepy town's Rockwellesque commons. The theater had graciously shelved its annual homegrown production of *The Nutcracker,* Travis told me, so that Albany's show could premiere, with all the attendant publicity, in her hometown.

Rather than take my rental car—and unleash my rusty winter driving skills—Travis drove us both to the theater in his rented SUV. He steered expertly through the snow-shrouded streets with leather-gloved hands, making me think about fingerprints.

"Do you think the police found much evidence last night?" I asked my advisor. "They closed up shop pretty quickly."

"Whatever they did find might be being buried as we speak." A quick troubled glance at me. "Did you see Roger Balthasar?"

We discussed him. Our joint conclusion was that the producer had pressured the police into slowing (or abandoning) their investigation. Travis agreed to look into the Balthasars' financials, in case he detected anomalies that might indicate, say, a bribe paid to the Sproutes police force. Then we arrived at the Sproutes playhouse and clambered out of the SUV.

I definitely needed different shoes, I realized. I'd worn my most rugged pair of moto boots, after my faithful canvas Converse had betrayed me on the icy walk last night, but even my boots were no match for the weather. Snow piled on the streets and sidewalks, on the roofs of the nearby buildings, and on the marquee of the theater, which announced *Christmas in Crazytown*.

EXCLUSIVE! the marquee trumpeted. LIMITED ENGAGEMENT! I pointed to it. "Seeing that must be pretty special for Albany." I wanted to give her the benefit of the doubt. Some people were tricky to warm up to. If Travis trusted her, so did I. "Did you two used to go to shows here when you were younger?"

A headshake. "We were honor-roll nerds, not drama geeks."

I tried to picture it. "Preppy? Serious? Competitive?"

"Check. Check." Travis locked his SUV, then glanced down the street while a few Sproutes residents (Sproutesians? Sproutessers?) passed by. I had the sense he was savoring the municipal Christmas decorations—strings of lights, wreathed lampposts, and red, green, and gold banners strung across the streets . . . the works. Businesses sported hand-painted Rudolphs, candy canes, and Santas on their windows. "Also, stop it."

I widened my eyes with overt innocence. "Stop what?"

"Stop fishing to see if Albany feels competitive with you." Briefly, Travis took my hand to help me cross the less than postcard-perfect snow piled up by the town's snowplows at the edge of the sidewalk. He let me go. "It's not a competition."

"If it was, then I'd win," I said. "Also, she started it."

There was no reply to that. Travis merely opened the playhouse door, ushered me inside, and spoke with the security person on duty about allowing me to accompany him backstage.

The response was a careless, hospitable wave. I wondered why, whoever the killer was, he hadn't chosen the playhouse as his murder venue. To say its security was meager was generous.

But now that we'd arrived fully inside, striding down the aisle between rows of velvet upholstered seats in the theater's beautiful Art Deco interior, I understood. Lax security was only one issue facing the production based on Albany Sullivan's tell-all opus. Since Melissa's death, no one had been working. Plenty of the cast and crew were present, but Albany was nowhere in sight.

"Well, the show's not canceled yet," I stage-whispered to Travis. Onstage, the lights were on. The stars were present, if not costumed. The stage was fully dressed. "Is everyone here?"

"Not everyone." He frowned, seeming preoccupied again. A few crew members nodded at him as he ascended the stage steps with me in tow, but no one spoke. Travis hailed a nearby dancer. "I thought rehearsals were being canceled today," he said to her. "Didn't Albany talk to everyone?"

She started, having been engrossed in her phone. Her hair was swept up in a pretty ballerina's bun, but her sweatpants and sweatshirt suggested she'd arrived to rehearse, not to perform.

It was safe to assume she was part of the production.

"Albany's not here. Or at least, I haven't seen her." Her concerned gaze met Travis's. "You haven't heard what happened?"

To enlighten him, she held up her phone. Travis peered at it. I did, too. I saw a grainy image—probably a cell phone photo snapped in dim lighting—and realized I recognized that place.

It was the B and B's dining room, with Melissa Balthasar's wassail-soaked body sprawled vulnerably in the middle of it.

"Someone took photographs last night?" Travis asked.

"I guess so." The dancer shrugged and wandered off while scrolling through her social-media feeds, leaving me gaping. Her blasé reaction to Melissa Balthasar's death surprised me. I understood that everyone might not necessarily be a friend of the producer's, but still . . . I'd have expected more seriousness than this. More sadness. Was anyone upset about Melissa's death?

All around me, the cast and crew were reading about it. To a person, they were riveted. I could glimpse enough of the coverage to see why. It included more ghastly photos and a few horrifying hashtags, too. I knew such "first-person reporting" was commonplace these days. But experiencing it relative to an event I'd lived through myself was disturbing.

It didn't seem right to mesh this kind of news with social media's usual fodder: photos of adorable puppies and spoilers about must-see TV shows. Doing so felt wrong. I glimpsed a stagehand in the wings, reading a printed copy of the *Sproutes Sentinel*, and felt even worse when I saw the paper's front page.

TRAGIC DEATH THREATENS HOLIDAY SHOW, the headline read. Below was a photo of Melissa Balthasar in her prime, looking every inch the Hollywood mover and shaker she was reputed to be.

Not even the traditional media had been able to resist the dramatic story. Sure, the *Sentinel* had strived for a more respectful tone, but the newspaper hadn't held back from its coverage. I knew much of it had to be speculation at this point.

All the same, I picked up a copy for myself from the craft services table. It featured coffee and all the accoutrements, a few greenish bananas, and a white baker's box full of donuts. All of them, regardless of flavor, had been decorated with red, white, and green sprinkles in recognition of the holidays.

You can see why chocolate—delicious but stalwartly brown—struggles to gain a foothold during the festive season.

Tucking my newspaper under my elbow, I studied the show's cast and crew. There were probably two dozen people of varying ages in the group. I tried to identify which actors might be portraying Albany's family. I knew Tansy was Albany's double in the show, but what about the rest? Given the nature of Albany's "lightly fictionalized" memoir, surely there were cast members on hand to portray Ophelia and Cashel, along with both of Albany's parents.

With all names and details changed to protect the innocent, of course. Or, more likely, changed to avoid legal action. From what I'd heard, Albany's memoir was a no-holds-barred account of her childhood Christmases. However humorously given, those representations could be grounds for lawsuits if they damaged someone's reputation. I had to consider *that* grounds for murder.

I had to actually dig in and read Albany's book, too. Soon. Travis had gifted me an autographed copy months ago. There were probably clues in it, if I could separate fact from fiction.

Exactly *how* "lightly fictionalized" was it, anyway?

A voice nearby startled me. "No. No, no, no. Bad Tansy!"

I glanced over to see Tansy Park standing there, gripped with indecision. Appearing agonized, she reached for a donut.

"No!" she muttered under her breath. "No more donuts!"

She whirled around, then put her hands on her hips. From my position, the actress appeared to be engaged in a Shakespearean struggle. To nosh on donuts, or not to nosh on donuts? That was the question. To me, they (bluntly) didn't appear worthy of debate.

"I'd hold out for a fresh batch if I were you," I advised with a smile. "See how the baker's box is soaked with grease? That means they've been sitting around for too long. It's like I always say, if you're going to treat yourself, do it up right."

Tansy's embarrassed smile flashed at me. "Sorry. I didn't know you could hear all that. It's exposure treatment. According to my therapist, I'll eventually become fully immune to donuts."

"Ha! If that worked, I'd never sneak another chocolate-dipped caramel while doing consulting work for a client. Color me skeptical. Good luck, though. I hope it works for you."

I really did. I had to admit, on the other hand, that if Tansy was fighting a bout of stress eating brought on by Melissa's unfortunate death, at least that made her sympathetic.

Tansy tossed her lustrous hair. Dressed in an oversize sweater with leggings and boots, she looked warm and stylish.

I'd worn my knit Breton chapeau from France, along

with my jeans and sweater, but I doubted I appeared half as chic as she did. Not that I'm obsessed with my appearance; I'm not. Most of the time, I'm busy troubleshooting chocolates in the back-of-house of a restaurant or devising desserts in the kitchen of a five-star hotel. I pack light. I like to be fast on my feet.

Just then, I needed to make tracks toward Travis. Where had he gone, anyway? I was headed to find out when Tansy stopped me.

"How do you do it, Hayden?" she blurted. "How do you work with chocolate all day, every day, and not eat every morsel of it?" Her voice sounded fraught with frustration. "Danny says you've been a professional baker and chocolatier for years now. Yet you don't look as though you eat chocolate, butter, and sugar for a living." Her hyper-observant gaze took in my jeans-and-sweater getup. "Do you have rules? A regimen? A detox plan?"

"If you count taste testing each creation only *once*, then sure, I do," I joked with a second grin. "It's the second, third, and fifteenth bites that do all the damage, you know."

To my surprise, Tansy's gorgeous eyes filled with tears.

Oh. She was seriously asking for help. I fumbled for a better answer, sorry that I'd been so glib. "Yes, I have a few techniques to avoid eating my body weight in cocoa butter every day," I shared in a more empathetic tone. "I have to. Aside from wanting to keep fitting into my favorite jeans, I have healthy arteries to think of. I want to perfect chocolate for *decades*."

Now Tansy looked more dismayed. "I thought chocolate was supposed to be healthy!" she cried with her hand in the air. "Now you're telling me it's not? That's just mean, Hayden."

I moved closer, then touched her arm. I met her gaze

straight on. "About an ounce a day *is* healthy. Especially if it's bittersweet dark chocolate, the kind that's rich in beneficial antioxidant flavonoids. You need phytochemicals."

The actress nodded. Despite her airhead reputation, she seemed to be following along. So I added more about how the stearic acid in cocoa butter doesn't raise cholesterol levels, about how chocolate can help fight a variety of health issues, about the fact that there's value in chocolate's ability to make people feel happy. But that's where I lost her, regrettably.

"It makes me happy until ten seconds after I eat it." She glowered. "Then I look at my ballooning thighs and regret it."

"It doesn't have to be that way." I hadn't intended to get caught up in any of this, but since I already was . . . "Tell you what. I promised Zach Johnson that I'd contribute a few things to the Sproutes holiday charity auction. Have you heard of it?"

Tansy nodded. "He hit me up for a contribution, too. I always travel with a few bikini shots, so I thought I'd sign some of them to be auctioned. My fans *love* swimsuit photos."

I just bet they did. You might have guessed that cheesecake photos of a certain globe-trotting chocolate whisperer aren't quite such a hot ticket. Unless they contain actual cheesecake, of course. There's always a market for chocolate cheesecake.

"My contribution is going to be a series of decorated chocolate houses," I confided. "Like gingerbread houses, only made entirely of chocolate. Zach said there's a converted barn where I can work, just a short distance from the B and B. I guess the owner donates its use to artisans and crafters each year so they can prep for the charity auction. It's fully equipped."

"Right." Tansy had clearly tuned out. "Um, and . . . ?"

"And I'm inviting you to come along and help me with a few of the chocolate houses. I'll show you how to manage chocolate."

Now I had her. "Without scarfing every single bite of it?"

"Exactly." I liked Tansy, but maybe her ditzy reputation was somewhat deserved. Even then, her gaze wandered longingly to the sprinkle-covered donuts. "We could meet in the mornings, before show rehearsals, or in the evenings. Whatever works."

"You'd really do that for me? That's so sweet, Hayden." She wrenched her attention from the craft services table and grabbed my hand. She daintily sniffled back her earlier tears. "Thanks."

Aww. Her gratitude made me feel like a hero. Awash in Tansy's glowing appreciation, I felt downright special. That was Tansy's unique gift. I'd heard that she made everyone around her feel smart, talented, and generous. Now I believed it was true.

You know, unless she didn't, I reminded myself. It was conceivable, it occurred to me unhappily, that someone might have meant to kill *Tansy* last night, not Melissa. Not Albany.

My working theory was still that Albany had been the most likely target, thanks to her inciting memoir and show. But I couldn't ignore the possibility that one of her doubles might have been the killer's true target. That included Tansy.

"As long as Danny agrees, of course," I told her, not wanting to step on my bodyguard buddy's toes. "Does he let you get out much without him? What's your arrangement, anyway?"

I held my breath, hoping Tansy wouldn't clam up.

She didn't. "Oh, he shadows my every move." A giggle.

"It's more than I counted on, really. See, I have this stalker . . ."

Tansy went on to describe the person who'd been harassing her—sending her threatening messages and mailing her photos of herself that were defaced with frightening drawings of knives and guns. "One time, even poison, complete with a skull and crossbones drawn on the bottle. I was pretty freaked out."

"Sounds scary." Poison could have been in the wassail.

"It was! It has been. Can you imagine? What a loser."

Tansy inhaled, then shook out her hair again. I wondered, suddenly, if it was a very expensive, very convincing wig.

"Anyway, I'm pretty sure I've dodged him." The actress noticed me noticing her hair (wig?) and grinned. "Thanks to my makeunder, I look like a different person. Everyone says so."

She glanced around. Now a few of the cast and crew were getting to their feet, clustering to discuss the news about Melissa. Backstage, something clanged noisily. I envisioned Travis and Albany knocking over props amid a torrid embrace.

The stage smelled of dust and floor polish, musty unpacked set materials and mingled assorted makeup items. *Greasepaint*, I thought in my best old-time vaudevillian. *Spotlights. Fame.*

I returned to Tansy. "So you're not worried anymore?"

"Not *as* worried. I mean, out here in the boonies, not even TMZ has found me. I've been to the grocery store, the motel, back and forth to the theater . . . nothing. No Perez Hilton, no TMZ." She gave me a beatific smile. "It's been wonderful!"

"So you're keeping Danny on call for . . . ?"

"Honestly? Eye candy, mostly." Tansy laughed, giving me a woman-to-woman, just-us-girls look. "I thought it might be fun to have Danny around. A friend of mine in L.A. used him for security during a red-carpet appearance. She recommended him." A pretty pucker. "She didn't say he was such a prude, though."

Danny Jamieson? A prude? I nearly died laughing.

On the inside, that is. I didn't want to offend Tansy. But I guessed that answered the question: they weren't involved.

The actress eyed me speculatively. "So, you and Danny—you've been friends for a long time, right? I mean, he talks about you nonstop, like you're his reference point for practically everything. I don't even think he knows he does it."

I shrugged. "We've been through a lot together, that's all. I knew him 'when,' as they say. But we're just friends."

"Have you *always* been 'just friends'?" Tansy pushed. "Or . . . ?"

Or . . . ? At her questions, I had a vivid, unstoppable memory of Danny. Me. Together. Tangled sheets . . . and morning-after regrets.

Yep. Sometimes chocolate experts can be real dummies.

"There's nothing going on between me and Danny," I said.

But Tansy's bright eyes and owlish expression told me she was more observant than she pretended to be. Was her dumbbell routine just an act? Was Tansy Park *that* skilled an actress?

If she was, how could I be sure she wasn't a complete psychopath? Judging by Albany's snide comments earlier, she and Tansy might have tangled once or twice regarding Tansy's acting.

Travis obviously thought there was some bad blood there. He was the one who'd suggested I add Tansy to my suspects list.

No one liked having their hard work dismissed. Most

people wouldn't go to murderous lengths to get revenge. Would Tansy?

I met the actress's forthright gaze and simply didn't want to believe she could kill anyone. *Finito.* Call me a patsy. I don't care. I didn't think Tansy Park was malicious enough to commit cold-blooded murder. Especially at Christmastime.

Which only made me wonder, if Melissa Balthasar *had* been murdered, exactly how had she died? Tansy's stalker talk had involved poison, something I ought to have considered before. But what else? There hadn't even been a murder weapon present.

I made a mental note to look into whether an autopsy was being performed and whether the police were investigating. I hoped the *Sproutes Sentinel* article might have information about Melissa's memorial service. Failing that, there was always Roger.

I needed a way to approach the show's second producer. Sensitively. In the meantime, I spotted Danny, making a beeline straight for me and Tansy and our burgeoning friendship.

"Donuts?" He seemed irked. "You dodged me for donuts?"

Guiltily, Tansy's cheeks colored pink. But she jerked her chin higher and eyed him regally. "I'm only getting coffee."

To prove it, the actress filled a paper cup with the murky brew. Yuck. I made a mental note not to rely on the production for my own morning java. Tansy bravely sipped it, nonetheless.

Danny's expression was knowing. "Fine. I guess that coffee is enough punishment for anyone." He nodded at me. "Sleep well?"

I couldn't miss the quick, approving way his gaze skimmed the contours of my body. I knew the reaction was automatic, like my mouth watering in the presence of fudge brownies. He couldn't help it. But I experienced a small, unnecessary thrill, anyway.

Hey, in the absence of a regular boyfriend, I have to take my excitement where and when it comes. *Had* I slept well?

"I've had better." I'd been haunted by Melissa's face.

"Jet lag is a killer," my security-expert pal theorized.

I didn't correct him. "Got time for a few questions?" I wanted to know what he thought about Melissa Balthasar's death. Plus, I wanted his take on Travis and Albany. "Privately?"

He got my gist immediately but didn't make a big deal of it. "We can talk out there." Danny's nod indicated the plush rows of empty theater seats. "It's private enough." He gave Tansy a fearsome look. "You stay onstage, where I can see you."

"Yes, sir." She offered him a sassy salute. Also, a grin.

"I mean it," Danny warned, looking unamused. "If you won't cooperate with my instructions, we can't work together anymore."

That got Tansy's attention. I knew why, too, as *her* gaze wandered very appreciatively over Danny. *Hubba-hubba*, it said.

"I think we all understand each other," I broke in.

Then I nodded at Danny and headed for the theater's remotest rows of antique velvet seats, trusting him to follow.

Five

Watching Danny slide his athletic form along the theater's narrow aisle and into the seat beside me was a pure pleasure.

Feeling the rush of sentiment that swamped me at the same time *wasn't*. Tears sprang to my eyes, leaving me overwhelmed.

Naturally, my bodyguard buddy noticed. "Hey, what's wrong?"

"Nothing," I croaked while swabbing away tears. "I'm fine."

It was possible I'd been affected by this new murder more than I wanted to admit. But I didn't intend to say so to Danny.

His stern, dark-eyed gaze met mine. "You don't look fine."

"Gee, thanks." I laughed, glancing away before he caught me studying his face. It was both appealing and rugged, full of macho angles and the beginnings of beard stubble, topped by his militarily buzz-cut hair. "I'm happy you're okay, that's all."

His worried expression eased. "It was only an eyeball."

While I'd been in Brittany, Danny had suffered a detached retina during a security-related skirmish for a client. He never hesitated to put himself on the line for the people he worked for. Sometimes, I wished he would. Having him out of commission, however briefly, had frightened me. I was glad he was back now.

"Yeah, but you need your eyeballs to work," I cracked, "otherwise you won't be able to tell me how nice I look."

"Not convincingly, at least," he allowed.

My smile broadened. "You'd pull it off somehow."

He would, too, I knew. Danny was nothing if not charming—in his own unique and occasionally brusque way. He could turn on the charisma when he needed to. I'd seen it for myself.

"You're all recovered now, then?" I wanted to know.

"I wouldn't be on the job if I wasn't." His gaze zipped over to Tansy, onstage, lingered a few seconds, then returned to me. "Although this is an easy one. The lookie-loos always are."

"Lookie-loos?"

"Come on, Hayden. You must have guessed." He crossed his arms, biceps bulging beneath his jacket. "Don't make me say it."

"Say what?"

A sigh. "That Tansy's keeping me around for the fun of it."

"Fun of it?" I gave my eyelashes a disingenuous flutter.

Danny almost growled. "Eye candy. That's what they call it. A certain segment of my clientele doesn't really need my help."

I tried not to guffaw. He was uncomfortable with being objectified for his good looks and buff physique.

I tugged his jacket, which covered his sweatshirt and topped his low-slung, beat-up jeans, worn with motorcycle boots. "Hey, if you didn't want anyone looking, you shouldn't have dressed so sexy."

That made him laugh. Danny knew I was referring to catcalling men who claim women are "asking for attention" because of what they wear. We both knew that was ludicrous.

"Yeah, well . . . look while you can, Mundy Moore," he invited with a certain edge, "because I'm thinking about retiring."

"And coming to work for me full-time?" He was free to work on his own, but I kept Danny's security services on retainer.

"And growing myself a big old beer belly, full-time."

"You wouldn't!" Now that I had a good excuse, I looked him over with no reservations. Yup. Danny was quite a man.

His laughter rang out. "Don't hurt yourself gawking."

Caught, I transferred my gaze to his smart-alecky face.

"Lightening up on the workouts would cut down on jobs like this one." His chin jab indicated Tansy, who was chatting onstage, amid the set's Christmassy accoutrements. "It gives her a kick to think she's dodging me, though. Plus, it's a living."

He was always interested in solidifying his finances, but that wasn't what was going on here. I realized the truth before he admitted it—not that I thought he would. "You're a fan!"

If I'd been hoping to suss out an embarrassing secret, I'd have been disappointed. "Damn straight, am I," Danny said. "Have you *seen* her? Plus, she's Tansy Park. Freaking *Tansy Park*."

"You own her swimsuit poster, don't you, D.?"

Good-naturedly, he scoffed. "Poster? Hayden, be real."

"What? You're a red-blooded adult male. You must—"

"It's the twenty-first century. I have Tansy's app."

Aha. It was my turn to smile. "Which includes photos," I surmised. "Well, working with celebrities comes with its perks, I guess. I'm happy for you."

Just don't sleep with her.

Huh? Where had that thought come from? I shook my head.

"You're not really going to retire, are you?" I asked.

The thought gave me chills. Not the good kind, either.

"I thought about it." Not looking at me, Danny rubbed the back of his neck. He shrugged. "I'm still thinking about it."

I guessed his recent detached-retina scare had affected him. It had to have been unnerving for him to realize he wasn't invulnerable. "Well, you're not bulletproof, you know. If you retired—to work for me, that is—you would be a lot safer."

At my obvious attempts to comfort him, Danny frowned. "I'm not *scared*." From him, the word sounded foreign. "But I've bankrolled some cash now, and I didn't need much to begin with."

I knew Danny had issues with money. With security. Growing up wondering where your next meal was coming from left its mark on a person—even on a person as strong and brave as my friend.

"Travis says you could retire on what I pay you alone."

Danny's profile turned flinty. He stared fixedly at Tansy.

Whoops. I'd forgotten, in my rush to reassure Danny that he would be okay (forever, if I had my say), that there was a certain friction between him and "Harvard" about his retainer.

Travis sometimes suggested that "the enforcer" was

taking advantage of my (newfound) need for amped-up security (in light of the murders I've run into lately) by siphoning off my trust fund in monthly retainer payments. Danny, as I've mentioned, sometimes suggested that Travis was interested only in using me to boost his profile at his company and earn a fat commission.

The thing was, they both could be correct.

But I didn't think either of them was. They were my friends. The fact that we were together at Christmas proved it.

I suddenly got it. "You deliberately took this job with Tansy so you'd be in Sproutes for the holidays. With me."

And maybe Travis. But Danny shrugged. "How was I supposed to know you'd be here?" Obdurately, he recrossed his arms.

I had him. Awww. That was sweet of him. "Travis told you."

At that, my bodyguard pal shook his head. "Look, I don't know what kind of crazy things you've been imagining, but Captain Calculator and I don't hang out. We're *not* besties."

"Of course not. You live in L.A. He's all the way up in Seattle. For the two of you to hang out, you'd have to be—"

"Two different people. But we're not. The only thing we have in common is you. That's the way it's going to stay."

I had my doubts. "Christmas changes people. It does."

"Yeah. Around here, it makes some of them murderous."

I didn't want to talk about that. Not yet.

"I've got it." I snapped my fingers. "You tracked Travis here, and then you took a job that brought you here, too. Right?"

I'd originally thought Travis might have recommended Danny to Tansy, for her protection. But this new theory worked better. It couldn't be a coincidence that we'd all wound up together in Sproutes during mistletoe time. However it had happened, I liked having the whole gang back together. It felt . . . right to me.

"Sure. I make it my job to know where Travis is, twenty-four-seven."

Danny's tone was sarcastic, but I'd have believed him. "You think Travis wants to defraud me of my trust fund." We didn't often talk about my inheritance from Uncle Ross. It's a sore spot between us. "It would be like you to keep tabs on him."

"I'll always have your back," Danny said. "You know that."

His gruff reminder warmed me. "And I'll have yours."

He chuckled again. "Nice try, scrawny. I know you're proud of that anti-mugger move of yours, but I'll protect myself."

A moment passed by, companionably, while we watched the goings-on onstage. The Sproutes playhouse was a fine theater.

"Travis told me that Albany was going to be pretty busy with the show's premiere. Someone suggested he invite *me* as his plus-one," I remarked casually. "That *someone* was *you*. So . . ."

"So I didn't want you to get your feelings hurt if he invited someone else," Danny explained. "That's not a crime."

No, but it *was* telling that Danny had pulled some strings to get us all together during the holidays. He wasn't especially sentimental. He wouldn't have wanted to appear that way, either. But I imagined that Christmastime was where the rubber met the road—where Danny's desire for togetherness went toe-to-toe with his urge to be tough. We'd spent plenty of previous holidays together, once (memorably) in Vienna. Another time in Thailand.

I was about to move on when Danny beat me to it.

"Albany and the number cruncher have been spending the nights together at the B and B." His gaze caught mine, full of concern. Was he worried I'd react badly to Travis and Albany's coziness? "That's how Albany got there so fast," he added, "after everything went down with Melissa Balthasar last night."

I'd been too anxious to notice her arrival, what with thinking the memoirist was dead. "They didn't arrive together."

"Right. *Conspicuously* not together. Like they planned it."

"Maybe they were just hanging out." *At 3:00 a.m.* All right, Danny had a valid point. "Do you think they're a couple?"

"Who knows?" Deliberately, Danny stared at Tansy again. "It's possible that Albany Sullivan is Harvard's, uh . . . you."

"Huh?"

When my buddy's gaze met mine again, there was a definite subtext there. "I think he had her once and wants her again."

Oh. A flush warmed my cheeks. Maybe other parts of me, too. Despite Danny's matter-of-fact way of referring to our past (let's just call them) indiscretions, I felt overheated. Breathless. Inundated with memories, sensations, longings . . .

"I think she wants the same thing," Danny continued in a more forceful, slightly husky tone. "So it's a matter of time."

A matter of time. My heart seemed to thud to a stop.

Did he mean . . . us? Was this some kind of oblique invitation?

Somehow, I managed to shake my head. "Just because Travis and Albany share a history and maybe a certain chemistry, that doesn't mean they're going to get together. Not inevitably."

There was a pause. Then, "Doesn't it? Are you sure?"

Okay, hold on. Was I imagining that seductive drop to his voice? Danny liked to tease me, but not about this.

Not about us. Not about our past together. Or our future.

We didn't even have a future—not in the usual to-have-and-to-hold, promises-and-rainbows way. I like to gridskip around the world, troubleshooting chocolate. He likes to stay in SoCal, where all his buddies from the bad old days can keep him grounded and in touch with his roots. Danny was proud of that.

"Very funny." It was time to shut down this line of discussion. Firmly, I asked, "Do Tansy and Albany get along?"

"Tansy's not your killer." *End of story*, his tone said.

Privately, I was glad we were on the same wavelength. "How do you know? Maybe Tansy is the world's best actress, and she's only pretending to be innocent." Also, fairly scatterbrained.

"I know because I know Tansy. She might have hired me on a lark, for the kind of job I don't usually take," Danny acknowledged patiently, "but you know me. Once I committed, I did all my usual reconnaissance. I don't work for murderers."

"Fair enough. But Travis says Tansy resented Albany."

"Who wouldn't? She's a pretentious twit."

Now it was my turn to laugh. "You think so, too?"

Our mutual grins felt vindicating. Just like old times.

We talked for a while about our impressions of Albany and her book. Danny *had* read it in full (research, duh). He had the temerity to give me a hard time about not having done so myself.

"Her dad sounds like a piece of work," he said.

"Always 'at the office.' Golfing when he wasn't. One of those useless upper-crust types." He gave me a cocky grin. "Reminds me of Travis."

That brought us around to Sproutes in general and Travis's upbringing in particular. This wasn't something I could easily discuss with my financial advisor, but Danny was more than game.

I told Danny about Travis's "honor-roll nerd" comment.

"Yeah, I can see that," he said. Activity onstage was ramping up now. The cast and crew of *Christmas in Crazytown* seemed to have become resigned to rehearsing. "You know Harvard was born with a slide rule in one hand and a grammar book in the other. His parents probably had tiny suits made for him."

"Danny!" His wicked look made me laugh, but I was too loyal to Travis to keep it up for long. "Don't be mean about Travis."

"I'm not being mean. I'm saying he's lucky. Privileged."

I hypothesized that Travis probably had grown up on the posh side of Sproutes, wherever that was. I pictured a small, studious financial advisor in training and smiled fondly.

"But we don't know the whole story," I warned. I shared a bit about the difficulties Albany had hinted about over muffins that morning. "It's possible Travis struggled, growing up here."

"Yeah," Danny deadpanned. "Perfect neighborhoods, friendly New England neighbors, and great schools are the worst."

"Because of his family, I mean. I'm worried. You didn't hear him. Travis cut off talk of his past right at the knees."

"So?" My bodyguard buddy didn't see the problem.

"He's hiding something. I'm sure of it—"

"Mmm-hmm," Danny interrupted. His rugged face

took on a warning cast. "I recognize that look. Don't start prying."

"It's not prying. It's concern. I want to help."

"He won't see it that way, trust me. Just back off."

That was impossible. "What if Travis needs help? Especially being here, where it all happened, at the holidays. Times like these have a way of bringing up old memories. It's—"

"It's none of your business. Let's talk about murder."

Hmm. Usually, Danny wasn't wild about digging into a potential investigation. I had a theory. "Did you already look into Travis's past?" I asked him. "Are you hiding something?"

He frowned. "Yes. And no. Now, let's move on. Suspects?"

I clung to our Travis talk instead. "What did you find?"

Danny's gaze hardened. "If he wanted you to know, he'd tell you. So don't ask me. Ask him. Until then, I'm not going to—"

"Was he abused? Abandoned? Neglected?" I conjectured, feeling sorrier for Travis by the minute. "Were his mom or dad workaholics? Is that why you were talking about Albany's dad? Was it a hint about Travis's secret past? Out with it, Danny."

He sighed. "If I tell you, can we get on with the job at hand? You can't tell me you're not planning on sleuthing again."

I couldn't. "Just tell me what you know, all right?"

"Fine." Dispassionately, Danny gave me the rundown. Travis had been born in the Pacific Northwest, in a town north of Seattle called Lynnwood. He'd moved to Massachusetts at the age of eleven, following his parents' divorce. He'd been raised by his newly single mother ("in an apparently happy home," Danny made sure to specify), excelled in school, earned a selection of scholarships, and gone on to Harvard. "After that, the records get muddier," my friend told me. "He's untraceable for a while. Then he shows up at Snooty, Snobby, Snotty & Sons, Ltd."

That was his nickname for my trust-fund management company.

"And turns into a big-shot financial whiz practically overnight," Danny said, "which brings us up to date. Happy?"

"I imagined a more personal take on the situation."

"This is me talking, not you, softy."

"I still think Travis is bothered about something."

"So ask him. In the meantime, what about Melissa B.?"

I could always trust Danny to get down to brass tacks. Last night, we'd arrived at the same conclusion regarding the four Albany Sullivan look-alikes. This morning, I wanted to know more.

"How do you think Melissa died?" I asked. "I didn't see a weapon of any kind, unless you count that silver punch bowl."

"There weren't any obvious injuries, either," my friend recalled. It seemed unlikely that Melissa had been bludgeoned to death, given the position of the punch bowl and the absence of wounds. "But calling it an accident feels like a stretch."

Danny described the tree-trimming party that had taken place earlier that night, an event sponsored by Zach and his B&B to celebrate *Christmas in Crazytown*. The people who'd been there read like a who's who of my soon-to-be suspects list.

I wondered why Zach hadn't cleaned up that leftover punch bowl after the party. Or why his catering staff hadn't. Either way, it seemed odd that it had been left out overnight.

In every other sense, I'd observed, the B&B was pristine.

"Any leads from the police last night?" Danny asked me.

I shook my head. "They took my statement, then cleared out. Honestly, all the officers seemed pretty keen to wrap up."

I described what I'd seen going on between Roger Balthasar and the police officer who'd seemed to be in charge. Danny found the timing of his "accidental death" announcement suspect, too.

"I don't see how we can prove it," I mused. "Without knowing the cause of death, we can't say it *wasn't* accidental."

I'd run into trouble too many times to take things at face value these days, however. There had to be more going on here.

"I have a contact who might be able to help," Danny volunteered. "If you're game, I'll set up a meeting."

"That would be fantastic." I gave him a cautious look. "Don't let on that I'm investigating. I want to be low key."

He pulled a face. "What do I look like? An idiot?"

"Right now? You look like my oldest, closest friend—"

I would have said more, but Danny cut me off. "Enough with the sappy stuff. And be careful while you're here. This place might look like a Hallmark Channel Christmas special gone wild, but there's a killer running around somewhere. Watch your back."

"Same to you." Glancing idly at the stage, I was reminded of something else. "Hey, were you here when Albany came in?"

"No." He looked puzzled. "She hasn't been here today."

He had to be mistaken. "Travis and I had breakfast

with her. She said she was coming down to talk to the cast and crew."

"Nope. Tansy and I were first in. We would have seen her."

I puzzled over that. "But she'd be in charge, right?"

"Not typically." Danny had been on enough sets to have a sense of the hierarchy. "Roger Balthasar is second producer. He and Melissa worked together to manage the production. He could do it without her. The question is whether he'd want to."

"Albany thinks he would. She says he's 'a machine.'"

Danny shook his head. "Years ago, maybe that was true," he acknowledged. "Roger built his rep on getting there first, hitting harder, and making anyone who crossed him pay."

More and more, Roger Balthasar looked like my top suspect.

"But lately, the real killer in that couple has been Melissa," Danny went on. "Without her, Albany wouldn't have published a memoir—and she definitely wouldn't have a show based on it. Melissa championed the whole thing, from start to finish."

"I would have expected Albany to be more broken up about losing her champion, then, if she owed Melissa that much."

"As far as I can tell, Albany doesn't think she owes anyone anything. Besides, don't go getting all goo-goo eyed. Melissa B. was nobody's heroine. Everything she did, she did for her own bottom line. Believe me, Melissa was a real shark. No holds barred." He cocked his head. "In fact, I think Melissa's your victim, cut and dried. No mistaken identity. She had enemies."

I wanted to know who they were. But just at that moment . . .

"Everyone, can I have your attention, please?" Albany had arrived. She stood center stage, hands clasped piously. The cast and crew turned to face her. "I'm afraid I have some bad news."

She prefaced the rest of her remarks by saying that she was speaking at Roger Balthasar's request. Then she made an official announcement about Melissa's death. "Please don't worry," she added afterward. "The police are working tirelessly to find out what happened. At the moment, it looks as though Melissa was the victim of a tragic accident. But you'll be glad to know that the chief of police has taken a personal interest in the case."

Reassured murmurs rose from the crowd. Yet I felt far from comforted. I'd seen that officer dismiss the case last night.

"In the meantime, out of respect for Melissa—and to allow us all time to grieve—we won't be rehearsing for a few days." Albany's voice wobbled with emotion. "I'm afraid, for now, that *Christmas in Crazytown* is in a holding pattern. If Roger decides to go forward with the show, then we should be able to premiere without further rehearsals. If not . . . well, I'll let you know. Thank you all." Albany swallowed hard. "Thank you all so much!"

She hurried offstage, into the wings . . . and straight into Travis's arms. Before I could do more than glimpse Albany's pale, teary face, my keeper whisked her away, out of my sight.

Was Albany upset because of losing Melissa? Had she been playing it tough for me, a newcomer, earlier? Or was she in tears because of (maybe) losing her show? It was impossible to know for sure. Aside from that, I wondered,

Had Albany been the killer's original target? Or had it been someone else?

Danny seemed reasonably sure that Melissa had been the intended victim all along, given her abrasive personality and famously ruthless business ethos. I still had my doubts. I couldn't miss the semi-disgruntled looks that the cast and crew threw each other in the wake of Albany's speech.

Maybe it was time, I decided, to meet my final "Albany."

Six

For me, there are few doors that chocolate doesn't open.

Doormen guarding deluxe high-rises are happy to step aside when I come along bearing chocolate. Security personnel at corporate headquarters get friendly when they catch sight of my usual take-along box of samples, giveaways, and demo products from appreciative chocolate-whispering clients. Potential consultees gain confidence in my chocolatiering skills when I offer them chocolate-praline truffles or mini mousse pots.

That day, it was a square of custom chocolate-peppermint bark that worked magic for me, wrapped in cellophane and tied with a bow, as I approached Albany's younger sister, Ophelia.

"Hi! Ophelia, right?" I gave her my sunniest smile. "It's Hayden—Hayden Mundy Moore. I'm Travis Turner's friend. I'm pretty sure we met at the tree-trimming party the other night?"

We hadn't, obviously. But it couldn't hurt to find out how much attention had been paid to the B and B's guest list that night.

"Oh, hey." Ophelia nodded a casual hello. "How are you?"

Okay, *not* very much attention had been paid to the guest list, I realized. Check. "Good, thanks. I'm just wondering . . ." I dug into my crossbody bag and pulled out my sample. "Do you know who I should give this to? I'm consulting for this new brand . . ."

At the sight of the chocolate-peppermint bark, Ophelia's eyes widened. She even ignored her phone for a minute. Making that happen was no easy feat when it came to anyone, especially a woman who appeared to be in her very early twenties, at most.

It was possible that Ophelia Sullivan's wide, gullible eyes, gangly frame, and trendy clothing made her look younger than her years. In fact, I frowned slightly as I looked at her, feeling increasingly worried for her well-being. She seemed so defenseless—and so oblivious to that defenselessness, too.

I wanted to protect her. I promised myself, there and then, that I would. If Ophelia had been the killer's true target, then I didn't want him to get a second chance at hurting her.

"I'll take it!" She wiggled her fingers in a classic "Gimme" gesture. Albany wasn't the only Sullivan sibling who wasn't lacking confidence. Ophelia seized the peppermint bark, then examined it from all angles. "I've never heard of this brand."

"Like I said, it's new." I'd created it myself, out of bits and pieces in my crossbody bag, amalgamating wrappers and labels and chocolate, then adding that bow. I explained about my job, glossing over the details. Often, my work for clients is top secret. Companies don't want it known that they need my help to improve their offerings or to develop new specialties. "I'm trying to get the word out about the company's seasonal products." That much could have been true. "They don't have a huge promotional budget." I lowered my tone conspiratorially. "I was hoping I could get Albany to put in a good word for it."

Ophelia rolled her eyes. "Albany's swamped right now. Ever since her book came out, it's been a total media juggernaut." She set down the peppermint bark, positioned it, then used her phone to take a photo of it. "I might be able to help you."

I made a regretful face. "I was really hoping for Albany."

For an instant, Ophelia's face clouded. "Sure, you and everyone else. I mean, she's got a list of sponsorship requests a mile long. By the time she sees this thing, it'll be July."

"Hmm. That won't work. This is a limited holiday item." I pretended to be flummoxed, then shrugged. "Oh, well. I just thought it was worth a shot, since I'm here in Sproutes, anyway."

With a disappointed mien, I reached for the peppermint bark. Inches from it, Ophelia's hand closed atop mine. "Wait."

I blinked at her. "Oh! Do you want it for a gift? Go ahead. I have a whole case of these. They're pretty, though, right?" I decided to take advantage of our varying perspectives. To a woman Ophelia's age, I knew, I was practically an old crone at thirty. "I wasn't involved in the packaging, but the product team assured me that it's . . . What's the word? Instagrammable?"

Ophelia's eyes lit up. She seemed like a sweet, pretty young woman. I felt bad for purposely misleading her. Given the circumstances, I needed an in with her. I needed it quickly.

Thanks to a briefing with Danny, I'd found my approach. "I'm an Instagram star!" She leaned forward with a certain urgency, stopping me from taking away the peppermint bark. "I can definitely help you." Her previously naïve gaze took on a shrewd glimmer. "I mean, I'm sure we can come to an arrangement about brand sponsorship with at least *one* Sullivan sister."

"I don't know," I hedged. "The client really wants Albany."

Another storm cloud darkened Ophelia's expression. I wondered if there was rivalry between the sisters. I wondered, too, how Ophelia was portrayed in Albany's memoir. Was her "lightly fictionalized" coverage of her sister favorable? Loving? Or was it mocking? Teasing? Somewhere in between?

I seriously needed to make time to read that book.

"Let me show you what I can do," Ophelia offered. She snatched the peppermint bark, then gazed around the theater's backstage, where I'd spotted her and enacted my plan. She bit her lip. "If we can just stage this properly . . ."

With a decisive, leggy gait that strikingly resembled her sister's, Ophelia strode across the cluttered area until she arrived at one of the waiting sets. It looked like a living room straight out of the sixties, with a silvery space-age aluminum Christmas tree and teardrop-shaped ornaments. Arranged beside it were a vintage turntable and several vinyl holiday records.

With a few deft movements, Ophelia created a tableau out of those materials. She placed the peppermint bark in its center, adjusted its candy-striped red-and-white bow, then buffed the package's cellophane to a high gloss. She snapped a photo.

On her phone, she looked at it. "Nope. We can do better."

As I followed, Ophelia energetically led the way through the backstage confusion. There were props and drop cloths, sets and ladders, lights and signs and equipment cables. Ophelia explained that the sets for *Christmas in Crazytown* entailed references to "like, old-timey Christmases," regardless of their relevance to the time periods covered in Albany's memoir.

"It's, literally, more arty that way," Ophelia informed me.

I nodded in understanding, watching as she arranged the items in yet another area into a suitable photographic backdrop. This time, we'd arrived at a Victorian Christmas scene, with a skinny tree alight with LED "candles" and ornaments. There was a mantel with knit stockings hung from it, plus milk and cookies for Santa. Ophelia replaced the cookies with the peppermint bark.

She snapped a photo, viewed her work, then grimaced. "Yuck. Talk about Grandma's attic," she said. "No way."

It was time to goose things along. "It's okay if you're not feeling super creative today," I assured her sympathetically. "You know, given the circumstances. I totally understand."

Ophelia arched one fashionably full, perfectly filled-in dark brow. "You mean because of Melissa? Don't worry," she said blithely. "We weren't that close. I mean, it's tragic and everything." Here, she adopted a somber face. Then she breezily snapped out of it. "And I'm majorly grateful to Melissa for letting me be Tansy's understudy. It's been great having access to all this." Her open-armed gesture indicated the backstage area, the stage beyond, and the whole theater. "But, I mean, life goes on, right?" She examined her setup. "Maybe one more."

At a near gallop, Ophelia took off for another set. This one was done up in flashy eighties style, with glimmering gold and white satin ornaments, fluffy metallic garland, and pure white mini-lights. She nodded her approval, then got to work.

"You're Tansy's understudy?" I repeated. "That's cool."

"Yeah, I guess so. I look the part. It's not like I'll ever be onstage, though. They'd close the show before opening without Tansy here." Ophelia moved her props a millimeter closer. She took some photos, then toyed with the filters on her phone. Her fingers moved rapidly over the screen. "This is my real calling, anyway. It's, like, fulfilling? Plus, I'm very good at it."

Well, she had an utter lack of humility in common with her sister, that was for sure.

Playing along, I nodded. "You are."

My approval made Ophelia smile. The quick, genuine grin she sent me was winning. I experienced another urge to protect her.

Stopping the killer would do that, I reminded myself.

"Of course, you'll have to get a real job someday," I said.

She snorted. "What? Go to college and start a career?" Ophelia rolled her eyes. "That's not how things work. For my generation, there are no guarantees—just the opportunities you create for yourself." She showed me a photo. "How about this?"

I barely recognized my humble package of chocolate-peppermint bark. It had been professionally styled to look twice as appealing as it did in real life. I could almost taste it.

Despite my subterfuge, I was impressed. Danny had told me that Ophelia was an aspiring "social-media influencer," someone who earned so many followers that companies paid him or her to flog their products. Ophelia Sullivan wasn't at that level yet. She hadn't quite reached Albany's celebrity status, for instance.

These days, though, you didn't need to be a superstar to garner fans. All you needed were a responsive target group and enough time and skill to connect with them, usually visually.

Satisfied, Ophelia uploaded the photo. She thumbed out an endorsement and a few seasonal hashtags, then regarded me seriously. "Hundreds of mentions within the hour," she promised. "Thousand more, if some of the better-known influencers I've partnered with pick up on the post. It's better than traditional marketing." Ophelia tapped her posted photo. "It's authentic."

"But you haven't even tasted the chocolate," I pointed out.

A shrug. "This time of year, half the people who follow me are just looking for holiday decoration or gift ideas. This fits both." She eyed the peppermint bark. "I don't need to taste it."

I felt a shiver run down my spine. If future customers didn't even want to taste the products I'd put so much work into, what good were chocolate-making skills and creativity? I appreciated beautiful packaging and word of mouth as much as the next person, but the bottom line for me was flavor. Forever.

Ophelia didn't agree. "So, do we have a deal?" she pushed.

I shook myself out of my musings. Right now, my job wasn't crafting amazing chocolate goodies. It was stopping a killer.

"I don't know," I hedged purposely. "You say you have some partners who are better known? Maybe I should contact them."

Ophelia's expression darkened once again. Despite her endearing enthusiasm, she seemed to be both impetuous and unpredictable. She also seemed to resent *not* being the center of attention at all times. Could she have resented Albany enough to want to kill her? It had been dark last night in the B and B. Maybe Ophelia had mistaken Melissa for Albany. Maybe she'd . . . done what?

I still didn't know how Melissa had died. I was stumped.

Then again, it would be very easy for the killer to mistake Ophelia for Albany. The two sisters had similar heights and hairstyles. They also moved with those spookily matching gaits.

"You can't ditch me," Ophelia said. "I won't tell you who they are. That's privileged information." Her disillusioned, accusing gaze met mine. "You seemed a lot nicer at the party."

As a burn, it was lacking, since I hadn't been at that party. I was interested to know that Ophelia thought I had been.

Suddenly, I wondered, Had *she* actually been there? I needed a guest list and some confirmation about who'd attended.

Maybe my B and B's host, Zach, could hook me up with that?

"Yeah, sorry about that." I gave her a conciliatory smile. "I'm under pressure to make this happen, like, yesterday. This client is pretty demanding." I didn't enjoy fibbing about my imaginary client (aka me), but desperate times called for desperate measures. "Tell you what. I'll think this over—"

"I'm actually considering other sponsorship offers."

"And I'll get back to you later. All right?"

Ophelia hesitated. Uncertainly, she rubbed her fingers over her phone screen. The gesture looked like a habitual tick to me.

"It's just that, with the show maybe shutting down, it's possible that endorsements here won't be especially valuable," I explained. "I have to take into consideration what's timely."

"*I'm timely*!" Ophelia almost screeched. She clutched her phone with whitened knuckles, then squeezed shut her eyes like a child having a tantrum. "Just pick *me*! I can do it, I swear!"

At her outburst, I took an involuntary, startled step back.

She saw. "I'm sorry. Sorry, sorry, sorry." She grasped my wrist, giving me a beseeching look. "It's just that if I don't make my influencer account work, my parents are going to make me enroll in school." Ophelia looked utterly trapped. "A whole semester will ruin me. Social media is *now*. I can't take a break. I just can't!" Her eyes filled with tears. "Okay?"

Her desperation caught me off guard. Was it sincere?

Chocolatiering meant that much to *me*, I reasoned. Maybe social media meant a lot to Ophelia, too. It was possible that I occasionally seemed obsessed with my work. So I relented.

"Sure." Encouragingly, I nodded. "Okay. Let's make this peppermint bark a success. Together. Let's do this thing!"

Instantly, Ophelia's expression cleared. "Seriously?"

Despite a few niggling doubts, I nodded again. "Yes."

She drew in a gulp of air, then grinned and waved her clenched fists with excitement. "You won't regret this, Hayden!"

I might. "The coverage needs to be tasteful," I reminded her. "No sexy selfies with the peppermint bark. Hear me?"

Another eye roll. "It's not that kind of account."

"Maybe you should give me the info, so I can make sure."

Ophelia gave me the details. I planned to log on later.

"In the meantime," I said, "you seem to know everything going on backstage. How about a tour? Is that allowed?"

"You haven't seen it yet? It's crazy elaborate!" She pocketed the peppermint bark I'd given her, careful not to crease the packaging or smash the bow. "Most people have already gone home, of course, so it won't be nearly as packed as usual."

"That's okay. I'm mostly interested in the sets, anyway."

"Yeah." She scrutinized me. "I guess you probably met everyone already at the tree-trimming party, right?"

I gave a noncommittal sound. Ophelia didn't seem to notice. She was already guiding me toward the next waiting holiday set.

Half an hour later, my head was spinning. Together, Ophelia and I had (essentially) time traveled through Christmas throughout the ages, starting with a feast-centered medieval holiday and ending with a futuristic, hi-tech Christmas. It seemed that no expense had been spared to stage the musical based on Albany's memoir-ish book. I'd seen mistletoe and holly, android angels and 3-D-printed snow globes, popcorn strung with dark red cranberries, and paper snowflakes the size of my torso. There were evergreens, wreaths, and fake wrapped gifts, too.

Ophelia snapped a photo of the two of us inside a faux gingerbread house. Amazingly, it was big enough to stand in.

I spread my arms and touched its realistic-looking walls. Somehow, someone had infused it with the Christmassy scents of cinnamon, nutmeg, and cloves. "Mmm. I wish I could take this home with me." Actually, I wished I had a home at all. "Yum."

"Don't move." Ophelia took another photo, this time of me alone. Then she handed me a prop—a gigantic cardboard Santa head. It was flat and glossy, printed with Old Saint Nick's face. "Okay, now one more. Just hold up Santa and say cheese."

Finding its size and heft awkward, I fiddled with it. I'd seen things like this at pro sports games. Usually, they were printed with the larger-than-life images of star players.

Exasperated, Ophelia lowered her phone. "You suck." She gave a joking eye roll. "We had these at the party, remember?"

Whoops. I found a way to improvise. "No, I may have had too much wassail." I successfully wrangled my prop. "Cheese!"

I was relieved to hear Ophelia laugh. "You and everyone else," she quipped. "That stuff was potent. I think we went through four bowls of it. It's a good thing for all of you that I have principles, otherwise I'd post all the damaging photos."

When I set aside my head prop, she looked somber.

"Maybe I should post some of them, anyway," Ophelia mused. "I could make them a tribute to Melissa, to honor her memory."

I was touched. So far, almost everyone else I'd encountered had seemed relatively indifferent to Melissa Balthasar's death. It was heartening to hear someone who'd known her express grief.

"My followers would go *crazy* for that," Ophelia enthused, squashing my newly refreshed faith in humankind. "I'd crush it with likes and new follows. Plus, Melissa is totally trending everywhere right now. It would be too easy to follow the wave."

I tried not to look appalled by her casual opportunism. I managed a nod. "Well, everyone wants to be remembered, right?"

"Exactly." Ophelia beamed. "Trust me, Melissa would have *loved* to know she was trending. The more places, the better."

Given what Danny had told me about Melissa, maybe Ophelia was right. Still, her plans to personally benefit from the producer's death—to funnel the public's prurient interest into traffic for her own "influencer" site—left me dispirited.

Maybe, I decided, Ophelia wasn't as innocent as she seemed.

There was only one way to find out.

"I can't wait to check out everything we did today," I told her, laying the groundwork. "Thanks, Ophelia. I'll bring some more of my client's products in tomorrow. Should we meet here?"

Ophelia looked at me as if I were crazy.

"Here? Again? Did you just land from another planet or something?" She snickered. "My account is fresh! We'll need a new location." She thought about it. "Maybe one of the covered bridges outside of town. Or a snowy brick storefront downtown?"

"I'll leave all that up to you." We swapped phone numbers so we could make plans. "After all, you're the expert here."

Ophelia's innocent face shone. It was evident that she didn't garner very many compliments—not off-line, at least.

I wondered why her "influencer" work was so important to her. Was she competing with attention-getting Albany? Did she hope to avoid going to college? Did she simply yearn to make her mark online and be "liked" a lot? I couldn't tell. I expected, with a little more time, that

I'd gain some insight about her. Meanwhile, my phone buzzed.

It was Danny. He'd already set up a meeting (which he jokingly called a "rendezvous") with the contact he'd mentioned.

I checked the date and time. Tomorrow evening couldn't come fast enough for me. Not because I needed a "rendezvous," either.

I was out for answers. I wouldn't stop until I got them.

Seven

Ordinarily, I would not have agreed to meet with a random stranger, especially not at his house. Thanks to Danny's longtime tutelage, I typically keep my meetings (business and otherwise) to safely neutral public sites where I can make a quick getaway if things feel dangerous or otherwise unusual.

But this time, Danny had vetted my contact himself. So as I parked my rental car the following evening and got out into the frigid weather to have a look at the site of my "rendezvous," I wasn't worried a bit.

Yes, there was a murderer in Sproutes.

No, Danny Jamieson hadn't set me up on a date with him.

I shivered and clambered up the shoveled-clear sidewalk, carrying my chocolate-whisperer bag of tricks with me. Inside were baker's bars of semisweet and dark chocolates, assorted decorative and flavored sugars, one extra-fine bar of milky white chocolate that I'd picked up in San Francisco, and a whole range of cookie cutters, thermometers, measuring spoons, and vanilla extracts.

Also, I'd brought some seasonal items and a culinary scale, just to have all my bases covered.

Once out in the cold December night, my breath puffed visibly in front of me, leading the way toward the fancifully decorated bungalow that was my destination. It turned out, Danny had promised to swap his source's information for an evening of personalized baking lessons with me. And a deal was a deal.

Technically, that meant that my friend had volunteered me for some extracurricular work, but I didn't mind. My supplies go wherever I do. Plus, creating delicious treats is something (the only thing) that clears my mind and calms my antsy soul. When engrossed in melting, whisking, stirring, and tasting, I'm not doing anything else. Quality cacao deserves full attention.

Speaking of which . . . this particular Sproutes homestead had earned its own share of the limelight. The place was impossible to miss. The small, snowy yard was full of glittering displays. Some of them moved. A glowing white snowman waved at me. A trio of lighted reindeer wearing red bows grazed in the snow. More of their kind gamboled along the icy rooftop, pulling Santa's sleigh. On the icicle-bordered eaves, multicolored chaser lights made the yard flash red, yellow, blue, and green. More lights covered the bungalow's white siding, delineating neat rows across its face. Those same lights spilled onto the snow-piled yard, blinking and flashing with over-the-top Christmas cheer.

I wouldn't have wanted my baking student's electricity bill, that was for sure. But as I neared the front door, with its pillared porch posts and showy beribboned holiday wreath, I did covet his snug household. Seasonal decorating is one of those things you don't realize you miss until you don't have it anymore. Even while globe-trotting with my parents, we'd all managed to add some Christmas cheer to our surroundings—and to enjoy whatever holiday celebrations were happening around us.

But once Uncle Ross had sadly passed on, my whole life had changed. I still missed him. I missed his eccentricities and his warmth. Most of all, I missed his wild, irrepressible smile.

As I stamped off my boots on the poinsettia doormat, the door itself whooshed open. A friendly-looking, thirty-ish man stood on the threshold, holding out his arms to me in welcome.

"Hayden, right? Thanks for coming! Come in, come in!"

He stepped aside to let me enter his home. Its interior wasn't quite as extravagant as the exterior, but there was a tall lighted Christmas tree in the corner. As I stood in the foyer to unwind my knit scarf and take off my hat, I noticed other seasonal touches, too—a row of painted wooden nutcracker figurines and a bowl full of antique glass-blown ornaments.

"The outside is a little much," he acknowledged with a rueful grin, "but I promise I'm not some kind of Christmas weirdo. I'm out to win the neighborhood decorating contest."

"Aha. Good luck, then. Josh, right?" I hauled in a breath, then smiled. "It's nice to meet you. Thanks for inviting me."

His genial face cleared. "I'm the one who should be thanking you! Especially for coming on such short notice." Josh indicated that I could leave my things on the foyer's coat hooks and the console table. I kept my crossbody bag and baking supplies with me, then followed him into his living room.

Bing Crosby was playing from a sound system somewhere. I felt myself relax another micrometer. Maybe this would be fun.

"Have a seat!" Josh's wave indicated a cushy-looking sofa with a snowman-printed flannel throw arranged on it. "I'll get us some eggnog. With a kick or without? I'm having it with."

His wink suggested I should do the same. Unfortunately . . .

"No, thanks. I'm driving, so I'll take it straight."

"Your loss!" he teased, touching his curly hair. With his khaki pants and button-down shirt worn with a crewneck sweater, he was the image of a classic New England preppy. "Maybe next time. Just make yourself comfortable. I'll be right back!"

Normally, I would have followed him to the kitchen and gotten down to work. But normally, I'm not swapping my culinary expertise for some off-the-books murder information. I felt acutely aware of my bizarre role— not quite a friend, not really a business associate, but something more. We were like spies, getting together to exchange top-secret information . . . except I was a good spy, working for the safety of all the Sproutesians.

I hoped that Josh was, too. *Josh Levitt*, I recalled.

Taking advantage of that unobserved moment, I shot a pair of quick texts to Danny and Travis, to let them know I'd arrived. I saw that I'd missed SMSs from Ophelia and Zach.

Ophelia's was a follow-up to the peppermint-bark photo shoot we'd done earlier, with Albany's little sister posing next to a horse-drawn sleigh. Zach's was a reminder about the chocolate houses I'd agreed to make for the town's auction.

Since neither was urgent, I left them for later.

"Here we go!" Josh returned, beaming, with a pair of eggnog cups in hand. Their china patterns didn't match. "Bottoms up!"

We toasted. I sipped. Mmm. Nutmeg and cream. Delicious.

"I swear, Danny saved my life." Josh Levitt's face was open and alert. That made it easy to trust him. "I wasn't getting anywhere with covering *Christmas in Crazytown*. Regional theater is my beat, but as soon as the Balthasars took over, they shut out the *Sentinel*. Usually, Donna gives me full access—"

"Donna?"

"Donna Brown. The theater's director."

I nodded, making a note to find out more about her. While briefing me, Danny had mentioned Josh and his work covering the Sproutes art scene for the local newspaper. The subject of Donna Brown hadn't come up, but I reasoned I might need to know more.

"Apparently, the Balthasars didn't think that a 'Podunk paper' like ours was worth dealing with." Josh rolled his eyes. "I was making zero progress. My editor is usually pretty mild mannered, but she was freaking out. There was *so* much interest in the show. We didn't want to be scooped by the national media. It was our big chance to serve our readers in a memorable way."

"And to score more advertisers, I'd imagine."

"Of course!" He sipped more eggnog, sending whiskey fumes wafting. "That's where all the pressure came in. The *Sentinel* is hanging on by a shoestring. If we don't maintain our readership, we're all unemployed. I didn't get into journalism for the money, but paying for groceries and electricity are nice perks."

I empathized. "I'm a freelancer myself. I have a financial cushion, but that doesn't mean I'm not serious about my work."

"Exactly." A nod. "Besides, it's Christmas! At this time of year, money is tight. I couldn't afford to risk getting fired."

"So . . . ?" Danny had been oddly discreet about this part.

"So I sneaked into the theater during rehearsals," Josh admitted. "I was planning to get a story about the show or die trying. Oops!" He covered his mouth with his hand, seeming (too late) to think better of his choice of phrases, given what had happened to Melissa. Cheerily, he waved away his carelessness. "Anyhow, I'm crawling in through the window—wearing all black, naturally!—and along comes the theater's security guard."

"Busted?" I gestured, urging him to tell me more.

"No! I would have gotten busted, sure." Josh's eyes went wide at the memory. "Except that's when Danny showed up."

"He has a way of doing that. Right on time."

"Yeah. He didn't even know me, but he bailed me out."

"He's always had issues with authority figures," I said. "I'm not surprised he'd wind up on your side of the situation."

"Whatever, I'm glad! He kind of swaggered over, saw what was going on and, in the most poker-faced way you can imagine, told the security guard that he'd been staging a test of the theater's policies and procedures. 'You failed,' he said."

Remembering it, Josh chortled. "I was about to pee my pants, I was so nervous," he admitted. "But Danny just hauled me the rest of the way over the windowsill, brushed me off, then took me backstage with him. It wasn't until later that I found out he was Tansy's bodyguard. After that, nobody said a word to me about reporting on the show. They just let me hang around."

I imagined Danny had a lot to do with that turnaround.

"Maybe the Balthasars didn't realize you were with the *Sentinel*?" I theorized. "If they had a blanket 'no press' policy, then their refusal to give you a story wasn't personal."

"It felt personal to me." Josh glowered into his eggnog. "It felt personal the whole time it was endangering my job."

I examined his brooding face. He had a right to feel bitter about the Balthasars having put his employment at risk, however inadvertently they might have done so. But had Josh felt bitter enough to try another break-in? Say, at the B&B two nights ago?

Had Josh Levitt wanted revenge against Melissa?

Hastily, I drowned those thoughts in another gulp of creamy eggnog. Danny wouldn't have let me come here if that was so.

I tried another angle. "I read your story about Melissa Balthasar's death." Josh's theater beat explained the slant he'd taken—that her demise had endangered the show's opening. "It's impressive that you manage to cover the local arts scene *and* crime, all at the same time. That must keep you hopping, right?"

Josh waved off my praise. "Well, around here, there's usually not enough crime to warrant a full-time reporter." He chuckled in the glow of his Christmas tree's lights. "Sproutes is a peaceful small town. Nothing much happens here. That's why it was such a big deal when the *Christmas in Crazytown* production came in. We were all hoping for big things—the paper, local businesses like restaurants and hotels, stores downtown."

I nodded, wishing (not for the first time) that I was a police officer or a detective—someone who could really grill a witness or informant and find out what I wanted to know. But I was only me, an itinerant expert in all things cacao related.

"It must be a boon having so many people working here now."

"It's got its ups and downs," Josh said cryptically. He peered into his now empty eggnog cup. "Would you like a refill?"

"No, thanks. I'm still enjoying this one. You go ahead."

He did, leaving me alone to scrutinize his living room while he puttered in the kitchen. I looked for signs of secret homicidal rage against the Balthasars but found nothing.

Unless owning several DVD box sets of TV murder-mystery shows made a person into a killer, Josh Levitt was in the clear.

"So your editor tapped you to write the Melissa piece because of your theater access?" I theorized at a shout toward the kitchen, keeping my voice casual. "Because you know people at the playhouse?"

Josh laughed as he returned with his second eggnog. "Hardly. It was because I know the police officers who responded to the scene. My brother works for the force," he explained, shoving aside a holiday-print throw pillow as he sat in the easy chair opposite me on the sofa. "Honestly, I know almost everyone in town, of course, but that was the critical connection."

"That makes sense. Your brother must be quite a guy."

"Yeah." Josh nodded. "I can tell you one thing, though. Things would have been *very* different that night if the chief of police had been on the scene." A wave. Another hearty slurp of eggnog. "In fact, that might be why Sproutes has such a low crime rate. Everyone around here is scared of the chief."

"Really?" I had to meet this super crime fighter. "But I thought Melissa's death wasn't being considered a murder, so—"

"Oh no you don't!" Josh's gaze took on an impish gleam. "Not so fast!" He got up, wobbling slightly. Exactly how strong had he made his spiked eggnog, anyway? "Danny told me you have a particular interest in Melissa's case, and I'm willing to play along, but finding out what I know is going to cost you."

Maybe I could shortcut this. "I have some chocolate samples with me," I tried. "I could offer you your pick. Fudge, caramels covered with chocolate, a variety of truffles . . . or all three?"

He seemed tempted, just as I'd intended. But no dice.

"What I need right now are *cookies*. Whoops!" Josh flailed his arms and narrowly avoided spilling his eggnog. He'd upset his balance while vehemently refusing my offer-slash-bribe. He laughed. "This is a trade, remember? I tell you what I know—"

"What *didn't* make it into your story," I specified.

Specifically, exactly how Melissa Balthasar had died.

"And you rescue me from looking like a loser at the annual *Sproutes Sentinel* Bake-Off and cookie swap to-morrow. Deal?"

I nodded. We needed to get started before he became too tipsy to chop or stir. I hefted my bag of supplies. "Let's go."

In Josh's small kitchen, the first thing we did was pre-heat the oven. Then I briefed him on my baking plans for the evening.

"Naturally, these are going to be chocolate cookies," I told him. "Chocolate cookies with white chocolate–peppermint icing and candy-cane sprinkles. Is that okay with you?"

"Sounds scrumptious!" He rubbed his palms together. "There's a prize, by the way. Did Danny tell you that? Winning would be even better than *not* being embarrassed. Last year, I got one of those boxed cookie mixes and tried to pass off the results as homemade. My editor took one bite and ratted me out."

"She must have a refined palate. Is she a good baker?"

"Her cookie-swap cookies are good," Josh specified with a meaningful look, "but I'm pretty sure she doesn't bake them herself. I'm told that her son is handy with a mixing bowl."

"Aha." I grinned at him. "Your next exposé, after you crack the Melissa Balthasar case?" I wanted us to get back on track.

But Josh appeared somewhat mystified. "There's nothing to 'crack.' Her death really was accidental, at least according to my brother. I know you're hoping for more, but . . . Hey, watch out!"

Josh yanked me out of the way. Heavy slabs of metal clanged to the floor in a jumble and landed with a loud crash.

I'd been opening and closing cupboard doors, trying to seem nonchalant about my questions while assembling supplies. One of the cupboards had indeed contained the baking sheets I was looking for, but several of them had almost crushed my skull.

"Sorry!" my friendly host yelped. "All my tidiness is just a sham, I'm afraid. I'm one of those people who jams everything into the closet, then calls it clean." Red faced, he scooped up the wayward cookie sheets and set them on the counter. "We'll just run those through the dishwasher before we use them."

My heart pounded. But I managed a wave. "No need.

A good rinse and towel dry will be fine. We're baking on parchment."

I showed him my roll of baking paper. It was one of my secret weapons, ensuring that my baked goods didn't stick to the pans and lightening my cleanup load. Temporarily derailed from my questions, I demonstrated how to measure the parchment paper to fit the sheet pans, how to roll it to easily trim it to size, and then—my super top-secret tip—how to crumple it and then smooth it, the better to ensure it lay flat beneath cookies.

Seriously, it works like magic. Without that final step, you'll find that your parchment paper wants to curl right up on itself, accidentally shielding your baked goods from the heat they need to bake and brown properly in the oven. It's genius.

"I have a box of that stuff, but I never use it," Josh admitted. "It's too much trouble. But you make that look easy."

"It is," I promised. We spent a few minutes clearing space on the kitchen countertop, removing rolls of holiday gift wrap, cellophane tape, and a bag of colorful bows. "So is baking, once you have a system. The first thing to do is read the recipe."

I'd already printed it while at the B and B's mini business center. I stuck it to the fridge with a Christmas magnet.

Josh glanced at it. "Okay, got it." He handed me an apron.

I laughed. "No, really *read* it. Start to finish, making sure you understand all the steps and have all the ingredients on hand. That's important. What if you get halfway through baking and realize you don't have a critical ingredient?"

A shameless grin. "That's what you're here for."

I liked his jovial attitude. "Not next year, I won't be."

"Fair enough." Josh pushed up his sweater sleeves. With his merry "Mrs. Claus" apron worn over his outfit, he looked up for the challenge. He read the recipe. "Okay. Got it. For real."

I gave him an approving smile. "Now, ingredients."

"Oh, don't worry! I already got everything you e-mailed me."

I'd sent a list earlier, so he'd be ready for the cookie swap.

"Let's get out everything, anyway. Right on the counter," I said. "This is where we make sure we have enough of everything, and it's in good shape to use. Ideally, we'd do this well in advance, in case we need to soften butter or bring eggs to room temperature, but the cookies we're making don't need either of those things." I smiled. "I wanted to keep it foolproof."

"I like that idea!" Complaisantly, Josh assembled flour, sugar, good-quality cocoa powder, leavening, and more. There were, of course, a few breaks for slurps of eggnog, but I was no taskmaster. It was important to enjoy time in the kitchen, too.

"Next, equipment," I said. "Bowls, measuring cups and spoons, wax paper, and a big ole wooden spoon for stirring."

"I have a fancy mixer." Josh nodded at it. He cracked a teasing grin. "It's barely used. Only a few minor disasters."

"For these cookies, you won't need it. They're easy."

His raised eyebrow indicated he doubted it. "I need 'stupid easy.' I burn toast. On the regular. I tried one of those 'easy mug cakes' in the microwave and almost started a kitchen fire."

I gave a knowledgeable nod. "Did you leave in the spoon?"

"So *that's* what did it!" Josh rolled his eyes and shook

his head. "I forgot you can't put metal in a microwave. Duh."

"This is easy," I assured him after offering to share my own (delicious) chocolate mug cake recipe. "Especially if you use my culinary scale." I showed him how it worked. "You just set your mixing bowl on the scale, add ingredients, and tare it in between." That step was necessary so that each ingredient could be weighed individually. We'd still need spoons, but . . . "No muss, no fuss, no sticky measuring cups to wash afterward."

"Cool. All right." Josh seemed game. He surveyed the scene we'd made, with ingredients and equipment strewn across the countertops. "I've gotta say, this actually looks worse than when I bake alone."

"There's a method to the madness, I promise."

It was time to show him. So I did. See, what trips up many bakers is the unfamiliarity of it all, coupled with the need to multitask. To beginners or part-time bakers, it often seems that a million things are happening at once. But it's possible to slow down the process. It's even possible (really!) to enjoy it.

All you have to do is take things slowly, step-by-step.

First, Josh weighed ingredients into a medium bowl set atop the scale. He carefully spooned in the flour, then studied it.

"Shouldn't I be scooping and sweeping or packing this into a measuring cup or fluffing it up or sifting or something?"

"No need. Whisking all the dry ingredients is as good as sifting, and when you're weighing, you don't have to scoop and level flour. You always get the right amount by weighing it."

"Okay. Next?" He shoved aside the flour bag and waited.

"Next, we put away the flour," I instructed. This was the next most important step in my practice. I'd learned it from my mentor. "That way, we won't add it to our cookie dough twice."

Hands on hips, Josh laughed at the very idea. "I'm not *that* drunk on eggnog. I can see that there's flour in that bowl."

"Sure, but what about baking powder? Salt? Baking soda? If you put away each ingredient immediately after using it, you'll never forget to use one—because it'll be there as a reminder—and you'll never double up, either. Plus, instant kitchen cleanup."

"Fair enough." Josh put away the flour; then we proceeded to add the rest of the dry ingredients. "Time to whisk?"

"You're a quick study." If only he'd spill some info. "Did you always want to be a reporter? How long have you been at it?"

His gaze met mine. "You already told me not to multitask."

Rats. I had. "All right, let's keep going." I regrouped. "Next comes sugar, then brown sugar." I watched Josh weigh both. The countertop was clearing rapidly. "Now cocoa powder, then a little milk. Just pour it right into the mix with the vanilla."

He frowned, with the milk held aloft. "Don't I need to cream this or something? Whip until light and fluffy? That's cookies!"

"Not these cookies. Trust me. This is the easy part."

A few minutes later, Josh had added all the liquids, including some vegetable oil. It doesn't have the flavor of butter, but it introduces a certain softness to cookies that is difficult to get any other way. It also offers easy baking.

Cookies made with butter—which contains water—spread a lot more.

"Using oil means less risk of 'one giant cookie' syndrome."

"When all the batter smooshes together in the oven, ruining all the hard work you've done?" Josh asked. "Yeah, been there."

I had been, too, but not for years. Now I showed Josh how to combine the wet and dry ingredients, portion the dough into equally sized balls using a small metal scoop, then arrange them on the lined baking sheets. We flattened each cookie slightly.

We double-checked the oven temperature. The oven was ready.

So was I. After watching Josh painstakingly slide his first sheet pan of chocolate cookies into the oven, I tried again to get the information I needed about Melissa's maybe-murder.

"So, about Melissa Balthasar," I said leadingly. "Do you know if there will be an autopsy? What was the cause of death?"

This time, I hit pay dirt.

"She drowned," Josh confided. "Smashed into that punch bowl—probably drunk or high, is what my brother said—and drowned."

I couldn't believe it. "Drowned? But there couldn't have been more than a few inches of wassail in that punch bowl."

A shrug. "That's all it takes, especially if you're too wasted to save yourself. Or if you've already passed out."

I shivered inwardly. Still . . . "Someone would have heard. There were more than a dozen people upstairs. A single shout—"

"Would have been impossible." Imperturbably, Josh peered into his oven. "The way my brother explained it to me, drowning is silent. Nobody can call for help. That's because all it takes is for the victim to inhale enough liquid to seal off her trachea. After that, there's no oxygen to shout—or to live."

Gruesome. Poor Melissa. She'd died all alone. If only I'd arrived at the B&B a little later that night. Maybe I could have saved her. "So the official cause of death is . . . ?"

"Cardiac arrest, brought on by drowning. *Accidentally*."

I couldn't miss Josh's emphasis on *accidentally*.

"Was Melissa known to drink a lot? Or take drugs?"

"Who knows? With these Hollywood types, probably."

"Were you at the tree-trimming party? Did you see her?"

"I wasn't invited." Josh sent me a chary look. "What makes you so interested, anyway? It's not as if you knew Melissa."

Whoops. I'd overstepped. I remembered the DVD box sets I'd glimpsed earlier and improvised. "Just curious. Is that morbid?" I pulled a jokey face. "I watch a lot of those TV crime shows."

That did the trick. Josh lightened up. "Hey, me too!"

We chatted about a few different series while moving on (at my prompting) to the next step of our cookie-swap contribution: carefully melting white chocolate for our peppermint icing.

Josh was ready to skip a step, though. He put the candy canes I'd brought into a sealable plastic bag, then tapped me on the shoulder. When I turned, he wielded a meat mallet overhead.

I took one look at his fiendish expression and yelped. He appeared ready to wallop *me* into dust, not the candy canes.

His expression cleared. "Oh, sorry! I was only kidding."

And I was overreacting if I thought harmless Josh Levitt was planning to meat-mallet me to death. "I know." I put my hand over my hopscotching heart, then grinned. "You wouldn't dare attack me. At least not until all the cookies are finished."

Josh laughed. "What kind of criminal mastermind would *I* be? You're already reading my mind." He sighed and squinted into his oven again, then turned to me. "Are they supposed to smoke?"

"What?" Panicked, I raced to the oven. I squinted, too.

"Gotcha!" His laughter rang out again, full of holiday merriness. "You're right, Hayden. Baking can be pretty fun!"

"I'm glad you think so." I shared his grin. "Let's make that icing. After that, we'll decorate and be done. Easy peasy."

Easy peasy. I wished I could say the same thing about investigating Melissa's death. After finding out what Josh knew, I was suddenly beset with doubts about my own sleuthing.

I had to admit, drowning did fit the evidence I'd seen.

More accurately, it fit the *lack* of evidence I'd seen.

Could I really be poking into an accidental death? Had I seen so much murder and mayhem recently that I was imagining things? Yesterday I hadn't thought so. But tonight . . . maybe?

I glanced at Josh, who was gleefully bashing the candy canes into the sprinkles we'd later use on our cookies. I was reminded that none of us ever really know what goes on in someone else's mind. Josh could have been a killer. Danny could have been wrong about him and set me up with a murderer.

Melissa could have been drugged before falling into that wassail punch bowl. She could have been the victim of an overdose that *wasn't* accidental. Someone could have held her head under the wassail until she drowned. There were still any number of ways that Melissa Balthasar could have been murdered.

Given the police's "accidental death" stance, it was up to me (more than ever) to find out what had really happened. So I shored up my resolve and decided to keep investigating.

My next step? Eating a couple of chocolate cookies with white chocolate–peppermint icing and candy-cane sprinkles (quality control, naturally). After that? I wanted to meet Roger Balthasar—because a death that was truly accidental definitely *didn't* require bribing the police to stop investigating it.

Eight

I was waiting for Travis in the B and B's snug parlor, enjoying its Christmassy ambiance (and a slice of fruit-cake), when opportunity knocked. I needed a moment with Zach, my B and B's host, so I could casually ask him about the guest list for the *Christmas in Crazytown* tree-trimming party. I wanted to know, too, about the lack of cleanup afterward. After all, leaving a potential weapon (the wassail and punch bowl) out in plain sight might have made things easier for Melissa's (maybe) murderer.

Sometimes, I reasoned, opportunity might be as important as motive. Even unpremeditated murder left catastrophe in its wake. I doubted that Melissa's loved ones and friends would feel comforted by knowing that her killer hadn't necessarily *planned* to cold-bloodedly drown her. Or maybe he had. I didn't know.

I was still mulling it over when an argument broke out at the B and B's front desk. Curious by nature, I set aside my fruitcake and swiveled to watch. A tall, dark-haired man was insisting on being given a room right away.

Zach, ever soft-spoken and apologetic, was . . . well, apologizing.

His remorse wasn't sufficient for the newcomer—who was handsome, I observed, with patrician features and an athletic appearance. His puffer coat framed his high cheekbones and almond eyes; his checkered scarf was worn with a rakish air.

Unfortunately, it didn't matter to me how good-looking he might have been. I don't like people who berate service workers. That was Zach's role at the moment. Looking on, I frowned.

"You *must* have a room!" the man complained, his shoulders slumped. He clenched his fists. "I drove for hours to get here."

"I'm sorry, but since you don't have a reservation—"

"I don't need a reservation! It's Christmastime."

"I'm afraid that's one of our busiest seasons." Zach seemed contrite. "Maybe the Sproutes Motor Lodge could—"

"Come on, dude!" the newcomer wheedled, changing tactics. "Can't I just crash up in the attic or something? Please?"

I'd never heard anyone call Zach "dude" before. More intrigued now, I took careful measure of the man. He was tall, I saw, and wore wrinkled canvas pants and lug-soled snow boots.

Whoever he was, he seemed familiar with snow—and with Zach. Was this a strategy, using a casual nickname on the spot? Or did they really know one another? They seemed about the same age. But where Zach Johnson was friendly, the stranger seemed aloof—at least when he wasn't pleading for a favor, he did.

Before Zach could answer, the unknown man's phone

rang. He moved away to answer it—without excusing himself first—leaving Zach standing, ignored, at the front desk. That was my cue.

I wandered over, then gave Zach a commiserating look. "Tough afternoon?" My meaningful nod indicated the demanding man. "I guess some people just can't take no for an answer?"

My host's expression looked faraway. Zach started, then flashed me a hasty, rueful smile. "It comes with the job. He's not such a bad guy. He's definitely not the first friend of mine to want a favor. Ordinarily, I'd help out, but I just can't."

I smiled in understanding, yet my mind was stuck on that word. *Friend.* This new guy *was* a friend of Zach's? He hadn't acted like one. "That's perfectly reasonable," I assured my B and B's host. "Especially with all that's been going on . . ."

I waited, hopefully, but Zach didn't volunteer anything more—especially not about Melissa's death. I forged onward.

"Now I feel doubly lucky to have scored a room here," I remarked. "I must have snagged the last one available, right?"

Zach nodded, but his pensive gaze remained trained on the newcomer. Naturally enough, I looked in that direction, too. Now he was pacing across the B and B's foyer, still looking beleaguered.

Snatches of his (one-sided) conversation filtered to us, albeit quietly. I gathered that someone was calming him down.

"Yes, all right," the man murmured. "I will. Thanks, Dad."

I nodded and hooked a thumb in that direction. "See?

Parents solve everything, especially at Christmastime. Right?"

Zach gave me a distracted nod. Then his gaze cleared. He focused on me. "Sorry, was there something else you needed?"

"Just the recipe for your yummy fruitcake, please."

We both smiled. "That's easily done," Zach told me. "I'll ask housekeeping to leave a copy in your room this afternoon."

I thanked him and turned away. Then I did a *Columbo*, trying to seem absentminded and nonthreatening as I doubled back.

"Sorry. Just one more thing," I said with a smile. "My friend Danny Jamieson is Tansy Park's bodyguard. He asked me to pick up a copy of the guest list from the *Christmas in Crazytown* tree-trimming party. He was planning to come over himself for it, but since I'm already here, I told him I'd try to help out."

"A guest list?" Zach blinked. It was obvious he was still eavesdropping on the newcomer's phone conversation. "Sure. I don't see why not. I thought the police might want one, so I wrote down everyone I could remember. But they never asked."

We talked for a while about the (non) investigation. Zach e-mailed me his list. I confirmed I'd received it on my phone.

"All right. Thanks, Zach! Have a nice day today."

I turned and deliberately passed close to the newcomer, who'd wrapped up his conversation now. He seemed visibly calmer as he put away his phone. He glanced up at me, then nodded.

I felt jolted. If Albany had had a male counterpart, it occurred to me as I nodded back, it would have been him.

He had her hair color, her rangy build, *and* her sense of entitlement.

I disliked him on sight. But then I caught a glimpse of Travis, descending the B and B's beautiful old carved oak staircase, and knew that he'd been right about me. I'd reacted badly to Albany and her closer-than-close relationship with my financial advisor. Now I was apparently projecting that reaction onto a total stranger. Zach had said he wasn't such a bad guy.

For all I knew, the newcomer had suffered a flat tire, gotten stuck in the snow, and nearly frozen to death on the way to Sproutes. It was treacherous out there. I was lucky I hadn't skidded into a snowbank myself. I shouldn't be too hard on him.

Still, it wouldn't have killed him to be a little nicer.

As if reading my mind, he smiled. "Sorry you had to hear all that." He gestured to the front desk. "I was out of line."

"The holidays can be stressful," I commiserated. I might not have liked him, particularly, but I didn't want to be rude myself. And he was apologizing, at least. I waved to Travis. "Sorry. That's my friend. I'd better run. Merry Christmas!"

And that, as they said, was that. Or at least it was until I glanced back at Travis and saw recognition on his face.

My financial advisor met me at the bottom of the stairs. With a hello nod for Zach, Travis herded me into the parlor.

"Whoa, whoa! Easy there, bruiser!" I rubbed my arm, where my (surprisingly strong) keeper had grabbed me. "What's up?"

"That was Cashel Sullivan. What are you doing with him?"

"Cashel Sullivan? Really?" I turned to look, but the

newcomer was gone. "The prodigal son? Albany's older brother?"

"The very same," Travis confirmed. He looked worried. "I didn't know he was in town. His family wasn't expecting him."

"His dad was. They just had a long and apparently bolstering phone call." I described what had gone on. "So he's come home for Christmas. Big deal." I leaned in, hoping to find a crack in the Sullivan family armor. I'm not as generous as I'd like to be. "Is he really the black sheep of the family?"

"You still haven't read Albany's memoir?"

"I've read some of it," I prevaricated. I'd taken a crack at it yesterday, after meeting with Ophelia and before going to Josh's house for our baking lesson. I'd made some headway. Then I'd gotten sidetracked watching Albany's interviews online and reading gossip sites' coverage about her. "It's a long book! Besides, the names and identifying details have been changed, so—"

"So 'my brother' still means one thing, as far as I know." My advisor's disapproving look swept over me. "Of all the people in Albany's memoir, he's probably the most closely represented."

"So shoot me, I didn't compile a dossier. That's your job." I gave him a "Lighten up" nudge. I wanted to move on from this. "So, you were looking into the Balthasars' financials?"

My brainiac advisor nodded, successfully diverted (as always) by talk of accounting. He adjusted his horn-rimmed specs, then dived in. He described Roger and Melissa's meeting and courtship, their prenuptial agreement and marriage, their business partnership, and their "extravagant" lifestyle.

"Then they weren't short on money," I summed up.

"Was there a huge life insurance payout available on Melissa's death?"

"A payout, yes, but nothing unusual." Travis looked up from the paperwork he'd brought. "I don't think it would have been sufficient to motivate a murder, if that's what you're asking."

"Lately? That's *always* what I'm asking."

"Yes." My keeper gave me a commiserating look. "How are you holding up, anyway? I've been busy taking care of Albany."

"That's what you should be doing. Your friend needs you." I remembered Danny's theory that Travis and Albany were sleeping together. My overactive brain offered up a vivid image of the two of them together. *Intimately.* I shook my head but couldn't get rid of it. That meant I had to act. "Especially now that you and Albany are a couple. You know, reunited. She needs you, and you're there for her. That's how love works, right?"

An excruciating silence followed my statement.

Okay, so technically, it was broken by the Bon Jovi version of "Please Come Home for Christmas" on the B and B's sound system. But I still felt those moments tick by in slow motion. Argh.

When I glanced up, Travis's dumbfounded look met mine.

Then he quirked his mouth. "I'm not in love with Albany."

"Oh, so it's just a fling, then. Sure." I managed an offhanded wave. "Well, you're a grown-up. And it's the holidays."

"And everyone has torrid romances during the holidays?"

Was he holding back *laughter*? I stiffened my posture.

"Some people do," I said defensively. "There are songs about it."

"And movies," Travis added with exaggerated solemnity.

But his eyes were sparkling at me. His sexy, husky voice had lowered to a seductive octave, too. Probably on purpose.

"Fine!" I blurted, sorry I'd brought up the subject. "If you and Albany aren't getting hot and heavy, then why are you sharing a room here at the B and B? Huh? Explain that, genius."

I folded my arms, waiting. Danny would have been proud. This was my best impression of his trademark no-nonsense stance.

Travis's face sobered. "The B&B was full. Albany and I doubled up so that *you* could have a room to stay in. Her parents don't have a guest room, so she can't stay with them while she's in Sproutes. Albany lives and works in New York now, remember?"

I knew that. I recalled it from reading her interviews and bio. But I wasn't quite ready to let this go. I opened my mouth.

Before I could do so much as take a breath, my financial advisor beat me to the punch. "You realize this is none of your business, right? My private life is just that. Private."

"I know. I'm sorry." This was Danny's fault. His conjecture about Albany and Travis had bothered me more than I'd realized.

Still . . . "Come on, though, Travis. I've seen the movies. When people come home for the holidays—or at any time of year—their childhood bedrooms are always perfectly preserved in their parents' houses." It was one of those things that I, as a perennial gridskipper, had never experienced . . . but had honestly yearned for. Having a permanent bedroom retreat sounded nice.

Now Travis appeared to be holding back a grin. "Sometimes, I forget about the gaps in your upbringing," he confessed.

"What's that supposed to mean?"

"It means that the movies aren't real, and neither is a childhood 'room shrine.' In real life, parents move on. They use that space for home offices. Gyms. Craft spaces. Or sometimes for guest rooms. But those guest rooms aren't typically frozen in time, decorated with someone's favorite posters from high school and filled with years of memorabilia and photographs."

I stared at him, stubbornly holding on to the idea.

"Kids tend to take that stuff with them to college," he added. "I know I did. What I couldn't bring went into storage."

Storage? That sounded so unfeeling. Sure, I keep most of my personal belongings in storage these days. But that's because I have to stay on the move, due to my trust fund's requirements.

"Just because you and Albany don't have childhood bedrooms to go to, that doesn't mean no one does," I argued. Something else occurred to me. "Maybe you both had unhappy childhoods?"

As soon as the words left my mouth, I regretted them.

A shadow passed over Travis's face. "Let's get back to Roger and Melissa's finances." He busied himself with his papers, then cleared his throat. "They had plenty of money."

"Then the motive wasn't financial."

"And there's no evidence of malfeasance."

"I'm sure Roger was making a deal with that police

officer, though," I maintained. "Were there any big payouts to anyone?"

"None directly linked to anyone here in Sproutes," Travis told me. He gazed across the B and B's parlor, toward the decorated foyer. "Although seeing Cashel here does make me wonder . . ."

"About?"

"About the expenses I noted for several Malibu rehab centers." Travis's candid gaze met mine. "We need to know more about Melissa's past. No one I've talked to mentioned her having a history of drug abuse, but those rehab stays bother me." He lowered his voice. "For one thing, they were paid at above the market rate. For another, they were all very brief—far too short to have accomplished anything as far as recovery is concerned."

"Maybe Melissa was in and out of rehab a lot. Maybe it didn't work for her." I frowned. "From what I've learned about her, Melissa wouldn't have had much patience for being told what to do. If she had a problem, then, she might not have kicked it in rehab. So she might still have been using in Sproutes."

"That would explain her passing out in the punch bowl," Travis mused. "She goes to the tree-trimming party, gets carried away with drinking or drugs, staggers into the dining room—"

And face-plants into a punch bowl of wassail. Forever.

I didn't want to think about it. "If there were multiple short stays," I said instead, "maybe they were for her clients?"

Travis nodded. "That's a possibility. I'll look into it."

"After all, if the Balthasars paid the rehab staff to keep quiet about their clients' treatment, that hush money would be paid 'above market rate.' We need to ask Danny about all this."

The whole thing seemed underhanded. It made me feel dirty.

It also solidified my hunch that Roger Balthasar was a strong suspect.

"So there's *no* proof," I pressed Travis, "of Roger having paid off the local police to stop or slow the investigation?"

He shook his head. "Not so far."

Hmm. Melissa's death had fallen off the media grid and social networks. Danny thought Roger's influence might have had something to do with that. I wasn't so sure that one man could have enough clout to suppress all those forms of communication.

"And what does Cashel Sullivan have to do with all this?" I remembered Travis's earlier comment but didn't understand it.

My financial advisor gave me a goading look. A familiar one. "You'd already know if you'd finished Albany's book."

"Cashel was in rehab?" I guessed. "And Albany wrote about it?" Instantly, I felt sympathetic toward her brother. I knew Travis cared about his longtime friend, but . . . "Addiction is a serious problem, Travis. Exposing him could hurt his recovery."

Travis gave a tolerant sigh. "Slow down, Sherlock. Cashel lives in Southern California now. That's all I meant. If you'd read Albany's memoir, you'd recognize him. He's 'the surfer.'"

Aha. In her book, Albany had used descriptive nouns—the surfer, the boss, the father, the underling, the teacher—to refer to people, without using their real names or mentioning their true roles in her life. "She didn't veer too far from the facts when 'lightly fictionalizing' her memoir, then. Good to know."

I vowed to speed-read through the rest of Albany's book immediately. As I may have mentioned, however, I tend to procrastinate. Plus, the online media coverage of Albany had been even more riveting than her (admittedly hilarious) memoir. She was a natural in the limelight. Some of the memes she'd inspired were definitely mean-spirited, but that's the Internet for you—full of people who believe that snarky takedowns are the ultimate in wit. Albany couldn't have helped that.

"Albany's memoir is fictionalized enough," was Travis's opinion. "There are fewer hurt feelings to worry about that way. Whether you think so or not, Albany is a good person."

I wanted to believe him. I truly did. But if embellishing the facts to make them more sensational (and salable) was "good," then I needed vocabulary lessons. I wasn't blinded by sentiment.

It was possible, I knew, that usually sensible Travis was.

"I'm sure you're right," I conceded. "At the moment, Albany might be a 'good person' who's being targeted by a killer."

"So we'd better keep digging," Travis agreed. He gathered his paperwork, then gave me an empathetic look. "Sorry to break the bad news to you about the childhood-bedroom movie scam."

I scoffed. "I was only kidding. I knew it was fake."

I wished I had. It was no fun having my illusions shattered. Thanks to my unusual upbringing, I knew how to speak several languages. I knew how to properly present a gift (with both hands) in Sri Lanka. I knew how to use a Bangalore squat toilet with no muss and no fuss. But a few gaps still remained.

"Anyway, duty calls!" I told Travis. "I've got to run. Josh Levitt invited me to the Christmas cookie swap at the *Sproutes Sentinel*, and it starts in half an hour. So while

I'd like to hang around here discussing tax returns and quarterly reports—"

"Go ahead." Cheerfully, Travis waved me away. "Believe it or not, I'd rather eat cookies than perform financial analysis, too. Have a few for me—especially if they have those sugar cookies with the frosting and sprinkles. They're my favorite."

I'd do better than that, I promised myself. I'd bring back those cookies for my friend. With that in mind, I headed out.

Nine

You might be surprised to learn that an official Christmas cookie swap is something I've never attended. Not in an expert capacity, and not on an amateur basis, either. In my mind, a traditional cookie swap is a very American type of event—and there's not much call for active experimental archeologists (and their inquisitive, chocolate-loving offspring) in the United States. That's why my parents and I traveled the world so much.

From the start, I was entranced. Josh Levitt graciously met me in the lobby of the *Sproutes Sentinel* offices, then escorted me farther in. We wove past cubicles and desks, TV monitors and meeting rooms, passing by and chatting with dozens of newspaper staffers. It was evident that Josh was well liked, and that he enjoyed his coworkers, too. The staff seemed like a family.

Someone had set up the Christmas cookie exchange in one of the largest meeting rooms. Danny would have found the place claustrophobic, thanks to its low ceilings, fluorescent lights, and overall air of nine-to-five clock punching. But I found the space was nicely upgraded by the ornamented Christmas tree in the corner, the multicolored lights strung from the ceiling, and the strands of garland that had been taped along the edges of the tables. The tables been pushed against the walls and topped with festive holiday-print paper tablecloths. Atop those were plates of different Christmas cookies, some humble and some elaborate.

There were so many offerings that it was almost impossible to detect the tablecloth pattern beneath them. Each plate bore a printed cookie description and an identifying baker's number.

"You weren't kidding about the cookie contest," I told Josh in an undertone, marveling at the setup. "I didn't expect all this—coded numbers, a secret ballot, professional taster cups."

"Spit cups" had been provided for the use of tasters who didn't want to munch their way through the entire selection, only to wind up with a winner several hundred calories later. Josh told me they weren't used much, though.

"It's a lot less formal than it looks, trust me," he said. "In fact, I'll bet you twenty bucks that my editor wins. Again."

I was affronted. "You're on! Because *you're* going to win. I helped you, didn't I? You've got this in the bag, Josh."

We each took paper plates, then circled the room with everyone else, talking while holiday music played. Everyone was friendly and lighthearted, jokingly evaluating the offerings and calling out teasing critiques of butter cookies, thumbprints, spritz, and peanut butter blossoms. I tried cookies shaped like candy canes, cookies flavored with nutmeg and other spices, and molasses cookies with vanilla icing. There were cranberry-orange cookies with white chocolate, sugar cookies with silver dragées, and impossibly thin, sugary creations shaped like snowflakes.

There, amid all the fun-loving *Sentinel* employees, I felt downright convivial. They welcomed me into their midst with tales of past cookie Bake-Offs, stories of Christmas decorating, and invitations to experience one of Sproutes's most traditional attractions: the annual Santa's locomotive ride for kids.

"All the kids show up in their pajamas—bundled up with all their warm winter gear on top, of course," Josh explained. "Then they jump onto a miniature steam locomotive, scream and go crazy while having cookies and hot chocolate, then get driven around by 'Santa' on a temporary track at the Sproutes town park."

"Aww, that sounds nice." I mentioned the municipal parade downtown that someone had told me about, with lighted floats and holiday balloons, and the charity ornament auction, too. "I'm volunteering a few chocolate houses. Zach asked me to."

I described my contribution, explaining that my houses would be similar to gingerbread houses, only 100 percent chocolate.

"Mmm. That sounds like my kind of thing!" someone said.

I turned to see a pleasant-looking woman of about fifty, wearing a tunic-length sweater with pants tucked into boots.

At her arrival, Josh practically saluted. He definitely stood up straighter. "Linda, this is Hayden Mundy Moore, the chocolate expert I told you about," he shared amid the holiday hubbub. "Hayden, this is Linda Sullivan, my editor."

"Linda Sullivan?" I grasped her hand, meeting her gaze

with a straightforward look of my own. "Any relation to Albany?"

Her smile warmed me. "She's my daughter. But don't worry—not everything in that book of hers is true!" she assured me.

If it had been true, I recalled, Linda Sullivan would have had cause to be resentful of it. The memoir's "mother" character was a manipulative control freak who cried at the drop of a hat.

"Still, it must be surreal to see your family depicted in a best-selling book," I chatted. "Especially a holiday memoir."

"A 'lightly fictionalized' holiday memoir," Linda reminded me gently. "It's really a work of fiction, with just enough grit to titillate and enough love to add verisimilitude. I'm a writer. Albany's a writer. I understand the impulse to exaggerate."

That made sense. Still . . . "But the holidays are sacrosanct!"

Her agreeable expression never faltered. But something in the perplexed way that Linda angled her head niggled at me.

It appeared very similar to the way that Travis had looked at me earlier, I realized, when we'd discussed the childhood room-shrine issue. Maybe I was culturally out of step again, I guessed. I was out of sync with my sleep schedule, still jet lagged. Probably, I wasn't thinking with the clarity I needed.

"Maybe to some people, the holidays are untouchable. We Sullivans are more freewheeling than that. It's a good thing, too! Otherwise, the past few months would have been very difficult for us." Linda gave me a confiding smile. "At this point, the whole family is making up new anecdotes to include in Albany's follow-up book. There's talk, you know, of a sequel."

I hadn't heard that. "A sequel?"

"Yes, with a summertime vacation theme." Linda glanced at Josh, bringing him into our conversation. "There's plenty of material there! In the meantime, I'm doing my part to help."

"Oh, are you Albany's cowriter? Or her editor?"

A jolly laugh. "Not a chance! Albany is very secretive about her work, at least until it's finished." Linda winced. She put her hand to her temple in what appeared to be a habitual, reflexive gesture, then gave me a pained smile. "What I'm doing isn't so much writing or editing as it is supporting."

I wanted to ask if she was all right, but Josh interrupted.

"The *Sentinel* is running a *Christmas in Crazytown*– themed crossword-puzzle contest to promote the show," he explained, unconcerned about Linda's ailment. "You have to complete all the weekly crosswords in the run-up to the show's opening, then submit them for a grand-prize drawing to attend the premiere."

Linda nodded while the cookie swap and Bake-Off continued around us. I have to say, that room full of cookies smelled scrumptious. Sadly, Josh's was the only all-chocolate entry.

"The contest is the least I can do," the editor explained. She carelessly shook out a couple of pain relievers and washed them down with some punch. It absolutely wasn't wassail. "Albany forbade me to give interviews or even have her book reviewed—which is unfortunate, given the readership the *Sentinel* has."

I'd been under the impression the newspaper was struggling. I was certain that's what Josh had told me. I puzzled over it.

Was Linda Sullivan hiding something about the *Sproutes Sentinel*? I couldn't quite envision it. Yes, she was exclusionary Albany's mom. Opportunistic Ophelia's mom. Rude Cashel's mom.

But frankly, Linda seemed much too kind to have raised three such self-involved twerps. Maybe her husband was horrible? Albany's dad remained a mystery to me—the final Sullivan secret.

I was starting to hope that *someone* in the family would justify my dislike of Albany. Cashel had almost done it, but then he'd apologized—seemingly sincerely. I would have preferred thinking that the Sullivans were awful people, just as depicted in Albany's memoir, rather than face my own shortcomings. My territorial feelings about Travis were embarrassing.

I've never claimed to be perfect. But I'm always striving to be better. To be kinder, more patient, and less suspicious.

My hopes for self-improvement stood at a crossroads with my sometime amateur sleuthing activities, though. It was tough to tamp down on suspicion when you needed to assess suspects.

Speaking of which . . . I pulled a regretful face at Linda Sullivan. "It's too bad all those readers will be disappointed."

Her gaze hardened slightly. "Disappointed?"

"Yes, when *Christmas in Crazytown* doesn't open. You can't win tickets to a sold-out holiday show that closes before it debuts." I imagined throngs of eager Sproutesians wielding completed crossword puzzles, storming the *Sentinel* offices.

"Yes, well, that can't be helped, can it?" Linda shot Josh an irked glance, as though blaming him for bringing me—and my pessimistic take on her prize drawing—to the cookie swap. "All we can do is hope that poor Roger is able to pull through this."

And that the show will go on, was the unspoken sentiment.

It was odd to hear someone express such sympathy for Roger Balthasar, though. He seemed so unlikable. I guessed that Linda was a more openhearted person than me, because she went on.

"And poor Melissa!" The editor heaved a melancholy sigh. "Without her, none of this would have happened for Albany. There would be no best-selling book, no holiday show . . . nothing at all."

I wondered if that was exactly what Linda wished were true. She couldn't *really* be as unbothered as she seemed by her daughter's tell-all memoir, could she? It couldn't be easy having your family's dirty (Christmas) laundry aired in public. She couldn't have prepared, either. As far as I knew, Albany's book had been a juggernaut, timed so that the holiday show followed very closely on the heels of the memoir's publication.

There were rumors of a Hollywood film in the works, too. Although that might change, I knew, now that Melissa was gone.

"Yes, it's heartbreaking," I said solemnly. "Melissa was so young to have died so suddenly. And at Christmastime, too!"

We three stood soberly, paying silent tribute to the show's second producer, with plates of gaily decorated cookies held incongruously in hand.

"Yes, well . . ." Josh piped up gamely, as cheery as he ever was. "You know what they say. The Christmas show must go on!"

Linda smiled. "You're right, Josh. Or at least, a few of our readers agree with you. We've received plenty of letters."

"Really?" I was interested, especially since public re-actions had plummeted elsewhere. "What kind of letters?"

But the *Sentinel*'s editor didn't elaborate. Instead, her focus pivoted to me with new attentiveness. Enlighten-ment, even.

"I just realized!" Linda exclaimed, pointing at me. "Hayden Mundy Moore! You must be *Travis's* Hayden," she guessed with a twinkle in her eyes. "He talks about you quite a lot, you know."

"Really?" I shouldn't have been sidetracked, but I was. *Travis's Hayden.* That was me. "What does he say?"

"It's not what he says. It's *how* he says it." Linda took my arm, waved away Josh, then guided us both to a more private corner of the cookie swap. "I've known Travis Turner since he was a gangly swim-team star working on the yearbook club."

I felt riveted. I'd always wondered about Travis's past. Now it looked as though Albany's mother might be the key to unlocking it. So far, Linda's story checked out. Travis had mentioned his love of swimming; it persisted to this day. I could easily envision my studious friend join-ing a club, too.

"Travis and Albany have been friends a long time, I know."

Linda's laughter was positively engaging. "More than friends! They're practically siblings. If I had a nickel for every time I fed Travis Turner spaghetti and meatballs after swim practice or kept him and Albany going through finals week, supplied with milk and oatmeal cookies, I'd be retired right now."

Aww, that was sweet. I pictured that wholesome scene, with Travis and Albany bent over schoolbooks and Linda whipping up homemade treats on the fly. My own mother hadn't baked much. She'd been busy making ground-breaking archeological discoveries and inspiring me to travel the world. I wanted to know more.

"Was he as serious then as he is now?" I asked. "Did you ever meet his parents? I understand Travis moved to Sproutes with his mom." His dad's whereabouts had gone unmentioned when Danny had briefed me about my keeper's past. "Where *is* the upper-crust part of Sproutes, anyway? I'm sure that's where—"

Linda looked startled. "Upper crust?" She gave me a baffled smile. "Travis didn't grow up anywhere fancy like that. He was one of those free-lunch kids. I think that's why he enjoyed my spaghetti and meatballs and oatmeal cookies so much, honestly."

Free-lunch kids? Travis had grown up poor?

The idea clashed so strongly with my image of "Harvard" that I couldn't speak for a minute. This new reality refused to mesh with my assumptions about Travis's privileged past.

I wanted to pepper Linda with questions—to find out all the details I could—but that was the moment when the cookie swap judging began. Someone paused the Christmas carols that had been playing. Several someones shushed the *Sentinel* staffers present. A dark-haired woman sashayed to the secret ballot box, then reached for the portable microphone being offered to her.

Transferring it to her was Josh Levitt. He fumbled with the device, clearly nervous, as he stood beside the newly arrived presenter. When I looked closer, I realized why.

Tansy Park was the judge. Her star power lent an electric air to the event.

"Thanks, Josh." Tansy seized the microphone herself, then raised it to her smiling, lipsticked mouth. "Hello, *Sentinel*!"

A raucous cheer rose to greet her. Several staffers applauded. A few wolf whistled. A man near me stood transfixed, gazing at Tansy with a mixture of incredulity and admiration.

The actress accepted the crowd's adoration, seeming perfectly at home in the spotlight—which, of course, she was.

"Humph," Linda groused beside me. "Some acting, right? You'd never know Tansy made Albany's life a living hell when she arrived to work on the show." Linda didn't seem able to help herself. "Not until *after* she'd won the starring role, of course. Until then, it was all sweetness and light. Like *that*." The editor grimaced at Tansy, annoyed at her presence.

Hmm. "I've heard that Albany didn't always appreciate Tansy's acting choices." I was careful to tactfully phrase Albany's slurs against Tansy's acting, using the same low voice that Linda had. "But not that Tansy was demanding in any way."

Linda's answering chortle seemed hostile. "'Demanding' is putting it mildly," she assured me. "Tansy wanted rewrites. She wanted more solo numbers. She wanted a fancier premiere venue."

Here, Linda harrumphed. I detected a certain amount of Sproutesian pride in her demeanor. Why not? It was a nice town.

She went on. "Melissa assured us that having the show debut here in Albany's hometown would be advantageous, but Tansy—"

A sudden quieting of the crowd reawakened me to

our surroundings. I'd been so engrossed in Linda's tirade that I hadn't been paying attention while Tansy addressed the *Sproutes Sentinel* staffers and (I presume) charmed their pants off.

Right on cue, Linda broke off and delivered a brilliant smile. She waved to Tansy, as though they were dear friends.

The actress must have acknowledged Linda in her remarks, I deduced, and Linda had realized it just in time to respond.

That meant it was my turn to harrumph. Inwardly. I didn't know who to believe anymore. Linda Sullivan, who seemed so devoted to her children and her newspaper? Tansy Park, who seemed so sensitive and honest . . . and had been vetted by Danny?

Reminded that he had to be present somewhere if Tansy was on the scene, I looked around. I spotted him at the back of the room, leaning with apparent nonchalance against the wall, arms folded over his muscle-bound chest while he watched Tansy.

I wasn't fooled by my bodyguard buddy's lazy demeanor. I knew he would be observing everyone present, alert for trouble.

Fortunately, the most disastrous thing likely to occur that day was a serious grumbling. The paper votes had been drawn from the ballot box and sorted into (revealingly) lopsided piles.

"And this year's *Sproutes Sentinel* Bake-Off and cookie swap winner is . . ." Tansy waited, letting the suspense build. "Linda!"

There were murmurs. Then a smattering of applause. It picked up intensity as Josh Levitt clapped more loudly himself.

It looked as though I'd just lost our bet. There went

twenty bucks. I watched, feeling dejected on Josh's behalf, as Linda Sullivan made her way to the front of the room, blushing and waving. With a smile, she hoisted the contest's trophy.

Although I liked her, I couldn't be entirely happy for her.

I shot Josh a consoling glance. "Next time!" I mouthed.

He shrugged and bit into a cookie. No lasting harm done. That made me feel better—but Danny's perceptive look didn't. He reached me seconds later, after shouldering his way through the crowd.

"The fix is in," he said. "The editor had a lock on it."

I appreciated him trying to make me feel better about Josh's defeat. Danny was the only one who knew I'd tutored him.

I changed the subject. "I didn't expect to see you here."

"They asked Tansy to make an appearance, so she agreed."

We both watched the actress. "She seems thrilled," I said.

"Yeah, she does." Danny crossed his arms again. His cynical gaze met mine. "Convincing, right? You'd never know I had to drag her here, kicking and screaming."

I was surprised. "Drag her here? Really?"

Danny gave a tight-lipped nod. Something in his unsettled expression made me worried. I thought I knew what was coming.

"Tansy told me she hates meet and greets like this, but you sure can't tell." Danny studied his vivacious, smiling client. His gaze transferred to mine again. Darkly, my friend added, "Looks like Tansy's an even better actress than I thought."

I nodded. We both knew what that meant.

We had to keep a closer eye on Tansy. I had an idea how.

"I'm on the job," I said. "Don't worry about a thing."

Then I went to assemble a Christmassy plate of frosted and sprinkled sugar cookies for Travis, exactly the way he wanted.

Things might have been heating up on Melissa's murder investigation, but that didn't mean I planned to shirk my duty to my friend and advisor. I'd sooner ruin a whole batch of fine chocolates than disappoint Travis— especially now that I knew that his childhood might have included very few treats at all.

With my heart in my throat, I hurried away before Danny asked what was wrong. I knew he'd be able to tell. I wanted to process what I'd learned about Travis's past on my own first.

The thing that bugged me most, though, was that Travis had never told me. As long as he was keeping secrets from me—maybe even many more secrets—what kind of friends could we really be?

Ten

When I returned to the B&B to deliver Travis's surprise plate of holiday cookies, my financial advisor was nowhere in sight. It wasn't like him to disappear without warning.

Thwarted, I checked my phone. It turned out that while I'd been making the white-knuckle drive between the newspaper offices and the B and B, I'd missed a series of texts from Travis.

Rehearsals are back on, said the first. More details later.

Then, Melissa's memorial service is scheduled for tomorrow.

I scanned the funeral details he'd provided, wondering if I could justifiably attend. Probably not, I decided. I hadn't known Melissa Balthasar.

I sighed and scrolled down to read Travis's final message.

Thanks for the cookies, it read. You're the best.

I laughed, shaking my head. My gaze fell on my plastic-wrapped plate of cookies, which I'd carefully selected to suit my keeper's preferences. How had he known I'd bring them?

You're too nice, came the next message, the first to

arrive in real time. Wherever he was, he had time to type. But thanks.

"Humph. 'Too nice,' huh?" Proving him wrong, I chose the most delectable-looking example of the buttery, pecan-filled, confectioners' sugar–dusted Mexican wedding cookies I'd brought.

Defiantly, I munched it. It tasted almost as delicious as my deliberate contrariness did. In this naughty-or-nice scenario, I vowed, this particular chocolate whisperer was getting a big lump of coal in her stocking, for a change.

I was tired of Travis and Danny accusing me of being "too soft" on my suspects and "too nice" in general. So what if I sometimes gave struggling chocolate-whispering clients extra time to settle up their invoices? So what if I slipped a bonus tip into the barista's jar when the person in front of me forgot? That didn't make me some kind of gullible nincompoop.

It made me human. That's it.

My phone vibrated. I glanced at the next message.

Very rebellious, it read. Tasty cookie?

All right. I swiveled around, planning to scour the area outside Travis's room. Instantly, I spotted the man himself.

He strode closer, laughing. "You should see your face."

Peevishly, I blamed Albany for my advisor's newfound prankster tendencies. "Just for that, no cookies for you."

Travis appeared repentant. "It's a joke, Hayden." His keen gaze lowered to the plate of cookies. "I really do appreciate these." He helped himself to the plate, deftly removing it from my hands. He bumped his hip on his room's door, unlocking it with what I assumed was his pocketed room key. "Come on in."

I was tempted. Me, Travis, alone . . . Why not?

"I'm supposed to be reading." I hooked my thumb toward my designated B&B room down the hall. "I have

this really strict required reading assignment. A memoir."
I made a "What can you do?" face. "If I don't finish, there'll
be hell to pay."

"I've heard procrastination is a good excuse." His voice
rumbled, washing over me with familiar, husky appeal.
"Plus, I have cookies to share. Someone's got to help me
eat these."

I caught a glimpse of the interior of Travis's B&B
room—the one he shared nightly with Albany—and
snapped to my senses. I had important things to do. For all
I knew, this was a test.

"Thanks, but if I eat another cookie, I'll burst." I put my
palms on my belly in joking demonstration. "You go
ahead."

"But everything's better shared," Travis cajoled.

When he talked to me that way, all I wanted to do was
agree. His voice was my kryptonite. It made me forget
reason.

But not today, I pledged. I refocused. "I have a feeling
you'll enjoy those more than I would." *Because you hardly
ever had treats when you were a teenager.* It seemed so
unjust. "But if you want to talk, I'm dying to know what
it was like growing up here in Sproutes," I remarked casually. "You know, as a person on the swim team or the
yearbook staff—things like that."

Travis's eyes narrowed. "Who have you been talking to?"

"Linda Sullivan." I raised my chin. "She's going to be
my source for all things teenage Travis Turner trivia related."

Comprehension darkened his eyes. "Of course. Albany's
mom works at the *Sentinel* now. I'd forgotten she'd be
there today."

"I'm told," I began, winding up to tease him, "that if

you'd actually finished Albany's book, you'd already know that."

"Har, har." Travis gazed longingly at his frosted cookies, then appeared to come to a decision. "You can't believe her, Hayden. There are things you don't know about the Sullivans."

"So tell me."

A headshake. "It's not my story to tell."

"Come on. Did you and Albany pinkie swear to hide each other's secret pasts or something? It's me, Trav! Trust me."

But there was no reaching him. Not then. "Thanks again for the cookies. I have to check in with the office. Talk later?"

"Sure." I recognized a brush-off when I experienced one. As I was about to turn away, I had another idea. "Hey, Danny and Tansy invited me and Josh to join them for a Santa pub crawl tomorrow night. You and Albany should come, too. It'll be fun."

I explained that we'd be dressing up in red and white Santa costumes with black boots and beards, then visiting local bars.

"On foot, in Sproutes's old-town district," I specified. "Where we can safely get around while toasting to Christmas."

"The enforcer has invented holiday beer. I'm impressed."

"I don't think Danny invented it, but I'll tell him you said you liked the idea. He'll be so happy you approve."

A wry grin crossed Travis's face. "I'll bet he will."

"So you'll come?" I pressed. "You and Albany?"

After meeting Linda and learning that Tansy might be a far more skilled actress than I'd counted on—one who could hide her nefarious intentions toward Albany or

Melissa, for instance—I had new interest in getting to know Travis's longtime friend.

Had I misjudged her? There was only one way to find out.

Travis kept me in suspense. "I'll let you know," he said.

Then he said his good-byes and left me alone in the hallway. I was no more enlightened about his past than I had been coming in, but I was no less determined, either. I had to know more.

Prompted by Travis's mysterious comment about the Sullivans (and all the things I didn't know about them), I spent much of the afternoon trying to track down Joe Sullivan, Albany's dad.

Joe was the only member of the cliquish clan whom I hadn't yet met. I scoured Albany's memoir for mentions of him. I inspected her interviews and media coverage for anecdotes about him. In a burst of frustration, I even flipped open the musty Sproutes phone directory and studied it for references to him.

By the time I realized I was obsessing about the issue, it was too late. I was already down the rabbit hole. I couldn't stop. See, one of the things that makes me a skilled chocolate expert is my ability to remain focused, even when the problems I'm troubleshooting are complex. Another is my passion for making sure that every detail is accounted for. Taken together, those qualities result in excellent chocolaty creations—when I'm working, that is. When I'm not, well . . . let's just say that my methodical, borderline fanatical nature can get me into trouble.

It can, for instance, make me focus too narrowly, causing me to overlook important things. That day, though, it merely brought me downstairs at the B and B, where I hoped to find out more about Joe Sullivan, aka the workaholic enigma.

I zeroed in on Zach Johnson, then smiled at my host. There were chocolates in my hands and a host of questions on my mind.

"Zach!" I called. "Hi! I have something for you."

Three minutes later, Zach had amiably accepted my gift of some hand-dipped chocolate-cherry creams. Then he'd called over one of his assistants to man the front desk, so he could answer the "few questions" about Sproutes that I wanted to ask him.

We settled together in the B and B's newly reopened dining room, with reams of paper and scissors on the table in front of us—part of a paper-snowflake-making project for the B and B's guests. That should have delighted me, since it was another holiday activity that I had heard about but had never experienced.

As it was, though, I couldn't stop seeing Melissa D.'s lifeless body there, crumpled on the floor, amid spilled wassail.

Zach was sensitive enough to notice my distress.

"It feels too soon, I know," he acknowledged, casting his own gaze to the scrubbed and spotless floor. "But it had to happen sometime. My guests were starting to feel uncomfortable, wondering about it. I thought, with the memorial service finally scheduled and things moving forward with the show, it was time."

Well, then, kindhearted Zach Johnson probably wasn't my Christmas killer, I mused. He wouldn't have wanted to risk damaging his B and B's business. Leaving a dead body in the dining room tended to cause low ratings on those travel-review sites.

That fact was as good as an alibi for my innkeeper friend. Also, as far as I knew, Zach had no motive for murdering any of the Albany look-alikes, despite having the most access of anyone.

"Ah, yes. I heard that Roger's decided to go ahead with the premiere," I chatted. Gravely, I asked, "How is he doing?"

"About as well as can be expected, I guess," Zach told me. "He seems to be holding up. It's possible he's still in shock."

"Yes, that's true. Anyone would have a hard time."

"I think Roger just wants to get back to work now." Zach gave me an opaque look—probably wondering why I was so curious about the show's producer. "Sometimes life really does go on."

"Yes." I'd seen—and lived—that platitude enough times lately to know it was true. "I hope staying busy will help Roger. Maybe Melissa would have liked that?" I was fishing.

"Maybe." Zach wasn't snapping at the bait. He glanced at the open box of chocolates I'd given him, then slapped his hands on his thighs and got down to business. "So, you said you have some questions about Sproutes?" His determination to change the subject was evident. "You're looking at a lifelong resident here"—he thumped his chest—"so I can probably help you out."

"Really? You've lived here your whole life?"

A nod. He picked up a piece of white paper and idly started folding. That alone made me feel like a kindred spirit with him. Sometimes, I find it hard to sit still myself. I need to act.

"That means you must know almost everyone in town!" I enthused. "Which brings me to the reason I'm here." Brightly, I leaned forward. "I'm told that Joe Sullivan,

Albany's dad, is one of the most influential people in Sproutes. And since I'm trying to bring attention to this new chocolate brand . . ."

I produced a cellophane-wrapped, ribbon-adorned sample of chocolate fudge. It was another impromptu creation, different from the chocolate-peppermint bark that I'd fabricated while searching for a way to meet Ophelia. "I thought I might give a few boxes to Mr. Sullivan, with the hope he'd share it at work."

"At work? That's a good idea. He's there all the time."

Right. I wondered where "there" was. In Albany's memoir, her father was referred to simply as "the father." His job was described as "the office." His favorite place was "the golf course." It had been fairly obvious that Albany resented him.

"That's what I've heard," I gushed in reference to Joe Sullivan's job. "I guess when you do such fascinating work—"

"Joe's the best at it, that's for sure."

"Then you never want to leave, right?" I laughed.

Zach completed another fold, then turned his paper. "Why not just give it to Albany? She can make sure her dad gets it."

Because I don't want Albany to ask why I want to meet her father, I thought. *Because I don't want her to know I'm trying to separate fact from fiction in her notorious memoir. Because I don't want Albany and Ophelia to compare notes about me.*

I couldn't say any of that to Zach.

I sighed. "Albany's so busy. I'd like to go straight to the source, but I, uh, haven't been able to make an appointment."

"You shouldn't need an appointment. Just go on in."

I was stuck. I couldn't agree to that idea without my

whole house of cards falling down. That was the trouble with sleuthing—with pretending to know more than you really did.

Beside me, Zach started snipping away bits of his folded paper. I watched, fascinated by the process, despite myself.

"But if it's an influencer you want," my host said while crafting his paper snowflake, "you should approach Roger."

An influencer. That was an interesting way to put it. Very Ophelia-like. Albany's sister and I were meeting again soon for another photo shoot. So far, her followers had responded well to the chocolate-peppermint bark she'd featured on her account. It hadn't seen a meteoric rise yet, but Ophelia remained hopeful.

She had mentioned trying "another approach" but hadn't specified what it might be—only that it might be "a big boost."

Setting aside my sham career as a purveyor of holiday candy for the moment, I considered Zach's suggestion regarding Roger.

"Oh, I definitely don't want to bother Roger right now!"

"I don't think he'd mind." Zach paused long enough to give me another unreadable glance. "He's all about business."

"But now, with all that's happened—" I fumbled for more.

"Stop," Zach interrupted. "You don't have to keep this up, Hayden. I know what's going on here. I can tell what's wrong."

A weird undercurrent rose between us, fraught with meaning.

The trouble was, I couldn't decipher that meaning.

I gulped. "Wrong?" My voice stuttered. I couldn't help it.

Zach smiled. Peculiarly. "Hayden, you can be real with me." He pointed his sharp scissors at me. "I've been there!"

Now I was thoroughly mystified. Also, a little nervous about Zach's lackadaisical handling of scissors. "You have?"

Was he another part-time amateur sleuth? I wondered crazily. Maybe there were more of us than I realized— more than I could imagine. I'd never expected to find myself in this role, after all. Yet here I was. Warily, I asked, "You've been there?"

"Yes, I have!" Zach assured me warmly. "Trying to build a business, feeling too shy to make the right contacts, desperate to succeed, anyway. I know! That was *me*, the first few years after I inherited this place." Zach shook his longish hair from his eyes, then smiled again. "The B&B used to belong to my grandma."

He crossed himself and glanced up, presumably paying tribute to Grandma Johnson. But I was still getting my mind around the fact that he thought I, Hayden Mundy Moore, was *shy*.

Danny, who knew me best, would have laughed his face off at the very idea. Travis might have enjoyed a good chuckle, too.

For the sake of expediency, I played along. I swallowed hard, then did my best to appear timid. "I'm sorry, Zach," I mumbled. "I feel so embarrassed. I'll leave now. Sorry again."

I pushed back my chair, planning a magnificently hesitant exit. Zach's laughter stopped me much too soon. "No, stay!"

I guessed Tansy wouldn't be getting any competition

from me in the acting department. Not today. "Seriously? You mean it?"

"Of course!" Zach offered me an indulgent smile. It was clear that he thought he was encouraging me. He pushed over a sheet of white paper and a pair of scissors. "If it helps, just keep your hands busy while we talk. That takes the edge off."

If I'd been truly timorous, I might have found that useful.

"Thanks." I picked up both, then mimicked the steps I remembered my host carrying out earlier. One fold. Two. Then a few snips. I sneaked a glance at him. "So you think I should . . . ?"

"Let me talk to a few people. I think I can hook you up."

"With Mr. Sullivan?" I let my eyes widen with gratefulness.

Zach chuckled. "Around here, most of us call him Joe."

"I couldn't possibly do that!" Was I taking my faux timidity too far? I couldn't be sure. "But if you could help—"

"I'd be glad to!" Magnanimously, Zach winked at me. "There are ways to 'hack' your shyness—to cope with it better." He seemed to enjoy his self-appointed mentor role. "For me, going online has been a tremendous help. For you, maybe having a personal introduction would be good. I'll put out some feelers."

Eww. "You can't just call Mr. Sullivan? I mean, Joe?" I'd been hoping Zach could expedite the process.

"I could, but the trouble isn't reaching Joe. It's convincing him to take a break long enough to take a meeting." Zach gave a resigned "That's Joe for you!" headshake. His gaze dipped to my festively wrapped fudge. "I'm not even sure he'd stop working long enough to taste test that fudge of yours."

"Wow. He's really that much of a workaholic?"

A nod. "Joe likes to call it 'dedication,' though."

Well, as a publicly recognized workaholic, he'd be likely to phrase it that way, wouldn't he? Clearly, the Sproutesians were enabling his bad behavior. If Albany had developed a grudge against her hometown homies, then she had a good reason for it. My own parents worked a lot, but they always had time for me.

"When Albany and I were dating," Zach went on informally, "I thought her parents must have gotten divorced, her dad was at home so infrequently." He gave me a wistful look. "I'm luckier, though. My own parents have been married thirty-four years now."

"Oh, that's sweet. Congratulations to them!" My thoughts were elsewhere. I followed them. "You and Albany, uh, *dated*?" I asked in as laid-back a tone as I could muster. "Really?"

I wanted to ask more. Much more. *Precisely when? For how long? Why didn't anyone say so before?* all sprang to mind.

So did, *Exactly who are you in Albany's memoir?* There had been a boyfriend or two mentioned, but none had been a B&B host.

Had Zach held other jobs? Could he be "the bartender"?

"There's no need to sound so surprised! Sheesh." He shook his head while slicing a few more precise cuts into his paper snowflake. Beyond us, Christmas carols played in the parlor. "It almost sounds as though you think Albany was out of my league."

He glowered. Whoops. I hadn't meant to insult him.

But I couldn't help wondering, *Had* Albany considered herself out of Zach's league? Had she dumped him before moving to the big city of New York? Did Zach harbor resentment over their breakup? If he did, was it the *murderous* kind of resentment?

It was possible, I had to concede, that jilted Zach had been in Sproutes all this time, feeling hurt and abandoned by Albany, only to seize his opportunity for revenge (he'd thought) when his former girlfriend returned home for the holidays.

Albany had been at the *Christmas in Crazytown* tree-trimming party, of course. So had Zach. Had he approached the woman he'd thought was his heartbreaker ex that night, after the party had finished, and shoved her head into the wassail punch bowl?

I still hadn't asked Zach about that nagging detail: the leftover full punch bowl. But I imagined that when (or if) you were planning on enacting an "accidental" death, cleaning up beforehand didn't rank high on the priority list. He'd certainly done a whiz-bang job of cleaning up the dining room afterward.

Or maybe it had been an impulsive murder, with no foresight beforehand and little remorse afterward. I still didn't know.

Back to Zach—and his hurt feelings that I'd suggested he was dating above his level when it came to Albany Sullivan.

"No! Oh, no, I'm sorry!" I gasped, hand over my mouth in pretend mortification. "Zach, I never meant to imply that." I put down my nascent paper snowflake and pushed to my feet. "I'm sorry. I really will leave you alone now. I understand if you don't want to help me meet Mr. Sullivan anymore. It's okay."

It felt unnatural to be so apologetic, but this routine had

already earned Zach's sympathy and cooperation once. Maybe it would do so again? Being too direct tended to backfire on me.

Nobly, Zach put his hand on mine. "No need for that. I understand. Albany and I might seem like an unexpected couple now that she's so famous. But it wasn't always that way."

"Oh no?" Timorously, I sat. "What was she like, anyway?"

For the next several minutes, my B&B host waxed rhapsodic about his relationship with the girl who'd become a best-selling tell-all memoirist. It almost sounded too idyllic to be true.

"You're a really good listener, Hayden." Zach sighed. His face glowed with nostalgia. "Thanks. This has been fun."

Yeah, fun. Finding out that someone I'd liked might be a secret Christmastime murderer was awesome. No, wait. It wasn't.

I had to tell Danny and Travis about this.

"So, are you and Albany back together now?" I inquired. A heartbeat later, I realized that if Zach were carrying a torch for his ex, then he might turn his homicidal attentions on his maybe-rival, my financial advisor, next. Uh-oh. "Or . . . ?"

"Oh, no!" Zach chuckled. "That's all water under the bridge now." He caught my skeptical look and added, "No, I'm not still carrying a torch for her. And I *don't* appear in her book."

"Are you sure?" More importantly, *Are you angry about that*?

If Zach considered himself Albany's first true love— and he still *wasn't* included in her memoir—that could definitely sting.

"Believe me, if anyone's read *Christmas in Crazytown* cover to cover, looking for signs of themselves, it's me," my host acknowledged. Then, "Also, everyone else in town, honestly."

He probably had a point. "I'd be looking over it with a fine-tooth comb, if it were me," I told him. "But then, I've never experienced a bad breakup," I added leadingly. "So . . . ?"

Zach sidestepped my trap. "So how's your snowflake coming along? Here's mine. Presto!" With a deft move, he unfurled it.

"Impressive!" Hoping for a similarly spectacular reveal, I made another final snip, then unfolded my paper the way he had.

It fell apart. I had no idea where I'd gone wrong.

But Zach only chuckled again. "Better luck next time. Maybe you're trying too hard—or maybe you're just a beginner." He winked. "I'll put the word out about Joe and let you know."

Eleven

I didn't see Danny or Travis at all the following day. While they and the cast and crew of *Christmas in Crazytown* were at Melissa Balthasar's memorial service, I stayed busy finishing Albany's memoir. Sitting beside my B and B's snow-shrouded upstairs window, with a cup of cocoa at my elbow and a halo of holiday lights to lend ambiance, I snapped shut the book at 4:00 p.m.

I'm not going to lie; I enjoyed reading it. Albany was a skilled writer, with a knack for evocative details and a genuine gift for economically getting to the heart of her characters.

In this case, though, the "characters" were her family, friends, coworkers, and neighbors. I wasn't so sure Albany's gift was a positive one, or that I could trust those depictions.

"The surfer," for instance, had seemed easygoing to a fault—not exactly accurate, when it came to impatient Cashel Sullivan. "The student" (a stand-in for Ophelia, I assumed) had flitted on and off the scenes like a sulky child—probably not a depiction that Albany's little sister would have appreciated.

I'd already noted that Linda Sullivan didn't much resemble the controlling matriarch shown in Albany's book. I suspected that Zach was wrong—or was purposely misleading me—about not being included in Albany's memoir, too, because it seemed likely that the frequently (but affectionately) mocked character of "the band geek," who played the tuba in the Sproutes High marching band, was him. Maybe Zach didn't consider his musical interests a part of his identity today, but it was possible Albany did. Or it was conceivable Zach hadn't been in the marching band at all.

Who knew? With so many details having been purposely obscured, fitting together all the pieces made my head hurt.

Speaking of solving puzzles . . . I picked up the copy of the *Sproutes Sentinel* that I'd found in the B and B's dining room, then flipped to the crossword. I couldn't miss it. The themed contest entry form occupied an entire page of broadsheet.

Since I had a backstage pass to *Christmas in Crazytown*, thanks to Travis's connection with Albany, I didn't need to win tickets. But I scrutinized the puzzle, anyway. It contained more than one reference to Albany's memoir, I saw. I noted references to her favorite holiday foods, to the Sullivans' sometimes kooky traditions, and even to the nonholiday-related background info given in the book about Albany's friends and schoolteachers.

One of those teachers, I remembered, had been mentioned in passing during one of Albany's late-night TV interviews. Goaded by the host—or simply prompted by her own inherent snarkiness—Albany had gone on record as saying that her former English teacher had doubted her "potential in life." The studio audience had booed loudly, the host had stepped in with a suggested uncharitable hashtag for use on his social-media feeds, and the whole incident had spread like wildfire. Potshots were taken. Memes were created. Albany's supporters struck hard and mercilessly. Before they were done, their defense of her had gone far beyond saying that her "life potential" was "amazing!"

I wished I could forget some of the meme images I'd seen. Most of them had used an old yearbook photo of the Albany-doubting teacher, doctored up with cruel words and suggestions.

What had begun as an impulsive "Take that!" to a less than adoring authority figure had quickly spiraled out of control. To her credit, Albany had tried to diffuse the situation once she'd realized what was going on. She'd taken to her own social-media accounts and pled with her followers to stop harassing her supposed high-school nemesis. But the Internet was permanent.

The damage had already been done.

Moving on from that unfortunate incident, I scanned the rest of the newspaper. My eye was drawn to the Letters to the Editor section, which ran for three pages. That seemed unusual.

Either the readers of the *Sproutes Sentinel* were uncommonly involved in their local newspaper or there was a controversy.

Controversy, I saw as I read through the letters. Some of them were in support of debuting *Christmas in Crazytown*, citing its "valuable trickle-down effects on Sproutes's economy." Others weren't so benevolent or so optimistic. One flatly stated that the annual staging of *The Nutcracker* should never have been shelved, even for a single year; another alluded disapprovingly to the "amoral attitudes" of the "deviant Hollywood types" who'd overrun their small town to work on the holiday musical.

Hollywood types. I'd heard that someplace before. . . .

If sentiments like these were common, it was a wonder the cast and crew of *Christmas in Crazytown* hadn't already been pelted with rotten cranberries and run out of town. I had to give Linda Sullivan credit, though. As editor, she'd managed to balance her support of Albany (the contest and puzzle clues) with her duties to the paper (the overlong letters pages). Someone less principled might have been tempted to downplay any differences of opinion to protect her daughter's show or to boost public support of *Christmas in Crazytown.*

It was possible, of course, that Linda didn't want the show to go on. I knew now that some of the funny holiday incidents likely to be included in it might embarrass the people who'd been involved in them. However much Linda insisted that the Sullivans didn't mind being slightly skewered for their oddball approach to the holidays, I wasn't sure I could believe her.

According to Travis, at least, I shouldn't believe her.

Reminded of my friend and financial advisor—and our plans for the Santa-themed pub crawl—I folded away the newspaper. Before heading out to Melissa's memorial service, Travis had let me know that Albany *loved* the idea of having a get-together. The two of them had agreed to come along. Albany had thought it would be nice to "rekindle the holiday spirit," because "everyone" would be sad after attending the producer's funeral.

Obviously, that take on *everyone* involved (conspicuously) excluded *me*, the one pub-crawling person who *wouldn't* have attended Melissa's funeral that day, sadly or otherwise. But I decided to give Albany the benefit of the doubt, anyway.

She probably hadn't intended to exclude me. Just as she probably hadn't intended to break "the band geek's" heart . . . and then write about their painful breakup for the world to laugh at. For a sensitive person like Zach, that could really wound.

Had he been nursing a grudge against Albany all this time?

Alternatively, had Tansy decided that no one was going to ruin her breakout role, including Albany? Had the actress gone out of her way to silence the woman she'd argued with so often on set, only to mistakenly attack look-alike Melissa instead?

Similarly, had Ophelia impulsively thought to rid herself of her clearest rival, her sister, alone in that dining room? She wouldn't have realized until too late that she'd actually drowned Melissa Balthasar that night, alone at the B and B.

I didn't think that Ophelia herself could have been the intended victim. She seemed far too harmless to have incited a murderous rage in anyone. I doubted, too, that Tansy could have been the target. She seemed universally idolized—except by Linda. Had Linda Sullivan cornered the actress at the B and B, then purposely drowned the woman who'd made her daughter's life "a living hell"? Or had Tansy's stalker followed her to Sproutes, only to attack doppelgänger Melissa after hours that dark night?

There were so many possibilities that I could hardly keep them straight—and that was ignoring the chance that the killer had in fact meant to murder Melissa Balthasar. The producer seemed to have infuriated as many people as she'd helped during her career. I couldn't overlook the likelihood that Melissa had made some very lethal enemies during her short, splashy life.

Reportedly, Albany had argued with Melissa about her

book's handling and promotion. Without his wife, Roger stood to gain a larger share of the show's profits, too. But if Travis was correct (Travis was always correct), he didn't need them.

The whole thing felt like a tangled mess. I'd been in New England for days now. I still wasn't sure *whose* murder I was supposed to be solving. Melissa's? Tansy's? Ophelia's? Or, as Travis insisted, had the whole thing been a missed attack on Albany? My financial advisor had scarcely left his friend's side in the time since Melissa's murder. His dedication moved me. It was no less than I would have expected, but I was proud of him.

Pacing across my B and B's room in thought, I caught a glimpse of myself in the old-fashioned cheval mirror. I was lucky I hadn't arrived any sooner than I had, it occurred to me, or gone downstairs any earlier than night. With my brunette hair and resemblance to the four Albanys, *I* might have been the victim.

I shivered and decided I needed a distraction. Given my jet lag, I wasn't thinking straight. I went downstairs to get a head start on making some couverture for use in my chocolate houses, but the B and B's kitchen was occupied with preparations for Zach's guests' annual gingerbread house–decorating activity. I found myself alone in the dining room, gazing morosely at the floor.

One of the housekeepers wandered by. She stopped. "Can I help you with something?" She frowned. "Is something dirty?"

I hadn't meant to worry her. I snapped out of it. "No! Everything is spotless, as usual. Believe me, the staff here is doing a wonderful job." I smiled. "I'm just feeling melancholy."

"Yep, well, the holidays will do that to a person." Her gaze brightened. "If you need anything, just let me know."

I promised I would. Then, as she made to leave, I asked, "The cleaning staff here . . . Does everyone work during the day?"

"Day? Night?" She laughed. "This time of year, it's dark when we get to work, and it's dark when we go home!"

I smiled in commiseration. "All the guests appreciate it, too." I paused. "I mean, if there were a party, for example, would someone on staff work extra hours to clean up afterward?"

Her gaze sharpened. "You mean the party where they found that poor dead woman? None of my girls were involved in that. We didn't even know it was happening!" She glanced behind herself. "Ever since Mr. Johnson took over this place, things have been different. He's always on his computer or his phone, doing God knows what. To tell the truth, I preferred his grandmother."

"Zach isn't a good boss? Why's that?"

"Oh, it's not that he isn't a good boss. Nothing like that," the housekeeper rushed to assure me. "It's just that he seems a lot more worried about this place's reputation than about what's actually going on around here. Things need fixing!"

Aha. We chatted awhile longer, while she described some of the B and B's maintenance issues. None of them sounded serious.

"You won't go telling anyone I said so, will you?" The housekeeper suddenly seemed to realize that she'd been talking out of turn to an outsider and guest. "It's just I needed to let off some steam, I guess, and you're really easy to talk to."

I promised her that her complaints would be safe with me.

"Whew! Thank you." With her hand on her heart, she

gave me a grin. Then she made her excuses and hurried away. "You have a nice day and a merry Christmas, too!" she called as she left.

After wishing her the same, I forced my feet to take me away from the scene of Melissa Balthasar's grisly death. It was time to get ready for the Santa pub crawl. I didn't want to be late.

The minute I walked into the Sproutes pub we'd designated as our meeting place, I knew I'd been had. I clomped in, gamely outfitted in the red-and-white velour Santa Claus costume that Albany had secured for me from the archives of the Sproutes playhouse, and realized that things weren't going to happen exactly as I'd hoped they would. That was because, while there were plenty of other Santa look-alikes at the local bar, none of them were my friends. I didn't even see costumed Josh yet.

I adjusted my red, pointy hat's white pompon and made the best of things. At the bar, I ordered my favorite (a nice dark porter), then maneuvered my black-booted self to the table where I'd spied Danny (no costume), Travis (no costume), and Albany.

She was wearing a costume, but it wasn't the kind I had on. Unlike me, Albany sported no itchy white tie-on beard, no bulky pillowed belly, and no overall unflattering ensemble—whereas I'd even given myself rosy-red Santa cheeks with a multipurpose tube of lipstick, endeavoring to match the famous description of Old Saint Nick in the Clement C. Moore poem. I was a real dope.

Albany, dressed as *sexy* Santa in a red-and-white cashmere sweater and matching skintight pants—both worn with high-heeled black stiletto boots—was the first to greet me. Possibly because my two best friends, Danny and Travis, were too busy laughing.

So far, my longed-for Friendsmas needed a little work.

"So, you just had that getup lying around, huh?" I asked Albany. Beside her I felt both lumpy and sexless, stripped of my femininity and my identity, too. "You look amazing, Albany."

I couldn't miss the fact that Travis and Danny seemed to agree. So did several other pub goers, costumed and otherwise.

Albany laughed. "Oh, this old thing? Just in my suitcase."

Humph. My suitcase contained things like kitchen clogs and spare spoons. There was no way I could compete with sexy Santa.

I directed my gaze at my friends—pointedly, at their everyday clothes. "In that case, I guess your luggage was lost?"

Danny laughed. "You didn't seriously think I'd do this."

"Yes, I did, actually." I'd thought it sounded like fun.

"The dry cleaner lost my Santa suit," Travis claimed.

"Likely story." Tansy gave me a breathless hello, then pointed toward the pub's distant ladies' room. "Important tip. Carefully secure your bowl full of jelly before pulling down your Santa pants, or you'll be sorry." The actress patted her flat stomach. "One pit stop and my realistic Santa is ruined."

I smiled. "I doubt your Santa was *that* realistic."

Because Tansy was, thankfully, outfitted in a Santa Claus costume. It was identical to mine. On the bombshell starlet, though, the effect was entirely different. Even with her face partly obscured by a shaggy white Santa beard and an oversize hat, she looked incredible. She'd cinched her wide black plastic belt tightly on her waist, probably to help hold up her velour pants.

"It was *highly* realistic!" Tansy informed me. Two hectic spots appeared on her cheeks—the real-life version of the Santa blush I'd mimicked with my makeup application. "It was *great*!"

Yikes. Her rancor caught me off guard. She seemed genuinely offended that I'd doubted the realism of her Santa portrayal.

"I'm sorry. I only meant that you're so stunning, Tansy! Nobody would ever mistake you for Saint Nick, believe me."

"Ha-ha. Gotcha!" Tansy hoisted a froufrou cocktail and toasted me with it. Its candy-cane garnish nearly stabbed me in the eye. "You should see your face, Hayden! I was only kidding!"

Grr. I was getting tired of hearing that.

Also, it occurred to me, Tansy seemed fairly tipsy. "How long have you all been here?" I asked. "Was the funeral very . . ."

Moving?

As one, they all groaned and held up their hands.

"For one night, let's *not* talk about Melissa!" Albany said. She rolled her eyes, as though fed up with conversations about her (former) champion and *Christmas in Crazytown* producer.

Danny saw me noticing her unkind attitude. "Some of the tributes today were pretty over the top. It was a lot to take."

Because Melissa was so unlikable, was the subtext. I understood. But that didn't mean she didn't deserve justice.

I must have looked indignant (and I was), because Travis stepped in next. "We can talk about it later," he promised.

Thus mollified, I did my best to relax. One porter later,

doing so got considerably easier. "I should have known better than to start drinking," I confided to Josh, who'd arrived late but dutifully in costume, leaving Danny and Travis as the only holdouts. "Jet lag always makes me more susceptible to alcohol."

"Hey, that's a good reason to travel right there!"

"You mean because I'm a cheap date? Maybe."

Danny was on duty as Tansy's bodyguard, so he wasn't drinking. That probably explained why he was the first to notice, each time it happened, when the pub we were in suddenly seemed to heave with costumed Santas getting to their feet. That was the signal for us all to head to the pub crawl's next stop.

We all trooped out onto Sproutes's decorated streets en masse, laughing and talking. I imagined we made a pretty funny sight: dozens of slightly wobbly, extra-cheery Santas, all marching along the town's light-bedazzled, decorated streets.

At every stop, Tansy was deluged with fans. She chatted and signed autographs and shared the bounty of drinks bought for her—and generally appeared to adore being in the spotlight. I had my doubts about the authenticity of her feelings, but I had to admit, I couldn't detect a single sign of deception in her.

Josh seemed captivated by her. His natural gregariousness found a good partner in Tansy's responsiveness. Only a few stops in, I was bereft of a date for the night, ditched by Josh for a more dazzling fake Santa. If not for Danny's observant nature, I would have been a true third wheel. But he kept me company at each stop on the pub crawl, telling me jokes and companionably slinging his brawny arm over my shoulders.

When he smiled at me, I couldn't help feeling that old attraction between us. I tried keeping it at bay with outrage.

"You implied you'd be wearing a Santa costume tonight."

His mouth quirked. "You assumed I'd be wearing a Santa costume tonight, because you are. That's not the same thing."

"It should be." I looked him over. "You'd make a good 'hot Santa.' You know the kind—the male counterpart of Albany."

Danny glanced at her. "Nope. The sweater looks itchy."

"Not the sweater! But the skintight pants might be okay."

"No thanks." My friend gave a pained look. "I'll pass."

Inadvertently, I let my gaze dip to his jeans. Very nice.

He saw me admiring him. Of course he did. His gaze took on a knowing glimmer. "You'd better be careful with that."

"Or?" I didn't mind playing with fire. Not after four pub stops and almost as many porters tonight. "Why's that?"

"Because something might happen that one of us re-grets," Danny told me amid the pub noise. His voice lowered. "Again."

I couldn't mistake the suggestive way he said *again*. I felt all tingly beneath my Santa suit . . . and realizing *that* brought me down to earth. Danny had to be kidding me. There was no way he thought I was regret-makingly sexy—not in this getup, anyway.

I put a lid on my feelings and got sociable with every-one else, hitching up my red velour Santa britches and heading out to the next pub stop with new resolve. Outside on Sproutes's snowy sidewalks, I promised myself I was going to be smart. I was going to be unshakably sensible. I was going to be focused.

I was going to be trapped in the headlights of an on-coming SUV.

Surprised and tipsy, all I could do was gawk. I was aware of the laughter of my nearby fellow Santas, of the holiday music spilling from the pub we'd just left, of tires crunching snow.

That SUV is going to hit me, I thought hazily. *Move!*

As I tried to make a break for it, Danny slung his arm around my well-padded middle. He tackled me from behind, putting all his weight into it. I landed with an "Oof!" on a patch of ice.

Ouch. Grimacing and shaky, I blinked in the dimness. I saw a dark SUV swerve crazily, then drive onto the curb. My fellow Santas yelped and scattered, some of them swearing loudly. I sensed weight on my right side, snowmelt penetrating my suit.

Screaming. It was Tansy. Danny had tackled us both.

"Calm down," Danny said as he rolled away. "It's over."

He helped up Tansy, then me. I crumpled. My knees were weak. Adrenaline surged through me. We'd almost been hit.

I squinted at the SUV just as its taillights vanished.

All around us, the other pub crawlers were talking and yelling. Several waved their fists and shook their heads.

"Somebody's had one beer too many," Josh said.

He shook his head with disgust, staring after the SUV. When I drew in a breath, Travis was there. "Hayden—"

"I'm okay." I gazed into his shadowed eyes and heard my own voice tremble. "What happened? Did you see who it was?"

He didn't look happy. "The driver was wearing a Santa suit."

"So it could have been anyone." I checked to be sure Tansy was okay. She was. So was Albany. No one was hurt. "Any of *us*."

My financial advisor didn't mistake my meaning. "You

think that was the killer?" he asked in his low, husky voice. His eyebrows drew lower. "I didn't get a photo. Nothing. I couldn't even see the license plate."

"It's okay. You were probably worried about me."

"Actually—" His gaze shot sideways. "I was pulling Albany to safety. It all happened so fast. Danny tackled you, and I—"

"Watched out for your friend. I understand, Trav."

He seemed inconsolable. "I couldn't believe what I was seeing. That SUV seemed to speed up when it neared you."

Sobered by that, I tried to reconstruct the scene. Me at the edge of the sidewalk. Tansy beside me. Josh just behind her, chattering about something. Travis and Danny bringing up the rear. My bodyguard pal had reacted quickly to tackle Tansy and me. Without Danny, I felt sure the night would have ended badly.

As it was, I still felt jittery. Scared. My knee hurt where I'd banged it on the ice. I could scarcely draw a clean breath.

Someone had targeted me. On purpose. Or they'd targeted Tansy. Or, on a wild tangent, some other costumed Santa. We all looked pretty alike, I admitted, role-playing in the dimness.

For all I knew, Josh was right. Someone had simply had too much to drink and shouldn't have been trying to drive home.

But if Josh was wrong, and either Tansy or I *had* been targeted, that could mean only one thing: we were getting close to finding Melissa's murderer, and they were reacting to that.

I couldn't stop now. I absolutely had to keep going.

Twelve

When I came downstairs for breakfast the next morning, bleary eyed and vaguely hungover, the preceding night felt like a dream. A bad dream. Well, parts of it did, anyway.

Okay, the last part of it felt like a nightmare.

Under ordinary circumstances, I would have dismissed my fears that someone had tried to run me over with a swerving SUV. But these weren't ordinary circumstances. I was investigating a murder. My part-time sleuthing occasionally made me a target.

I couldn't stop hearing that loud crunch of snow beneath the SUV's tires. I couldn't quit imagining myself pinned beneath its wheels. Tansy and I both could have been seriously injured.

We weren't, though, I reminded myself as I grabbed a coffee and a pain au chocolat, then left the dining room in favor of the parlor. Today Tansy would be back at work in rehearsals for *Christmas in Crazytown*. I'd been planning to get together with Ophelia for another chocolate-peppermint bark photo shoot, but now our plans had been scuppered. I wouldn't be gathering any additional clues or background information from Albany's sister.

Rehearsals sure did put a crimp in my plans, I thought as I sipped my coffee. I tried to relax, looking out the B and B's window at the peaceful landscape, but my shoulders felt tight. My knee still throbbed, most likely injured during Danny's tackle.

He would be at the Sproutes playhouse himself today, keeping watch over Tansy. Necessarily too. After last night, the potential for peril felt all too real to me. What if Tansy's stalker had been driving that runaway SUV? If so, Danny had earned his security-service salary twice before midnight.

He'd saved Tansy's life. Mine too. But in the aftermath . . .

Well, the significant look he'd given me afterward didn't bear thinking about, much less dissecting. We'd been shaken, that's all. We'd been friends for ages. He'd been concerned.

I savored my pain au chocolat, then went back to the dining room sideboard for another. What can I say? Danger makes me hungry. Returning to the parlor, I heard voices at the front desk. They sounded just secretive enough to pique my interest.

I sauntered closer and took a peek. Albany was there, her head close to Zach's. Both of them were laughing softly. As I watched, Zach turned his face to hers. He looked enraptured.

Then he pulled a goofy face. Albany's laughter rang out.

Had Zach only been kidding about swooning over Albany? I couldn't tell. A moment later, someone else arrived at the desk.

"Morning, kids! What's new? On with the show, eh?"

I started. This was Roger Balthasar, freshly showered and shaved, wearing jeans and a hoodie with trendy sneakers—the kind you have to be on a waiting list (or know a collector) to score.

He looked like somebody's "cool dad"—the kind of guy who was happy to allow the neighborhood teenagers to raid his liquor cabinet, share his stash, and lounge around his L.A. swimming pool all day. I couldn't get over his overtly cheerful demeanor.

If Roger Balthasar had wanted to, he could have made his living as an actor. Unless, that is, he really *wasn't* sad about his departed wife. It would have been decent to pretend he was, in either case. Roger was supposed to be bereaved!

Albany and Zach seemed unfazed by the producer's jolliness. They all chattered for a while. Their conversation centered on *Christmas in Crazytown* and its resumed rehearsals. Roger's vociferous voice made every word clearly comprehensible.

I went back to the parlor and listened in comfort while I relished my follow-up pain au chocolat. A short while later, having learned nothing more useful from that overheard conversation than the fact that Sproutesians loved to gossip, I stared at the buttery crumbs, jam, and chocolate smears on my plate. I sighed. Tansy would have been disappointed in me.

I'd been honest with her; ordinarily, I make it a practice to stop at one. But today I was worried. No one is *always* immune to stress eating, not even a professional chocolate expert.

While I contemplated my dietary foibles, Roger strode into the parlor as though he owned the place. His gaze lit on me.

I felt uncomfortably pinned to my upholstered armchair.

For better or worse, my reaction to feeling trapped tends to be immediate and impulsive—much like Ophelia's reaction to being passed over in favor of her sister, only with less animosity.

"Good morning! You're going to enjoy the pain au chocolat. It's well done, with just enough *bâton de choco-lat* in each one." I nodded at Roger's plate, which contained one of the pastries. "The addition of cranberry jam makes it nice and Christmassy."

That was a culinary twist I'd approved of, so I explained in further detail exactly what made it perfect. My hat was off to Zach's pastry chef. I really needed to start my chocolate houses, though. They would need time to set before decorating.

"Eh, it'll do in a pinch." With that casual dismissal of my expertise, he set down his coffee. His face brightened as he got a better look at me. He offered his hand. "I'm Roger Balthasar!"

It was an announcement as much as anything else, and it led to an awkward moment between us. He seemed to expect me to know him. Of course, I did, but not for the reasons he probably wanted: his famous exploits wheeling and dealing as a producer.

"Yes, I'm so sorry for your loss," I said in a respectful undertone. "I can tell that everyone will really miss Melissa."

In response, Roger's face fell. He frowned, clearly let down. "Me, most of all. She's left me quite a mess to sort out."

A mess? His disgruntled tone was obvious. I gawked, not wanting to believe I'd heard him say something quite so callous.

He saw and actually grinned. "Believe me, she would

have had a few choice words for me, too, if our roles were reversed."

"Really?" His glib remarks left me feeling flat footed. Yes, I suspected Roger of being a potential murderer, but I expected him to try a little harder to hide his shadowy side. Weren't all the best criminals super devious? "Is that so?"

"Hell, yeah!" With a low groan, Roger settled onto the armchair beside me. A round occasional table and a lamp served as barriers between us. His profile was self-assured, with his gray hair arranged in a short, up-to-the-minute style. He wasn't hiding that he was older, but he seemed far from fusty. "That's how Melissa was," Roger confided easily. His voice boomed. "My wife was a real shark—a go-getter to the bone. That's what first attracted me to her. Her ruthless nature was so . . . unique."

He said this wistfully, the way another man might have remarked on his wife's gift for writing ingenious software code or her talent for hosting an effective networking get together.

I must have misheard him. "Her ruthless nature?"

"Absolutely." This was spiced up with a few curse words. "When I met Melissa, she undercut me on a deal. The rest, as they say, was history." Conspiratorially, Roger leaned closer. I smelled coffee on his breath as he tipped his head toward the B and B's front desk, where I'd noticed Zach and Albany earlier. "So, you think those two are bumping uglies?" He winked.

I was appalled. Sure, I'd wondered if Albany and Zach might still have feelings for each other, but not nearly so crudely.

"You do!" Roger chortled. "You don't have to say so. The look on your face gives it all away. Ha-ha-ha!" He gazed at me with new interest. "What's your name, croissant expert?"

Technically, pains au chocolat—"breads with chocolate" in English—weren't croissants, I knew. It's a misperception shared by lots of people. While pains au chocolat are made with the same type of laminated pastry dough as croissants are, the shape is necessarily different, to better contain the chocolate.

I stopped myself from geeking out on pastry specifics any further and instead met Roger's gaze squarely. If I could take charge of this conversation, maybe I could learn something.

"I'm Hayden Mundy Moore. I should have said so before." *But I was busy thinking you needed consoling over your wife's recent death*. I nodded at him. "I'm a friend of Albany Sullivan's."

Okay, I was name-dropping. But I doubted he knew Travis.

"One of Albany's peeps, eh? Cool, cool." Roger munched a bit of his breakfast, then washed it down with coffee. I doubted he tasted a morsel of it. "She's a nice girl. Very pretty."

"And witty," I couldn't resist specifying. "So talented."

Roger waved away those qualities. I should have expected his assessing gaze to run up and down my figure next, and it did. Even curled up in my armchair, wearing (my usual) jeans and a warm sweater with moto boots, I felt uncomfortably exposed.

"Her memoir is remarkable," I pushed. "It was smart of your wife to recognize its potential. Did it make the rounds much?"

"No more than usual." Roger's eyes narrowed. "Hayden Mundy Moore. I've heard that someplace . . ." He snapped his fingers. "You're the hot-to-trot one! The one who needs an influencer!"

Somehow, he made *influencer* sound exactly like *lech*. Ugh.

This had to be Zach's doing—his way of putting out feelers. He'd suggested that Roger Balthasar was exactly what I needed.

I regretted every minute of trying to get Zach to help me. Next time, I vowed, I'd be more circumspect and avoid jams like this one. "I'm in the market for sponsorship opportunities for a client," I agreed smoothly, ignoring Roger's weird hot-to-trot comment. Zach must have garbled the message somehow. I put on my best innocent look. "Do you know someone who's influential?"

I stopped short of batting my eyelashes, but only barely.

Roger's poorly concealed annoyance was its own reward. He smiled, but it looked more as though he'd gritted his teeth. Given what Danny had told me about him, I knew he was an L.A. big shot.

I couldn't help thinking it was people like Roger B. who put the "deviant" and "amoral" in the "Hollywood types" that people had mentioned in their letters to the *Sentinel*'s editor.

"*I'm* influential," Roger informed me testily. "Although you can be forgiven for not knowing that yet, since we just met."

"Oh? Really?" I frowned. "Um, who do you influence?"

"Everyone. *Nobody* crosses me. Believe me, that's a fact."

This time, I did bat my eyelashes. "It sounds as though your wife crossed you. You said she undercut you on a deal." I let that reminder sink in while I finished my coffee. I studied Roger Balthasar over my coffee cup's rim. "That must have hurt."

For a moment, he seemed to be dumbfounded. Or seething.

Was he reliving an incident that had made him murder his wife in a punch bowl of wassail? I couldn't forget the possibility of his having bribed the police.

I hadn't lingered there solely to annoy him, but at this point, it was a nice side benefit. I didn't like Roger at all.

Quickly enough, he rallied. "Like I said, I liked that about Melissa. I loved her ambition *and* her ruthlessness."

He seemed to genuinely mean it. I found that creepy. What kind of person treasured their beloved's ruthless side?

Maybe the kind of person who'd kill their own spouse? In which case, I didn't want to stick around. Not without backup.

"Yes, well, they say there's someone for everyone."

I no longer had the heart to needle him on purpose. All I wanted was to leave and get on with my day. With that in mind, I uncurled myself from my chair and grabbed my bag.

"Don't you want to know what *she* loved about *me*?"

Roger's brusque voice stopped me. I had my back to him, but there was no mistaking the sense of wounded entitlement there.

I reasoned that the best thing to do was play along.

"Of course." I put on a smile, then turned. Maybe I was being too hard on him, I told myself. Maybe Roger B. couldn't help being crass, insulting, and oblivious to his effect on people. Maybe that was what grieving did to him. Agreeably, I asked, "What did your wife love about you?"

I nearly cringed while awaiting his answer, sure it would be something even more ribald than "bumping uglies" had been.

My imagination ran wild. I wanted *so* much to rein it in.

In all solemnity, Roger said, "She loved my sensitivity."

I knew I was gawking again. I simply couldn't help it.

"Nah, just kidding! She loved my big, fat wallet! Ha-ha!"

Yes, the "big, fat wallet" he'd used to bribe the police into not investigating her likely murder. If the afterlife existed, Melissa had to be looking down on us in fury just then.

I was stumped for a response to that. I truly hoped he was kidding. In the end, no reply was necessary. That was because Roger Balthasar had already taken out his phone and was ignoring me while swiping through his notifications and messages. Rude.

"Break a leg today," I told him, then made my escape.

Whatever Roger had been looking at on his phone, I saw a few minutes later, it had a dramatic effect on him. I was leaving my room key with Zach when the producer barged past.

Beneath his stylish hair, Roger's face looked pale, as though he'd had some bad news. I wondered what it might be.

I'd just finished with my B and B's host, so impulsively, I followed Roger Balthasar. He flung on a jacket while striding out onto the B and B's decorated porch. His breath made plumes in the frosty air; so did mine. Hastily, I dragged on my coat.

I'd planned to go to the shared work space that Zach had mentioned artisans and crafters used to prepare for the charity auction. Now I made a spur-of-the-moment decision to trail Roger instead.

He didn't look back as he stomped down the B and B's steps and hurried to his vehicle. I did a double take as I saw the one he chose: a dark-colored SUV, similar to last night's attack model.

Hmm. As far as I remembered, Roger hadn't been part of the Santa pub crawl. Had he lingered nearby and attacked afterward?

I could easily imagine him attempting some light vehicular manslaughter. It was a little trickier picturing him in a borrowed velour Santa suit and tie-on beard. I wasted a moment examining the SUV, trying to discern if it was the same vehicle.

I couldn't tell, and now I had no time to lose. I got in my own rental car and pulled out, teeth chattering in the cold.

Ahead of me along the road to Sproutes, the taillights of Roger's SUV swerved and dipped. He was speeding. His erratic driving worried me, but I had no choice except to keep up.

I wanted to know what had Roger in such a tearing hurry.

It was possible, I thought as I clenched the steering wheel and peered through the blustery snow that had begun falling, that a self-important big shot like Roger always drove this way. He was from Los Angeles, after all. There you had to keep up on the highway, or you'd be a danger to yourself and others. But rural Massachusetts wasn't Southern California. If anything, the weather and slick conditions should have demanded more caution.

Instead, Roger sped up. Because he'd noticed me?

Warily, I fell back. I pulled my knit cap lower, hoping to hide my face. My thoughts went crazy. Was I really engaging in a car chase? I caught a glimpse of Roger's harried-looking face in his side mirror. He was yelling into his phone, red-faced, now.

I wished I could have called Danny or Travis. But that would have been foolhardy—just as dangerous as following Roger might turn out to be. Who knew what he was up to? Was he leading me out into the wilderness as an ambush? Was he Melissa's killer? He'd already warned me that *nobody* crossed him. . . .

On the next turn, my rental car lost traction. For one terrifying instant, I skidded crazily. The nearest snowbank seemed to zoom toward me. I steered with my heart pounding, trying to remember the driving instructions for this situation.

Instinct told me to slam on the brakes. I steered into the skid instead. A second later, the car's tires regained traction.

Whew. I had control again. I blinked and gulped in some air, hoping to calm my racing heartbeat, as I sped along. As I looked ahead, though—now that the crisis was past—I saw that the road was empty. Somehow, Roger Balthasar had slipped away.

I swore and shook my head. Some amateur sleuth I was. I'd bombed out on my very first car chase. I had almost wrecked my vehicle in a snowbank—or worse—and had nothing to show for it. Dispirited but abuzz with adrenaline, I pulled over to catch my breath.

I probably made an odd sight, there on the road into town, with my head cradled in my arms atop the steering wheel, scared.

I was scared about what I'd just done. Scared about the lengths I'd now go to try to solve an overlooked murder. I didn't want to be changed by what had happened to me lately, but there was no mistaking the truth: I was changed forever now.

After a few minutes, my phone buzzed. I dragged it out

of my crossbody bag, then checked its screen. It was Danny calling.

"You might want to get down here," he said when I answered.

"Down to the Sproutes playhouse? For rehearsals?"

My bodyguard buddy gave an affirmative sound but no further details about what was going on. "Gotta run. See you soon."

I glanced at my dash clock. "I'll be there in ten minutes."

By the time I arrived at the theater, Danny's call made sense. First of all, I couldn't park. In fact, I could barely approach the venue for Albany's sold-out holiday show at all. That was because Sproutes's charmingly decorated downtown was thronged with what appeared to be gathering protesters.

I sized up the situation, then changed tactics. A few streets over, I was able to park my rental car and climb out. As I did, I noticed several more Sproutesians heading toward Main Street. They carried signs but hadn't yet adopted the official protest posture—they were laughing and smiling, as though they were about to attend a music festival or summertime street fair.

I puzzled over that as I made my way toward the theater, edging between clumps of protesters. Most of them seemed to be student age—college freshmen or maybe high-school students.

BRING BACK *THE NUTCRACKER!* one of the signs read.

WE DON'T WANT *CHRISTMAS IN CRAZYTOWN!* said another.

Okay, then. I understood what the protest was about.

This jibed with what I'd read in the *Sproutes Sentinel*, at least from the faction of residents who hadn't wanted their beloved production to be canceled this year. In fact, I saw there were now slightly older Sproutesians among the protesters. A few of them had children with them. Little girls wore tiaras and were dressed up in spangled ballerina costumes beneath their coats.

I found myself below the theater's dazzling marquee, being shoved from all sides. Chants rang out against Albany's musical.

It was a mostly peaceful event, but there was strength in numbers. It felt as though the crowd was gathering energy.

"Everyone, please!" a feminine voice rang out, amplified through a bullhorn. "Let's keep this Christmassy, all right?"

I half expected the protesters to launch into a holiday carol. Instead, they became louder. More animated and forceful.

I'll admit, I was nonplussed. Who knew that a home-grown production of *The Nutcracker* could engender such loyalty?

Although, it occurred to me, those cute mini ballerina wannabes and their parents would be missing what was likely an annual holiday tradition this year, so I felt sympathetic.

Curiously, I turned and looked for the woman I'd heard through the bullhorn. Hmm. I'd seen her before, I realized.

Once I remembered where, everything became clear to me: the perfectly timed opposition to *Christmas in Crazytown*, the largely student crowd, and the real purpose of this protest, too. Because that wasn't just *any* Christmas-loving bullhorn holder I caught sight of on the other side of the sidewalk.

That was Albany's former high school English

teacher—the very one who'd been targeted so mercilessly by all those ugly online memes a few months ago. Apparently, she hadn't been deterred by those malicious Internet attacks—or at least, I estimated, her past and current students were undeterred.

Decisively, I maneuvered in her direction. It was time to finally meet Donna Brown—full-time English teacher *and* part-time Sproutes playhouse director. She looked ready to fight to the end to bring back *The Nutcracker* . . . and everyone knew that would require ridding Sproutes of *Christmas in Crazytown* first.

Thirteen

Once I'd gotten close enough to Donna Brown to see her face clearly, I thought I realized what was going on. A few minutes' conversation with her inside the Sproutes theater confirmed it.

"I'm just so overwhelmed!" the playhouse director told me inside the ornate lobby. "I swear, I never meant for any of this to happen! I came down here today to try to calm everyone down."

"Well, no worries, then!" I said cheeringly. I nodded to the small crowd, still milling around beyond the theater's decorated-for-the-season windows. "Everyone seems peaceful."

In fact, they seemed positively upbeat, for a protest.

"Do you really think so?" Donna's gaze looked apprehensive.

I nodded. I felt for her; I truly did. She reminded me of a few of my clients—particularly the ones who were small-business entrepreneurs. They were perpetually overextended, juggling too many responsibilities and feeling they were doing nothing well.

As the playhouse director and a teacher, Donna Brown

could easily feel the same way. Compared with the photos I'd seen of her, she appeared much older than I would have expected. She was probably only sixty, but her face seemed drawn and creased with worry. Her movements were jittery; her hands restless.

I guessed months of online bullying could be tough on a person—especially one who, like Donna, seemed so delicate. Behind her eyeglasses, her blue eyes were teary and hesitant.

Beneath her knee-length puffer coat, I glimpsed her sequined holiday sweater, dressy trousers, and snow boots. She wore gloves, so I didn't spy a wedding ring, but I knew from my research that she was unmarried. Her dog had shed on her coat; an unraveled thread on its hem told me she'd been wearing that garment a long time. Maybe she couldn't afford to replace it?

"What I don't understand is how things got to this point." I gave her a steady encouraging look. "You have a real fan club out there! But I thought you agreed to cancel *The Nutcracker*?"

"I did." Donna shuffled her booted feet, then glanced at the nearby security guard. He had recognized me and let us in.

The crowd, believing that I represented someone who wanted to negotiate the closure of *Christmas in Crazytown*, had cheered.

"But something has changed since then?" I pressed. This was none of my business, really. But I was afraid Roger Balthasar would show up at any moment and terrorize Donna. He had to have caught wind of the protest and come here to deal with it.

I doubted he would handle the matter with any compassion.

"Honestly, I was happy to shelve this year's production," Donna admitted. Her gaze sought mine. I nodded in affirmation. "I'm positively overloaded with work and projects right now. I would have canceled it for nothing! It was a relief not to have to coordinate one more thing." She studied the snow melting from her boots onto the theater lobby's marble floor. "It's been a difficult year," Donna added with enviable understatement.

I understood. "That's too bad. Work pressure?"

Her face took on a venomous cast. "Not exactly."

Yikes. Apparently, Donna Brown had a dark side, too.

Was Donna dark enough to murder someone? Being under public attack might have made her want to strike out in some way.

After all, she'd never asked for a public feud with Albany.

I swallowed hard. "Oh? What happened?"

My nonchalant tone seemed to convince her that I was unaware of the awful online situation. Donna shifted, glanced outside at the protesters, then looked at the security guard again. She was certainly uneasy. Her gaze returned to me. She looked unhappy. "I had a disagreement with one of the students I mentored."

"A disagreement?" That was one way to describe the situation. I wanted to keep her talking. "Really?"

"Yes. While she was a student in my class, I thought she appreciated all the guidance I gave her," Donna explained. "All the extra time I spent encouraging her and editing her work after hours. She was gifted, you see, but needed discipline."

She had to be talking about Albany. That made alarm bells go off in my mind. Albany's own mother had said that Albany was touchy about having her work edited. I doubted she would have reacted well to Donna Brown's well-meaning critical feedback.

"I *loved* my mentor," I shared, thinking fondly of Monsieur Philippe Vetault in Brittany, France. "He taught me so much. Without him, I never would have found my true calling in life."

"Exactly!" Donna brightened as she gave me a vigorous nod. "That's all I wanted to be for this student. Once she *did* succeed, I liked to think that I'd played a part in that, however small. I thought that maybe the help I'd given her had sunk in, after all, and she simply hadn't wanted to admit it."

"Sometimes that happens." My next statement was a risk, but I had to know. "But not this time? Not after the book came out?"

I was referring, of course, to Albany's memoir. But either Donna didn't notice we'd switched from the abstract to the specific or she didn't care. Outside, the protesters chanted.

"After the book came out, I couldn't wait to read it. I knew I'd find some sign, some subtle hint, that I'd made a difference." Donna's gaze turned pleadingly to mine. "Isn't that what everyone wants? To make a difference to someone?"

"I know that's what I want." That much was true. "I do a lot of freelance consulting work. I want to leave my clients happier and more confident than I found them, every time."

"See? You understand." Donna gave a relieved nod. "I don't have children of my own, but in a way, I like to think of all my students as my children. I care so much about each of them."

"Of course you do," I told her and hoped I didn't sound unbalanced.

"This particular student was a favorite of mine," Donna told me. "She was challenging, but I was so proud of her!"

"Of course you were!" Had pride turned to resentment? "If I'd mentored someone successful, I'd have been shouting from the rooftops about it." Especially if they wrote a tell-all book.

At that, Donna blushed. She shifted again. "Well . . . I did."

I gave her a playful, friendly look. "Really? You did?"

Abashed, she said, "I told everyone I knew! I'd mentored a famous writer—you must know it was Albany Sullivan—so of course I told people about it. But then, when Albany's book came out . . ."

Donna had been scarcely mentioned, I knew. Albany certainly hadn't recognized her teacher as a cherished mentor. "The appreciation just wasn't there?" I guessed sympathetically.

"No." Donna's gaze turned stony. "Quite the opposite."

Her demeanor had taken a decided turn for the furious. Despite her harmless appearance, I suddenly believed Donna capable of a Christmastime punch-bowl death by drowning. That was worrying. I had enough suspects already. Also, too many victims.

I waited a few seconds, in case she volunteered more.

She didn't. Instead, Donna swiveled expectantly to me. "So, you said you might have a suggestion for fixing this mess?" Her arm wave encompassed the Sproutes playhouse, the protestors outside, and possibly the entire holiday season.

I gulped. That was what I'd promised on the sidewalk a few minutes ago, when I'd swept Donna inside with me. Now it was time to make good on that declaration. I thought I had a good idea, but I needed Albany's participation to make it work.

"All I want is to put all of this behind me," Donna pushed, looking beleaguered. "But I honestly have no idea how."

I empathized. "Don't worry," I said, hoping I wasn't

accidentally consoling a murderer. "I think we can work out everything—and in a way that makes everyone happy, too."

"A compromise?" Donna seemed skeptical. "Not likely."

"That's what everyone says before they realize where the common ground is." I channeled my inner Travis, trying to seem like an expert negotiator. "Now that I know what you want, I can go have a chat with the *Christmas in Crazytown* folks and find out what they want. After that, we'll all reconvene."

"And in the meantime?"

"In the meantime, I have just the thing for everyone."

When I arrived backstage after my chat with Donna Brown, Danny was waiting for me. He spotted me and shook his head.

"You shouldn't have done that," he growled.

I knew he wasn't referring to my impromptu conversation with the teacher. "Why not? It was fun. Everyone enjoyed it."

"I agree with the enforcer," Travis boggled my mind by saying. "It's a bad idea to make a splash around here."

"Come on! It was a peaceful protest full of teenagers and tiaraed children. All I did was defuse the situation outside."

"Yeah," Danny grumbled, "by taking the whole crowd to the local donut shop and treating them to all the free donuts they could eat." He tsk-tsked. "Nobody likes a show-off, Hayden."

Hey, I didn't have a trust fund for nothing, I reasoned. What good was all that money if I couldn't share sometimes?

But I knew better than to say so to tightfisted Danny.

"It's not even a tax-deductible business expense," Travis pointed out dampeningly. "Or a principally sensible expenditure. There were dozens of people outside. Conservatively figuring one donut per person, at an average of three dollars per donut—"

Danny snickered. "*One* donut? Be real. Try five apiece." He scowled at me. "People take advantage of things that are free."

"Good point." Travis resumed his calculations. "Let's say three dozen people times five donuts each, at three dollars—"

"That's a damned expensive donut," Danny grumbled. "What's in there, anyway? Solid gold? Sugar is cheap. So is fryer oil."

"It's not a big deal," I protested. "I was in a jam. I needed a diversion. Goodies are the best diversion out there."

I hadn't had an appetite for deep-fried, sugar-dusted treats myself. Not after my two-pastry breakfast. Especially not when I hadn't yet figured out a way to get in my usual heart-healthy, calorie-burning run while on the road in wintertime.

It had been fun, though, watching all the kids running around, choosing donut flavors. Fun seeing their contented parents. The students had required no urging at all to indulge.

"The important thing is," I went on, squaring off with Danny and Travis simultaneously, "that I learned a few things."

I told them about Donna's perception that she'd nurtured and mentored Albany—and her disappointment that Albany hadn't seen their relationship in the same way. I mentioned her dark look when referring to the publication of Albany's memoir.

"Donna felt ignored. Unappreciated!" I explained.

"She'd bragged to everyone in town about mentoring Albany, especially after Albany's book deal was announced. Then, during Albany's press tour, the social media and meme attacks happened. Donna was publicly broadsided by someone she sincerely tried to help. You can see where she'd have an ax to grind against Albany."

"*I* can see where she'd have a murder motivation," Danny said.

I expected Travis to leap to Albany's defense, as usual. Instead, he said, "You think Donna is dangerous, and you made a promise to her, anyway? A promise you know you can't keep?"

I raised my chin. "Keeping it is partly up to Albany."

I still intended to talk with the memoirist about it. Also, with a few other people—including, regrettably, Roger Balthasar.

My financial advisor looked dubious. "You're meddling."

"You're being negative! Who knows? It might work," I insisted as rehearsals kicked off nearby. "Also, you're ignoring the most important part. When I was talking with Donna about the show, she told me she 'would have canceled it for nothing.'"

"So?" Danny kept an eye on Tansy, who was safely onstage.

"So that means she *didn't* cancel it for nothing," I said.

Travis caught on. "Someone paid Donna Brown to cancel her production of *The Nutcracker*." He looked up at the stage lights, lost in thought. "If that's true, why stage a protest later?"

"That's adorable, Trav." I grinned. "You can't even conceive of anyone going back on their word." I loved that about him. "But Donna didn't stage that protest. Her current and former students did. The ones who *did* love and appreciate her"—unlike Albany—"took advantage of their Christmas break to march downtown." I thought of their eager faces when I'd gone outside to announce that a solution to the situation was in the works. "They were protesting for Donna, because they care about her."

It would have been heartwarming if Donna weren't (potentially) murderously rage filled and fueled by betrayal.

Danny harrumphed. "The bottom line is, who paid her?"

As if on cue, Roger Balthasar barged onstage. Until that moment, I hadn't seen him anywhere, despite thinking that he must have raced away from the B&B to deal with the protest.

"Hey, hey, hey!" He flung his arms wide. "Daddy's home!"

Ugh. Nevertheless, the cast and crew applauded him.

"Let's get down to work!" the producer said, rubbing his palms together. "I heard that nutball theater director was outside doing crazy stuff, but I guess I scared her away!"

Travis, Danny, and I exchanged meaningful glances.

"I'll look into that payment," Travis promised.

I glanced at Danny, anticipating a similar "Go get 'em" comment from him. Instead, he quirked his mouth. "Hey, I'm still pissed you didn't bring me a damn donut. I've got work to do."

They both left me alone, standing offstage, in the wings.

Unfortunately, their joint departure drew Roger Balthasar's attention to me. He spied me in the wings, then grinned widely.

"Hey, it's hot-to-trot Hayden Mundy Moore! How ya doin'?"

As one, everyone involved in *Christmas in Crazytown* turned to gawp at me. I wished I could hide behind the stage curtains.

"Aww, don't be so unfriendly! Ha-ha-ha!" Roger waved off my (probably obvious) mortification. "No hard feelings! It takes a while to warm up to me. That's what everyone says." He grinned, unbothered by that characterization. "Come out and say hi!"

I shook my head, then gestured that I had to be going.

Given Roger's manic behavior, it occurred to me, he might well be on medication—something to help him cope. Poor guy.

"Hayden Mundy Moore wants to hook up with somebody!" Roger announced next, loudly, seemingly oblivious to that phrase's double meaning. To someone his age, it merely meant "meet."

To someone my age? It was more analogous to "sleep with."

I couldn't believe this was happening. Nearer to the stage, Danny, Travis, Tansy, and Albany all had the nerve to chuckle. Behind them, Ophelia had stopped in the midst of taking a phone photo, wearing a look of utter disgust. *Old people still do it?*

"Anybody know someone Hayden Mundy Moore can hook up with?" Roger boomed. He seemed under the impression that he was making amends—righting the wrong foot our relationship had started on. "She's especially interested in Joe Sullivan. Albany, you ought to introduce Hayden to your dad." A wink. "Go on. Do it!"

Albany's expression morphed from one of amusement to confusion.

Ophelia's switched from one of disgust to indignation. I could discern the exact moment when she thought that I was trying to ditch her for an alliance with Albany and/or her own father.

Not that any of those outcomes made sense. We'd already discussed Albany's overloaded schedule, and Joe Sullivan wasn't an influencer—not beyond Sproutes, at least. But with an emotional young woman like Ophelia, sometimes the facts didn't matter. She shot me a malevolent look, then stormed offstage.

I caught up to Ophelia near the sixties Christmas set.

"Ophelia, wait." I moved aside a plastic Rudolph figure that was blocking my path, then hurried to her. "I think you misunderstood what was going on out there with Roger."

"I think it was pretty obvious." Albany's little sister fussed with her trendy outfit, not meeting my eyes. "You still want to connect with Albany. *And* you're into my dad! Gross!"

"No. And double no." I held out my palms in a pacifying gesture, then smiled. "I'm happy working with you! In fact, I was hoping to schedule another chocolate-peppermint bark photo shoot soon. I heard people go sledding on a certain hill outside town. Maybe that would be a good spot? You could wear a cute hat, pose next to one of those vintage sleds?"

"Mmm." Ophelia gave me a reticent glance. "Maybe."

Progress. "And as far as your dad is concerned—"

"Stop. I don't want to know." She made a revolted face. "I know everyone thinks he's at work all the time, but I'm smarter than that. You should know, I'm not as naïve as I look."

I nodded, unsure where this was going. "Of course not."

A moment passed as Ophelia stared stubbornly at the holiday decorations. Beyond us, the show's rehearsals had resumed.

"Did you really buy donuts for the whole town?" she asked.

I was surprised she'd heard about it. That must have shown.

Proving it, Ophelia raised her phone. "It's already all over social media. Hashtag free donuts. People are coming from all over Massachusetts. I hope you have really deep pockets."

I didn't want to discuss my finances. "You should go pick up a few for yourself," I urged instead. "I hear they're tasty."

Her gaze lingered curiously on me. "So you don't care?"

"About . . . ?"

"About people taking advantage of you. I'd be mad."

She tipped up her chin, her eyes glimmering. It occurred to me that Ophelia was a lot more sensitive than she let on.

"No, I'm not mad," I assured her. "I like treating people. It's my job, after all, making sure people have lots of delicious chocolate to enjoy. What's not to like?"

A shrug. "Nothing, I guess!" She smiled, then appeared to shift gears. "Hey, let's get out of here. You want to?"

"Aren't you supposed to stay for rehearsals?"

"Nah. I half expect the whole thing to be canceled still. Plus, my priorities are *not* with *Christmas in Crazytown*."

They were with her social-media influencer account, I knew. But still, "Roger is back today. Won't he notice you're gone?"

A grin. "Not hardly. He thinks I'm a bratty kid." For a moment, her face darkened. "Melissa was worse, though. She wanted to get 'someone with experience' as Tansy's understudy."

That seemed reasonable to me. But I already knew how poorly Ophelia reacted to being doubted, passed over, or overlooked.

Had Melissa made the fatal mistake of pushing her too far?

Looking at the young woman then, I couldn't believe it.

Until I cornered Albany and Roger to discuss a truce with Donna Brown, though, I had no particular reason to stay at the theater. I nodded. "Sure. Let's go! Another photo shoot?"

Ophelia grinned. "This one's going to be sick. I was, like, looking at my follower analytics the other day, and I realized—duh!—we're ignoring a whole huge demographic!"

"You analyze your followers?" That was news to me.

"Duh. How else can I monetize them? Come on. Let's go."

Fourteen

Fortunately, I had mocked up a whole case of my faux product, in the event I found an opportunity to meet with Ophelia. So I was prepared with loads of ribbon-wrapped chocolate-peppermint bark in the backseat of my rental car.

Before heading over to the Sproutes sledding hill, though, Ophelia and I drove to her parents' house. She had a few props in mind for use in our photo shoot and wouldn't be deterred.

I didn't mind. I was curious to see the household where the oddball Christmastime events depicted in *Christmas in Crazytown* had really gone down. I'd imagined the place while reading, of course, but my mental image was an amalgamation of sitcom and movie sets, polished up for the holidays and inhabited by the Sullivans instead of by TV and movie stars. It had been unlikely to be accurate, and it wasn't. The real Sullivans lived in a small Cape Cod–style house just beyond Sproutes's town common.

"Wait here." Ophelia practically had the passenger-side car door open before I parked in the drive. "I'll be right back."

I'd already caught a glimpse of someone moving around inside, visible yet unrecognizable through the

Christmas-light-trimmed front windows. I saw a decorated fir tree, too.

So far, so normal. In case that was Joe Sullivan—and I could wrangle a casual chat with the family's paternal missing link—I jumped out of the car right behind Albany's sister.

"Don't be silly! I'll come with you."

I scampered around the parked car in her wake and hurried up the drive. Someone had shoveled the snow recently; it was piled up along the driveway's edge and at the base of the porch, leaving a clear path straight to the holly-wreathed front door.

I admired its ribboned and ornamented finery for a split second, before Ophelia pushed open the door and rushed inside.

Beyond her, I heard someone call, "Ophelia? Is that you?"

"Yeah, it's just me, Mom." Looking exasperated, the young woman glanced over her shoulder at me. "I'll be right back."

She hurried upstairs, leaving me in the narrow foyer. So far, the Sullivan household seemed patently normal. Fir garland wound around the bannisters; twinkly lights sparkled in the next room. I glimpsed a fireplace with stockings, the Christmas tree I'd seen through the window, assorted wrapped gifts arranged underneath it, . . . and, through the passageway, Linda Sullivan.

"Linda, hi!" I was surprised to see the *Sproutes Sentinel* editor home during the day. I was even more surprised to see her wearing sweatpants and a T-shirt covered by a knee-length cable-knit cardigan. Its pockets bulged with tissues. Above that ensemble, Linda's face looked weary. "It's Hayden Mundy Moore," I reminded her. "Josh Levitt's friend from the cookie exchange."

"I remember you." There was startling malice in her tone. "Don't think I don't!" Linda winced and touched her temple. I recognized the gesture that had preceded her painkiller dose at the newspaper offices. "I know what you're up to, too! How dare you come here?" Despite her pain, Linda advanced on me. Her face darkened with obvious suspicion. "You leave my Joe alone!"

Oh no. Sproutesians really *did* love to gossip, I realized, if word had already spread to Roger B. *and* Linda that I was some kind of hot-to-trot hussy, eager to "hook up" with Mr. Sullivan.

I put up my palms. "I'm not interested in your husband!"

"That's what they all say . . . to my face." Linda's eyes narrowed. Upstairs, Ophelia thumped around. "I'm watching you!"

The vehemence in her face frightened me. Stripped of her workplace pleasantries and her usual aura of professionalism, Linda seemed like a different person—a deeply malicious person.

I was sorry to have found myself on her bad side.

Before I could formulate a response, Ophelia reappeared.

"Mom! What are you doing up? You're supposed to be resting." She slung her tote bag full of props higher on her shoulder, then slipped her phone in her coat pocket. With a caring demeanor, Ophelia hurried to her mother's side. She took her elbow. "Come on. Let's get you settled. Did you take some of your medication? Do you need more of it? I want to help."

"Cash is picking up a refill for me." Behind Ophelia's back, Linda gave me one of those "I'm watching you" gestures.

She did seem to be in pain, so I forgave her ire. If I'd

been suffering from an ailment requiring medication, I'd be cranky, too. Plus, Ophelia had hinted that her father spent his time doing something other than working. It didn't take a mental leap to think Joe might be having affairs. That was too bad for Linda . . . although I don't think I'd have wanted to hold on to him.

You leave my Joe alone! Or what? came to mind. Yikes.

I couldn't help wondering if Melissa Balthasar and Joe Sullivan had fooled around. If so, had Linda Sullivan known?

"Cash was supposed to have done that yesterday," Ophelia complained. She made a production of getting her mother settled on the sofa, where a snowman-print throw and several holiday accent pillows awaited. "I can't believe you keep asking him."

"One of these days, he's going to come through. You'll see." Linda gave a slight groan as she settled onto the sofa.

"I'm seeing him in a few minutes." In a tellingly sarcastic tone, Ophelia added, "I'll tell him you're still waiting."

"Oh, don't do that! You'll only antagonize him."

There was no reply from Ophelia as she arranged the throw over her mother. I expected that antagonizing her siblings gave her a reason to get up in the morning. Feeling suddenly aware of my eavesdropping, I politely slipped back toward the front door.

On the other hand, eavesdropping had become my bread and butter as an amateur sleuth. I crept a little closer. I waited.

"But you need your medication!" Ophelia said. "Your head—"

"Will be fine. I've already taken a dose. I just don't have another one ready," Linda soothed, although it was obvious from her slightly labored breathing that she was still hurting. "You go ahead and have fun today." Her tone changed. "What are you doing with *that woman*, anyway? Is she trying to win you over?"

"Mom, come on. It's nothing like that."

"I heard about her donut trick! She can't buy us!"

Catching the obvious resentment in Linda's voice, I frowned. Travis had warned me it wasn't smart to "make a splash" in Sproutes. Maybe he'd been right. All I'd wanted was to defuse the protest. Somehow, I'd sparked a social-media frenzy and stoked resentment instead. It was so easy to make a misstep here with these supersensitive folks. Had Melissa done the same thing?

I vowed to avoid punch bowls full of wassail from now on.

"Shh. Hayden's not trying to buy anyone," Ophelia soothed. "We're doing a social-media campaign together, that's all."

Linda gave a harrumph. "You're still doing that? I told you, Ophelia Jane, and your father did, too. You have to go to college! That's what Albany did. Look how well it's worked out!"

A pause. Then, "Yeah, really well. For the whole family."

Before I could be sure of the reasons behind Ophelia's acerbic tone, the young woman reappeared. She strode toward me as she made a stompingly dramatic exit from her mother's side.

"Don't put all your eggs in one basket!" Linda called from her place on the sofa. "Internet fame is fickle, Ophelia. It's toxic! Look at what happened to poor Ms. Brown."

Now rejoining me, Ophelia rolled her eyes. "Let's go."

Stuck on Ophelia's side of this mother-daughter divide, I felt torn. My sympathies lay more with Linda than with her influencer daughter. I knew people sometimes made a good living being "Internet famous," but that type of celebrity was like every other—likely to be short lived and quickly forgotten.

Awkwardly, I popped my head around the passageway. I gave a brief wave. "I hope you feel better soon, Linda. Bye!"

The editor gave me a killing look, then ignored me.

"Be sure to bundle up, if you're going to be outside long!" she yelled at her daughter. "Don't forget your scarf again!"

Ophelia turned pink. Her frown deepened. "Later, Mom!"

She stomped to the door, opened it, then scowled at me.

I recognized my cue. Feeling off kilter, I stepped through. I didn't want to be on Linda's bad side, especially on such specious grounds. How could Zach have suggested I was looking for more than a sponsor? He'd made me sound downright tarty.

While I'd been ruminating over my unfortunate new (and unearned) slutty reputation in Sproutes, Ophelia had reached my rental car. She stood beside it, staring at me accusingly.

Sheesh. This whole family was out to get me today.

I remotely unlocked the doors, then followed Ophelia. We might as well get on with our photo shoot, I decided. Until rehearsals ended, I couldn't speak with anyone. Until I'd done that, I couldn't return to my B&B to ask Zach to please stop spreading the word that Hayden Mundy Moore wanted to "hook up" with Joe Sullivan—and maybe a few other Sproutes men, too.

I didn't want to make that treacherous drive twice, if I could avoid it. My memory of nearly sliding into that snowbank this morning remained strong. Even frightened by that car chase and slowed by a knee injury, though, I'd been lucky so far.

For Melissa B., visiting Sproutes had been fatal. I couldn't forget that. The producer had come here only to get some work done. She'd probably had good intentions, good ideas. . . .

"Hey! Earth to Hayden!" Ophelia rudely snapped her fingers. "Are we, uh, getting out of here anytime soon, or what?"

I started, then laughed. "Sure. Let's go."

I eased the vehicle into motion, my tires briefly sliding as I did so. The back end of my car fishtailed. I glimpsed a car creeping down the Sullivans' street with the kind of care that the snowy wintertime weather demanded, and hit the brakes.

We skidded harder across the driveway.

Ophelia yelped. "Hayden, look out!"

My car smacked into the snow-shoveled snowbank. The impact scarcely jolted us, but my heart pounded all the same. That was because as I looked over my shoulder to make sure I hadn't hit that passing car, I caught sight of its occupant.

The driver was wearing a Santa suit. Plus a hat and beard.

After last night, that particular ensemble felt menacing.

I scrambled for my phone to take a photo, oblivious to our crazy crooked parking position and any damage to my bumper.

I looked at the result. A blurry, useless snapshot.

My eyes filled with tears. I wasn't sad, though. I was mad. I was frustrated by my own inability to crack Melissa's case *and* my inability to save my own skin—say, by not sliding into snowbanks. How long had sinister Santa been following me?

Ophelia snapped out of her tantrum. "Are you okay?"

"Yeah." I sniffled, then tried to smile. I sneaked a glance

in my rearview mirror. Santa's car had already vanished. *Santa's car.* Hmm. Last night our attacker had driven an SUV. This had to be a coincidence—a department-store Santa driving to work. "I'm fine." I looked at Ophelia. "I'm sorry. Are you okay?"

"I'm good. If I had my driver's license, I'd take over from here. But I don't, so I can't." She smirked. "Sorry. My dad has been badgering me to get it for years, but I don't see the point." She held up her phone. "All my friends are right here."

I nodded, understanding. Also, I wondered, if Ophelia didn't have her driver's license, how did she get around? Was Sproutes's public transit system comprehensive enough to take her to the B&B to murder Melissa, then bring her back home again?

I didn't know. If not, it seemed that Ophelia had an ironclad alibi for the night of Melissa's murder. Either that or Albany's sister had had an accomplice in any wrongdoing.

I inhaled, put my head on straight, then carefully backed up. "No need. I've got this. I just need to go more slowly."

I did just that and made it successfully to the street.

Inside the Sullivans' house, someone moved. Linda?

I imagined her hobbling to the window to snicker at my disconcerting almost crash into the snowbank. Well, at least my mistake had probably brightened her difficult day, right? Linda seemed so dedicated to her work at the *Sentinel*. I was sure her discomfort must be severe to have sidelined her for the day.

Either that or Linda was faking it. But to what purpose?

I sighed and kept driving to the sledding hill, chiding myself for being purposelessly suspicious. Now I was imagining Ophelia taking the bus to pull off a murder?

Linda faking an injury while staying home to . . . do what, exactly? Plan another one?

Hmm. Now that I thought of it, it wasn't that crazy.

But as much as my mind was swimming with theories and horrible instant replays of the night I'd found Melissa dead beside that wassail punch bowl, our morning plans distracted me.

At the top of the Sproutes sledding hill, Ophelia and I parked the car, then gathered all our supplies. She carried her tote bag full of props. I brought along my faux "product."

"We should probably try some of this," Ophelia suggested with a mischievous nose wrinkle, "just to make sure it's good."

I didn't argue. It had been hours since my two-pastry nosh. By the look of things, we were going to miss lunch, too. I doled out cellophane-wrapped packages to both of us, then I nibbled.

Ophelia took her first bite. Her eyes widened. "OMG!"

I was proud enough of my work to smile. "You like it?"

"Like it? I, like, want to marry it or something!"

I laughed while Ophelia went to town on the rest of her chocolaty confection. The crushed candy cane topping made it festive; the high-quality chocolate beneath made it delicious.

We brushed off the snow from the fence bordering the sledding hill area, then leaned on it while we munched. Idly, I watched a dilapidated pickup truck rumble into the parking lot.

Beside me, Ophelia stiffened almost imperceptibly.

More curious now, I examined that truck. I thought I recognized the dark-haired man in the passenger seat. Cashel.

"Looks like our model is here," Ophelia said with

forced cheerfulness. It sounded as though she'd gritted her teeth.

I wondered at the source of her annoyance. She'd known Cashel was coming to meet us. Her plan, as she'd explained it to me during our drive, was to enlist her brother as today's photo-shoot model and pose him with the chocolate-peppermint bark in a variety of social-media-friendly scenarios. Cashel, as an older man, could broaden Ophelia's "female-centric" demographics.

At least that was her theory. In practice, Ophelia seemed less than thrilled with her choice of male model. She frowned as the ramshackle truck parked, offering us a perfect view of the bedraggled Rudolph-style plastic red nose affixed to its front bumper. Moments later, Cashel climbed out of the passenger side.

As before, he wore an athletic puffer coat and canvas pants, with a dapper red and green flannel scarf twisted around his neck. His face was chiseled, his dark hair topped by an ivory knit cap. Given his physique, I thought he'd make a good model. He exchanged a few muffled words with the truck's hat-wearing driver, then waved and slammed shut the passenger door.

As Cashel came toward us, I couldn't miss his cheery demeanor. It stood in marked contrast to the demanding way he'd dealt with Zach at the B&B the other day. I vowed to view him with fresh eyes. He'd had a momentary outburst. It wouldn't be fair to hold it against him, especially when I barely knew him.

Ophelia wasn't big on introductions. I wasn't sure if she was aware that Cashel and I had already met or if she just didn't care.

She stormed over to her brother, then poked him right in the chest with her non-chocolate-bark-holding hand.

"Cashel! You're supposed to be staying away from those guys, remember?"

"That's not 'those guys.' It's just one guy," he said, in an obvious effort to appease her. "He's helping me deliver some stuff for Dad. Besides, I'm not 'supposed' to be coming home for all the Christmas drama right now, either, but I did just that."

Cashel looked past Ophelia and saw me. He smiled. "Hey, we meet again!" He trod closer and offered me his gloved hand.

I shook it, then studied him while I gave him my name.

"So you're my little sister's benefactor, eh?" Teasingly, Cashel gave Ophelia's shoulder a light shake. "I'm happy she's found someone. Albany isn't the only one in the family with talent to spare." He cast her a fond look, then met my gaze. "I still feel bad about the way we met, Hayden. That wasn't me."

As he said so, Ophelia scrutinized him. Her gaze traveled from his boots to his scarf, then lingered on his face. Her expression of sisterly concern was as touching as it was unexpected. Most of the time, she strived to seem nonchalant.

Apparently, Cashel brought out Ophelia's caring side. As we got to work setting up photo opportunities, I began to see why.

In marked contrast to the man I'd met at the B and B, today's Cashel Sullivan was far from entitled, difficult, or rude. On the slope of Sproutes's sledding hill, with a rented metal-runner sled and many, many packets of chocolate-peppermint bark, the eldest Sullivan sibling seemed positively engaging. He joked around with the little kids who were sledding that day, tossed snowballs, and helped them haul their plastic sleds up the hill.

While doing that, Cashel comically huffed and puffed. His antics drew delighted laughter from several of the children.

"Whew!" With a dramatic gesture, he pretended to wipe his brow. "I'm knackered! That's a really heavy sled you've got!"

"No it's not!" Its owner, a boy of four or five, giggled. He hefted his sled's towrope, lifting the apparatus an inch from the sparkling snow. "See? I can lift it all by myself!"

"Wow. You must be superstrong!" Cashel crept closer and jokingly squeezed the boy's tiny, coat-covered biceps. He gasped. "Are you a superhero or something? I can keep a secret."

Cashel glanced up at the boy's mother, then gave a wink. She tittered, obviously charmed. The little boy explained that he got his strength "from vegables!" pronouncing that tricky word minus a few of its syllables. Nearby, Ophelia snapped away with her camera. She'd switched from her cell phone to a professional rig with multiple lenses to capture the scene.

She really was serious about all this, I realized. For me, showing off "my client's" chocolate-peppermint bark was a means to an end. For Ophelia, it was a part of her future—she hoped.

"All right, let's broaden the scope of this thing," Cashel announced. He headed straight for me, then posed at my side.

"Whoa. Nope! I'm not part of the photo shoot," I protested.

I tried to step aside. Cashel's grasp around my waist stopped me. It wasn't as firm as Danny's had been while saving me from the marauding killer Santa Claus, but it was close.

I felt his hair tickle my earlobe. Then he came even nearer. "Just a few snaps," he coaxed. "For Ophelia. Okay?"

I relented. Cashel misunderstood my initial reticence and seemed to think I wanted to be cajoled into participating. That meant he did his utmost to persuade me. He laughed and sweet-talked, posed and hammed it up. Eventually, I enjoyed myself.

Not a single suggestion of Ophelia's went unfollowed. Uniquely among the Sullivans, Cashel actually seemed to fit his depiction in Albany's memoir. Under the right circumstances (that is, while *not* being denied lodging), Cashel really was an easygoing guy. Nothing fazed him— not slipping downhill, not falling off the sled we shared, and not even spilling (tepid) hot cocoa all over his puffer coat when I accidentally jostled his elbow during a break in the action.

"Oh! I'm so sorry." I grabbed a napkin and tried to sop up the mess. Marshmallows and milk foam smeared over his puffer coat's shiny surface. "Ugh. This is only making things worse."

Cashel grabbed my wrist. "It's okay. Seriously."

I felt something odd pass between us. Momentarily stymied by that, I peered into his face, then withdrew my hand. I was aware that this was the first time he'd touched me while not posing for the photo shoot. I didn't know what to think of it.

He chuckled. "You can just buy me a new coat. How's that?"

"Cash!" Ophelia groaned. "Wow. Obvious much?"

I glanced from one to the other of them, bewildered.

Ophelia noticed. "Cash got wind of your donut bonanza," she explained dryly. "Now he thinks you're some kind of big-city billionaire." She rolled her eyes, then gave her brother a nudge. "He thinks he can cash in if he charms you hard enough."

Aha. "That explains the Mr. Nice Guy routine. I get it."

"No!" Cashel protested immediately. "That's really me!"

I looked at Ophelia for confirmation. She shrugged, but her face was alight with mischief. I didn't know whom to believe.

I sensed there was a longtime complex camaraderie between these two. It wouldn't be me who cracked their sibling code.

"Let me prove it to you," Cashel urged. We all leaned on the fence again, having nearly wrapped up our photo shoot. "I'll take you to dinner. I'll make you dinner! Whatever you want."

I hesitated. I didn't want to be unkind, but I also felt keenly aware of my (unfair) racy new reputation in town.

In the meantime, Ophelia cracked up. "You're going to cook a multicourse meal on the hot plate in your room at the Sproutes Motor Lodge?" she guessed. "Nice try, Romeo, but I doubt it."

"Shut up, pip-squeak," Cashel shot back. "I might."

"I'm afraid I'm booked solid with work," I refused gently, not mentioning that my "work" wasn't chocolate making but amateur sleuthing. "Sorry, Cashel. Today has been fun, though."

"I'm not giving up," he warned with a grin. "Not ever."

That made me smile. "My friend Travis would say that makes you sound exactly like my kind of guy," I joked. "Danny too."

"Danny?" He blinked. "You mean that jacked-up dude who's working as Tansy Park's bodyguard? You know him? Small world!"

It wasn't such a stretch that Cashel made that connection. Travis, Danny, and I were all conspicuously new in town—and it turned out that Danny and Cashel had met at the Sproutes Motor Lodge. Apparently, their assigned rooms weren't far apart. Plus, I imagined that being with Tansy made a person extra noticeable.

Cashel swore, looking impressed. "We've only nodded at each other, mostly, but that guy looks like he'd be just as happy to break your arm as shake your hand. Is he always like that?"

Danny? Not with me, he wasn't. He memorably wasn't.

Forcibly, I shook off those memories. "When he's working, he is. When he's not . . ." I considered it. "Yeah, he still is."

We all laughed. I was surprised to have shared even that much personal information with Cashel and Ophelia. Here in Sproutes, I'd almost felt undercover. I still felt guarded, but I guessed that our productive afternoon together had relaxed me.

I'd been sledding once before in Switzerland. The memory made me think about my parents, who were busy working on a site. Later, I promised myself, I'd fire up a video chat with them.

We would miss each other at Christmas this year, but it was comforting having Danny and Travis nearby. My mom and dad still didn't know all the ins and outs of my sleuthing activities.

If I had my way, it would stay that way. Permanently.

"Well, I think I've got all I need for today," Ophelia announced. She looked up from her ever-present phone. "Hayden, can you drop me off at the theater? If I'm lucky, no one will even notice I've been gone. I'm pulling a paycheck, after all."

Her casual mention of deliberately sneaking in instead of earning that paycheck surprised me. But, apparently, not Cashel.

He only smiled. "And maybe a lift to the motor lodge?"

I'd become the Sproutes chauffeur. "Sure." I gestured to my rental car, then gave Cashel a teasing glance. "I'm guessing *none* of the Sullivans have licenses, then? Is it family policy?"

"Not officially," he replied with a grin. "But you know we're all a little unusual. You've read Albany's memoir, right?"

When I nodded, Cashel seemed pleased.

"Then you can't be surprised by anything about us," he kidded. "Now, can you?"

Then we all piled into my waiting car, and I drove us away.

Prudently, slowly, and with all possible caution, too.

Fifteen

I was still pondering Cashel's remarks when I met Danny and Travis that night for mulled cider and Christmas bowling.

That's right. We'd descended on the Sproutes Star Lanes, along with Tansy and a starstruck Josh Levitt, who seemed less bummed than ever about losing the *Sproutes Sentinel* Bake-Off. Every moment spent in the actress's golden company seemed to make him glow just a little bit brighter.

I was happy for him on a personal level. Even more so on a semiprofessional level. Having Josh nearby helped take the load off of Danny and his bodyguard services. That meant we could talk freely, my two best friends and I, about Melissa's murder.

It wasn't the subject I would have chosen to discuss there, amid the bowling alley's multicolored lighted decorations, holiday music, and individual lane tables wreathed with garland and tinsel. Ahead of us, down the lanes, the pins were painted to look like reindeer, with center pins resembling Santa Claus.

It was kitschy, sure. I liked it, though. Of a differing opinion was Albany, who'd skipped out on tonight's gathering owing to a headache. I had my doubts about her supposed ailment. Privately, I believed she was simply too snobby to participate in something as lowbrow as Christmastime-themed bowling.

On the other hand, I reflected, Linda Sullivan had clearly been in pain earlier. If her absence from the *Sproutes Sentinel* was due to migraines, for instance, then maybe Albany was prone to headaches herself. After dropping off Ophelia at the theater, I'd agreed to Cashel's last-minute request to stop at the local drugstore. He'd forgotten about his mother's pain medication.

"I was so psyched about the photo shoot with you that I totally spaced," he'd said with a regretful expression. "I feel like the worst kind of loser—the kind that lets down his mom."

Seeing his downcast face, I would have been churlish to refuse. I didn't ask why Cashel's truck-driving friend hadn't helped him pick up his mother's prescription. There was no point in berating him. I had the sense that forgetfulness was a long-standing issue for Cashel. I commiserated. I'm often sorry about my procrastinating, too, but no one understands.

Unfortunately, after Cashel made it to the drugstore, he emerged with a crestfallen look. "Albany picked it up. Again."

"Oh." I felt sorry for him—and partly responsible for having distracted him earlier, too. "Maybe next time, right?"

"Maybe." Cashel sent me a mopey glance. Then he grinned. "You're so optimistic. It's obvious you don't know me yet."

"It's obvious you don't know me, or you'd know that about me already. My friends can't stop giving me a hard time about it." I grinned back, then dropped him off at the Sproutes Motor Lodge, not altogether sorry the day hadn't included another hostile encounter with Linda Sullivan. I couldn't shake the weird memory of her glaring at me from her living room window.

Now, surrounded by bowling Sproutesians and sipping spiced cider from a Christmas-printed paper cup, I tried to perk up.

Travis was late—a rarity for him—so I turned to Danny.

Not surprisingly, my bodyguard pal watched alertly while Josh helped Tansy improve her bowling form. I was pretty sure hurling an eight-pound ball didn't require that much hip swing.

"That's a gutter ball for sure," Danny predicted drily.

"I don't think they care," I offered as a rejoinder.

"You're probably right." He swung his dark-eyed gaze to mine. "You look like you want to dish about Travis. So spill."

"Me?" I blinked in pretend innocence. It went over about as well as I expected, which is to say, not at all. "Okay, fine."

I'd actually been dying to discuss Travis's unforeseen upbringing in Sproutes, along with the comforting cookies and spaghetti and meatballs he'd found at the Sullivans' household.

I got as far as "He was a free-lunch kid! Poor Travis!"

Danny's opaque gaze darkened. "Having a tough childhood doesn't make someone a pity case," he said in a hard voice.

"I know that! That's not what I mean." I struggled to explain my reaction to learning that Travis's family had been—must have been—fairly destitute. They'd had to accept public assistance. That couldn't have been easy. I said as much.

Danny wasn't having it. Irritably, he crossed his muscular arms. "You can still be happy even if you don't have much."

"Of course you can." I knew that's what he'd done, as a child and beyond. "The thing is, between poverty and divorce—"

"Mmm-hmm?" His expression sharpened dangerously.

I had to tread carefully or risk stepping on Danny's (understandably sensitive) toes. "It can be difficult, that's all," I wound up saying. "I'd always imagined Travis growing up in, if not the lap of luxury, then comfortable circumstances. I didn't know he'd gone to Harvard on a scholarship! You know how secretive he can be about . . . everything. Then, to find out he was raised here in Sproutes by a struggling single mom—"

Danny cleared his throat. "Again, not necessarily a problem." His posture became even more defensive. "For anyone."

No way. I was *not* about to inadvertently dis Mrs. Jamieson and the rest of Danny's extended family. I loved all of them.

"I just hate thinking of anyone struggling, that's all."

He looked away, his expression impervious as he watched Josh and Tansy give a heartfelt "Oh no!" Their latest attempt at bowling didn't so much as teeter Rudolph or his brethren. The ball rolled harmlessly and unbearably slowly down the gutter.

A moment later, Danny grinned at me. "I'm just messing with you, Hayden. I was surprised about Travis, too."

I could have smacked him. "You were 'messing' with me?"

A shrug. "It's hard not to when you're in crusader mode." He stretched his neck. "Plus, I'm still waiting for that donut."

Argh. He wasn't the type to bear a grudge. Like me, Danny fell into the live-and-let-live category. Most of the time.

"You don't even like sweets," I objected reasonably. "Unless the donut shop has some kind of superhot habanero-filled, bacon-topped, salted cruller, you won't be satisfied."

"Sounds tasty. And it's the principle of the thing."

"I'm sorry I left you out. Okay? Are we square now?"

His lighthearted glance said we were. "Let's go back to Melissa B.," Danny suggested. "That night at the B and B, who do you think she was getting high with after hours by the punch bowl?"

I frowned. "You make drugs sound like an inevitability."

"They're not *not* an inevitability. Maybe she was using."

"Maybe she wasn't."

"Now you're just being contrary." He gave me an indulgent look, then got up for his turn at bowling. A strike. "I'm back." Danny settled into his allotted plastic chair, one arm spread along the back of mine. "If Melissa was on something that night, it would explain a lot. Maybe not why she died, but how."

At the touch of his arm on the back of my neck, I balked. I left our conversation hanging while I took my turn (not a strike, but I did knock down a few reindeer and one Santa). Afterward, I argued, "I don't see how Melissa possibly could have done her work as a producer if she were using drugs."

"Then you haven't known very many addicts," Danny

said. "Plenty of them find ways to use while earning money to buy. This isn't an after-school special, Hayden. It's real life."

"Maybe Roger destroyed Melissa. Got his wife addicted?"

"It's not an afternoon soap opera, either." Danny gave me a grin with that quip. Then his expression changed as he nodded toward Star Lanes' shoe-rental zone. "Now I've seen everything. Harvard's here. He brought his own ball *and* shoes. It figures a brainbox like him would have had all his stuff custom made."

A few seconds later, Travis arrived. He set down his bowling bag, then surveyed the scene. His gaze lingered on Tansy and Josh, then returned to Danny and me. "Sorry to be late," my financial advisor said as he hooked his thumb toward the scoreboard. "But I see there's still time to beat both of you."

Danny guffawed. He took a swig of cider. "You're on."

I wasn't so confident. "You barely glanced at the board."

"There are only so many probable outcomes." Travis took a seat and got ready. His shoes came out. I thought I saw him look at them with near fondness. "These were at the Sullivans' house. I left all my bowling gear there when I went off to college."

"You did? Why's that?" I asked while he put them on.

"Didn't think I'd need them. I was aiming for the dean's list, not the bowling club. Anyway, the whole setup was a gift from the Sullivans one Christmas." Travis unzipped his bag, then carried his ball to its place. "I'll jump into the next game."

"Best two out of three?" Danny suggested confidently.

"As long as you feel like losing," Travis agreed.

Uh-oh. It appeared their rivalry wasn't over.

Nor was I off the hook in any way, as it turned out. Because while Danny left the seating area to bowl another strike amid the jolly Christmas music, the decorations, and Josh and Tansy's increasingly frisky flirtation, Travis turned to me.

"I scrolled through Ophelia's social-media accounts this afternoon at rehearsal," my financial advisor told me in his gravelly voice. "I was looking for anyone who seemed threatening or unstable enough to want to strike out against Ophelia."

"Good idea. Were there any likely candidates?"

"Thousands. The comments section of almost any Internet site is a cesspool," Travis said mildly. "But you know how it is. As I was scrolling, new content was constantly coming in."

"That's how social media works, Trav," I joked. "I know you're new at this stuff, though." I recognized my moment and took it. "Speaking of which, why don't *you* have any profiles?"

Travis wasn't biting. Instead, he went on. "Imagine my surprise when these lovey-dovey photos of you and Cashel Sullivan appeared at the top of the feed. Care to explain?"

Damningly, he held up his phone. There we were, the eldest Sullivan sibling and I, caught in what looked like a clinch. I held a package of chocolate-peppermint bark in a carefully posed position; Cashel nuzzled my ear while making goo-goo eyes.

Travis's censorious gaze suggested he did not approve.

"I have to admit, that looks pretty real, doesn't it?" I joked. "But it's all acting. You already knew about my approach to meeting Ophelia. That's not news. This is the next step."

"The 'next step' is making out with Cashel Sullivan?"

Travis put away his phone and devoted his attention to giving me an intelligent, super-serious look. Those were his specialty. "He's bad news. There's a history there that you don't know about."

I already knew he wouldn't share that history. So I didn't ask him to. Instead, I felt my innate contrariness kick in.

"People change, Travis. It happens all the time."

If anything, his serious expression deepened. "Not in Sproutes."

I was flummoxed. "Really? Is this town that bad?" I waved at the earnest, fun-loving bowlers around us. "It looks okay."

"Looks can be deceiving," Travis said as Danny returned.

The three of us exchanged glances while Danny tried to decipher what had gone on in his absence. Nearby, Tansy giggled.

I sighed. "This is *not* the Friendsmas I was hoping for."

I didn't enjoy feeling at odds with either of them. Even if our occasional argumentativeness hadn't upset me, there was also its impact on our investigating to consider. Just then, I felt too annoyed to follow up properly on the issue of Ophelia's nasty social-media commenters. Had she known any of them in real life? Had any of them known her? Had any of them lived nearby?

Just then, I didn't care. Leaving my "Friendsmas" comment dangling, I got up to take my turn. I hurled my bowling ball with extra force . . . and threw my first strike of the evening.

When I turned around, Danny and Travis both pretended to huddle in their chairs, struck dumb by my bowling prowess. As I walked back to them, they broke into perfectly united applause.

Danny's wolf whistle drew every eye to our area. "Booyah!"

I couldn't help laughing. They were sometimes difficult to deal with separately. But together in this way? Impossible.

I knew when the two men in my life were making amends for something, though. Usually, they joked around exactly this way.

My derrière was inches from my seat when Danny spoke up.

"Hey, let's go look at the Christmas lights sometime," he said in a casual voice. "I hear there's a hayride you can take."

That sounds like the kind of cornball thing you'd like, was the subtext. Danny Jamieson was definitely not the hayride type.

"There's a showing of *It's a Wonderful Life* at the Sproutes independent cinema," Travis said, piping up simultaneously. "Let's go."

I looked at their identically (implausibly) guileless faces and nearly burst out laughing. "You've got to be kidding me."

"What?" they asked in unison, looking like choirboys.

I knew what was going on here. Danny and Travis were competing again—competing to give me the very best Friendsmas.

Theoretically, it was a bad idea to encourage that. But I couldn't quite stop. "I like Christmas lights and hayrides," I told Danny. "And I like classic Christmas movies," I told Travis. "You're both on. Who wants to take me gift shopping?"

They both blanched. It was an effort not to guffaw.

"I can see why you two give me such a hard time. It's fun."

They glared at each other, then back at me. Rivalrous, as always.

"Whatever works," Danny said agreeably. "I'm here for you, Hayden. Any time." He lowered his voice. "Day or night."

Whoa. Was it me, or was it getting hot in here?

"I'll take you gift shopping," Travis volunteered. "Unlike some offers on hand, mine can't be misconstrued. It's *shopping.*"

The deliberately quelling look he gave Danny next spoke volumes. I didn't know how much Travis understood about my (let's call it romantic) history with Danny, but evidently, my keeper had more than zero knowledge about it.

I honestly wasn't sure how to feel about that realization.

But back to Christmas—or, this year, Friendsmas. A less scrupulous person might have taken advantage of Danny's and Travis's ongoing competitiveness for her own personal gain. But I didn't. Not much, at least. We'd all enjoy ourselves, right?

Through sheer will, I resisted the urge to line up a few more Christmas-themed entertainments for myself. I knew I could prod Travis and Danny into trying to one-up each other, but that would happen without my interference. Why not be surprised?

Setting aside what they might come up with next Friendsmas-wise, I got back to the problem of solving Melissa's murder.

I described my day and everything I'd learned, starting with meeting Roger Balthasar. I downplayed my high-speed car chase (although Danny's narrowed eyes suggested he'd guessed I'd run into trouble) and emphasized exactly how smarmy the producer had seemed instead. "I still don't know where he went, though."

Danny seemed lost in thought. Then, "I have an idea."

Travis and I listened interestedly.

With evident reluctance, my bodyguard friend went on. "You know that Tansy and I are staying at the Sproutes Motor Lodge," he began.

I nodded, unsure where this was going. Clearly reluctant to say whatever came next, Danny rubbed the back of his neck.

"So is at least one drug dealer," he acknowledged. His wary gaze met mine and Travis's. "Some guy with a big old truck."

I froze. "Does it have a Rudolph nose on the front bumper?"

My oldest friend looked at me as if I'd lost my marbles.

"How should I know that?" he asked with an edge. "I wasn't painting a watercolor of it. I was surveilling its driver for Tansy."

I understood. "How do you know he's a drug dealer?"

This time, Travis joined in on that "You're crazy" look. "It's Danny." He angled his chin at his adversary. "He'd know."

"Hey." Danny's eyebrows drew together. "I'm not a thug."

"Not anymore," I couldn't resist saying. We all knew the truth. At one time, Danny had been living very much outside the law. Still, Travis's point was well taken. "So, go on," I urged.

"So I've seen Roger near that truck," Danny said. "Watching him make a connection . . ." He trailed off. "It's laughably obvious. I can't believe he hasn't already been arrested. Or doesn't have a better supplier. This happened before Melissa's murder, but still, Roger could have paid to have something couriered to him."

I didn't want to know about that. Travis, however, nodded

sagely. Apparently, my keeper contained multitudes—and hid them all. I trusted Travis, but why was he so hard to get close to?

Grumpily, I realized that Albany probably knew everything about him. Their shared history gave her an advantage I couldn't hope to duplicate. All I wanted was to understand the man who'd been such a mystery to me for so long. Was that so unreasonable?

But while I was thinking about that, Danny kept talking.

"Which means Roger could have been at the motel, meeting him, this morning, during the protest at the theater," my bodyguard pal was saying, "after he gave Hayden the slip."

"Hey, I'm new at car chases!" Whoops. I'd outed myself. "And, anyway, Roger didn't seem—"

To be on drugs when he got to the theater, was what I intended to say. But, actually, the show's producer *had* been acting oddly. I regrouped. "To be on anything that couldn't have been prescribed by a physician."

Reminded of Linda Sullivan and the medication Cashel had tried to pick up for her—only to be scooped by his sister—I told Travis and Danny about what I now suspected was the editor's migraine issue. Out of some sense of protectiveness for Cashel, who'd truly seemed to be struggling with making his family respect him, I omitted the part about his failed mission to pick up his mother's medicine. My friends hadn't seen Cashel's face when he told me that Albany had beaten him to the punch . . . again.

Besides, I didn't want to hear Travis gush about Albany.

I told them about Ophelia. "She doesn't have a driver's license, which seems almost as good as an airtight alibi to me," I theorized. "Unless Sproutes has a superior public transit system?" I looked pointedly at Travis, who would know.

He shook his head. "There's no budget for 'superior.'"

"Serviceable is good enough for most people," Danny argued pugnaciously. He looked at me. "I'll check for surveillance cameras at the transit stops. Most cities have them these days."

"That sounds good." I was starting to feel that things were coming together. Maybe in a few more days, we'd have answers. "In the meantime, I've got some chocolate making to catch up on." I told them about the converted-barn work space not far from my B and B. "It's time to make some *Theobroma cacao* holiday magic!"

"Be careful," Danny warned. "It's a public work space. You don't know who you'll find out there. I shouldn't leave Tansy, but I could work out an alternative during rehearsals, when she's not in any real danger."

"Josh would volunteer to watch Tansy," Travis noted.

I waved off both of them. "No problem. I'll keep an eye out for homicidal ornament makers and killer crafters."

Speaking of being watchful, I saw Josh and Tansy eyeballing us suspiciously. If they only knew that Danny, Travis, and I were engaged in (unlikely) amateur sleuthing. Although, it occurred to me, *someone* must know what we were up to.

Otherwise, why would SUV-driving Santa have targeted me?

Maybe he hadn't, I reassured myself, reflexively reaching to rub the ache in my knee, still sore from hitting the ice. Maybe he'd targeted Tansy. Or someone else in a Santa costume.

Maybe he'd been an ordinary, reprehensible drunk driver.

But I couldn't shake the feeling suddenly that I was

being watched—that Travis and Danny were being watched, too.

I looked around the bright, noisy bowling alley. Plenty of people were there. None of them seemed to be paying particular attention to me and my friends. Except maybe . . . that guy?

Alarmed, I felt the hairs on the back of my neck stand at attention. I knew my face must show my suspicion as I quickly averted my gaze. He was fortyish, I estimated, with blond hair and a penchant for flannel shirts. I sneaked another peek.

He winked at me, then raised his glass of spiced cider in a coy invitation to join him. Oh, no. My tarty rep had struck again.

Feeling provoked, I shook my head no. I'd already tested the waters with Albany and Roger about resolving the Donna Brown issue earlier. Next, when I got back to my B and B, Zach Johnson was getting an earful from me about his so-called "helpfulness."

Sixteen

I'm afraid I unleashed a few of my murder-investigation-related frustrations on my B and B's host when I retrieved my room key that night. I wasn't quite my usual diplomatic self as I asked Zach to please stop "helping" me "hook up" with a sponsor for my second phantom holiday product: my chocolate fudge.

Even though I forgot to put on my (fake) timidity for him, Zach didn't notice. He also had the good sense to apologize.

"I'm sorry! Someone must have misunderstood," he told me immediately. "Around here, sometimes gossip gets out of hand."

With that, the issue was sorted, at least as far as I was concerned. But when Zach was still apologizing the next morning—wearing an expression that definitely seemed more embattled than contrite—I began to have my doubts about his sincerity.

It was my turn to make amends. "I'm sorry if I offended you last night," I said as I headed out post–pastry breakfast. "I didn't mean to be accusatory. I was tired. It was a long day."

"Oh?" my host asked archly. "Long day doing what, exactly?" His irked gaze pinned me. "Not making chocolate houses for the charity auction, I know that much. Was I wrong to count on you?"

Uh-oh. It was evident that Zach was holding a grudge. But I couldn't exactly offer the best and most truthful excuse.

"I was investigating your guest's murder," just wouldn't fly.

Besides, I was still bothered by my impression that I'd been being watched last night at Star Lanes. It was like an itch I couldn't scratch. Maybe I was being paranoid, because I *knew* what Danny, Travis, and I were up to, but I didn't think so.

We'd done our best to be circumspect so far. Still, Danny's bodyguard security work for Tansy meant that the three of us couldn't meet in complete privacy. Either we had to bring in Tansy (impossible, given that she was technically a suspect or potentially a Melissa-look-alike victim) or we had to speak in public. It was always possible we'd been overheard, I knew.

Back to Zach's question. *Long day doing what, exactly?*

"Oh, you know—this and that. Making connections." I gave him a breezy wave. "I'm working on helping retool *Christmas in Crazytown* to address some of the protesters' issues."

"Ah, I heard about that. I'm friends with Donna Brown."

"Really?" That was interesting. Not to mention unexpected.

Zach noticed my puzzlement. "We work together on a lot of the same Sproutes town committees and volunteer organizations. The charity auction"—another meaningful, chiding look—"the pj's and hot cocoa Santa's locomotive ride for kids, the arts council, the Christmas parade. You name it, we're on it."

"That's very admirable," I told him. "Was Ms. Brown your high-school English teacher, too, along with being Albany's?"

His frown deepened. "You mean, did she mentor me, too?"

Actually, I wanted to know if Donna had truly mentored Albany—if she'd originally had cause to resent Albany and her memoir. I liked the playhouse director and teacher. I wished there was some way to see her come out ahead in all of this.

Zach didn't wait long for me to answer. Instead, he gave a rueful chuckle. "Nah, I didn't really get to know Donna until way after high school. I wasn't exactly a straight-A student."

"You and most of the world," I told him encouragingly.

"Yeah. There's a reason I'm trying to make a go of it in the hospitality business." Zach's wave encompassed the cozy B&B and its Christmas decorations. "I'm pretty good at the publicity side of things, though. And the decorating is coming along."

"Absolutely." That much was true. "So, Ms. Brown was . . ."

"A really good teacher." Zach picked up the conversational thread I'd left dangling. "At least for the honor roll kids, she was. You know what I mean? If you were one of those brainiacs, there wasn't anything Donna wouldn't do for you. Stay late after school, offer extra credit, do one-on-one tutoring for college admissions tests. Me?" My host gave a self-deprecating laugh. "I'm pretty sure she thought I was a lost cause from the start."

"Oh, I doubt that." I remembered to try to seem shy. I didn't want to let on that Zach had wrongly pigeonholed me.

"Hey, the truth hurts, right?" He laughed, seeming very much cheered up. He glanced at my bag of chocolate-making gear. From the top, my Moleskine notebook peeked out. "You, on the other hand, seem like the studious type. Are you taking notes?"

"Just on my chocolate projects," I hurried to assure him, still preoccupied with thoughts of being watched—of being found out as a part-time amateur murder investigator and paying the price for that somehow. "Nothing more . . . nefarious," I hedged.

Too late, I realized how suspicious that sounded.

Indeed, Zach gazed at me perplexedly. "Nefarious how?"

Everything seemed to become extraordinarily still around us all of a sudden. I noticed the way his shoulders squared.

Was Zach . . . *defensive*? Did he suspect me of sleuthing?

I heard cutlery clatter against a plate in the dining room, smelled freshly brewed Christmas blend wafting from that same space, heard ordinary conversations being carried on by guests nearby, and realized how ridiculous I was being. I hadn't even been in contact with the Sproutes police, because I suspected those officers of being susceptible to Roger's bribe. How could anyone possibly guess that I was looking into Melissa's murder?

Stuck for a response, I settled for an off-the-cuff one.

"Oh, you know, sleuthing," I joked with a grin. "Carrying on a part-time amateur investigation into local murders, that kind of thing." I gave a silly eye roll. "It's important to keep careful notes under those circumstances. Sherlock does it."

At my knowing nod, Zach's gaze wandered to my notebook.

"Sherlock? You mean Sherlock Holmes?" he asked. "I don't think he needs a notebook, actually. He doesn't on TV."

Zach launched into a ten-minute tangent about the two versions of Sherlock Holmes that had aired, both of which he was a fan of but for vastly different (numerous) reasons. As someone who spent her time flying between time zones and perfecting chocolate, I had a tricky time keeping up, but I did my best.

I was relieved to have thrown Zach off the track, however. Once, Danny had told me that the truth can be the best dodge. No one is ever expecting you to baldly confirm their suspicions.

"Anyway, I'm off to get started on those chocolate houses." I surreptitiously tucked my Moleskine deeper into my bag and vowed to keep it hidden from now on. It really did contain my suspects list and notes on the case. "Have a nice day, Zach!"

He wished me the same, and we parted. Sadly, now that my B and B's host had confirmed Donna Brown's practice of choosing favorites from among her students—Albany included—I had to move the playhouse director and teacher higher on my suspects list.

I could never know if Albany had ever used any of her former English teacher's advice while writing her book, but I did know that the memoirist had never acknowledged her mentor. I also knew, even more significantly, that Albany *had* mentioned Melissa Balthasar's support and stewardship in a few interviews.

If mousy Donna Brown had watched those interviews,

she'd know that Melissa B. had taken *her* rightful place in Albany's public acknowledgments. Had that realization made her resent *Christmas in Crazytown*'s producer? Was Donna capable of murder?

If I wanted to find out, I needed to see Donna again. The next time I did, I still hoped to have good news for her on the playhouse front. So, after I hauled on my winter coat, a hat, and a warm scarf and grabbed my gloves, I picked up my cell phone.

"Hi, Roger!" I said when the producer answered. "It's Hayden Mundy Moore. About the changes to the show we discussed . . ."

Four minutes later, I had his loudly voiced agreement.

"Hey, it's simpatico with me if it's simpatico with Albany! Ha-ha-ha!" the producer boomed. I could hear him chewing his breakfast. Gross. "Ordinarily, the writer of the source material doesn't have veto power on casting and script changes, but Albany got into Melissa's head with some 'girl power' stuff."

Except he didn't say "stuff." He used a stronger pejorative word. I gave an inward groan at his crudeness, then kept going.

"Then you'll talk to the cast and crew?" I pushed.

"Sure, sure!" Roger's voice carried to me in duplicate.

Huh? Then I heard other sounds being repeated— silverware clanking, footsteps clomping, holiday music. He was near me.

There was a reason I'd called, rather than seeking him out. I didn't want to wind up in the producer's lecherous sight lines.

"For you? Anything, anything!" Roger bellowed. He laughed.

To me, frankly, he still seemed *too* cheerful. If the producer was on antidepressants to help him deal with his wife's death, someone needed to adjust his dose. He was out of hand.

"In fact, we should get together sometime!" Roger went on. "I've got some other projects you might be interested in!" He broke off and shushed someone near him with no tact whatsoever. "Can't you see I'm on the phone, moron?" Roger complained in a beleaguered tone. Then he returned to me, employing a noticeably more solicitous (for him) voice. "So? Whaddya say, Hayden?"

Was he asking me on a date? He couldn't possibly be.

If he was, I intended to duck him. Forever. But not until things were official at *Christmas in Crazytown*. I hesitated.

Apparently under the impression that I was driving a hard bargain, like Melissa, Roger clarified. "There are better things to spend your money on than donuts!" he informed me. "Like bankrolling Hollywood productions with yours truly! Ha-ha-ha!"

Aha. It all made sense now. Roger, too, had heard about my donut-based largesse. It seemed he wanted to personally cash in.

I heard him coming even closer and made my getaway.

"No, thanks. I'm tied up with other investments right now."

"Well, don't forget about me! I'm just a phone call away!"

I could tell he was closer than that. I slipped out the B and B's front door, onto the porch. In the distance, rows of snow-dusted pine trees marched along the landscape, fronted by pure white fields and a few houses and barns. I saw my destination.

If my boots held out, I wouldn't even need to drive there.

"Don't worry," I told Roger. "I'll never forget you."

I wished I could. I hung up after his next few hearty chuckles, feeling lucky to have escaped further entanglements.

Next up? Albany. Since I wasn't driving to the converted-barn work space where I'd be making my chocolate houses, I was free to phone her, too. It was still too early for rehearsals. I hadn't run into her in the B and B's dining room during breakfast.

She had to be upstairs in Travis's room when she answered my call. I felt a little weird about that. My keeper had led me to believe that he and Albany were platonic friends. Linda's characterization of their ongoing friendship had seemed to confirm that. All the same, I couldn't help picturing Albany and Travis in bed together, naked and snuggly, in a loving embrace.

Albany's crisp, guarded tone suggested quite the opposite.

"I'm a little busy at the moment. What can I do for you?"

"Just checking in on the *Christmas in Crazytown* ideas we spoke about yesterday." I kept my tone upbeat as I made my way past the low fence separating Zach's B&B from the pasture that bordered it. I gave a slight "Oof" as I landed in the snow.

"Are you all right?" Albany asked. I heard holiday music in the background, then an electric razor. Travis's? "Hayden?"

Whoops. "I'm fine. I hurt my knee the other night."

We chatted briefly about the SUV Santa and his scary swerve toward us. I didn't think Albany had been the intended victim (if there had been one), given that the driver had seemed to target those women who were wearing red-and-white velour costumes, but it was understandable that Albany would be concerned.

The snow underfoot got deeper, more powdery beneath a faint icy crust that glittered in the sunlight. I squinted toward the distant painted barn, wondering if I should have driven instead.

There were a couple of vehicles parked there already.

"So, have you thought about the changes?" I pressed, still trudging onward. It was cold out. "Roger says he's up for it."

A laugh. "Roger is up for anything." Albany heaved a sigh while the razor buzzed in the background. "I don't know. It's very late in the process now. With the other delays we've experienced, I'm not sure it's a good idea to disrupt the cast and crew any further. We're lucky the show wasn't canceled."

I acknowledged that while I reshouldered my bag of chocolate-making supplies, regretting my huge chocolate blocks.

I've become pretty strong while working in professional kitchens. I can capably hoist fifty-pound sacks of cacao beans and equally heavy bags of sugar and flour, but I'm not typically called upon to do those things while sinking in fresh snowfall.

Apparently, Albany thought I was only paying lip service to the threat her holiday musical was under, because she dug in.

"I'm serious!" she assured me. "Bringing my book to press was hard enough. There were legal threats, editorial changes, contract disputes—the works. Thank goodness for Melissa." It sounded as though Albany was moving around now, maybe packing her things for the day. The razor and the Christmas carols had both stopped in the background. "Then the show! First, Ms. Brown said she wouldn't cancel *The Nutcracker*. Later, she agreed, totally out of the blue. She had to make me sweat first, just because she could. She was maximally mean about it."

"I doubt she was being mean," I murmured. "She's nice."

The feud between the two of them was at the crux of this.

Albany gave a frustrated sound. "I *know* she's nice! But so am I! I don't appreciate being forced into the role of bad guy in all this." More moving around. "Honestly, I resent it."

"I know you do. It's not fair." It wasn't fair, actually. Albany hadn't started those memes. I put myself in her shoes and realized how upset she'd probably felt on Donna's behalf. "You're not powerless, though. You can do something about it."

Another heavy sigh. "I already tried that. Look, I've got to get down to the theater." A playful note crept into her crisp voice. "Travis tells me he's taking you to the movies tonight?"

Our date to see *It's a Wonderful Life*, aka the opening salvo in my keeper's rivalry with the enforcer. I was looking forward to it. But I didn't want to be sidetracked just then.

"Yes. That'll be fun," I agreed. "Also, I know you did your best after your interview, when things got out of hand online with Ms. Brown." Legions of Albany's fans versus the small-town high-school English teacher: it had never been a fair fight. "There wasn't much more you could do," I told her. "Not then."

"That's right!" Albany sniffed. "I really tried. But it was already out of control." Her voice lowered. "After I came home to Sproutes for Christmas, I tried to make amends again."

"Really? When was this? What happened?"

There was a pause. In the background, I heard a door slam over the phone. "The day after I flew in," Albany told me. "Then again, a few days later, after Melissa died. Losing her made me rethink things. That could have been me! I didn't want my legacy to include unleashing an online mob on an innocent woman, not even accidentally. But Ms. Brown barely listened to me."

"Did you try apologizing?" Sometimes, that was overlooked.

Belatedly, I realized Albany must have disappeared for a while before going to the theater that day because she'd been covertly meeting with Donna Brown, and she didn't want to say so.

"Of course! Believe me, I said *all* the right things."

I pictured the scene as I reached the outskirts of the converted-barn work space. Because of the weather, its doors were shut tightly, but I heard hammering inside. Also, holiday songs.

"I'm sure you did," I soothed. "And you're right. Sometimes it's not enough to *say* the right things, Albany." I knew she'd made no such statement. "You have to *do* the right things, too."

There was a moment of silence while she considered that.

I'd learned while working with my clients that almost everyone was concerned with protecting their reputations. Yet almost everyone also wanted to do the right thing. Sometimes I had to convince people that doing the latter was worth risking the former. In the end, my clients' reputations were usually strengthened by the very act of behaving honorably.

I could name names, but it would violate my contracts.

"I don't care what you say, Hayden!" Albany blurted. "I'm going to do it! I'm going to change *Christmas in*

Crazytown." She hauled in a breath, then rushed on. "Ophelia thinks it's a good idea, too. She says that since the sets are so arty, anyway, no one will notice that the show is slightly different from the book, and if they do, they'll love it! Plus, all those little ballerinas who were at the protest? They'll be amazing."

I nodded, studying the vehicles parked outside the barn. If one of them was a dark-colored Santa SUV, I was leaving. But no.

"They danced last year, so they'll be in form," I agreed.

By now, you may have guessed my idea. To ease the tension between the Sproutesians who wanted *The Nutcracker* and those who wanted *Christmas in Crazytown*— and to mend some fences with Donna Brown in the process—I'd suggested to Roger, Albany, and some of the show's cast and crew that the character of Albany's high-school teacher be included in a couple of newly penned scenes.

The public was interested in Albany's onetime mentor, anyway; their curiosity would spur ticket sales (that's where the appeal to producer Roger came in). Those scenes would, crucially, skew positively toward Donna— thereby silencing the "haters" for good (that's where the appeal to Albany came in).

As far as the tiny ballerinas were concerned . . . well, they were simply adorable. No one could object to their inclusion.

At this point, all sides of the issue were coming together.

"I'm so glad we could work this out, Albany." I watched my frozen breath float toward the barn door. "Hey, do you want to come see *It's a Wonderful Life* tonight with Travis and me?"

What was good for the goose was good for the gander,

right? It was time I truly buried the hatchet with Albany Sullivan.

"That sounds like fun, Hayden! Okay, I'll see you then."

We ended our conversation on an buoyant note. I made one more phone call to Donna Brown, to let her know that everyone needed to meet to hammer out the details, then said good-bye.

I was pleased that things were working out for the better. But as a chocolate whisperer, I still had a lot to do. The huge bars of chocolate in my bag wouldn't become houses without me.

I stepped inside the work space and got down to business.

After several hours' work, I'd made substantial progress on my chocolate houses. I'd made several new Sproutes friends, too.

There was Lawrence, who owned the property the barn was situated on and who was in charge of maintaining the floats for the annual Sproutes Christmas parade downtown, several of which were parked in the barn itself. There was Ginger, Lawrence's wife, who crafted exquisite handmade ornaments using glassblowing and metalworking techniques. Ginger informed me proudly that they were always a big draw at the charity auction.

Also on-site were two retired women who made quilted holiday stockings. They donated some of them to the charity auction and sold the rest at a weekly handicrafts market. I also met Sarah, whose hand-poured artisanal candles made the whole place smell amazing, and her girl-friend, Josie, who used light strings to create freestanding sculptures. They were all talented and all very nice—and all *very* interested in my chocolatiering.

I described my process to them as I followed it, starting by making a big batch of chocolate couverture. That's what it's called when you precisely melt a quantity of chocolate until it reaches the right temperature to retain its structure. If common candy bars didn't go through this process, they would be dull and prone to melting, almost impossible to shape properly.

The air was thick with the luscious fragrance of cocoa butter after I'd created my couverture. Next, I set about molding it. Bakers need cookie-dough "walls" when making a gingerbread house; similarly, I needed chocolate walls—plus roofs, shingles, doors, and shutters. Today I was concentrating on the essential building blocks, though. So it was walls only.

I poured melted sweet chocolate into flat, rectangular molds of various sizes. They would need a while to come to the correct temperature for construction, so this had to be completed ahead of time. It was tricky finding space for all my walls, even though I was building only a couple of chocolate houses for the charity auction. Ginger helpfully moved aside some of her tools to make way; so did Josie, who consolidated some of her light sculptures so I could lay out my molds.

"Hey, if chocolate isn't a good cause, I don't know what is," she joked. "Are you sure you don't need an assistant?"

"I'm afraid I've already got one," I told Josie. Tansy had agreed to meet me after rehearsals for an hour or so. I planned to dig deeper into her fractious relationship with Melissa B. "We're going to be working on decorating, probably after hours."

Lawrence and Ginger nodded, confirming what Zach

had told me about having made special arrangements for me to work late in their converted barn. I'd been unable to refuse that privilege, now that I was (a teensy bit) late with my chocolate houses. See what I mean about me and procrastination? We're old pals.

"Well, if you change your mind, just let me know!"

I promised I would. Then, grateful for the welcome I'd received from these artisanal Sproutesians, I reached for my bag. I doled out a variety of delicious chocolate samples as thank-yous to my new friends, then said my good-byes for the day.

It was time to find out how the cast and crew of *Christmas in Crazytown* were reacting to all the script changes involving Donna Brown and the junior ballerinas. If we were lucky, no one would have, say, a *murderous* reaction to any of the changes. . . .

Seventeen

I'd barely stepped into the Sproutes playhouse before Travis strode purposefully toward me, dressed in his usual suit.

"I've been trying to call you," my financial advisor said.

"Sorry. I was in the car." Driving to the theater had consumed all my attention for that half hour or so. While I'm traveling, I generally don't drive much — something you might have guessed, given my difficulties with the snowy roads. Especially when I'm working abroad, in European or Asian cities, it's more efficient to use trains and public transit. "What's up?"

"I thought you said you'd brokered a deal between Albany, Roger, and Donna Brown to change the show going forward?"

"I did." I was fairly proud of that fact, too. "Move over, top negotiator! I think I'll be joining your ranks soon."

At my joke, Travis didn't even smile. "Are you sure that everything was settled? You didn't misinterpret things?"

"Of course I'm sure. I know better than to make assumptions about business." His irked expression bothered me. I looked past Travis, toward the stage. "Why? What's going on?"

"Isn't Donna supposed to be here?" he pressed.

"Yes." I nodded, perplexed. "To work out the details with Albany and Roger, and to start rehearsing her role. It's going to be a minor walk-on, but she wants to do a good job."

"Something's gotten lost in translation, then."

"What are you talking about, Travis?" I gestured toward the stage. Rehearsals were still under way, complete with singing and dancing. By now, the cast and crew would be wanting to break for lunch. "Everything looks fine up there." I squinted. "Except—"

"Except Donna Brown never showed up. I tried calling her, but I haven't been able to reach her. Nobody has." Travis cast a concerned glance toward the stage. Albany stood there with her arms crossed over her chest, biting her lip. "Albany's worried."

So was I just then. I didn't think that mild-mannered Donna Brown would trick us into believing we'd reached an accord when we hadn't. "There must be a misunderstanding. I spoke with Donna on the phone just a few hours ago."

"Well, she's been unreachable since then." Travis seemed concerned. "If this is the way things are going to be going forward with those changes to *Christmas in Crazytown*, it's not going to work. The show is set to premiere this weekend."

Only a few days away, I knew. I'd spotted the new banner saying exactly that, that someone had hung in the theater's window.

"Don't worry. I'll handle this," I promised Travis.

I spotted Danny, gesturing for my attention. He was

inviting me to join him in the wings, where he stood keeping an eye on Tansy, as usual. I gave him a nod of acknowledgment, then shook my head. I would have liked nothing more than to kick back with my friends while enjoying a chorus of holiday tunes and a nice catered lunch, courtesy of the theater's craft services. But I'd apparently created a new crisis by brokering a deal with Donna that had hit a snag. I'd have to handle that first, then meet up with Danny later.

I gave my bodyguard buddy one of those "I'll call you later" signals, then headed for the lobby. I pulled out my phone.

"Hi, Zach! Listen, can I ask you for a favor, please?"

"Will you pay me in chocolate?" my B&B host asked.

"Is there any other way?" I made sure to keep my tone a bit tremulous, as though I was almost too timid to make the call.

"What do you need?" I heard guests chatting nearby him.

"Well, I'm supposed to meet with Donna Brown in a few minutes," I fibbed shyly, "and I, um, thought I'd written down her address someplace, but now I, uh, can't find it, and—"

"And you're stuck not wanting to call her and say so?"

"Something like that." My fake shyness was filling in all the blanks. That was pretty handy. "Can you help? Since you two are friends? I thought the address was, um, nineteen eighty-nine South—"

Zach's laugh interrupted me. "Not even close! You should actually use that notebook of yours next time." Genially, he supplied the correct address. Chidingly, he added, "Not that I should even tell you that, since this means you *won't* be working on my chocolate houses for the charity auction."

"Oh, I've made loads of progress on those. No worries."

"I want to see you there in Lawrence's barn, burning the midnight oil later!" Zach pushed. "I've already publicized your contribution to the auction. People are very interested."

"My work isn't *that* well known," I told him, mystified by my apparent popularity. "Not to the general public, at least."

"But you're working with Tansy Park on this," Zach countered instantly. "These are Tansy Park chocolate houses! You haven't decided to stop working with Tansy Park, have you?"

A note of alarm had crept into his voice. I understood.

"No, it's just as I promised," I assured him as I left the theater for my parked car. "Tansy will help decorate those houses with her own two celebrity hands. Don't worry a bit."

A sigh flowed over the line. "Whew! That's a relief!"

"I appreciate your including me in the event, Zach," I told him sincerely. Then something else occurred to me. "You said you're publicizing Tansy's participation in the auction?"

"I'd assumed you'd seen it." My B&B host sounded wounded.

I wasn't sure why. Or what he meant. "Seen it?"

"Online!" I heard censure in his voice. "You've seen my site, haven't you? Isn't that what brought you to the B and B?"

Honestly, Travis's suggestion had brought me there. But Zach seemed so indignant that I hadn't seen his site that I didn't want to say so. I pictured a modest Web page featuring the B and B, homemade, with a basic template. That was the sort of thing you saw often while researching independent lodging.

Big hotel chains might have the money to finance

whizzy Web sites with all the bells and whistles, but I knew that someone like Zach might not have the resources for that.

"I'd heard such good things from Travis and Albany," I hedged, letting my unfinished statement suggest that I'd heard those things in addition to viewing Zach's site. My host seemed satisfied by that. "I just hope you're not publicizing Tansy's participation to your readers too much." There had to be dozens of them. "She's trying to keep things low key here in Sproutes."

It wasn't my place to mention Tansy's stalker. But he remained an ongoing concern, especially after opening night, when the media and audience members would descend on the town.

Zach gave a carefree chuckle. "My readers are all awesome!" he guaranteed me. "Don't worry. They'll be cool about Tansy."

"Okay." That had to be good enough for now. I made myself a mental reminder to tell Danny about Zach's site, just in case, then said, "Thanks for your help with Donna, Zach. I really appreciate it. I'll stop by with some chocolate for you later."

After my promise of chocolate compensation, we said our good-byes. Then I pulled out into traffic. It wasn't far from the theater downtown to the playhouse director and teacher's modest house in east Sproutes, so I drove straight there.

I'd been impressed by the variety and razzle-dazzle of Josh Levitt's Christmas decorations when I'd visited his house for our cookie-baking session. But I was reminded, as I pulled up and parked at Donna Brown's place, that everything was relative.

That included Christmas cheer. Donna had outdone herself with a show-stopping tableau. The herd of reindeer in her snowy front yard was lighted and animatronic; her lights were arranged in an exacting grid that encompassed her yard, her house's front exterior wall, and her roof. She'd hung reams of lights on the eaves, twined them around each porch pillar, and spelled *Merry Christmas* on her garage door in huge letters.

Every one of those lights was on and flashing as I made my way up the sidewalk. That was odd, I thought. Most people didn't keep their lights on all day, even if they were home. I'd sort of hoped that Donna had passed by me, unnoticed, on her way to the theater, and that I'd find her house empty. The day had turned overcast, though. I reasoned that if Donna's fancy holiday light setup was on some kind of timer or sensor, it might have turned on automatically. I couldn't deny that it would have been nice for Donna, after a long day of teaching or playhouse directing or Christmas parade volunteering, to come home to a merry house.

On the porch, standing atop a Christmas kitten–printed doormat that started playing "A Holly Jolly Christmas" in meows when I stepped on it, I eyed Donna's huge wreath and rang the doorbell.

It chimed to the tune of "Christmas Is A-Comin'," an old Bing Crosby song. I caught myself humming along. What can I say? I'm a sucker for an old standard, especially during the season.

As jolly as that doorbell chime was, it didn't summon anyone. I tried again, then used my phone to try calling Donna.

No answer. I glanced around for a neighbor I could ask for clues to her whereabouts, but the weather seemed to be keeping everyone indoors. A snowstorm was definitely threatening.

I shivered, then peered through the door's side windows. They were frosted liberally with fake snow. I couldn't see a thing. I moved down the porch to the closest window; it was also artificially frosted, with a glowing border of Christmas lights.

A third ring of the doorbell, coupled with a hearty knock on the door, drew no response. Neither did a hasty text to Donna.

I was starting to get annoyed. I'd gone out of my way to try to defuse the situation yesterday   to mend fences between Donna and Albany. Now I felt punked by the whole experience.

Had Donna been merely pretending to go along with me?

Wishing I'd had the foresight to ask Danny to trail her—not that he could have, with his duties to Tansy—I tried the door handle. Nada. The door was locked tight. My bodyguard buddy had the skills to pick the lock, but I wasn't Danny. I hadn't once specialized in burglaries. Travis would have been appalled by my line of thinking, but my financial advisor had the luxury of access to most things. He didn't need to break in anywhere.

Maybe the back door? Deeming my moto boots sufficient for the job, I picked my way through the snow, carefully avoiding all the twinkling lights and decorations. It was a tight squeeze between the houses to Donna's side gate. Thankfully, I unlatched that barrier easily with my gloved hands, then kept going.

As I rounded the corner, I spied something in the snow. *Someone* in the snow, very close to the house. Oh no.

With my heart in my throat, I raced over. Donna Brown lay motionless in her backyard, her body twisted at a horrible angle. I thought I saw blood pooled beneath her in the snow.

I definitely saw her eyes staring sightlessly upward.

No, no, no. Not Donna. My hands shook as I reached for my phone. I dialed for help. I could barely get out the words.

I felt on the verge of hysteria as I spoke with the police. Maybe that was why I found myself feeling so angry. Given what had happened with Melissa Balthasar, I did not expect anyone to genuinely seek out answers to this. I felt embittered. Helpless.

I blinked up at the sky, trying to clear my head. It was no use. I felt hideously aware that there was *another* dead body at my feet. This was the second in less than a week! There was no telling when this would stop. Donna hadn't even been an Albany look-alike, I babbled to myself. Her death didn't make sense.

I hauled in a breath, then looked around. Before anyone else arrived, I needed to try to figure out what had happened.

Okay. There was a metal extension ladder propped against the siding, just a few feet away. There were several packages of Christmas lights on the snowy ground nearby. Inspired by them, I looked up. At the peak of the roof, there was a Santa's sleigh with lighted reindeer. Unlike the front side, though, the rest of the roof was bare . . . all except for one unplugged light string.

It dangled there, seemingly forgotten. I imagined that Donna had been finishing her holiday decorating, with all the lights on to help her place them, when disaster struck.

Here, there were no Christmas lights on the eaves, as there were up front. Tellingly, the snow at the roof's edge had been dislodged. Icicles had broken off from the roofline. A few of them had probably landed in the snow moments before Donna had.

She'd fallen from her roof, I surmised. Something akin to relief mixed with my shock and horror. As bad as this was, maybe it *wasn't* another murder. Maybe I was getting carried away.

I gripped my phone more tightly, then risked another glance at Donna as I tried to reconstruct the scene. On her way to the ground, she must have struck her head on her snow-shrouded metal barbecue grill. Its waterproof cover seemed to have been dusted with snow until a few minutes—hours?—ago, when Donna had fallen.

Judging by the blood in the snow, she must have landed with considerable force, I guessed with a shudder. I was surprised none of her neighbors had come to investigate the sound . . . not to mention whatever ghastly sounds poor Donna might have made as she fell. She must have desperately grabbed her slick, icy roof shingles, I thought, while searching with her sliding feet for something to stop her fall. She must have known the danger.

The realization made my heart pound. I felt dizzy, too. I would never become blasé about this scenario—about finding dead bodies, especially of people I'd known and liked. I felt sad and overwhelmed, sorry I hadn't arrived early enough to save Donna.

While I'd been contemplating picking the lock on Donna's front door, had she been sliding to her doom back here? The thought was horrific. I didn't think that was the case, though. I thought I would have heard something. But the idea haunted me all the same. I wheeled around, feeling queasy. When I'd come to track down Donna, I'd never expected to find anything like this.

All those people at the theater—I'd have to tell them.

I heard sirens in the distance. Help was coming, I realized. In a last-ditch effort to amass all the information I could while I was still alone, I tried to take in everything. There were footprints in the snow. Footprints! Those were almost as good as fingerprints, right? People's shoes were unique. Sure, these footprints were a mess. Someone had tromped down the snow in multiple directions. But if I could compare them . . .

I wished I could take photos of them, but I was stuck on the phone with the 911 operator. So I did the next best thing. Shakily, I took a tentative step, then compared the result of my own moto-boot print with the other prints. Some of the impressions were smaller; those were likely Donna's. She was—*she had been*—more petite than me. A few prints, though, were larger.

I examined them, trying to discern any patterns. Wasn't that what the police did? Identify what kind of footwear had made the prints, then figure out where those shoes had been sold, then pinpoint the murderer, using that information? It was likely that situation was nothing more than a television fantasy, I reminded myself, thinking of the conversation I'd had with Zach earlier—and even the similar chat I'd had with Josh—about TV crime dramas. There was no question that TV shows sacrificed accuracy sometimes for the sake of storytelling. But I was desperate for a lead. Any lead at all.

The sirens screamed closer. I couldn't help wishing Donna had been even slightly *less* conscientious about hanging her holiday lights this year. She was supposed to have been at the Sproutes playhouse. What had possessed her to do this first?

Trying to figure out exactly that—ideally, before the authorities arrived—I stepped toward Donna's kitchen window. On my phone, the operator said something soothing yet businesslike. I barely heard her. I focused on placing one foot after the other, stepping inside Donna's footprints to determine her movements. I placed my gloved hand on the windowsill for leverage.

I peeked. Inside Donna Brown's kitchen, something moved.

Alarmed, I reared back. I gave a startled cry. A moment later, just as I realized it was Donna's cat that I'd seen inside, I sensed a whoosh of air behind me. *What the . . . ?*

I heard a faint swishing sound, then smelled . . . milk? That was the last thing I remembered before the world went black.

When I opened my eyes, Danny was there.

Typically enough, he was frowning at me. "Welcome back."

"Hi." Confusedly, I blinked at him. "What's happening?"

His expression took on a darker edge. "You're concussed."

I tried to sit up. *Ouch.* Pain speared through my skull. Also, something cold and clanking arrested my movements. Huh?

Dazedly, I realized I was no longer at Donna Brown's house. I wasn't even outside. I was someplace fairly chilly, in a bed.

"Try not to move, dummy." Danny sounded aggrieved. "That's the universal reaction to being told you're concussed. It's as if everyone thinks they can run away from it or something."

His gaze focused on me. He looked . . . *tender*. Clearly, I was woozy if I thought tough-guy Danny Jamieson was going soft on me. I mumbled something to him. My mouth felt papery. Yuck.

If I wasn't outside anymore, then where was I?

"Huh?" Danny leaned closer. "Do you need something?"

I needed him to listen. I must have said so, because I saw his mouth quirk. Heartened, I added, "I wasn't running away. I was sitting up, to prove that you're wrong. This is probably just a headache, not a concussion. It'll go away in a few minutes. You'll see."

"Nice try. It's not a headache. The doctor's already been here. You definitely have a concussion." After that discouraging statement, Danny glanced at someone who stood just beyond my view. Travis maybe? "Tansy wants to know if this will affect your plans to decorate those chocolate houses of yours. She's hoping some of them won't be good enough for anything but eating. I've gotta say, she's a beast when it comes to sweets." He added a grin. "Worse than you, and that's saying something."

I felt too foggy to keep up with his teasing. "Where am I?" He'd mentioned a doctor. I glimpsed industrial-looking acoustical ceiling tiles and dingy yellow-painted walls. "Is this a hospital? Danny, am I in the hospital? What happened?"

I had a dim recollection of being at Donna Brown's house. Of finding her lying there, lifelessly and tragically. Oh no.

"You're lucky." Danny nodded, as though hoping to convince us both of that. "It was an outdoor Christmas Santa statue that you got walloped with. It was pretty light. It could have been worse. Probably, whoever did it thought it was heavy ceramic."

Yikes. "A Santa statue?" I imagined one of those decorative garden gnomes, except made to resemble shorty Santa Claus, in Donna's yard. *"Walloped with?"* I couldn't remember that at all.

"It didn't even smash. Your big old noggin held up

pretty well," my closest friend encouraged me. "Only a few stiches."

"Stitches?" I tried to put my hand to my head. No dice. Whatever had clanged before did so again. I looked down. Uh-oh.

Danny's breezy tone remained unaffected. That was how I knew the situation was serious. My closest friend was many things, but he was never *breezy*. I knew he was trying not to worry me.

I appreciated the sentiment. However, "Where am I?"

"The good news is"—Danny inhaled, then ducked another glance at whoever was in the room—"you're not in the hospital!"

As he said so, Travis came into view. At the sight of his resolute, concerned face, I nearly burst into blubbering tears.

Did a concussion make you emotional? Maybe I did have one.

"Hayden, you're in jail," my financial advisor said.

He went on explaining, but I didn't hear a thing, I was too busy listening to my heart pound in fear. *Jail?* I felt numb.

Danny gave Travis a shove. His expression was formidable. "Don't tell her that way!" he barked. "You're scaring her!"

Too late. There was no help for it now. The fact that my bodyguard buddy leaned solicitously toward me and gave me the most purely reassuring look I'd ever seen on his face didn't help a bit. I was *in jail*? How? Why? What was wrong with my arm?

"It's going to be all right, Hayden," Danny told me gently. "This is only a city jail. It's not even a county lockup!"

He smiled, as though that was excellent news all around.

Tears rushed to my eyes. That was when Travis gave Danny a shove right back. My keeper held my hand. "You're not being charged. Not right now." A reassuring smile made his face look twice as handsome. "Getting coldcocked really saved you today."

I squeezed shut my eyes, willing my tears to stop. I felt a couple of them trickle down my cheeks instead. "You two are the worst at reassuring somebody," I cracked hoarsely. "I'm scared."

They gave each other identical accusatory looks. Beyond them, I now heard people talking. A door slammed. Keys jingled. *I was in the slammer.* That explained the clanging I'd heard.

Handcuffs. I raised my arm to confirm I was a prisoner.

Travis saw my rising panic and squeezed my hand. "The police found you in Donna's backyard when they responded to your call," he explained. "They are pretty sure, given that you were the one who called nine-one-one, that you weren't there with criminal intentions. In fact, the nine-one-one operator heard you get clobbered."

I shuddered. I still didn't remember that part clearly.

"Since you couldn't very well crack a decorative holiday gnome over your own head, especially from behind," Travis said, "the police decided you were probably blameless in whatever happened to Donna Brown. Or, at worst, criminally stupid."

Humph. "That doesn't explain why I'm here, locked up."

Travis looked even more troubled. "You don't remember?"

"Remember what?" I swabbed overwhelmed tears from my eyes.

He and Danny traded wary glances. Then Travis said,

"The doctor told us that you'd probably remember things gradually."

That didn't help right now. "Remember what?" I repeated.

My advisor looked trapped. He stammered, "Well, you, uh—"

"You accused the police of not caring about 'Donna's murder,'" Danny interrupted brightly. There was a definite "That's my girl!" gleam in his eyes. "You were yelling about Melissa B.'s murder, Roger's bribe—the whole nine yards. At first, they thought you were drunk, since you were so crazy."

"Then they saw that your scalp was bleeding," Travis added evenly, apparently having thoroughly briefed himself on the circumstances, "put two and two together, and called a medic."

"They should have taken me to a hospital, not here." I frowned, still not understanding. "What am I doing in jail?"

I gulped after I said it, wishing I could remember.

Danny looked chipper. "You're here for the attempted assault." He brightened further. "It was pretty intense."

"Attempted assault?" I stared at them both, astonished.

Travis held up his hands to calm me. "You didn't assault anyone. It's a legal statement." He threw Danny a reproachful glance. "You said a few things, made some accusations . . ."

"Made some enemies at the local PD," Danny put in. It occurred to me that he, notorious avoider of police stations everywhere, had come to one to be with me. On purpose. He cared.

"Got a little out of line," Travis finished staunchly, "but everyone understands you were injured. I spoke with a few of the officers already. They've agreed not to press charges."

That was a relief. "Then I have to stay only overnight?"

I tried to keep the telltale tremor from my voice. I failed. I didn't want to spend a night in jail. Any jail.

"Nah." Danny's grin lit the room. "I already bailed you out. You're free to go whenever you feel ready to walk out."

I could have hugged him. "I could hug you." More tears.

He only shrugged. Then, to my bewilderment, Danny leaned nearer. Very gently, he thumbed away a tear from my cheek.

"You'd do the same for me," he said. "Hell, you have."

"It was a good use of his retainer salary," Travis added.

My financial advisor seemed much less thrilled with Danny's generosity than I was. At that moment, I didn't care. "Thanks."

Danny grinned. "You're not cut out for the big house."

I laughed. "Are you saying I'm not tough enough? You just watch, mister," I threatened. Then I remembered something. I switched my gaze to Travis. "Our movie date! Did we miss it?"

"Don't worry about that," he said immediately. "You're more important than any old movie." His throaty tone had deepened.

I was lucky that both of them cared about me. I inhaled.

"I'm happy you think so," I said honestly. "Now, let's get out of here!" I looked straight at Danny. "I just thought of something that needs to be done." I glanced at Travis. "And sorry, Trav. But this is something only Danny can help with."

Eighteen

As cover for our mission, Danny and I moved our Christmas lights–viewing hayride to that night. My bodyguard buddy wasn't thrilled about putting me on a quaking, stopping-and-starting vehicle while I was still (mildly) concussed, but I insisted.

"I feel fine now!" Which wasn't strictly true. My headache persisted, joining my achy knee in making life difficult for me. I still had gaps in my memory, too. But I was resolute. "Plus, if anyone questions us later, I want us to have an alibi."

"I'm already intrigued." Danny's eyes gleamed.

I told him my plans. "It's simple," I said. "Donna had a cat. I saw it through her kitchen window." I'd glimpsed evidence of the little critter's furry existence on her coat, too. "Did anyone at the police station talk about rescuing her cat?"

My friend frowned. "Nobody reported seeing a cat."

That was what I'd thought. "But the police searched the house?" I still wanted to know what had happened. "For clues?"

"It's not an official crime scene. They think Donna's fall might have been an accident." Of course they did. "On the other hand, the police might still be watching the place, so—" Danny broke off, then eyed me with something close to apprehension. He'd guessed my intentions: a break-in, obviously. "Seriously?"

"Yes, seriously. We have to get into Donna's house and rescue her cat. It's probably scared half to death in there. It's abandoned now! No one will be coming to take care of it."

Eventually, I assumed, Donna's next of kin would arrive. Someone close to her would take possession of her cat. But Donna had been single; a casual questioning of Travis had told me the police hadn't yet reached anyone. That left an unknowable number of nights for Donna's poor cat to hide, all alone, in her house.

I couldn't bear the thought of it. I'm an animal lover through and through. The fact that I don't have any pets of my own (yet) doesn't change that. I'm sure I'll adopt a lovable golden retriever the minute I quit gridskipping for good.

Also, given the police's seeming indifference to Melissa Balthasar's murder, I wasn't sure anyone in Sproutes would go out of their way to care for Donna's cat. Plus, I wanted a look inside her place for clues. If anyone caught me doing that, rescuing Donna's cat would be my excuse.

Which was a long way of saying that, yes, Danny and I jumped off the Christmas-lights hayride that night and sneaked over to Donna's street in east Sproutes.

We made our getaway while the hayride was stopped for carolers. I doubted that even Tansy and Josh, who'd come along, noticed. It was a dark night in mid-December, after all.

I did have one lingering concern. "Won't Tansy need you?"

Danny shook his head. "Not for the few minutes this will take." He glanced over his shoulder at me. I saw his mischievous grin flash in the darkness. "I told Josh I wanted to sneak away with you to make out. He said he'd watch Tansy. I trust him."

"Okay, cool." I crept in Danny's wake down the dim street. Fortunately, some of the residents hadn't lighted their houses with quite as much Christmas zeal as Donna had; we were nearly invisible. Belatedly, Danny's earlier remark registered. I did a double take. "You told Josh you wanted to make out with me?"

He nodded. "Why not? I thought it was believable."

"You couldn't think of anything else as an excuse?"

A shrug. "It was expedient." Danny led us along Donna's side yard. He made his way to the back door. "Here. Hold this."

"This" was his lock-picking gear. I fumbled to catch the small pouch he carried it in, trying not to envision all the less than lawful black marks on Danny's record. Thievery. Forgery. Bar brawls and general criminal misbehavior. Next to them, a simple bump key and torsion wrench were nothing, right?

"I'm a little disappointed you're still carrying this," I murmured, low enough that we wouldn't be overheard. "You were supposed to be reformed, remember?" I was worried about him.

He paused to toss me an ironic look. "Is it okay if I finish breaking into this house, the way you asked me to, before we have a heart to heart about my life on probation?"

My heart leaped to my throat. "You're still on probation?"

"Nope. That's how little you know about it. Also, you're missing the point." Danny wiggled the doorknob. The lock popped open. He gave me a sarcastic, chivalrous wave. "After you."

Duly chastened, I stepped inside. Instantly, I felt enveloped in Donna Brown's mousy, trinket-stuffed life.

I'd brought a pocket flashlight (Danny forbade me to use it while he handled the job), but I didn't need any extra light to see that the theater director and teacher's small house was packed with overstuffed furniture and tchotchkes. There were souvenirs of shows at the Sproutes theater, a bulletin board crammed with reminders, a calendar full of volunteer events, crafting projects in various stages of completion, and more Christmas décor than I'd seen anywhere short of a boutique.

The realization that Donna would never again enjoy the bits and pieces of her busy life—or her Christmas tree!—made me sad.

Danny distracted me by saying, "The police found one of those Santa Claus costumes in here. It was Donna's size."

I thought about that, squinting as I searched for the cat. "I don't remember seeing her at the Santa pub crawl. Do you?"

My friend gave me a headshake. He crouched to look under the floral-print sofa. It was chockablock with holiday pillows.

"That doesn't mean Donna wasn't there, though," Danny said as he straightened. "That's the whole point of a costume."

"We could have overlooked her. She was involved in a lot of community events." I hurried down the hallway, past a litter box, following my nose toward the cat's likely hiding place. I told Danny about what I'd learned from Zach—that Donna had, indeed, favored some of her students. That she definitely had considered herself Albany's unappreciated creative-writing mentor. "If Donna blamed Melissa for taking her place with Albany—"

"She might have wanted revenge for that."

I agreed. "As recently as today, Donna was my top suspect." I reached the bedroom and experienced a new wave of melancholy. It was intrusive to be there. Spooky too. "It's going to be harder to prove anything now that Donna is gone, though."

"Why?" Danny dropped to the floor, agile and stealthy. That cat didn't have a chance of staying hidden.

"For one thing, Donna can't confess," I told him.

My buddy crawled farther, his torso half enveloped by Donna's ruffled Christmastime bed skirt. I heard the cat yowl.

Lights shined against the bedroom window. Car headlights. I felt momentarily trapped in their glare. Donna had died before closing her drapes for the evening. She'd let in the whole world.

Had she also let in a murderer? Or had her fall from the roof been an accident? Panicked, I threw myself onto the carpet.

At my side, Danny graciously ignored the *oof!* sound I made upon impact. He continued coaxing the cat. "What's wrong?"

"Someone's outside," I whispered. "Hurry up!"

"Persuasion takes finesse. It can't be hurried. That's going about it all wrong." His voice dropped into a pet-friendly register on that last remark, turning singsongy. "Here you go!"

I saw him reach into his jacket pocket for some kibble. It disappeared beneath the bed. "I didn't even see you grab that."

"You need to learn to pay attention, Miss Marple." Soon after that, Danny emerged with Donna's pet cradled against his burly chest. I heard the cat purr. My security-expert pal stood, then scratched the cat between its furry ears, making friends.

"Nice finesse." I was impressed. "Let's get out of here."

"Okay." In the dark, Danny led the way. "Grab the kibble."

I balked. "How am I going to explain carrying a bag of kibble on the Christmas-lights hayride a few minutes from now?"

"How am I going to explain carrying a fifteen-pound cat?"

Hmm. It appeared that we hadn't thought this through.

"You just got out of jail," Danny pointed out, smiling at the cat as he cuddled her more closely. "You're an official badass now. You can pull it off. No one will dare question you."

"Really?" Maybe there were unforeseen benefits to having a bad reputation. If anyone knew about them, it was my friend.

"No, not really." He flashed a grin as we rushed into the living room, still alert for any clues. "Not for you, at least."

"Hey!" I objected, stopping on my way to the back door. Danny wasn't in the mood to humor me. "Go wait outside."

He veered in the opposite direction from the back door. I watched him go, feeling indecisive. I still needed kibble.

But where was he going? I heard the subtle whoosh of air as he opened a door somewhere nearby. Defiantly, I followed him.

"If you're getting yourself arrested, I am, too!" I hissed at him in an undertone, still worried about the headlights I'd glimpsed through Donna's bedroom window. "We haven't even found any clues here. It's not worth spending time in the hoosegow."

I'd tried to lighten the mood with that cheesy jailhouse

slang, but it was no use. Not after I saw what Danny had found.

I wheeled to a stop in the doorway he'd passed through and looked around. At my feet, in the small mudroom I found myself in, were a broom, a dustpan, and an unopened bag of dry kibble. Ahead of me, in the garage that had been adjoined to the mudroom, was . . .

"Is that Swerving Santa's dark-colored SUV?" I asked.

"Maybe so." Gravely, Danny looked over his shoulder at me, trying to gauge my reaction. "I had a hunch we might find this here. I was trying to keep you from seeing it, just in case."

Just in case I broke down in tears again or something, I guessed. That explained his detour. "You don't have to baby me."

"I might." He appeared unyielding. Then, "You didn't know?"

"About Donna's SUV? We've spoken only a handful of times."

None of those times had taken place beside her incriminating vehicle. All the same, it occurred to me that my ongoing sympathy for Donna might be misguided. Maybe she *deserved* to be at the top of my suspects list. If so, what now? Now that she was dead, I couldn't get any answers from her.

"Feeling all right?" Danny swaggered to my position on the landing, still holding the cat. His gaze searched mine. "You were almost mowed down by this SUV that night. Don't freak out."

"Yes, sir." I looked at it, expecting terror to strike. It didn't. It could have been the same SUV. Or not. "This doesn't technically prove anything." Although it was chilling to think that I could reach out and touch an SUV that had been used in an attempted vehicular attack. "We have to find out if anyone saw Donna at the Santa pub crawl. She must have been with someone."

I doubled back to the kitchen, not sorry to leave behind that dark-colored SUV. Danny and I were both wearing gloves—because of the cold and because of our covert mission—so I was unconcerned as I seized a few things from the area.

The unopened cat food. A canvas tote bag. A crumpled, mostly used-up bag of kitty litter. One of those disposable foil pans used for baking cakes.

Don't use those pans for baking your own chocolate goodies, by the way. Not if you can help it. They don't conduct heat efficiently. That means you might wind up with mushy brownies or soggy-bottomed chocolate cakes. There's no reason to gamble with your best cacao, is there? I planned to use that foil pan as an improvised kitty litter box, so that was different.

Last, I grabbed Donna's electronic tablet, where I hoped to find her full schedule. "Maybe she kept a diary," I theorized. "If she detailed her resentment and her murder plans, we've got it made." I felt my mood worsen. "*If* the police will listen."

In Sproutes, it seemed, that was a big *if.*

For once, Danny didn't join me in bad-mouthing the local police force. "They weren't that bad at the station earlier."

"They essentially chained me to a hospital bed," I reminded him with renewed ire. "They weren't that great, either."

"If we're lucky, something will break soon."

I headed for the door. "Am I hearing things, or are you actually being optimistic about solving a murder case?"

A pause. Then, "You'd better have your ears checked."

I smiled, then slipped out the back door.

* * *

As it turned out, the best excuse for our brief absence from the Christmas lights–viewing hayride was the thing we most wanted to hide: the cat. On Danny's suggestion, we brazened out our return, showing up at the next stop with Donna's cat in full view. Rather than becoming suspicious, everyone applauded.

"You got Hayden a kitty for Christmas? That's *so* sweet!" Tansy squealed, reaching out to pet the black-and-white cat.

A few more hayriders joined in. Danny cast me a triumphant look, reminding me of our conversation a few minutes earlier.

"Won't people suspect we're up to something?" I'd asked when my friend suggested this plan while offering me the cat to hold on to. "What if someone recognizes Donna's cat?"

"It's a cat, Hayden. No one will recognize it."

"But if someone does, we won't have a good excuse."

"No one will recognize the cat, especially in the dark," my bodyguard buddy had insisted. "Cats are pretty interchangeable."

"Not to their owners, they aren't!"

Danny's expression had said it all. *This* snuggly cat's owner wouldn't be there tonight, or ever again. So I'd agreed.

Well, Danny had been right. No one had even blinked.

Partly, that was because everyone accepted the idea that Danny would give me a cat as an early Christmas gift. Partly, it was because it really was dark outside, aside from the holiday lights up and down the streets we toured, and it was difficult to make out any details of the cat's appearance. Partly, it was because the hayride ended early, and on a semi-threatening note.

"Sorry, everyone!" the driver announced a few minutes after Danny and I rejoined the group. "We're going to have to head back early. The snowstorm is headed this way, earlier than expected. I'd suggest everyone go home, for safety's sake."

There was a unified groan of disappointment, mingled with resignation. As one, we all glanced up at the gloomy sky.

There really was a new chill in the air. A few snowflakes had started falling, too, swirled by the steadily rising wind.

"I'll take you back to the B and B," Danny told me.

"No need for that. My car is parked a few streets over, remember? Just outside Donna's place. I can make it by myself."

His expression remained unyielding. "I'll bring you back into town tomorrow morning so you can pick up your car."

"But what about Tansy?" I objected with a glance at her. "You have to take her back to the Sproutes Motor Lodge."

"You have a concussion, Hayden. You're not driving."

"I can get someone else to do it for me. Maybe Josh?"

My friend's hard look disagreed. "It's settled."

But I persisted. "I don't want you to shirk your duty."

"*You're* my duty," Danny told me. "First and foremost."

That was touching. It was. But . . . "I feel fine. Really!"

That was when Tansy gave Danny a poke. I couldn't tell if the actress had overheard us. "I'm spending the night with Josh," she said with a lift of her chin. "You're *not* invited."

Beside her, Josh cuddled Tansy on the hayride bench.

He seemed thrilled with her decision. Warily, Danny studied them.

I couldn't help thinking that this was awfully convenient. At the same time, Tansy was a grown woman. She'd hired Danny.

She could give him the night off at her discretion.

My pal shrugged. "You're the client. It's up to you."

Danny had already told me that Tansy was one of his "lookie-loo" clients. He didn't think she genuinely needed protection. The actress had essentially confessed as much to me, too.

"Whatever we do, we'd better hurry up about it," Josh put in as the hayride lurched down the street. "The ride's ending."

I saw that it was. We were nearing the Sproutes town common, where the hayride had kicked off. A short while ago, the area had been packed with shoppers, Christmas lights viewers, and children begging their parents for candy canes and chocolate Santas. Now it was almost empty. Cradling the cat, with my tote bag full of borrowed cat supplies at my feet, I shivered in the cold.

Danny didn't notice. He was busy giving Tansy a warning look.

For her part, the bombshell laughed him off. "Danny! It's fine." She clung to Josh's arm. "You can't tell me you haven't already researched Josh. If you hadn't, we wouldn't be here."

She had a point. I had to lift my estimation of Tansy's intelligence. Danny was always hypervigilant while working.

"You'll call me if anything happens," he told Tansy firmly. It was emphatically not a suggestion. "Anything at all."

"Well, not *anything*." Tansy tittered. "I like my privacy!"

"I can be there in twenty minutes," Danny reiterated.

"Wow. You're relentless," I joked as the hayride stopped moving. "Remind me not to hire your security services anytime soon."

"*You* don't have to pay." Danny gave me an unreadable look. Those were his stock-in-trade. "You're always covered."

Travis would have said that was obvious, since Danny was on a semipermanent retainer as my (sometime) bodyguard. But I knew there was more to it than that. There was friendship, above all.

So, just for the night, I decided to let friendship take the forefront. For the first time in a long while, I relaxed.

"I'm in your hands," I told Danny truthfully.

Then we all parted ways before the blizzard encroached.

Nineteen

There was something comforting about letting go. Since arriving in Sproutes, I'd been on my guard, watching for danger, alert to any chance that a killer might be tracking me.

That night, as I unlocked my B&B room to let in myself and Danny, I finally felt (somewhat) at ease. Ever since I'd discovered Melissa's body, I'd been creeping inside my room, hitting the light switch to illuminate the place as fully as possible, then examining it for signs of intruders. I'd been tense and alert, steeling myself for a potential fight.

I didn't creep in or tense up that night. But Danny could tell what I'd been going through anyway. He noticed the B and B–logoed umbrella I'd stashed in the miniscule foyer, moments before I reached for it—one handed—on autopilot while holding the cat.

"Expecting rain?" he asked with a quirk of his mouth.

"Just being cautious." I left the umbrella where it stood.

"You might do better hurling the cat at any intruders," my friend added jokingly, but his gaze seemed to approve.

He noted the heavy lamp I'd moved from the bedside table to the credenza, which was closer at hand. "The lamp is a solid idea, though."

I nodded, then realized, "Hey, my headache is almost gone."

"That's a good sign." Danny pushed the door shut, then secured all the locks. He studied my room, seemed to find it acceptably safe, then grabbed one of my boxes of improvised chocolate "products." Fudge packets rained onto the desk.

"Hey! What are you doing? I'm going to need those."

"I'm taking care of the cat." He put the empty box on the floor, stuffed in a hand towel, then eased the cat from my arms.

I watched as he got her settled with water and kibble and the foil litter box nearby. His efficiency was impressive.

"How do you even know how to do all that?" I asked him. As far as I knew, Danny had never owned a cat. Or any pet.

A shrug. "It's not exactly genius territory, now is it?"

Outside, the winter wind howled. I heard the icy snow scour the lighted windowpanes. We'd beaten the blizzard by moments.

As though reminding me that we'd tempted fate by coming all the way from Sproutes to the relatively remote B and B, the lights flickered. Danny lit both of my travel-size bedside candles.

The sweet aromas of fig and cloves wafted into the air.

"You're pretty handy in a crisis," I told him.

But I'd already known that. One of the things I like most about Danny is his willingness to put himself on the line for people. He might seem like a tough guy, but deep down, he cares.

He frowned at me. "Now you should get some rest."

I laughed. "It's nine o'clock." The Christmas lights–viewing hayride had started promptly as soon as it got dark. We'd enjoyed one of its earliest excursions. "I'm not ready for bed."

But we would need entertainment, and the B&B wasn't a hotbed of nightlife. Looking for something to keep us busy, I dropped my gaze to the minibar. Its contents looked tempting.

"Feel like a drink?" I asked as I took off all my warm winter gear. "I already have eggnog stashed in the mini-fridge."

"You're not drinking with a concussion."

"I feel fine. Besides, that doesn't mean you can't enjoy a nightcap." I realized he would need to get back to the Sproutes Motor Lodge later and relented. "Maybe some straight-up eggnog instead? That's driver friendly."

Danny had gone to the window. He studied the weather.

I studied him. He'd shucked his coat, hat, and gloves. His dark hair was mussed just a bit, staticky from his knit hat. That imperfection lent him a slightly less intimidating air.

I smiled, thinking of all the good times we'd shared.

"I'm not driving anywhere in this weather." He turned, his muscular frame covered in a sweatshirt and his ubiquitous jeans. He raised his eyebrow. "Is it a problem if I stay here?"

"Of course not." I waved. "Please, you take the sofa."

He grinned. "And you'll have the big, comfy bed?"

"It's *my* room. Besides, you're man enough to handle it."

Feeling lighthearted, I got busy pouring a pair of eggnogs for us and suggested a few holiday movies we could watch on the B and B's TV. I presented him with one of the glasses, then offered him a toast. "It won't be the wildest night we've ever spent together," I admitted, "but our options are limited. Cheers!"

Danny didn't toast back. "Our options aren't limited."

I felt confused. "You just said we're basically stranded."

"That's not a problem." He took the eggnog from my hand, then set it beside his on my room's desk. I protested, but my longtime friend made a face. "Eggnog tastes terrible. It's like getting socks for Christmas instead of a new video game. I'll pass." He came closer to me. "No need for a movie, either."

"Not even something short? *How the Grinch Stole Christmas!*"

That was his favorite. I'd known that for years.

Another smile. "Not even the Grinch. Not tonight."

"Huh. Well, I'm stumped for what to do, then."

"I'm not." Danny lowered his gaze to my lips.

Aha. I started getting his drift. It was . . . dangerous. I took an automatic step backward, giving myself room to think clearly.

He followed me, scrambling my thoughts anyway. "Are you *sure* this won't be the wildest night we've ever spent together?"

Even as he asked that, his hooded gaze suggested it might be. It *might* be wild between us in a way it hadn't been—not for a few years now, not since we'd agreed to keep things platonic.

But tonight *wild* was on the table. I already knew it would be good between us. After all, a lack of satisfaction wasn't the reason I'd stopped being with Danny. An excess of caution was.

I didn't want to endanger our friendship. Or my heart.

I recognized his invitation for what it was. Somehow,

I found a way to shake my head. "You know that's a bad idea."

I can't say I wasn't tempted, though. Between the romantic ambiance in my B and B's Christmassy room and the attractiveness of the man who was about to share it with me for the night, I felt very tempted.

"Is it?" Danny closed the distance between us. "It doesn't *feel* like a bad idea." He brought his hands to my jaw. He cradled my face, then lifted his gaze to mine. "I was worried about you today," he confessed. "Seeing you like that—" He broke off, then closed his eyes. "I should have been there for you."

I wanted to reassure him. To remind him I felt fine. But all I could do, instead, was feel. I felt his thumbs, callused but gentle; his fingers, familiar and inviting. Seductive.

If you think I wasn't wooed, you're wrong. I was.

I resisted by closing my eyes, too, just the same way Danny had done. For only a few seconds. I reminded myself of all the reasons it would be foolhardy to take this step again.

I thought of all the reasons it would be amazing, too.

When I opened my eyes, Danny was watching me. Waiting. For a long moment, we shared the same breath. Then I looked away.

"We can't," I finally said in a rush. "Travis would—"

"Know," I was about to say. *He'd be disappointed*, was my next fuzzy thought. But before I could voice any of that, Danny's mouth was on mine. I couldn't think of anything at all.

He kissed me as though he really *had* been worried about me today—as though he'd worried about me all the months I'd been sleuthing around, semi-recklessly endangering myself in the process. I'd been hurt a few times. I'd been in genuine danger.

I'd never wanted more to forget about all of it.

Danny caught me in his fierce gaze. "This isn't about Travis," he told me. "It's about you and me. That's it."

Travis? Not Harvard? A joke occurred to me, but I couldn't make heads or tails of it just then. I could tell that Danny was about to move in for another kiss. I had a moment to refuse. But the first one had been so good that I didn't. I couldn't.

Instead, I grabbed two fistfuls of Danny's sweatshirt and pulled myself against him. This time, I kissed him.

This time, it was even better. How had I ever stopped?

I wanted more, and I took it. I didn't care if it was dangerous. I ran after danger these days, didn't I? Wasn't that part of what had changed about me? I was braver now. I embraced every risk.

If there was a bigger risk than Danny, I didn't know what it was. So I murmured something seductive, and I smiled with satisfaction at the husky sound he made in response, and I used those handfuls of sweatshirt I'd grabbed to yank even higher.

Seconds before I pulled off Danny's shirt, all the lights went out. The blizzard must have gotten worse, I realized.

In the flickering, insufficient glow of my travel-size candles, Danny smiled at me. "Too bad. I wanted to see you."

"You'll see me," I promised. I'd make sure of it.

"Not in this light, I won't. Not well enough." He rested his forehead against mine, both of us breathing raggedly. His dark gaze lifted to mine. "This is really happening?"

"So far, so good," I acknowledged, but that was all the talking I wanted to do. Unlike Danny, I had no interest in being clearheaded. Not then. Maybe not for a long time to come.

I felt gripped by urgency. Not just because of what was happening between us, but also because I knew how easily it could be shattered. A phone call, a knock on the door . . . even, at that point, the lights coming back on could do it.

When would we have another chance like this?

"Keep talking, and I'll break out the eggnog again," I warned with a grin. I took Danny's hand and headed for the bed.

Even as I moved in that direction, I worried that something would happen. I'd trip on the rug. Danny would get an urgent message from Tansy. Donna's cat would wake up and distract us.

But nothing interrupted. The B&B was silent, and so was I.

So was Danny, it occurred to me. Alarmed, I looked at him.

Elaborately, he pantomimed zipping his lips and throwing away the key. He was always kidding. I'd told him to be quiet.

The threat of eggnog had accomplished something that few things ever had. I smiled over the realization, then squeezed his hand. It was about to get real between us. I might not even bother getting either of us fully undressed first, I decided.

For the next several hours, there would be no risk of me *or* Danny making Santa's nice list, that was for sure. I intended to keep us both on the naughty slate, at least until morning.

* * *

I awoke with my head aching, startled awake by . . . what?

I jolted upright, tangled in the bedclothes, unsure where I was or what I was doing. *Sleeping* was what I'd have preferred.

Muzzy-headed, thanks to my old friend jet lag, I frowned. I took in the darkened room. Aha. The B&B in Sproutes. Of course. I was spending Christmas in Massachusetts with Travis and Danny.

Danny. Everything came rushing back to me, including the preceding few hours. I momentarily forgot whatever had awakened me, and looked down at myself, awash in a thousand divergent feelings. I looked over at Danny, sprawled beside me on the mattress. All my feelings became ten times more complicated.

Typically alert, Danny cracked open one eye. "You okay?"

"I heard something."

"The B and B's front door. Go back to sleep."

But I was already far too awake for that. "Hey."

"Hey, yourself," came the mumbled response.

"Some night, huh?" I wanted to make sure we were okay. For us to remain friends, we had to carefully work through this.

No, I'm not spelling out what *this* is, precisely. Suffice it to say that things got pretty heated for a while.

Danny sat up, then ran his fingers through his sleep-tousled hair. He wasn't wearing a shirt. "We agreed," he reminded me huskily. "This doesn't have to be weird between us."

"That's funny," I observed interestedly. "When you're half asleep, your voice is almost as deep and husky as Travis's is."

That did it. "All right, now it's weird." A scowl.

"Sorry! Just thinking out loud." I climbed out of bed, then went to my room's window, aware the whole time of Danny's gaze fixed on my bare legs . . . and maybe more. I pulled down my shirt.

That was as good as a minidress, right? No problem.

"I'm sure I heard something," I insisted, taking a look.

Outside, the B and B's grounds were more snow covered than ever. A fresh blanket of white had cloaked the whole place. At the moment, though, everything was still. Almost spookily still.

You might have guessed by now that I'd been kidding about making six-foot-plus Danny sleep on my room's miniscule sofa. It wasn't the first time we'd shared a bed, platonically or not.

"You were dreaming," Danny told me in the darkness.

I smiled. It felt very much as though I had been. Also, as soon as I had that thought, I couldn't be sure that wasn't *all* it had been. Just a dream. I did have that mild concussion to think about. Maybe, it occurred to me, it wasn't entirely healed.

"Was I?" I decided to play along while I looked around.

"Must have been a good dream, though." There was a smile in Danny's voice. "Judging by all the moaning that was going on."

"Well, I don't dream like ordinary people. I go all the way," I boasted nonsensically. "If you're going to do something, you might as well do it up right. That's my philosophy."

"Hmm." His throaty rumble left me wondering what he was thinking. "Good philosophy. How's that working out for you?"

"Pretty well so far." I strived to keep my tone light,

so Danny wouldn't guess that I was seriously starting to wonder.

Exactly what *had* happened between us a few hours ago? I couldn't ask him. Of course I couldn't. Whether we had been indiscreet and impulsive—or whether we hadn't—I knew that Danny would follow my lead in handling the aftermath. If we'd gotten frisky, he'd want me to feel comfortable. If we'd put on the brakes, the same theory applied. That meant that, short of out-and-out interrogating him, I couldn't know for certain.

I thought we'd stopped in time, before anything serious had happened. At least that was my (admittedly) hazy impression.

Before I could figure out anything for sure, I glimpsed movement outside my window. I glanced at the bedside clock to gauge the time and saw that it was almost two in the morning.

Into the hushed stillness of the B and B's front yard, someone stepped outside. I recognized her faux-fur-trimmed coat and pompon-topped hat, worn with mittens and a lot of lip gloss.

Ophelia. Albany's little sister flounced into the snow, her pretty face and long dark hair lit by the Christmas lights that again illuminated the yard. She stopped below one of the B and B's old-fashioned wrought-iron lamps and gazed expectantly toward the front door. Despite the late hour, Ophelia didn't seem the least bit sleepy. In fact, she seemed downright effervescent.

An instant later, Zach Johnson emerged, dressed in warm winter wear like Ophelia. My B and B's host moved with much less vivacity than she had, though. In fact, he seemed to creep toward Ophelia, as though he were in

pursuit of her. He held something behind his back—
something I couldn't see clearly.

"Danny!" I called in an undertone. "Come here!"

Was I about to witness an attack? Could Zach really be
dangerous? My heart leapt to my throat as I signaled for
Danny.

He was beside me in an instant, holding aside the
curtain.

"What's the matter?" He looked at the scene, then at me.

I couldn't believe he didn't see the threat. Worriedly, I
pointed at Zach. "He's got something behind his back."
I zipped my gaze to Danny. "Should we go down there and
intervene?"

"*You* shouldn't." His expression was wary but un-
worried.

A few seconds later, I saw why. Zach did creep up on
Ophelia, but she clearly knew he was coming. She sneaked
a peek just before he reached her . . . and produced a gaily
wrapped gift.

Ophelia's expression of astonishment seemed genuine
all the same. Maybe she'd been picking up acting tips
from Tansy at the *Christmas in Crazytown* rehearsals? Her
face positively glowed. So did Zach's, for that matter. He
presented his gift.

For a moment, the two of them seemed frozen in that
tableau, like a couple on the front of a Christmas card.
Coyly, Ophelia accepted Zach's gift. Holding it at arm's
length, she admired its fanciful wrapping. It appeared to
be a velvet bow, wrapped around elaborate paper, both of
which caught the light.

Zach came nearer, then pulled Ophelia into his arms.

I gawked. Albany's little sister . . . with Albany's ex-
boyfriend? Until now, I'd assumed their rendezvous was

entirely innocent. I'd reasoned that they were together because of a party at the B&B or a holiday event they'd both volunteered for. But as my B and B's host and Ophelia came together in that radiant Christmassy light, alone in that late-night world of silent snowfall, their togetherness seemed anything but chaste.

I watched the two of them canoodle for a minute, then realized I was shivering. I hugged myself and sidled closer to Danny, who threw off warmth like a portable furnace. The heat must have gone out along with the lights, I realized tardily. The power had been restored, obviously, but the furnace was taking its sweet time warming up the place. It felt distinctly nippy in here.

"So why are we watching these two make out?" Danny asked.

"At first, I thought Zach was sneaking up on Ophelia," I told him. "Now . . . I don't know. Do you think they're an item?"

Below us, the couple in question were locked in an embrace.

"If they're not, they're giving a good impression of it."

I agreed. Surprisingly, I felt indignant on Albany's behalf. Everyone knew that exes were supposed to be off limits.

Also, I couldn't help thinking that Ophelia was in over her head with Zach. She was younger than him and far more gullible. Given her competitive feelings toward her sister, I shouldn't have been completely surprised this had happened, but I was.

First, Joe Sullivan and his apparent sleeping around when he was supposed to be working. Now Ophelia Sullivan and her clandestine relationship with Zach. Was there something in the eggnog in Sproutes that nudged people toward indiscretions?

Maybe I just wanted to believe that to cover my own tracks. I couldn't be sure, and Danny definitely wasn't helping.

Down in the yard, Ophelia and Zach finally parted. The young woman gave my B and B's host a flirtatious fingertip wave; then she pranced just to the edge of the Christmas lights' glow.

She blew him a lip-glossed kiss, then darted away, out of sight—off, I assumed, to catch the Sproutes city bus home.

I looked at Danny. He answered my unspoken question.

"There are no municipal cameras on the transit lines."

I was about to turn away and try to get some shut-eye when another movement outside caught my attention. I looked down.

Albany had emerged from inside the B and B. Wrapped only in a heavy sweater, she hurried to Zach's side. The two of them shared an affectionate look. They embraced. I stared at them, unable to believe my eyes. I'd forgotten, temporarily, that Albany was staying at the B and B. She was accessible to Zach at any time.

Day or night, as Danny was fond of saying suggestively.

"Hmm." He crossed his arms beside me. "Interesting."

I glanced at him. "Interesting, as in you have an idea?"

"Interesting, as in that looks like a weird arrangement to me." Danny frowned. "Albany had to have seen Zach and Ophelia together. She doesn't seem to care, though." He switched his gaze to me. "In my experience, sisters can be competitive."

At his deliberate understatement, I laughed. I remembered a few specific instances that had given him that idea.

"Especially those two," I agreed, thinking of Albany and Ophelia. The Sullivan sisters were anything but mutually supportive.

If nothing else, Albany's memoir had proven that much.

So what were they up to? It would be bizarre for me to go downstairs in the middle of the night, I knew. I couldn't confront anyone at the moment. But when morning finally dawned . . .

Watch out, Zach Johnson, I thought. *I'm coming for you.*

Twenty

If I told you I have an insatiable yen to know how things work, what's going on behind the scenes, and what might happen next, you wouldn't be surprised. That's why the next morning, I was awake before sunrise, determined to get a jump on things.

Bleary-eyed, Danny blinked at me. "What are you doing?"

"Reading Donna's tablet." I lifted the electronic device to show him. I felt weird about doing it, but I was hoping to find some clues. I'd curled up in one corner of my room's sofa with a mound of throw pillows, a knit throw, and Donna's purring cat on my shoulder. "Go back to sleep. I'll fill you in later."

My bodyguard buddy required zero convincing. He slept.

While he did, I flipped through Donna Brown's schedules, getting familiar with the way she handled things. Judging by the myriad reminder schemes, organizational apps, and complicated filing systems and filters in her e-mail program, the teacher had been juggling a lot of priorities—and she'd been determined to ace them all. To say she seemed like a perfectionist was putting it mildly. Donna had had a system for everything in her life.

Tellingly, hanging her Christmas lights had indeed been broken into multiple segments, one for each area of her home. There'd been one day for preparation and bringing down all her decorations from the attic. One day for double-checking her neatly spooled lights and replacing any broken bulbs. One day for sourcing her Christmas tree and stringing lights; another for placing ornaments on the tree and distributing knickknacks.

Donna's to-do lists were never-ending. Literally. Most of the events and tasks she'd scheduled were set to repeat at defined intervals, like clockwork. As far as I could tell from scrutinizing her records, she hadn't missed a thing for at least three years. In fact, that was when Donna had first gotten serious about becoming systematized. Her routines put Travis to shame.

I felt a kinship with my financial advisor, actually, as I sorted through all the details with my Moleskine at my side for my notes. Examining the specifics of Donna's life offered an insight into her days that nothing else could have done, short of speaking with her. Since that was no longer an option, I kept on going. Gradually, I assembled a picture of a woman who was conscientious above all else—a woman who wanted to be flawless.

The reason Donna hadn't been at the Sproutes playhouse on the morning of her death, I discovered, was that she'd had an existing appointment. She'd planned to finish her Christmas lights on that fateful morning. The Donna Brown I now knew would not have been swayed by *Christmas in Crazytown*. She would have finished what she'd started or what she'd planned, then gone.

Sadly, she'd never had the opportunity to do that. Even

her task of hanging her backyard Christmas lights would remain unfinished now, a black mark on her otherwise spotless record.

I hesitated, then touched the screen. A tick mark appeared, designating that task as complete. That felt better. With a glance at the cat—Georgie was her name, listed in multiple tasks and appointments—I also ticked off feeding and litter-box duties.

As I did so, I felt a subtle *zing* of accomplishment. I smiled, understanding then why Donna had kept so many lists and calendars. It was rewarding to see everything fall into place.

A multitude of upcoming meetings remained out of reach, however. I couldn't mark all of them as finished; they wouldn't be. There were crafting get-togethers and parties, volunteer commitments and doctor's appointments—even a more cryptic activity, coded to recur every Wednesday evening. Indefinitely.

I puzzled over it. Why the code? Did Donna have a lover?

If Zach, Ophelia (and Albany) were any indication . . . maybe.

I blinked, suddenly aware I was being watched. Danny had gotten out of bed. He eyed me as he lowered himself companionably onto the sofa's opposite side. Georgie, the feline traitor, abandoned me to paw her way across his lap and onto his chest. She had the discourtesy to cover his incredible six-pack abs. Too bad.

Danny gave me a sleepy look. "What are you up to?"

Wondering if I dreamed . . . everything. I set aside the thought. For now, I'd have to be comfortable not knowing, the same way I was trying to be relaxed about the hole in my memory caused by the Santa-gnome-shaped blow to the head I'd taken yesterday.

"Wondering if Donna Brown had a secret lover." I showed Danny the tablet's screen. "If so, they both loved punctuality."

He studied her calendar. "That's not a lover. It's A.A."

I was startled. I turned the tablet around. "As in rehab?"

"As in the program, yeah." He pet the cat. Georgie purred. "Have you got anything to eat around here? I'm starving."

"Just the fudge you dismantled last night."

"Ugh." He made an "I hate sweets" face. "No, thanks."

I stared at him. "That's it? You drop a bomb like meek Donna Brown was in A.A., then start scrounging for breakfast?"

"It's not a big deal. How about the minibar? Any chips?"

Given his hopeful, handsome face, I hated to disappoint him. However . . . "I asked housekeeping to clear all the food from the minibar," I confessed. It was one of the ways I made room on the road for higher-priority snacks. Like all things chocolate. "But Zach should start serving breakfast in an hour or so."

When he did, I intended to have a few words with him. I wanted to know what he'd been doing with Ophelia *and* Albany.

I wondered if Travis knew his friend had had a rendezvous.

I tapped Donna's tablet screen. The appointment I'd puzzled over contained nothing more than the date, an address, and the initials A.A. I suppose I should have guessed what that meant.

"It could be Albert Anderson," I said. "Arturo Alvarez?"

"It's an A.A. meeting." Danny moved the cat, then got

up. He was shirtless, stripped to his boxer shorts. I'm not sorry to report that I ogled him. "I recognize the address," he told me.

I dragged my gaze from his flexing muscles. Danny had a way of pulling on a pair of low-slung jeans that was *fascinating*.

"You recognize the—" He'd been there? "Oh. I'm sorry."

He frowned at me. "It's treatment. It's not embarrassing."

I was still taken aback. "But we've been drinking. We just went to the Santa pub crawl together. How does that jibe with—"

Your in-depth knowledge of meeting places for alcoholism treatment programs? Danny's deepening frown stopped me from asking.

Surely I would have known if my friend needed help?

"It's not for me. But I know how the program works." He waved at Donna's tablet. "All that stuff, it's how some people deal with their recovery. By controlling everything."

"Donna's strict schedule was meant to keep her sober?"

Kindhearted Donna had been in ongoing treatment for addiction issues? I couldn't quite wrap my head around the idea.

"Could be," Danny said. His fingers made short work of the button fly on his jeans. He hauled on his sweatshirt. "I have clients in the program. Friends too." He frowned. "*Not* me."

Whew. I thought of all the times I'd offered Danny a beer or a tumbler of something stronger—including last night—and felt relieved. I believed him, too. Danny's friends from his bad old neighborhood included all kinds of people. Of course, his celebrity clientele was sometimes dealing with addiction issues, too. I'd forgotten about that aspect of his work.

It would be like Danny to plan for the possibility of needing to take a client or a friend to a nearby A.A. meeting.

I switched course. "Do you think Donna was buying drugs from the dealer you saw at the Sproutes Motor Lodge?"

Danny shook his head, then tucked his wallet and keys into his pocket. "Not if she was actively in treatment, I don't."

Hmm. That made sense. Mulling it over, I glanced at Donna's tablet again. "It's too bad," I mused. "Donna was a generous person. She would have made someone a wonderful sponsor."

Danny scoffed. "Yesterday you thought she was a murderer."

"That was before I knew she had problems like these," I informed him. "The kinds of problems that make you meet with a bunch of strangers week after week to talk about your troubles."

"You're right," Danny deadpanned. "You'd never make it."

"I would if I wanted to," I disagreed. "Or needed to."

"Nope. People in recovery are supposed to avoid drama in their lives. You *love* drama." My buddy's grin told me he was joking. "Come on. Let's go break into the B and B's kitchen."

"Danny!"

"What? You didn't mind a little rule breaking last night."

Was that a reference to what might have—or might *not* have—happened between us? I couldn't tell. He had the gall to grin.

"You know *I* don't have to break in," I settled on saying. "Zach gave me free access to the B and B's kitchen, remember?"

Danny smiled. "I remember *everything*," he taunted.

My frustration that *I* didn't must have shown, because he stopped with one hand on the door. He studied me, then shook his head. "Nothing happened, Hayden. Nothing big, anyway." Another curious look. "You were pretty out of it. You didn't really think I'd take advantage of your concussion, did you?"

Hmm. When you put it that way . . . "No! Of course not."

"Because I didn't. All I did last night was tuck you in."

I remembered kissing him. Leading him by the hand to the bed. "There had to have been a little more to it than that."

"Okay, slightly more," Danny acknowledged. He gave me a wicked look. "You were . . . enthusiastic. Let's just say that."

"That sounds like me." I *was* attracted to him, after all.

"But I managed to keep things in line—the way you would have wanted if you'd been thinking straight." A pause. "Right?"

"Right." *Right?* I felt . . . vaguely disappointed.

Danny wasn't *all* gentleman, though. "Don't worry. When it happens between us, you'll definitely remember," he promised.

Then he swaggered out the door and, with that settled for now, led the way to our soon-to-be (stealthy) breakfast.

I was staring at a partially unwrapped box of Christmas chocolates, thinking about my unfinished chocolate houses, when it happened—the call came in that would have interrupted me and Danny last night, just when things were getting steamy.

Danny's phone didn't ring. He always kept it on silent. I did hear it vibrate, though, thanks to the B and B's unusually quiet kitchen. It seemed that no one was awake yet, except for Zach.

I'd spent a few minutes alone with him. It had been an enlightening conversation, but I still wanted to confirm a few details. For that, I would need Albany and her sister, Ophelia.

"Yeah, I understand." Speaking into his phone, Danny shouldered shut the open refrigerator door. He'd been staring into it, looking for something to nosh on, when the call came in. His gaze met mine as he spoke to whoever had called. "No, don't worry about that. I'll be there in thirty minutes."

"Tansy?" Assuming it was his client, I raised my eyebrows while Danny pocketed his phone with his back still to me. "Yesterday you said you needed only twenty minutes to get to her," I reminded him. "Those are ten extra billable minutes."

The instant Danny turned, I regretted joking with him. Something was seriously wrong. His face looked drained.

"That was Josh. He's at the hospital with Tansy."

The Sproutes Regional Medical Center was a modest hospital, quiet and antiseptic, with a friendly staff. Danny and I arrived in record time, having sped through the silent, snowy streets.

Hoping to keep up Danny's strength for the drive, I'd grabbed the box of chocolates I'd seen in the B and B's kitchen. But when I offered my security-expert pal a bonbon, he blanched.

"Are you kidding me? Thanks, but I'll be fine."

I had to take his word for it. I held on to the chocolates, anyway, in case of emergency. What can I say? A chocolate whisperer has to be prepared. I stuffed them into my tote bag as we made our way inside the hospital. There, Tansy's ward seemed nearly deserted. We found Josh at her bedside, looking stricken.

My gaze shot to Tansy. She lay unmoving in her hospital bed, just as beautiful as ever, sound asleep. At least I *hoped* she was asleep. I listened to the myriad monitors nearby. The actress seemed to be resting, not dying. That was a relief.

I rushed to hug Josh. "What happened?" I asked him.

"Tansy woke up ill early this morning," Josh explained to me and Danny. "She was woozy, vomiting, headachy. It was so bad, I brought her here." He sent her a devoted, concerned look. "She was fine when we went to sleep. I don't know what happened."

"What do the doctors say?" Danny asked.

"They think it's some kind of food-borne toxin."

"Toxin?" I repeated. "As in food poisoning?"

Josh nodded. "We both ate the same things yesterday, though, and I'm fine." He pulled something from a hospital-issued plastic bag. "I did find this in the trash. Tansy was collapsed on the floor next to it. It's the only thing we didn't both eat. I'm not sure if Tansy had any of it—you know how she is with constantly dieting—but I brought it with me, just in case the doctors needed it."

It was an elaborately wrapped box of chocolates. Or at least it had been at one time. Now it was a raggedly unwrapped, empty box of possible poison.

I couldn't believe it. Had Tansy been the Christmas killer's target all along?

If so, Donna's death did not fit the pattern at all.

"All that was left were chocolate-covered cherries," Josh told us. "Tansy doesn't like those. They were in the trash."

"And the rest of the box was gone?" I asked Josh. If Tansy really had been struck with food poisoning—and she definitely seemed to have been—*not* eating every last morsel of chocolate might have saved her life. "Do the police know about this?"

"About the candy? No. No one's been here to ask any questions. The hospital tested the contents of Tansy's stomach. That's how they knew what was wrong with her," he explained. "They think she'll pull through all right, but . . ." Josh's face crumpled. He gave Danny a shame-faced look. "I'm sorry. I thought I had it under control. Everything was fine! If this was Tansy's stalker, he definitely chose the right moment to strike."

When Danny wasn't on duty. I imagined we were all thinking it. I didn't want to say so. I felt responsible enough already.

If I hadn't gotten concussed . . . That probably wouldn't have made any difference, anyway, I realized. Danny wasn't aware of Tansy's binge eating. He wouldn't have been able to stop her.

I envisioned the actress sneaking into Josh's kitchen in the middle of the night, indulging in those chocolates, picking out the chocolate-covered cherries . . . then falling ill mid-nosh.

She must have been trying to hide the evidence in the trash when Josh found her. I figured there must be several other chocolates that Tansy hadn't eaten but had thrown away in a rush. I knew she struggled to manage her consumption of treats.

When we'd spoken about it, I hadn't imagined this.

"I don't think it was Tansy's stalker," I told Josh and

Danny. "I think it was the Christmas killer—the same person who attacked Melissa Balthasar, and maybe Donna Brown, too."

Both men frowned at me.

"I thought Donna fell," Josh said.

But I didn't have time to argue about it. Because I'd been staring contemplatively at that unwrapped box of toxic chocolates, bothered by a niggling detail. I'd just recognized what it was.

"Can I borrow your car?" I asked Danny. "There's something I have to do, and I assume you'll want to stay here with Tansy."

My friend handed me his keys. "Have it back by midnight."

"Or what? It'll turn into a pumpkin?"

"Or I'll come looking for you myself." Danny's attention focused tellingly on Tansy, then me. "This could have been you."

Did he always have to go there? "It's not, though." I gave Josh another hug. "This isn't your fault. Hang in there, Josh."

He nodded. "Thanks for coming, you two." His distraught gaze sought out Tansy. He sighed. "Tansy's going to be so bummed if she doesn't recover in time for the show's premiere. She was counting on *Christmas in Crazytown* to change her image."

That was the crux of it, wasn't it? Whatever else happened, it always came down to the holiday show based on Albany's outrageous memoir. I thought now that was the key to it all.

Before I could deal with that, though, I had something else to do. I waved to Danny and Josh. "See you two later!"

As I left Tansy's hospital room, I wasted no time taking out my phone. First, I called Ophelia. I had to meet with

Albany's little sister, and I had to do it right away. Then I phoned Travis. My financial advisor answered immediately.

"I was just about to call you." His deep, husky voice held a note of accomplishment. "I have news about Melissa's rehab."

That could wait. "I have news about the Christmas killer." But first . . . "Does Albany have a box of chocolates anywhere?"

I described the unwrapped box that Tansy had eaten from. It was easy to do, because it matched the box I'd taken from the B and B's kitchen. I was still carrying it, like a live bomb, in my tote bag. I heard Travis and Albany confer in the background. Good. That meant that my friend's memoirist pal was all right.

My keeper came back on the line. "Yes. It's here." He confirmed the wrapping's details. "Why? What's wrong?"

I told him about Tansy. An instant later, Travis put me on speakerphone. I could hear Albany's distressed voice.

"We're going to have to cancel the show again!" she wailed.

I wished she was worried about the lead actress in her holiday show, rather than its (repeatedly) deferred opening.

But the fact that *Christmas in Crazytown* had been canceled again and again was important. So I overlooked her attitude.

"Don't eat any of that candy!" I ordered Albany and Travis. I spoke to Albany briefly about the things Zach had told me. Then, to Travis alone, I added, "Trav, can we talk privately?"

He agreed.

When he came back on the line, on his own, I got down to business. "You've got that box of chocolates, right?"

"Of course I do. It's safely sequestered."

"Well, unsequester it and turn it over. What do you see?"

After a few tense seconds, Travis told me. I wished I was surprised by the result, but I wasn't. Not this time.

"That's what I thought," I said. "Talk to you later?"

"I haven't told you what I found out about Melissa's rehab stays," Travis objected. "There was definitely more than one."

While I braved the snowy winds in the hospital parking lot, he explained that Melissa Balthasar had had a legitimate drug addiction problem. She'd been in treatment multiple times.

"But Melissa didn't just use her rehab stays to get better. She used them to make connections, too." Travis told me about the financial trail he'd followed to uncover that information. "In essence, Melissa used those exclusive Malibu rehab centers as personal lead generators. That's how she scooped everyone. That's how she rose to the top so quickly, too."

"By taking advantage of people in treatment?" I got into Danny's rental car, feeling disgusted. "That's awful."

"By taking advantage of *talented* people in treatment," Travis specified. "That's how you get to the story first—while it's still being formed. Or, in certain cases, while it's winding down to its tragic conclusion. It's unethical but expedient."

That must have been how Albany's "lightly fictionalized" memoir came about, I assumed, its potential contents whispered about to Melissa while she was trolling rehab centers for projects to produce.

"Color me unimpressed." I pictured Melissa Balthasar in group therapy, coolly evaluating her fellow rehab inpatients, deciding who had the best story to sell. Roger was right. His wife *had* been a real shark. "Thanks for digging, Travis."

"Just playing my part. I'll keep an eye on Albany." There was a pause. "She's calling everyone in the production now, to let them know there might be another show cancellation."

I hoped it wouldn't come to that. For Tansy's sake.

"While Albany's doing that, can you do me a favor?"

I needed to know what was in those chocolates that had made Tansy ill. *Exactly* what was in them. If Travis could obtain that information . . .

"I'm on it," my keeper promised. His voice lowered. "Hey, be careful out there, all right? Call me if you need me."

"Hey, I'm not crazy. I'm not going to rush into trouble."

"You've been known to do that before," Travis reminded me.

"There were extenuating circumstances then." And I'd been a first-time sleuth. This time, I hoped, things were under better control. "Thanks for having my back, though. I appreciate it."

"Always," Travis said. "You know that."

The warmth in his voice made me smile. Suddenly, I felt a little bit glad that things hadn't gotten out of hand between me and Danny last night. Travis really would have known eventually. I wasn't so sure I wanted to change our relationship that way.

I hung up the phone, then drove straight to my meeting place with Ophelia: the local diner in scenic downtown Sproutes.

Twenty-one

As I'd requested, Ophelia had brought her wrapped box of chocolates. Of course, it was identical to Tansy's and Albany's.

It was identical, too, to the box I'd found in the B and B's kitchen with Danny earlier—the one now stashed in my tote bag. I'd recognized its distinctive embossed foil paper and glitzy velvet ribbon. I'd remembered seeing them hours earlier, when Ophelia had held a matching package while canoodling with Zach. Then, its gaudy decorations had caught the light perfectly.

Now, they did the same as Ophelia waited in a booth for me. I glimpsed her through the diner's window as I hurried up the sidewalk, shivering in my warmest clothes and moto boots.

There was nothing like murder to lend a chill to the air.

Inside the diner, it felt warm and welcoming. Classic Christmas pop music played; the long counter and cash register were both adorned with holiday lights. I strode past booths full of hungry Sproutesians, nodding and waving to people I knew.

When I reached Ophelia, she was frowning into a cup of hot cocoa. Her face looked pinched with lack of sleep.

I tucked myself into the booth opposite her. The fragrances of hot cocoa and marshmallows rose to meet me. That familiar aroma wasn't entirely pleasant; I felt too queasy for that. After all, I still hadn't eaten anything. I'd been too worried about Tansy. Now that I'd arrived at the diner, I wasn't hungry.

Ophelia noticed my perturbed expression. "Oh! Do you want one?"

I considered it and felt even worse. I waved away her offer. Ordinarily, my love of hot chocolate is second only to my fondness for a delicious peppermint mocha. Not today, though.

In fact, the idea of hot cocoa seemed oddly repugnant. I felt a niggling sensation in the back of my mind, like there was something I'd promised to do and later forgotten. I set aside the feeling.

"I need to meet with your dad, Ophelia," I said instead. "I think you're the only one who can help me get to him."

"My dad?" She blinked in surprise, then set down her phone on the table between us. "What's he got to do with any of this?"

I'd told her about what happened to Tansy. I'd warned Ophelia not to eat any of the (potentially) tainted chocolate herself. So what did Ophelia's dad have to do with any of that?

To answer her question, I flipped over her box of chocolates. I pointed at the label affixed to its underside.

"These chocolates were community gifts from the Sproutes Police Department. That's their insignia." I'd recognized it from my brief stay in the clink. "And that's your dad's name right underneath it."

You've probably guessed it already: *Joe Sullivan. Chief of police.*

The reason I hadn't been able to reach the Sullivan family patriarch was that he'd been dodging me on purpose. Joe Sullivan really was a workaholic, just as depicted in Albany's memoir. He really was busy, just as everyone in town insisted.

But Joe wasn't busy doing what everyone thought he was doing. And, as they insisted, the police investigation into Melissa Balthasar's murder would have been *very* different if Joe had been there that night. He hadn't been, because he'd been too busy covering up the crime. I was sure of that now.

But I still needed a way to get close to him. How was I supposed to take down the crooked chief of police? Especially in a town as close-knit as Sproutes? I needed subterfuge.

Ophelia looked trapped. "I shouldn't have come here."

She slid out of the booth, abandoning her hot cocoa and almost colliding with the concerned-looking server in her haste.

"Are you all right, honey?" The waitress put her hand on Ophelia's arm. She gave her an uncertain smile, then glanced at me. Her eyebrows drew downward. "Is there a problem here?"

Suddenly, I felt acutely aware of my status as an outsider. Not to be paranoid or anything, but the Sullivans were a big deal in Sproutes. The whole family was known. Albany was famous. Cashel was infamous. Linda was admired as the editor of the *Sentinel* newspaper, and Joe was universally beloved. Ophelia was the odd one out, but her influencer account was changing that.

"No! I'll, uh, be right back." Ophelia bolted, head down.

The server's suspicious gaze returned to me. I had the

bizarre feeling she was about to sound an alarm. *Alert! There's a secret sleuth here, stirring up trouble. She doesn't even like hot cocoa!* I imagined the whole diner full of people rising up, pitchforks at the ready. But that was silly, wasn't it?

Nobody brings a pitchfork to a small-town diner.

"So." She whipped out her order pad. "What would you like?"

Whew. There would be no mobbing of outsiders today in Sproutes, I guessed. I ordered a black coffee, then shakily executed the rest of my plan while the server went to fetch it.

As I'd hoped, Ophelia had left in such a hurry that she abandoned her cup of hot cocoa *and* her cell phone, too. It lay right there on our booth's table. She'd always kept it at the ready during our photo shoots. I'd hoped she would today, too.

I had no compunction about snooping. Within seconds, I had the information I needed. When Ophelia came storming back after realizing she'd left her precious phone behind, I was ready.

I held up her screen. "You've been blackmailing Zach."

Ophelia took one look and caved. "He deserved it," she informed me as she flopped herself onto the opposite side of our booth. She rolled her eyes. "Zach could have just helped me. I literally asked him to. I said please! But he was so selfish! He didn't think about me at all. I *had* to do it, you know."

What she'd "had to do," I'd had a hunch, was snap several grisly photos of Melissa's murder scene, then later upload them via a secret account. Ophelia had watched them go viral, then had made another demand on Zach to cooperate with her. After he'd agreed, she'd closed that account. Shortly thereafter, most of the social-media frenzy about Melissa's death had died down. I'd thought that was because of Roger's influence. It turned out, it had been Ophelia's influence—*coupled* with Roger's, of course.

The producer was still a Hollywood big shot. He still held sway over certain media outlets. Because of that, Roger had unwittingly helped Ophelia conceal what she'd done to Zach.

"You should have deleted the photos from your phone." I thumbed through a few more images, then brought up another social-media account: Zach's account for his B and B. "You'll need to learn to manage your resources better if you want to match Zach's popularity someday. I mean, look at all these sponsors!"

I showed her a few of the posts on Zach's account, all of them featuring merchandise and paid publicity from well-known corporations. Those companies were interested in Zach's travel-savvy readers, a demographic keen to experience new things—and averse to frequenting traditional advertising channels. For the privilege of reaching them, those businesses tended to pay well.

Ophelia made a haughty face. "Zach's a sellout."

"If so, he's a popular sellout." I accepted my coffee from the server with a thank-you, then blew on it as I contemplated Zach's perfect images of idyllic Christmastime bed-and-breakfast stays in Massachusetts. "Ten million followers strong."

I'd finally remembered to look up my host's Web site for his B and B. What I'd found had astounded me: an entire community of people who were interested in Zach's take on small-town living.

His latest posts featured the deceptively romantic images that he and Ophelia had posed for last night in the B and B's snowy yard. She was described as "a friend." I knew better. I knew now that Ophelia was a thorn in Zach's side.

"Sure, he'll take money to pimp all those products, but he won't lend a hand to his ex-girlfriend's little sister!" Ophelia snorted, then gave an infuriated pout. "That's not okay! We were practically family when Zach and Albany were going out. He could have spared a little cross-promotion, just enough to bring attention to *my* accounts. It wouldn't have hurt him one bit!"

"But letting Zach's followers know that someone had gotten murdered at his B&B *would* have hurt him, is that it?"

I didn't need Ophelia to answer that. I already knew.

"You published those photos, but you cropped them first," I theorized. "It was impossible to see exactly where Melissa had died. None of Zach's followers connected her death with the B and B, so there was no commensurate fall in traffic. But if Zach hadn't agreed to help you, you were planning to publish the originals."

"It was only a threat. I never did anything wrong."

That was debatable. No, wait. It wasn't. It was awful.

"Blackmailing someone into helping you isn't exactly 'right.'"

"It was only encouragement! Besides, Zach's online image was a lie, anyway!" Ophelia protested. "It's all editing and props and excellent camera angles. You're staying at his B and B. You know it's nothing special. But his stupid followers—"

"Did they at least visit your site? Did they follow you?"

"Some did," Ophelia told me vehemently. The look on her face said otherwise. *Not enough* had. "It was worth it."

"Was it?" I pressed. "Or was it something you were just a little bit sorry for?" I sipped my coffee. "Albany knew, you know. She and Zach are still close. He told her about you." I remembered seeing them laughing and talking at the B and B's front desk that day. "He wasn't blowing you off. He just didn't want to commit to helping you until he got Albany's okay."

"Got *her* okay?" Another snort. "Who needs *her* okay?"

Apparently, the Sullivan sisters' rivalry was alive and kicking. At least it was on Ophelia's side. "Zach did, obviously. He didn't want Albany to see the pictures of your fake online relationship with him"—because that was what Ophelia had pitched for their "collaboration" project—"and be misled into thinking that the two of you were really dating."

The way *I'd* been misled last night, regrettably. It turned out, Zach was aware of the unspoken dating rules. Hooking up with your ex-girlfriend's sister was absolutely off limits.

Ophelia rolled her eyes. "That's, like, so unnecessary. I mean, Albany and Zach were over with a long time ago." Another eye roll. "He didn't need her approval for anything."

"He did if he still cared about her feelings." I drank more coffee, trying to kick-start my brain. The pieces were starting to fall into place, but there was still a lot I didn't know. "Just the way Albany cared about your feelings." I wound up for the big one. "Zach didn't agree because he was afraid of your blackmail. Your sister asked Zach to help you as a favor."

That was why Albany had been outside with him last night.

Ophelia's eyes bugged. "As a favor to *her*? Ha!"

"Albany was embarrassed for you," I said gently, hoping I could make her understand. "You'd gone so far, for so little—"

"Embarrassed for *me*?" Ophelia's hooting laughter

cut me off. "After all the things she said in her book? That's rich!"

I expected her to reveal more. Instead, Ophelia slumped on her side of our booth, arms crossed over her chest. She stared broodingly at her cell phone, still in my grasp. She exhaled.

I gave her a moment. Then I got down to brass tacks. "The things in Albany's book aren't true?"

Ophelia rolled her eyes so hard I thought they'd rattle. She gave another gusty sigh. "Whether they are or whether they aren't, it doesn't really matter, anyway. Not in this town."

That wasn't the first time I'd heard someone speak about Sproutes that way. Travis often took the same cynical tone. The difference now was, I understood what he meant. When it came to Sproutes, what was true mattered much less than what was believed. For instance, my own sullied reputation was a fiction. But you wouldn't have known that to talk to Linda Sullivan.

Linda's take on my interest in Joe Sullivan had seemed extreme. Now I understood. For Linda, the rumors about my relationship with her husband might as well have been true, just as long as her friends and neighbors believed they were.

Just as the dirty (Christmas) laundry Albany had aired in her memoir might as well have been true. It had been believed.

"I'd like to help you, Ophelia," I said in a milder tone. She was too young to be headed down this path. "If you would only trust me, maybe we could make a difference. Together."

"Nice PSA." She sneered at me. "Tell someone who cares."

Okay, then. I guessed I wasn't getting anywhere with

her. It was time for plan B. Danny never has a backup, but I always do. When you're elbows deep in liquefied chocolate, sometimes you have to embrace unexpected results—like the melted mousse that inadvertently led to my most successful consultation ever.

I can't tell you what it was, but you'd definitely know it.

"All right." I shrugged, then tipped back the last of my inky diner brew. I tossed down enough money to pay for my coffee, plus more to cover a tip and Ophelia's hot cocoa—which, as I looked at it, suddenly jogged my memory. Because of that, I barely managed to add, "I guess I'm off to my next lead, then."

I still needed to get to Joe Sullivan somehow. But I was distracted by the memory that had just reoccurred to me. Could I trust it? Or was it just another trick, like the "Did we or didn't we?" merry-go-round I'd jumped onto with Danny earlier?

Ophelia's eyes lit up with malice. "By 'next lead,' you mean, Cashel, I assume?" It was the next logical step after Albany and Ophelia. "Ha! Nice try, loser. My phone, please."

She arched her eyebrows, silently demanding I hand it over.

When I hesitated, Ophelia laughed. "I don't have to remind *you* who my dad is, do I? Would you rather just get arrested?"

I'd been there, done that. I handed over Ophelia's phone. She seized it with a gloating expression, then tucked it away.

"You don't think Cashel will help me?" I asked guilelessly.

"Help you?" Ophelia chuckled meanly. "My brother can't even help himself. Like, literally. He can't get out of his own way. That was, like, the only thing that was true in Albany's book."

My pretense of being timid for Zach's sake was truly handy. It was certainly keeping Ophelia talking. I still needed info.

"Maybe, but Cashel seemed pretty close to his dad," I said. "I overheard them on the phone one time. It was really sweet."

I'd even remarked about it to Zach at the time, about how parents solved everything when it came to Christmas troubles.

That was when I had first met Cashel and didn't know how he fit into this group.

Not surprisingly, Ophelia scoffed. "If there's one thing my brother *isn't*, it's close to my dad. As far as Dad's concerned, Cashel can't do *anything* right. He never has and never will."

Bingo. "Sounds like a well-worn family truism."

"Whatever." She eyed me. "Weren't you leaving? I'm busy."

I glanced at the hot cocoa Ophelia was "busy" with and almost shuddered with distaste. But since Danny and Travis weren't entirely wrong about me being softhearted, I lingered a minute. "If you ever want to talk, after all this is over, just let me know," I volunteered. "Sometimes life is hard, Ophelia."

"It'll be easier the minute *you're* gone," she huffed.

Fine. This time, I really was moving on to plan B. And since Ophelia had confirmed my instincts about Joe and Cashel Sullivan, I had a better idea what I was getting into, too.

After a busy morning, I headed back to the Sproutes Regional Medical Center to check on Tansy. What I wanted to do was charge down to the police station and forcibly extract a confession from Joe Sullivan (somehow), but I knew I had to be smarter. I had to plan. I had to confab with Danny and Travis. Together, the three of us were better than any one of us alone.

The blizzard had left its mark on the hospital's parking lot; snowplows had been through now and had left piles of dirty snow in some of the parking spaces. Exasperated, I parked around back, near the industrial trash bins. I was hurrying past them, huddling in my coat for warmth, when I smelled something sweet, herbal, and familiar from my time in Amsterdam: marijuana smoke.

Automatically, I glanced in that direction. Roger Balthasar stood with a lighted joint in his fingers, eyes closed as he smoked some. He held his breath, then exhaled a plume of smoke.

He opened his eyes and looked right at me.

I was flabbergasted. Wasn't this illegal?

The producer, however, was indifferent to my reaction. He waggled his eyebrows and held up his joint, offering me some.

I didn't want any, but I joined him. "This isn't where I'd expect to find someone like you." I nodded at the trash bins.

"Eh, usually, I hide out in gyms—hotel gyms, airport gyms, hospital gyms. Take your pick. As long as I'm not in SoCal, they're usually deserted." Roger took another hit. He seemed beleaguered, his eyes red-rimmed and almost teary. "Today, some old lady was racking up her ten thousand steps on the hospital treadmill, so . . ." He spread his arms to indicate the grimy enclosed trash area. "Here I am! Sure you don't want some?"

I shook my head. "You seem . . ." *Upset.* "Are you okay?"

"Okay? Me? Ha-ha-ha!" His laughter sounded forced, though. I almost felt sorry for him. "My wife—my partner—is dead. I'm knee-deep in a disaster of a show that may never open. And my local connection just called it quits. Why wouldn't I be okay?"

I seized on the part I didn't already know about. "Your connection?" I nodded at his marijuana. "You mean for that?"

"Yep. He had the supremely bad timing to need rehab just when I needed him to come through with a new supply." Roger held out his joint and gave it a fond look. "Thank God for this. I've been hoarding it for an emergency, and, well, here it is! Ha!"

"Emergency?"

He squinted in the smoke, then croaked, "Tansy. You heard?"

I hadn't heard anything *new*. I was suddenly seized with panic. "She's all right, isn't she? She's not any worse?"

"Well, she *looks* like hell, that's for sure." Roger shook his head with evident dismay. "Nobody would have hired her looking the way she does today. But Melissa had a soft spot—"

At his mention of his departed wife, Roger broke down. Deep sobs racked his body. His shoulders heaved. Caught off guard, I looked around, not sure what to do. His grief seemed genuine.

Tentatively, I patted his arm and tried to reassure him.

Soon enough, the storm passed. Wearing a sheepish look, Roger wiped his eyes, careful not to drop his joint in the snow.

"I guess Tansy getting sick was the last straw," the producer confessed in a ragged voice. "I've been trying to keep it together, trying to be strong so I could lead everyone." He swore, shaking his head. "But this is all so freaking hard!"

I commiserated. "You've seemed very strong," I told him honestly. *Strong enough to maybe murder someone without remorse.* But I no longer thought that was true. "It's been difficult for everyone. It's only natural that this would weigh you down."

"I know!" He sniffled, then took a final hit. I'd be glad when that sickly smell subsided—I still didn't feel very well. "Melissa would have wanted me to keep the show going, so I've been trying, but I've gotta say . . . I couldn't care less about it."

I was surprised. "Really?"

A shrug. "Albany's memoir wasn't my thing. Too mean."

I boggled. If something was "too mean" for insensitive Roger Balthasar, that was saying something. "Too mean?"

"All that stuff about her family—that's private!" The producer shook his head. "The fallout from it has been brutal." He gave a cautious look around the hospital parking lot. "I grew up in a town a lot like this one. I know how gossip works. Ugh!"

He waved away that thought, but I couldn't. It was integral to my case. At this point, I didn't think Roger was guilty. I did think he'd been abusing antidepressants in an effort to keep up with *Christmas in Crazytown,* and it had all caught up to him.

"So now what?" I asked him. "Will Ophelia go on for Tansy?"

Maybe Albany's sister had been wrong about her undervalued role as the actress's understudy. But Roger only laughed.

"Ophelia? That twerp never even learned her lines. She tried a few of the dance routines, took photos, then scrammed."

That sounded about right. "So if Tansy doesn't recover in time . . . ?"

"Then we're all screwed," Roger announced. "But you know what? It's going to be okay." He drew in a deep breath. "It's almost Christmas, right? I'll go back to L.A., maybe drop in on some of my kids, try to think about what's important in life."

"That's a good idea." After all this was over, I hoped to do something similar. I'd spoken with my mom and dad, but that wasn't the same. Maybe after the holidays, I'd hop a plane to their latest jobsite. "I didn't know you had kids."

Roger hooted. "So many kids! Melissa was my fifth wife."

"Oh." Wow.

"Yeah. That's what everyone says. 'Oh.' Ha-ha-ha!" He gave me a look that seemed almost fond. "Hey, thanks for the chat."

I was only sorry we'd reached this rapport so tardily. "I misjudged you, Roger." I'd considered him a suspect because of it, too. But even if the producer *had* bribed the Sproutes Police Department to slow their investigation into Melissa's death, Roger had met a willing coconspirator in Joe Sullivan. I couldn't hold Roger entirely responsible for the aftermath.

Nor could I completely blame myself for mistrusting Roger. I was still trying to strike a balance between suspicion and trust, fear and foolhardiness. I've already said I'm not perfect. The fact that I was so willing to add Roger to my suspects list—partly because he was unlikable— was proof of my fallibility. I'd almost missed a chance at the real killer, too, because I hadn't wanted to own up to my own darker impulses.

I'd wanted to meet Joe Sullivan to confirm my dislike of Albany—to uncover what I'd thought would be the sordid truth about her "lightly fictionalized" memoir. Because of that, I hadn't told Danny and Travis what I was up to. I hadn't asked for their help. I hadn't wanted them to delve too deeply into my motivations for meeting Joe.

Now I was scrambling to make up time at the last minute, caught flat-footed by circumstances.

The ironic truth was, any one of us could have done an Internet search for Joe Sullivan at any moment and uncovered his role as the chief of police. I hadn't had to put out "feelers" with Zach Johnson at all. I was still kicking myself for that.

As I said good-bye to Roger and headed inside to Tansy's bedside, I started to feel better, though. That was because Travis greeted me in the hospital corridor. He was smiling.

He had the last piece of the murderous puzzle, too.

First, he assured me that Tansy was improving rapidly. Then my financial advisor added, "I found the source of the toxin that sickened Tansy. You'll never believe where it came from."

I smiled right back. "I bet I will." I nodded toward Tansy's room. "Is Danny still in there? We've got a lot to do."

"He is." Travis arched his eyebrow. "You've decided to plan your approach this time?"

"I've always planned!" Then I backpedaled. Sometimes things went haywire at the last minute. "But this time, I'm going to plan a little more carefully. I guess you're rubbing off on me."

Twenty-two

Of course, my plans fell apart almost immediately.

I didn't plan on bringing Albany to my big showdown with the Christmastime killer, but nothing I did dislodged her. I tried sprinting to my rental car; Travis's longtime friend beat me there. To add insult to injury, she did so by thirty seconds.

"Track and field star in college," Albany boasted in the car, pointing to herself with both thumbs. "Let's get going!"

Her chipperness stood at odds with the job at hand. "This isn't a party, Albany." I started the car and backed out, headed for the rendezvous I'd set up earlier with Cashel. "I'm about to have a very serious confrontation, with serious consequences."

"No problem! All I want to do is help." Albany gave me a look that suggested we bond like sisters, starting now. "It's possible you don't know what you're in for. I need to be there."

I frowned, still driving. Despite the meeting I'd had with Travis and Danny, I hadn't thought to ask my keeper how much Albany knew. Surely, she was still in the dark about some things.

"Maybe we could go out for drinks afterward," I suggested as I drove through the snowy streets, under holiday banners and past decorated storefronts. "Or Christmas shopping? That would be fun." I glanced at her, then added, "You probably finished your Christmas gift shopping last August, though, right?"

She laughed. "Are you kidding me? I'm still not done."

Her gaiety set my teeth on edge. I'm not going to lie. I was nervous about meeting Cashel—and even more anxious about confronting Joe Sullivan. I had some proof now, thanks to Travis and his useful connections, but would anyone listen to me?

"I really appreciate all you're doing, Hayden." Albany surprised me by sounding absolutely earnest. "I can see why Travis thinks so highly of you. I understand your friendship a lot better now."

She sighed, then fidgeted in the passenger seat. "I'll confess," she confessed, "that I was jealous of you. That's why I was so exclusionary at first. Sorry about that."

I gave her a sidelong look. "Jealous? Of me?" I gripped the steering wheel in my gloved hands, feeling dubious. "But you're practically perfect, Albany. The whole world thinks so."

"Not everyone." Her face darkened. "That's why I'm here, too. I want to set that right. And I want us to be friends!"

All at once, I wanted that, too. "No worries. We are."

"Really?" Albany beamed at me. "Travis said you'd say so."

My keeper thought he knew me so well. That's because he does.

We spent the rest of the drive in silence, each of us lost in thought. I wasn't sure what Albany was thinking about (her hopes for a Pulitzer, probably), but I was thinking how sorry I was for everything the Sullivan family was about to go through.

It wouldn't be easy for them, having a murderer in their midst. I wished I didn't have to be the one to expose him.

When we arrived at the Sproutes city park, things were hopping. There were pajama-clad children everywhere, bundled up with coats, hats, and winter boots on top of their pj's. They ran atop the snowy landscape, some of them having snowball fights.

"Aww, cute! Cashel and Ophelia and I used to come to this event every year," Albany told me as we made our way inside the park. "Cashel always wanted to ride Santa's locomotive first." She nodded toward the nearby steam train, currently parked on its tracks while ticket-bearing children clamored to board. "Ophelia always wanted to take pictures with Santa first." She indicated the park's Victorian-style gazebo, where an official photo station had been set up. "But I always wanted to get hot cocoa first." Albany gave me a mischievous look. "Do you mind? It's awful and watery, and the mini marshmallows are always stale, but it's nostalgia." She paused. "Do you want one, too?"

"No, thanks." I felt queasy with apprehension. I'd managed to down a sandwich earlier, but that was all. "You go ahead."

She did, hurrying toward the lighted and decorated hot-cocoa hut like a glamorous grown-up five-year-old in a knit hat and fur-lined boots. I watched her go with pure uneasiness.

Why hadn't Travis tried harder to help me dissuade

Albany from coming here? If things went as planned, the repercussions would be difficult for her—for all the Sullivans.

I looked around for Cashel and saw him waving to me from across the park. He was volunteering at the event and had agreed to meet me there. The eldest Sullivan sibling didn't know his role in bringing down his dad, of course. I wasn't that dopey—I'd disguised my interest in meeting Cashel as simple curiosity about Sproutes's pj's-and-hot-cocoa Santa's locomotive ride.

It had been a long few hours since that initial phone call, though. Now it was already dusk. It was getting darker fast.

All the Christmas lights were on, flashing merrily, as I went to meet Cashel. I weaved my way through throngs of children and their paper-cup-wielding parents. It was cold outside. Like Albany, everyone wanted hot cocoa or coffee to stay warm.

Holiday music burst from nearby loudspeakers. The children shrieked happily, too busy playing to notice the frigid weather.

"Hi!" I was finally close enough to speak with Cashel. I wanted to chat with him quickly, before Albany saw us together. "Thanks for meeting me. I didn't know you volunteered here."

"I'm taking Donna's place today." Cashel's gaze grew somber. His eyes filled with distant memories. "She used to volunteer here every Christmas. Someone had to do it this year."

I couldn't help noticing that Cashel seemed absolutely wrecked. His beard stubble was overgrown; his face was pale; his hands were tremulous. I thought I knew the reason for that, too.

I also thought his subbing for Donna was only appropriate.

"It's pretty crazy, isn't it?" I indicated the boisterous crowd around us. "Is there someplace quieter we can talk?"

Cashel looked surprised—almost pleased by my suggestion. Under other circumstances, I would have thought he wanted to be alone with me for romantic reasons. As it was . . . I didn't.

He conferred with another volunteer, then returned to me. Gently, he touched my shoulder. "Okay, I'm all set. Let's go."

"Over there?" I pointed to a small equipment shed.

"I have access to the whole park," Cashel bragged, leading the way there. He glanced over his shoulder, nervously checking in with someone. He saw me watching him and frowned. "Come on."

Cashel grabbed my arm, no longer seeming like a man who hoped for a romantic rendezvous. He hustled us both across the snow at a pace much too forceful to be considered friendly. I glanced backward as we moved through the snow, looking for . . .

Joe Sullivan. Bingo. I spied the chief of police at the edge of the locomotive entrance, watching me and Cashel. His face was hard; his demeanor even harder. *He knew.* I could tell.

He knew what I was there for, and he didn't like it.

I swallowed hard and let Cashel haul me closer to that shed. I was counting on him doing exactly that, in fact. I couldn't risk having this face-off with him near all those children. I didn't want another ghastly scene in Sproutes.

I remembered finding Melissa. Later, finding Donna. Those memories would haunt me forever. I needed this to end today.

It was going to, if I had anything to say about it. As we reached the shed, I put up just enough resistance to convince Cashel that he had the upper hand.

He didn't, though. Because Joe Sullivan wasn't the only one whom I intended to bring down that day. Cashel was guilty, too.

If I'd had any doubts, the aroma that hit me as Cashel grabbed me would have dispelled them. I inhaled a lungful of the smell that had nagged at me for a while now—the same smell that had jogged my memory at the diner while I was talking with Ophelia.

The rank odor of old chocolate and sour milk was hard to overlook, a remnant of the hot chocolate I'd accidentally spilled on Cashel's puffer coat during our photo shoot with Ophelia.

That telltale smell was what I'd noticed right before being bashed in the skull with that Santa gnome. Preceding it had been the swishing sound of Cashel's ever-present puffer coat as he moved to hit me. I'd finally recognized both for what they were.

"You never had a chance to have your coat cleaned, huh?" I nodded at it. That chocolaty stain had basically fermented. "Sorry again about that. I would have paid for dry cleaning."

He glanced down at the mess, eyes narrowed. "Sure. I'd be happy for you to pay, Hayden," Cashel said in a bizarre voice.

I detected liquor on his breath. My instincts were correct.

Cashel Sullivan was an addict. He was using again, too. Even if I hadn't been able to smell alcohol, I'd have noticed his unsteady steps and vaguely slurred words. I'd already observed his trembling hands. Cashel had been drinking heavily.

"How about if we make a deal?" I asked while he fumbled with the door of the equipment shed. I looked around and saw Albany watching us curiously, hot cocoa in hand. Uh-oh.

"A deal?" Cashel peered over his shoulder at his dad again.

I didn't want too much of that going on. Not yet, anyway.

"Yes!" I turned the doorknob and gave the door a shove. I stepped inside the shed. Cashel followed me. "I'll pay for your dry-cleaning bill, and you'll confess to killing Donna."

Silence. Inside, the shed was gloomy, lit by a pair of windows that showed the Christmas lights, and filled with lawn mowers and rakes, fertilizer bags and shovels. I turned around.

Cashel was staring at me in disbelief. He glanced over his shoulder, mouth agape, then made an uncertain motion. He wanted to leave. To check with his dad about this. I couldn't let him.

Instead, I slammed shut the door. "Donna was always there for you, wasn't she? All those A.A. meetings." I angled my head and adopted an inquisitive tone. "I'm guessing it must have been weird to run into your former teacher at a meeting, huh?"

That got to him. A hesitant smile cracked his mouth. He messed up his hair, then shook his head. "She didn't recognize me. That's how far gone I was then. But when she did . . ." Cashel's face looked wistful. "Donna didn't care. She knew what it was like, trying to stay clean. She knew how hard it was. How everyone is watching. How no one thinks you can do it."

"Is that why Donna offered to be your sponsor?"

Cashel gave a guilty nod. "We went to meetings together

whenever I was in town. It wasn't often, believe me." His voice took on a sarcastic bent. "Addicts are supposed to avoid drama."

"There's nothing more dramatic than a family visit."

"You're not kidding." My commiseration loosened him up. "I thought I could handle it this time. I knew I had to be here, on account of Albany's stupid memoir, but—" He swore harshly. In a broken voice, Cashel added, "I wish I'd never come back."

"I'll bet it's been a complicated visit," I agreed. "Coming all the way from California, too. It's so cold here. Brr!"

We laughed together. It was odd. But for the moment, he seemed willing to listen to me. I had the feeling that, without his father to pull the strings and cover his tracks, Cashel would have gotten better eventually. He would have *done* better.

Regrettably, he hadn't had that chance.

As though realizing that, Cashel shivered. "I'd rather be in L.A. right now, that's for sure. But this is the way things went, so . . ." He looked around. Saw a rake. Moved toward it.

I didn't think he'd bludgeon me with it, but I wasn't taking any chances. I glimpsed movement under the shed's closed door—just a pair of shadows crossing the threshold—and inhaled.

I had to be brave enough to finish this. So I kept on talking. "L.A. wasn't that great for you, either, though, was it? Not after you met Melissa at the rehab facility in Malibu."

Cashel stopped to frown at me. "You know about that?"

I raised my palms. "Hey, I'm on your side! That was a terrible thing to do, pumping you for info about Albany."

His mouth twisted. "All I said was that my sister had this wacky book she was shopping around. It was fiction then. I've never been any good at artistic stuff, but I like talking."

That was fortunate for me. I'd noted that about Cashel during our photo shoot and surmised he might help me now.

"Group therapy is like that. You find yourself spilling stuff you never intended to," he explained. "I didn't think much about it at the time. And Melisa could be really nice! You wouldn't think so, to see her in full-throttle mode. But sometimes . . ." He sighed. "When you had her attention, you *really* had it. You were the only person who mattered. That was me as soon as I opened my big, fat mouth about Albany and her memoir."

"Group therapy isn't supposed to be about other people."

"You're telling me!" Cashel gave me an aggrieved look.

"For Melissa to use you that way . . . It was wrong."

I held my breath, hoping for an outright confession. But it wasn't going to be that easy. Cashel paced around the shed.

I tried another tactic. "But you're probably used to that, right? I mean, all these years, you should have been getting the credit for your mom's cookie-Bake-Off trophies at the newspaper." I watched as his shoulders stiffened. "You're very talented. Those cookies you made for your mom were really delicious."

Josh had told me that his editor's son was "handy with a mixing bowl." From there, I'd put two and two together . . . and come up with a whole lot of questions. Starting with, if Cashel hadn't arrived in town until after the *Sproutes Sentinel* cookie swap—which was when I'd first met him at Zach's B and B—then how had he baked his mother's prizewinning cookies for her?

The answer had to be that he'd been in Sproutes all

along, possibly hiding out with his parents, avoiding any questions.

Questions like, where were you the night Melissa died?

"Yeah, well . . ." Cashel ducked his head bashfully, wordlessly acknowledging his contribution to Linda's cookie victory. "I'm not a screwup at everything. Even my mom has to admit that."

"The truth is the truth," I said. "It always comes out."

His eyes narrowed again. "Not this time." He hauled in a breath. "I'm sorry, Hayden. You seem like a nice person." Cashel scrounged in his pockets and came up with some capsules. Pills? I guessed they were Linda's prescription pain medication. "Unfortunately, like I told my volunteer buddy back there, you showed up here all upset today. Suicidal, even." He shrugged. "I'm not going to be able to stop you from taking all these."

He grabbed my hand, preparing to force those pills into my grasp. I twisted away, suddenly scared. His grip was painful.

"Cashel, stop!" I kicked his leg. My heel connected with his shinbone. He let me go. I wheeled around, arms out to ward him off. His eyes were crazy; his hands even more tremulous. "You don't have to do any of this. I can help you, I promise."

He gave a bitter laugh. "Nobody ever helps me."

"Donna did."

"Yeah, and look what she got for her trouble."

Her horrible death hung between us, all too tragic. For the moment, Cashel seemed broken up about that. His shoulders fell.

I wondered if her death had caused him to start drinking again. He definitely seemed remorseful about Donna in a way he hadn't been about Melissa. Today he seemed absolutely ruined.

"That was an accident," I reminded him. "Donna slipped off her roof, that's all. It was a terrible, awful accident."

"She fell because of me!" Cashel yelled, finally confirming my suspicions that he'd been there that day. He pounded his chest with his fistful of pills. "Me! She fell because I messed up at the Santa pub crawl. We were arguing about it while she was on her roof." He frowned. "I went to her place to apologize that morning. Donna wouldn't let me off the hook, though."

I frowned. "She must have really cared about you."

His eyes filled with tears. He nodded. For a minute, Cashel seemed unable to speak. Then, "She followed me to the pub crawl. She tried to talk me out of staying. It was bad for my recovery, being there, even though I wasn't drinking that night. But I got mad and I stormed out and I took her SUV. I'd lifted the keys from her purse. I'm pretty good at that. She didn't like that."

"You didn't just take Donna's SUV," I theorized. "You drove it onto the sidewalk." I kept my voice calm, hoping to calm Cashel, too. That was the way I'd imagined things had happened. Albany had confirmed seeing Donna at one of the pubs, wearing a Santa costume and holding a club soda, but she hadn't thought it was important to say so. I looked steadily at Cashel. "It's a good thing you weren't caught driving without a license."

He looked abashed. "You guessed mine was revoked? You've thought of everything." He gave me a rueful headshake. "I remember you asking about that at the photo shoot with Ophelia."

I had. We'd joked about the Sullivans having an unlikely "no driver's license" policy. I hadn't realized then that Cashel had a record of disorderly conduct and driving under the influence. Those were just a few of the things

Travis had been referring to when he'd warned me Cashel Sullivan was bad news.

"Yes, I did," I agreed. As a chocolate expert, I was nothing if not meticulous about details. "I also noticed you telling Zach that you'd driven 'for hours' that day you tried to check into the B and B. You made such a fuss about him not having a room available, I forgot to wonder until later why you hadn't taken a flight all the way across the country from California."

"Hey, I've never been a good liar," Cashel admitted blithely. "All I needed was to make a scene. That's what I did."

"That's what your dad told you to do? To cover your tracks, so no one would guess you'd already been in Sproutes for days?"

Cashel turned jittery. He stepped away, then back again.

He glared at me. "You don't know what I've been through!" he yelled. "Everything I touch falls apart! No matter what I do, it's not good enough." He gave a wild wave. "Albany betrays the whole family, makes us look like losers, and gets applauded. I go into rehab a couple of times, and suddenly, I'm the bad guy forever. I can't win, ever. End of story. Bad, bad Cashel."

He swore, looking infuriated. I wanted to run for the exit, but I stayed in that shed, sticking to the plan I'd devised.

I figured he might keep talking as long as he thought I was going to die before I could tell anyone what he'd said.

Besides, didn't everyone say I was really easy to talk to?

I gulped. "You're not a bad guy," I soothed, trying not to let the quaver in my voice seem too apparent. "Just because bad things happen to you, that doesn't make you a bad person."

Cashel closed his eyes. I thought I saw him flinch.

"You don't know anything," he said in a low voice.

"This wasn't the way it was supposed to happen. Melissa was supposed to go away, and the show was supposed to go away, and I was supposed to be the hero—the one who shut down the whole thing."

I blinked. So that really *was* what this was all about. It all boiled down to *Christmas in Crazytown*—and Cashel's desperate need to stop it from happening. I guessed Linda Sullivan hadn't been as tolerant of Albany's writing as she'd pretended to be.

She'd probably been ranting to her family for months, upset that the whole town—the whole world—was gossiping about them.

"The hero who shut down the whole thing?" I asked.

"That show made my family miserable!" Cashel seethed. "Not Albany, but the rest of us. My mom's migraines got really bad. My dad started 'working' more. Ophelia went way off the rails, ditching her college plans and taking up pro selfies instead."

Outside, I heard children whooping. I heard Santa's locomotive start puffing along its tracks. Had I really been in that shed with Cashel for only a few minutes? It felt like days. Whatever else happened, though, I had to keep going.

"You felt responsible?" I asked him carefully.

"*Responsible*?" Cashel scoffed. "None of it would have happened without me. None of it!" He shook his head. "Believe me, nobody let me forget it, either. Albany was off the hook—I guess because she's 'talented'—but not me. My dad was pissed."

Any second now, I expected Joe Sullivan himself to crash into that shed, guns blazing—or, you know, whatever the small-town Sproutes equivalent was. I had to move things along.

"For what it's worth, I don't think you meant it," I said. "With Melissa or with Donna. I don't think you meant it."

Cashel stared at me.

Say it, I silently begged him. *Say it.*

Say you killed Melissa Balthasar that night, Cashel.

We were staying there in the gloominess until he did. There was no way I was quitting. Not when I'd come this far already.

Maybe I could goose him along somehow?

"You should have drawn the line at delivering those candy boxes for your dad, though," I went on, picturing those gaudily wrapped police department gifts with their velvet bows. "He was taking advantage of you with that one. Tansy is pretty sick."

Cashel looked gutted about that. He hung his head. "Yeah, my buddy told me that seemed fishy when we were driving around, doing it. Why would my dad trust me to do that? Nobody even thought I could pick up my mom's medication." He swore again.

I couldn't wrap my head around his mood swings. So I decided to go for broke, before he made another threatening move. "The toxin that was in that chocolate came from the police evidence room," I told Cashel. "It was part of a criminally negligent recall effort involving a local manufacturing plant."

I mentally thanked Travis for that timely information.

Cashel blinked at me, sobering up now. "So? So what?"

"So you might have delivered those killer chocolates, but only a police officer could have gotten a hold of the toxin to make them. Only your dad." I gave him a firm look. "He's going down for that. For everything." I paused to make sure Cashel understood the implications. "He set you up, Cashel, by making you deliver that box of chocolates to Tansy." Zach's box had tested clean already. So had Albany's and Ophelia's. Tansy had been the sole target. "He won't be able to protect you anymore."

Cashel digested that. Then his voice turned panicky. "I don't need protection!" he blurted. "Melissa was an accident, anyway. I was only there that night to deliver something."

"To deliver drugs? For your truck-driving friend?"

A nod. "By the time I got there, Melissa was already out of her mind, she was so high. She didn't need anything else, believe me, but she wanted it, anyway." Cashel chuckled darkly at the memory. "But I didn't kill her! I didn't!" His gaze begged me to believe him. "I just didn't pull her head out of the punch bowl when she passed out in it. That's it! That's all. That's not murder. I even thought she was joking at first."

I shuddered, imagining the horrible scene. "You should have tried to help her." I raised my gaze to Cashel's. "When you realized what was going on, you should have tried to save her."

Wild-eyed, Cashel disagreed. "If I hadn't been there, Melissa would have died, anyway! It's not like I held her head in the punch bowl on purpose or anything." He offered his hands in supplication. "Come on, Hayden. Do I look like a murderer?"

Just then? He absolutely did. I hoped that by now I wasn't the only one who'd heard him confess to everything.

Evidently, my horror at what he'd done showed, because Cashel's scruffy face suddenly tightened with fury. He gritted his teeth, then grabbed my gloved hand. I was too surprised to prevent him from shoving those narcotic pills into my grasp.

"You'll never understand. I shouldn't have told you a thing." Cashel's whole body trembled as he tried to force my hand to my mouth. "I just want all this to be over with!"

I resisted, but Cashel was strong. His intoxication gave

me a slight edge—enough that we were still struggling when the shed's door burst open. I took my chance to drop those pills.

Breathless and contorted from fighting against Cashel, I saw uniformed police officers rush in. Then Travis was there, looking stern. Danny too. I'm pretty sure my body-guard buddy was the one who hauled Cashel away from me. I grabbed Danny before he could do something rash, like punch a murderer in full view of the Sproutes police force. I couldn't stop shaking.

Danny saw. He frowned. "Are you all right?"

"I am now." I promised Travis the same thing. "You?"

They both nodded.

"All we had to do was wait outside while you extracted a confession," Danny reminded me of the plan we'd made while at the hospital. "We had the easy part."

"The hardest part was not rushing in to help," Travis said.

I believed that. Outside, I saw a few more officers with Joe Sullivan. The chief of police had been handcuffed. Now, so had Cashel. It was a relief to watch them both being taken away.

This time, the whole town had something new to gossip about—except it was true. Apparently, I'd learned from my friends, my concussed rant in Donna's yard had caught the attention of certain critical members of the Sproutes police force. Combined with Danny and Travis's question-ing, that incident had caused them to come clean about a few things.

With a little prompting from my financial advisor, the officers had admitted that they'd suspected Joe Sullivan of being crooked for years, but they hadn't had the means to prove it.

Thanks to the toxic chocolate box connection—and my

chat with Cashel in the equipment shed, which had been recorded and listened to by the authorities—those honest, ethical officers now had the means to arrest, charge, and prosecute dishonest Joe and Cashel for their crimes. The shadows I'd seen under the shed's door belonged to the officers, who had been moving around while setting up.

It was over, I realized, with a wobbly sense of relief. I looked down at those scattered pills as two of the police officers marked them as official evidence. It felt surreal. Things hadn't gone *exactly* as I'd planned, but in my line of work, I'm used to improvising.

While the police took Cashel and Joe into custody, Danny and Travis and I headed out into the park. Its jolly atmosphere felt unreal, too; so did the sight of Ophelia and Albany, standing near the hot-cocoa hut, hugging each other. The sisters ignored everyone around them as they spoke together, united at last.

I'd expected Ophelia to show up at the park—or at least to alert her dad that I suspected him of something. I'd hoped my talk of "leads" at the diner would raise doubts for her. I'd even hoped Zach might have jokingly mentioned our conversation about my amateur sleuthing activities to Ophelia during one of their photo shoots. However it happened, I'd been counting on Ophelia to serve as my backup plan for flushing out Joe.

That seemed to have worked. What I hadn't counted on, though, was that this crisis might bring together the two sisters. Yet that was exactly what seemed to have happened.

"I told Albany you were staging an intervention with Cashel about his addiction issues." Travis was watching Albany and Ophelia, too. "That's why she wanted to come with you."

Aha. "That's why she was so nice to me."

"She was nice to you because she likes you."

"I like her, too." Despite myself, it was true. Especially after our recent car ride, when Albany had explained some things to me. I nodded, then glanced at Danny. "I guess we're off to the police station, then? We'll have to make statements."

My burly pal shrugged. "Making a statement is better than being arrested." He nodded at the police officers, who were currently putting Joe and Cashel into cars. "You should have seen the chief's face. He thought he was untouchable in this town."

"Yes, well . . . no one's untouchable." That was what I hoped.

It was what I would always hope. That was what kept me going on my surprising new sleuthing path. I always had hope that justice could be done. If I could help with that, I would.

If I couldn't, then I'd be happy making amazing chocolates.

We pulled ourselves together and went to wrap things up.

Twenty-three

There were three curtain calls on opening night for *Christmas in Crazytown*. The media showed up in droves to cover the event. They were united in their adoration of Tansy.

"A revelation!" one news outlet raved. "Astonishing!" wrote another. Cheering fans lined the streets of Sproutes, hoping for a glimpse of their favorite star—who was now, everyone agreed, a bombshell with twice as much talent as anyone had ever suspected.

Tansy reacted to all the brouhaha with enviable equanimity.

"This is what I hoped for," she told me backstage after the premiere, still in full stage makeup and breathing hard from her exertions during the final dance number. "I always knew I could do it." Tansy smiled at Josh. "Especially with so much support."

The newspaperman beamed right back at her. "I'm just happy you're okay." His arm encircled her costumed figure tightly. "You really scared me with that hospital stay! That chocolate—"

"Don't say chocolate!" Tansy held up her hands to ward off any mention of it. "I'm never touching that stuff again."

As aversion therapies went, being food poisoned by chocolate was a pretty effective means of avoiding it. I doubted Tansy would have very many more midnight snack raids.

I smiled and squeezed her hand. "Congratulations on your performance. You were fantastic," I told her honestly. "I guess that 'show must go on' mentality is a real thing in showbiz?"

"It is for me!" Tansy laughed. "I was opening this show if I had to crawl here! Besides, I had excellent care." She aimed a besotted look at Josh. "Money and fame can't buy that."

Her relationship with Josh actually seemed as though it might last. Partly, I gathered, that was because he'd proven he would stick by her, whether she was in a sold-out show or not.

Fortunately, the show *had* gone on, though. And Tansy wasn't the only one who'd pulled positivity out of adversity. On the other side of the Sproutes playhouse backstage area, I glimpsed Albany Sullivan talking with some reporters about her show.

At her side stood Zach Johnson, who was looking adoringly at her. Apparently, my B and B's host and Albany had rekindled their former relationship during the holidays. That was partly why, I'd learned courtesy of Travis, Zach hadn't cleaned up the wassail punch bowl after the party. He'd been upstairs, tipsy from the celebration and intoxicated by being reunited with his long-lost Albany at last. Because of that, Ophelia's blackmail attempt had wound up only bringing them closer together.

Danny saw me watching them. "It's too bad Cashel didn't have the talent to write Albany's book himself. He was already the family black sheep. Things couldn't have gotten any worse for him. He might as well have enjoyed the fame for a while."

I boggled at my buddy. "You don't really think that."

"And the money. The royalties would be nice, too."

"Danny!"

"I'm kidding. But I can relate to the black-sheep thing."

"*You're* not a murderer. That's an important point."

"True." Danny crossed his arms, then glanced at me. "I'll bet Albany and Zach hooking up makes things easier for you."

"Easier for me?" I batted my eyelashes. "What do you mean?"

"I mean, it's hard for you to carry on an infatuation with Harvard when you *know* it has to be one sided." Danny nodded at Albany and Zach. "If the brainiac had been banging her, you'd—"

"Danny!"

"Have a different take on the situation, believe me."

I remembered the kiss that Danny and I had shared at the B and B. And his insistence that that kiss was about *us*. Not Travis.

I scoffed. "If you're suggesting that I have a thing for my financial advisor, you're barking up the wrong tree." Because I didn't intend to admit any such thing. However true it might be.

Danny gave a perceptive laugh. "I know what I know. But it's all right. I still win Friendsmas, hands down."

"Look, it *was* a pretty good kiss, but Travis didn't even—"

"Have a chance to compete with you," I'd been about to say.

"If nothing else, I win for finding a home for Georgie," my security-expert pal butted in. He gave me a look that said I should quit talking about my soppy feelings for Travis for the moment. "That cat is going to be completely spoiled with Josh."

"And Tansy," I agreed. "She's already buying little outfits and accessories. The two of them really took to pet parenting."

I was relieved that Donna's cat was settled. I'd attended the memorial for Donna, along with what had seemed like everyone else in Sproutes. I wondered if the teacher and playhouse director had known how beloved she was. Tonight's performance had been dedicated to her, with a special presentation by all the junior *Nutcracker* ballerinas, who'd carried white flowers.

Still moved by that, I sniffled, then pulled myself together. Briskly, I looked at Danny again. I was surprised to find him frowning intently at me.

"What's the matter?"

"I'm waiting for you to say I win. I win Friendsmas."

Aha. "I knew it! You and Travis *were* competing about that." It had all kicked off at the Sproutes Star Lanes bowling alley.

Before I could address the issue, though, Travis turned up, looking extra handsome for the occasion in a dark fitted suit.

"We weren't competing to give you the best Friendsmas," he informed me, obviously having overheard a bit of what I'd said.

"But if we were, I won," Danny put in. "I was the best. There was the Christmas-lights hayride, the Santa pub crawl—"

"We were *teaming up* to make sure you wouldn't run into too much trouble while investigating murders," Travis went on staunchly. "Just the same way we always do." He aimed a quelling look at Danny. "Also, *I* was part of the Santa pub crawl, so—"

"So even if that doesn't count, the cat counts double."

"*It's a Wonderful Life* counts triple," Travis countered. We'd finally caught a matinee together. "That means I win."

I held out my hands before their bickering went too far.

"You know what? It's not quite Christmas yet," I told my two favorite men, with a smile. "You'll both have more chances to wow me over the next few days. So let's see what you've got!"

I was kidding. But I still hoped they'd give it a shot.

All around us, the cast and crew were dispersing, getting ready to head to the *Christmas in Crazytown* afterparty. The general sense of exhilaration and merriment felt revitalizing.

"You can start at the after-party," I urged, grabbing Danny and Travis by the elbows so they could escort me. I'd broken out my one and only cocktail dress (a classic LBD) for the occasion. I didn't want it to go to waste. "There's going to be dancing!"

"Dancing?" Danny grumbled. "No way. My, uh, retina hurts."

That was an excuse. I knew his eye injury was healed.

"I'm pretty sure I have some accounts to review," Travis put in, getting ready to make a break for it rather than rumba.

But I wasn't letting either of them off that easily.

"There'll also be a great big pot of my famous peppermint mochas for a crowd," I coaxed. "Everyone loves those!"

I'd developed the recipe for a certain never-to-be-named corporate consultee several years ago. It had begun with a melted peppermint mousse fiasco, but I'd managed to persevere and, to my client's delight, create something entirely new. The version I'd made for tonight wasn't identical (the original recipe was protected by copyright law and my own privacy guidelines), but it was close.

"A treat for a crowd, huh?" Danny echoed. He harrumphed. "I'm still waiting for you to make good on the last time you treated an entire state to something and didn't include me."

"Oh yeah?" I'd been waiting for my cue. I pulled out a small white bakery box and handed it to him. "Merry Christmas!"

Danny took it. His eyebrows drew downward.

Impatiently, I poked him. "Go on. I think you'll like it."

He opened the box. Seeing its contents, he snorted with laughter. "It's a three-dollar donut." Looking at its perfectly round, chocolate-frosted form, he smiled. "You remembered."

You remembered me, I heard and nodded in agreement.

I would always remember him. He was my closest friend.

As the cast and crew continued chatting and filing toward the after-party—and Danny gamely took a bite of his long-awaited donut, after declaring that maybe *he had* changed some, too, and now liked sweets—I became aware of a certain "cat that ate the canary" look on my financial advisor's face. Curiously, I turned to him.

"Travis? What's up?" I nudged him. "Can't wait to dance?"

He shook his head. "I can *always* wait to dance. Forever, if necessary." He waved to Albany, gesturing that he would see her later at the party, then returned his focus to me. "I just remembered that I forgot to tell you something, that's all."

Beside us, Danny raised his eyebrows in question. He

hadn't yet spit out his donut. That was an encouraging sign, I thought.

"Oh yeah?" I asked my keeper, as thrilled as ever to hear his deep, seductive voice saying something to me. "What's that?"

"Just that at the charity auction yesterday," Travis said with a distinct gleefulness, "*I* was the top bidder for Hayden's chocolate houses." I'd found time to finish them at the barn work space as expertly as I could. Technically, Travis was telling *me*. It was obvious this news was for Danny's benefit, too. "So I think you'll find that *I* win Friendmas this year."

Travis looked pleased. Danny looked disgruntled.

And me? I'm fairly sure I looked positively merry.

And why not? I'd helped to solve a murder and to take down a killer—and this time, I'd stopped a crooked cop, to boot.

I'd overcome some pretty steep odds. I'd earned a record bid for charity. I'd seen two couples start on their way toward what appeared to be fantastically romantic Christmases together. I'd been on the inside at a sold-out, smash holiday show, too.

Next, I had dancing all night long and peppermint mochas to look forward to. What wasn't there to like about that?

On top of everything else, Danny actually finished his donut and appeared to enjoy it. I raised my eyebrows. "It's a Christmas miracle! You like sweets now, Danny?"

My bodyguard buddy gave me a cryptic look.

"I like you," Danny said as an excuse for scarfing that donut. He tossed away the empty box. "Let's leave it at that."

Travis glanced from Danny to me and then back again. He matched Danny's enigmatic look with one of his own. I was sure that my financial advisor (and friend) knew there was something going on between me and Danny. But then Travis only shrugged.

I stepped in decisively anyhow. I didn't want to give anyone more time to think about things. It was better that way.

"Hey, Merry Christmas!" I told them both. . . . Then we headed out together to put all the troubles behind us and enjoy the season.

Recipes

PEPPERMINT-MOCHA COOKIES
WITH PEPPERMINT-VANILLA ICING
& CANDY-CANE SPRINKLES

Makes about 2 dozen cookies

- 1¼ cups all-purpose flour
- ⅓ cup cocoa powder
- 1 teaspoon instant espresso powder (or your favorite instant dark roast coffee)
- ½ teaspoon baking soda
- ¼ teaspoon baking powder
- ¼ teaspoon salt
- ½ cup salted butter, softened
- ½ cup granulated sugar
- ¼ cup dark brown sugar
- 1 large egg
- 1 teaspoon peppermint extract
- 1 teaspoon vanilla extract
- ½ cup semisweet or bittersweet chocolate chips

- ½ cup salted butter, softened
- 1½ cups confectioners' sugar, sifted
- 1 teaspoon peppermint extract
- 1 teaspoon vanilla extract

- 3 candy canes, coarsely crushed

GET READY: Grease 2 baking sheets or line each with parchment paper. Preheat the oven to 375°F.

MAKE COOKIES: In a medium bowl, whisk together the flour, cocoa powder, instant espresso powder, baking soda, baking powder, and salt.

In a large bowl, cream together the butter and both sugars with an electric mixer until light and fluffy. Beat in the egg and both extracts. Add the dry ingredients and beat just until blended. Stir in the chocolate chips.

Scoop up about 3 tablespoons of cookie dough and place it in a mound on a prepared baking sheet. (A #20 scoop—which holds about 3 tablespoons—is handy here.) Repeat with the remaining dough, spacing the cookies about 2 inches apart. Flatten the cookies slightly.

Bake for 7 to 9 minutes, or until just set. Transfer the cookies to a wire rack and let cool while you make the peppermint vanilla icing.

MAKE ICING: In a medium bowl, beat together the softened butter, ¾ cup of the confectioners' sugar, and both extracts until combined. Add the remaining ¾ cup confectioners' sugar, and then beat until light and fluffy, about 2 minutes.

DECORATE COOKIES: Frost each completely cooled cookie with the peppermint vanilla icing, and then decorate with candy-cane sprinkles. Enjoy!

Notes from Hayden

To add coffee flavor to desserts, I use superfine versions of instant coffee, which dissolve easily. Good choices include Medaglia d'Oro Instant Espresso and Starbucks VIA Instant French Roast or Italian Roast. Make sure whatever variety you choose doesn't contain added sugar! These cookies are plenty sweet.

Crush your candy canes by placing them in a sealable plastic bag and whacking it (gently!) with a hammer or the flat side of a meat mallet. Starlight mints can be substituted for the candy canes and crushed in the same manner. You can also skip the crushing step by using candy-cane sprinkles (easy!). Each of these options will make your cookies look super festive!

EASY PEPPERMINT-MOCHA FUDGE

Makes 4 dozen pieces

- 1½ cups granulated sugar
- ⅔ cup (one 5-ounce can) evaporated milk (not low fat or fat free)
- 2 tablespoons salted butter
- 1 teaspoon instant espresso powder (or your favorite instant dark roast coffee)
- ¼ teaspoon salt
- 2 cups miniature marshmallows
- 1½ cups semisweet or bittersweet chocolate chips
- 1 teaspoon vanilla extract
- 1 teaspoon peppermint extract
- 2 candy canes, coarsely crushed

GET READY: Line an 8 x 8-inch pan with foil and/or parchment paper (see note below).

MAKE THE FUDGE: In a medium-size, heavy-duty saucepan, combine the sugar, evaporated milk, butter, instant espresso powder, and salt. Bring to a full, rolling boil over medium heat, stirring constantly. Boil for an additional 4 to 5 minutes, stirring constantly. Remove from the heat.

Add the marshmallows, chocolate chips, and both extracts, and stir vigorously for 1 minute, or until the marshmallows are completely melted. Pour the fudge mixture into the prepared pan, and sprinkle evenly with candy-cane sprinkles. Refrigerate for 2 hours, or until firm.

Lift the chilled fudge from the pan, remove the foil or parchment paper, and cut the fudge into 48 pieces. Enjoy!

Notes from Hayden

Don't use sweetened condensed milk in this fudge! Evaporated milk is unsweetened and adds a lovely richness to this candy.

An easy way to line your pan with foil is to flip over your pan so that the underside is showing and then to press a piece of foil around the outside. Then flip over your pan so that it is right side up and press your perfectly shaped foil inside it! For added insurance, you can also line your pan with parchment paper, too—or simply use parchment paper on its own. Either way, this is one time when a disposable foil pan liner works perfectly!

To easily cut your cooled fudge, try using a bench scraper.

PEPPERMINT-MOCHA DIPPED PRETZELS
WITH CANDY-CANE CRUNCH

Makes 2 dozen small pretzels

1 cup semisweet or milk chocolate chips
1 teaspoon instant espresso powder (or your favorite
   instant dark roast)
1 cup white chocolate chips
24 small pretzel twists
12 candy canes, coarsely crushed

GET READY: Line a large baking sheet with parchment paper.

MELT CHOCOLATE: Pour the semisweet or milk chocolate chips in a small microwave-safe bowl (Pyrex is good). Microwave on high for 1 minute. Remove and stir in the instant espresso powder. The chips should melt while you stir. If not, microwave for an additional 15 seconds, and then stir again. Repeat this process with the white chocolate chips. (Don't add instant espresso powder to the white chocolate! It will make it look dirty.)

DIP and DECORATE: Dip half of a pretzel twist into the melted semisweet or milk chocolate, and let the excess chocolate drip back into the bowl. Set the pretzel on the prepared baking sheet, and then sprinkle the chocolate coating with the candy-cane sprinkles. Repeat until you've coated all the pretzel halves with the semisweet or milk chocolate and candy-cane sprinkles. Once the pretzels are dry, dip the bare half of each in the melted white chocolate and sprinkle with candy-cane sprinkles, using the same technique.

Let the pretzels dry completely before serving, about 2 hours. Enjoy!

Notes from Hayden

These treats are great for kids to help with! The melted chocolate isn't too hot, so kids can have fun dipping and sprinkling.

To add coffee flavor to desserts, I use superfine versions of instant coffee, which dissolve easily. Good choices include Medaglia d'Oro Instant Espresso and Starbucks VIA Instant French Roast or Italian Roast. These dipped pretzels are also delicious without the espresso powder, so feel free to omit it.

Crush your candy canes by placing them in a sealable plastic bag and whacking it (gently!) with a hammer or the flat side of a meat mallet. Starlight mints can be substituted for the candy canes and crushed in the same manner. You can also skip the crushing step by using candy-cane sprinkles (easy!). Each of these options will make your pretzels look super festive!

PEPPERMINT-MOCHA
NO-BAKE MINI CHEESECAKES
WITH CHOCOLATE-COOKIE CRUST

Serves 4

¾ cup finely crushed chocolate wafer cookies
2 tablespoons melted salted butter
1 tablespoon granulated sugar
Tiny pinch of salt

1 cup heavy cream
8 ounces cream cheese, softened
½ cup confectioners' sugar
¼ cup cocoa powder
½ teaspoon instant espresso powder
½ teaspoon vanilla extract
½ teaspoon peppermint extract

Sweetened whipped cream (optional, for topping)
Chocolate-peppermint bark (optional, for garnishing)
Candy canes, coarsely crushed (optional, for
    garnishing)

GET READY: Preheat the oven to 350°F. Have at hand 4 individual 8-ounce baking dishes (4 ovenproof stoneware ramekins are ideal).

MAKE CHOCOLATE-COOKIE CRUST: In a small bowl, combine the crushed chocolate wafer cookies, melted butter, granulated sugar, and salt. Stir with a fork until well combined. Next, divide the cookie mixture into four equal parts and press each portion into the bottom of a baking dish to form a crust. Place the 4 baking dishes on a baking sheet. Bake until the crusts smell chocolaty and have darkened slightly, about 7 minutes. Cool the crusts while you prepare the cheesecake filling.

MAKE CHEESECAKE FILLING: In a large bowl, whip the heavy cream with an electric mixer until stiff peaks form. Set aside. In another large bowl, beat the cream cheese with the electric mixer until smooth. Add the confectioners' sugar, cocoa powder, instant espresso powder, and both extracts to the cream cheese and beat until very smooth. Gently fold in the whipped cream until combined.

ASSEMBLE MINI CHEESECAKES: Spoon an equal amount of the filling atop the 4 reserved crusts. Cover and refrigerate the mini cheesecakes until ready to serve.

To make your mini cheesecakes extra special, before serving, top each with sweetened whipped cream and garnish with chopped chocolate-peppermint bark or candy-cane sprinkles. Enjoy!

Notes from Hayden

Okay, so you *do* have to bake the cookie crust (but *only* the crust) for these mini cheesecakes. It's worth it, I promise!

You'll need about 14 chocolate wafer cookies (about 3 ounces) to make ¾ cup crushed cookies. I like Nabisco Famous Chocolate Wafers. If you can't find chocolate wafer cookies, you can substitute 8 crushed Oreo cookies, either regular or peppermint flavor, to make the crust.

When it comes to peppermint extract, preferences differ! I usually go with classic McCormick Pure Peppermint Extract. You can also find excellent options from Nielsen-Massey, Wilton, and Watkins. If you'd like something more potent, try a peppermint oil, such as LorAnn Peppermint Oil. Make sure it's food-grade culinary oil (not for aromatherapy) and adjust the quantities accordingly. You'll need approximately ⅛ to ¼ teaspoon of peppermint oil for each 1 teaspoon of peppermint extract. Be cautious—this stuff is very strong, so it's easy to overdo it!

SUPERSIZE PEPPERMINT MOCHA

Serves a crowd

1 cup water
1 cup granulated sugar
2 teaspoons peppermint extract

8 cups whole or low-fat milk
2 cups semisweet or bittersweet chocolate chips
8 shots espresso
½ cup peppermint syrup
2 teaspoons vanilla extract

Freshly whipped heavy cream (for topping)
Chocolate shavings (optional, for garnishing)
Candy canes, coarsely crushed (optional, for
    garnishing)

GET READY: Have at hand a 4-quart or larger slow cooker.

MAKE PEPPERMINT SYRUP: In a small heavy saucepan, combine the water, sugar, and peppermint extract. Heat over medium heat (don't stir!) until the sugar is completely dissolved. Set aside.

MAKE PEPPERMINT MOCHA: In a slow cooker, combine the milk, chocolate chips, espresso shots, ½ cup of the reserved peppermint syrup, and vanilla extract. Cover and cook on low for 2 hours, whisking occasionally. The peppermint mocha will be steaming hot.

TO SERVE: Whisk the peppermint mocha just before ladling it into individual cups. Top each cup with whipped cream and chocolate shavings and/or candy-cane sprinkles. Serve at once. Enjoy!

Notes from Hayden

This recipe makes more peppermint syrup than you'll need. Save the leftover syrup to make individual peppermint mochas for someone special (like you!) by refrigerating it in an airtight container for up to one week. If you don't want to make your own peppermint syrup, you can also buy it ready-made. Torani and Starbucks are brands you might like.

Pick up to-go espresso shots from your favorite coffee shop, or substitute 2 tablespoons plus 2 teaspoons instant espresso powder for the espresso shots and stir it in thoroughly. Be sure to top each drink with whipped cream and crushed candy canes for that festive Christmas touch!